## About the Authors

With over two million copies published in over twenty-one countries, **Sarah M. Anderson** has published over fifty books. Sarah's book *A Man of Privilege* won an RT Book Reviews 2012 Reviewers' Choice Best Book Award. *The Nanny Plan* was a 2016 RITA winner for Best Contemporary: Short, and *Seduction on His Terms* won the 2020 Bookseller's Best Award for Short Contemporary. Recently, she's branched out into writing YA under the name Sally Sultzman. She lives in rural Illinois with her family, her rescue dogs, and a collection of oversized tea mugs.

**Nicole Helm** writes down-to-earth contemporary romance and fast-paced romantic suspense. She lives with her husband and two sons in Missouri. Visit her website: nicolehelm.com

**Charlene Sands** is a *USA Today* bestselling author of contemporary and historical romances. She's been honoured with The National Readers' Choice Award, Booksellers Best Award and CataRomance Reviewer's Choice Award. She loves babies, chocolate and thrilling love stories. Take a peek at her bold, sexy heroes and *real good men* on Facebook.

# In The Spotlight

# In The Spotlight:
# Desired Melodies

SARAH M. ANDERSON

NICOLE HELM

CHARLENE SANDS

**MILLS & BOON**

First Published in Great Britain 2026
by Mills & Boon, an imprint of HarperCollins*Publishers* Ltd
1 London Bridge Street, London, SE1 9GF

www.harpercollins.co.uk

HarperCollins*Publishers*
Macken House, 39/40 Mayor Street Upper,
Dublin 1, D01 C9W8, Ireland

In The Spotlight: Desired Melodies © 2026 Harlequin Enterprises ULC.

*His for One Night* © 2019 Sarah M. Anderson
*Wyoming Cowboy Bodyguard* © 2019 Nicole Helm
*Her Forbidden Cowboy* © 2015 Charlene Swink

ISBN: 978-0-263-42112-5

Printed and Bound in the UK using 100% Renewable Electricity
at CPI Group (UK) Ltd, Croydon, CR0 4YY

MIX
Paper | Supporting
responsible forestry
FSC
www.fsc.org
FSC® C013604

# HIS FOR ONE NIGHT

## SARAH M. ANDERSON

To my mom. Here's to new beginnings and fresh starts! Love you!

# One

"It's a good crowd tonight," Kyle Morgan said as he slipped down the narrow hallway that qualified as the backstage of the Bluebird Cafe in Nashville, Tennessee. He winked at Brooke Bonner. "But I don't think any of them came for me."

Brooke gave the older man a shaky smile but didn't stop humming to herself. The Bluebird was usually full—it was a small space where songwriters and singers came to test out new material. She'd been coming here for a decade now—first as a patron, then as a performer. She hadn't been back in almost a year and a half, though.

She hadn't been anywhere since she'd had Bean.

This night marked the beginning of her official comeback. After almost seven months of what felt like house arrest, she was walking back into the spotlight.

She was done hiding.

Mostly done, anyway. No one but a few select people knew about James Frasier Bonner—who she still called Bean, even though he definitely had grown. At three months, Bean was already smiling and cooing at her.

He had his father's smile.

Kyle wasn't in the know about Bean. Which made Brooke feel bad because Kyle was almost a father figure to her. He'd been at the Bluebird for her very first show and had taught her more about songwriting than anyone else. At every step of Brooke's journey from "girl with a guitar" to "country music phenomenon," Kyle had been a cheerleader, giving her advice and gentle pushes forward.

"Missed seeing you around," Kyle said. "Been quiet without you."

If she could've picked a father, Kyle might've done the trick. Sadly, Crissy Bonner would never tell Brooke who'd sired her. And the fact that she was walking in her mother's footsteps by keeping Bean's father a secret was a huge problem for Brooke.

But what choice did she have?

She didn't *want* to repeat the mistakes her mother had made. She wanted to do better.

But first, she had to get back out into the music scene.

Kyle's smile crinkled the lines around his mouth. It was a damn shame he refused to even talk to Mom. They could've made a good couple, and Kyle was rocking a silver-fox thing. Plus, if Mom had had a boyfriend or a husband, it might've taken some of Crissy Bonner's focus off Brooke. But the few times Brooke had managed to get them in the same room, the barely concealed hatred had been enough to crush any dreams of an instant family.

Of course, if Kyle and Crissy had hooked up, that might've meant Brooke wouldn't have a Grammy and a couple of chart toppers to her name. And it also might've meant she'd never have performed at that All-Stars Rodeo where Flash Lawrence had been riding, which would've meant no Bean. And she loved her son with her whole heart.

"Does this show mean you're off hiatus?" Kyle asked as he packed up his guitar.

"Yup. I'd been touring for almost four years straight before I hit big last year. It just wiped me out."

That was the official position her record label and family had cooked up. Brooke had needed a break to work on her new material. There might have been something in there about resting her vocal cords, she couldn't remember.

It'd all been a load of crap.

No one *rested* during the last three months of pregnancy. New mothers with fussy babies didn't *rest*.

Not for the first time, Brooke wished they'd just announced she was pregnant and dealt with the issue head-on. Yeah, the press might've been brutal—but there was no such thing as bad PR, and she'd argued that her surprise pregnancy might've taken her second album, *White Trash Wonder*, from double to triple platinum. After all, an unexpected pregnancy was on brand.

She'd been overruled because of one fact and one fact alone: she wouldn't tell anyone who Bean's father was. Not that it was any of their business, because it wasn't.

Her mother hadn't forgiven her yet for sitting on that particular secret, as if Crissy hadn't done the exact same thing by refusing to acknowledge Brooke's father.

Which meant Brooke was stuck lying, which she hated.

Kyle stood and wrapped an arm awkwardly around her shoulder. "Welcome back," he said, giving her a friendly squeeze before he headed out to the front to watch. "You need anything, you just give me a call. I mean it, Brooke—anything at all."

Brooke's eyes stung with unexpected emotion at Kyle's thoughtfulness. She forced her shoulders down and started humming again, keeping her vocal cords warm.

Alex Andrews, her bodyguard and friend, squeezed her big frame into the hallway and handed Brooke a mug of hot tea. "They found some honey," she practically growled.

Brooke accepted the tea gratefully and took a sip. Ah, the perfect temperature. "Thanks, hon."

Alex was big and gruff, but underneath her tanklike exterior she was a softie with a heart of solid gold. They'd been friends since junior high, back when Brooke was a band geek just starting to perform and Alex had been the first girl to play offensive lineman on the football team. Long before *White Trash Wonder* had hit big, Alex had been right beside Brooke in every dive bar and county fair, doing her best to keep away grabby, drunk assholes.

Thirteen months ago, Alex had stayed home because her girlfriend had the flu, instead of joining Brooke in Fort Worth for the All-Around All-Stars Rodeo. If Alex had come, would Brooke and Flash have spent that white-hot night together? Or would Alex have been the voice of reason, keeping Brooke far away from cocky cowboys who were good in bed? And against the wall? And on the floor?

Brooke must have been frowning, because Alex asked, "Worried?"

Damn it—it was hard to get anything past that woman. Especially since Alex was one of the few people who knew about Bean. "It's fine. He's home with Mom," she said, stretching her facial muscles to loosen them up.

"They'll do great. Crissy only wants what's best for him," Alex replied, which was probably supposed to be reassuring. Except it wasn't and Alex knew it. Her eyes widened as she realized what she'd said. "Oh, crap—I didn't mean…"

"It's fine," Brooke repeated, taking this opportunity to test out her fake smile. Crissy Bonner's favorite saying was 'It's for the best.' Brooke starting singing lessons at the age of five was *for the best*. Guitar lessons at the age of six was *for the best*. Hours of practice every day were *for the best*. Slumber parties, birthday parties, pets or boys— they *weren't* for the best.

Knowing who her father was? That definitely wasn't for the best.

Brooke kept humming. She was the last act of the night and she was surprised to realize she was nervous. It had been almost seven months since her last public appearance. Seven months since cleverly cut dresses and long, swingy cardigans hadn't been enough to conceal her baby bump. Seven months since she'd sung in public.

After years of constantly touring—starting with bars on Nashville's Music Row and then to county fairs to state fairs, to being the opening act for some of the biggest names in country music—Brooke had paid her dues early and often. And it'd all paid off last year when *White Trash Wonder* had hit. Suddenly, sold-out rodeos like the All-Stars had led to sold-out arenas. Years of lessons and performances and navigating the business world as a teenager had suddenly paid off, and Brooke had officially been labeled an overnight success, country music's Next Big Thing.

And she'd ruined it by getting knocked up by Flash Lawrence.

She'd had to miss the Grammys, for crying out loud. She'd been in labor when she'd won Best New Artist.

She wanted to be home with her son right now, she realized. She wasn't ready to do this again—the long and lonely nights, the negotiations, the travel and, most especially, the constant media scrutiny. But she didn't have a choice. Her uncle and former manager, Brantley Gibbons, had embezzled not just most of her money but a great deal of his other clients' funds and invested them in the Preston Pyramid Scheme—which had, of course, collapsed around his ears just about the time Brooke was breaking out.

Brooke and her mother weren't penniless—she still had royalties coming in on her two albums and had managed to keep the bulk of her profits from the last few months of touring after Uncle Brantley had "relocated" to Mexico to avoid criminal charges. But she couldn't afford to stay out of the spotlight any longer. She had to strike while the iron was hot.

Getting back out there was for the best, her mother had said. Because of course she had.

"Ladies and gentlemen," the MC began. "Our final act tonight is none other than the Grammy and Country Music Association winner, Brooke Bonner!"

Brooke took a final sip of her not-quite-hot tea and locked her smile in place. She'd been fourteen when she had first performed at the Bluebird, just a scared little girl and her acoustic guitar. It seemed fitting to start over where it had all started.

Brooke stepped out of the hallway to an impressive roar of applause. She smiled and nodded and tried to turn her body so no one would make a grab at her ass as she worked her way to the center of the Bluebird, where chairs and mikes had been set up.

As she settled into her chair, the hairs on the back of her neck stood up and she had the strangest feeling that *he* was here—Flash Lawrence. Which was ridiculous. In the thirteen months since their one-night stand, she hadn't heard from him. And she hadn't contacted him, either. She'd come so close when she'd realized she was pregnant. But she'd Googled him and seen all these horrible headlines about barroom brawls and trials and…

And she'd passed.

Her life was crazy enough with her career. A baby would make it crazier still. But a violent, immature cowboy? That was a hard *no*. She wanted her son to know his father but not at the risk of his well-being. Or hers.

A shiver raced down her back. She was imagining things, that's all there was to it. There was no way that her one-night stand was in the audience. It just wasn't possible.

Just to be sure, she turned in her seat to wave at the people behind her who were still clapping.

Damn. There, at the bar—a long, lean cowboy was perched on the last seat, the brim of his black cowboy hat throwing his face into deep shadow. He wore jeans with an absolutely huge belt buckle, with a leather biker jacket over a black Western-style button-up shirt. She couldn't see his eyes, but she could feel him looking at her.

Oh, no. Oh, *hell.*

Maybe she was wrong. It wasn't like cowboys of a certain height and weight wearing black hats and big belt buckles didn't exist around Nashville because they absolutely did. But her blood pounded in her veins and her hands shook, and there was no mistaking the flight or fight reaction.

Because she wasn't wrong.

The cowboy shifted in his seat, tilting his head back. His gaze collided with Brooke's, and even though she hadn't seen him for thirteen months, even though she'd only ever spent one amazing night with him, heat pooled low in her belly and she trembled with want.

Her big mistake was sitting less than thirty feet away. The one time she'd gone off schedule and done something just for herself—not for her career or her mother or anyone—and she'd been paying the price ever since. She loved her son, but...

She wasn't ready. Not for Flash Lawrence.

Not for any of this.

The lights dimmed and an expectant hush fell over the crowd.

Well. The show had to go on, so Brooke did the only thing she could.

"It's so good to be back, y'all. I've been working on new material for my next album—should be out in a few months—and we're thinking of calling it *Your Roots Are*

*Showing.*" The crowd laughed appreciatively as she flipped her hair back with an exaggerated toss of her head. "Aw, you guys are great."

She desperately wanted to turn in her seat for this next part. If that was Flash, what would he think when he heard the song title? But she didn't. She was giving him nothing to work with, and, besides, there was a literal audience here tonight. All it would take for the wildfire of gossip to catch and burn would be one too-long look, one touch, one wrong move, and her comeback would be forever tainted.

So she didn't turn, didn't even acknowledge that there was anyone behind her. She played to the people she could see when she said, "So the first song that'll be on the new album that I want to sing tonight is called 'One-Night Stand.'"

# Two

God, she looked amazing.

Brooke Bonner wasn't wearing the skintight crop top and leather miniskirt she'd had on the last time Flash had seen her. For this small crowd, she was wearing a black hippy-style skirt that came just below her knees and showed off her turquoise cowboy boots. A long sweater vest thing without sleeves was held in place over a deep-cut white shirt with the kind of studded belt that Flash's sister Chloe sold for her Princess of the Rodeo clothing line.

Turquoise dripped off her ears and around her neck but—he had to lean to the side to see—her fingers were bare. He couldn't tell for sure, but he didn't think there was even a tan line for an engagement ring on her finger.

Thank God.

When she'd disappeared from the public eye a few months ago, Flash had been terrified to think she might have met someone, might have gotten married. If she had, he'd have had to walk out the Bluebird's door without a look back. He wasn't going to screw up a marriage. But no ring meant he settled in and ordered another ginger ale. He was here for the duration.

Had he ever seen a more beautiful woman? He'd met a lot of hot women and slept with his fair share of them, but there was something about the way Brooke was put together that drew his eye. He couldn't look away, hadn't been able to since the very first moment he'd seen her in Fort Worth. He'd kissed her hand and that had been that.

Brooke wasn't wearing a hat tonight, so he could see the glory of her dark red hair as it flowed down her back in long waves. His fingers itched to bury themselves in that hair, wrap it around his fist like he'd done the last time, holding her head so he could kiss her again and again.

Apparently, absence really did make the heart grow fonder, because Flash was so glad to see Brooke right now that he wanted to sweep her into his arms and carry her far, far away from this crowded little place and show her how damned glad he was to see her.

He'd spent a year trying not to miss this woman. A year of trying to put the most intense sexual experience of his life out of his mind. He'd tried to pick up buckle bunnies since that night, but he hadn't succeeded. Not once in thirteen months.

He was afraid Brooke Bonner had ruined him for any other woman.

And that would be a damn shame.

No way in hell he wanted to be tied down. Especially not this year, when the All-Around All-Stars Cowboy of the Year was in his sights. After a wreck of a year—mostly brought on by Flash's own hot temper and alcohol-fueled brawls—he was back and ready to prove he wasn't just a chip on his shoulder with a good right hook.

For too long, people had assumed that Flash only won the All-Stars because the Lawrence family owned the circuit, and he understood now that most of his fights had been about proving he wasn't just a Lawrence, but that when it came to the rodeo, he was one of the best.

Getting suspended from the rodeo after that last fight—along with forfeiting his winnings up to that point—had been a blessing, although it sure hadn't felt like it at the time, especially not with the busted jaw Flash had gotten brawling. But it'd forced him to come to grips with his temper and grow the hell up. Plus, it'd shown everyone the All-Stars wasn't just a family business coddling the baby of the family. The rodeo family understood now that Flash had earned his place in the rankings.

This was *his* year and, for once, he wasn't going to shoot himself in his own foot. That included this thing between him and Brooke.

He just wanted...well, he wanted another night with her, to see if there was still that same electric current between them.

Best case, they'd make an effort to meet up on the road a few times a year, whenever his rodeo was in town during her concerts. He wouldn't say no to something like that. Not with her. He could focus on winning it all and she could focus on her career, and they'd get the chance to enjoy themselves during their downtime, like they had in Texas.

Then she announced the name of her first new song. "One-Night Stand."

The tips of Flash's ears went hot. That wasn't about him, right?

Couldn't be. It was the height of egotism to think that one night with him had left Brooke with anything other than a fond memory.

"Everyone should have one good night stand, don't you think?" Brooke went on, and the crowd chuckled approvingly. Someone to his left wolf whistled. Flash didn't see who, but he'd like to bust whoever it was in the jaw.

But the moment that thought crossed his mind, Flash clamped down on it. He was not going to lose his temper here. People were allowed to be jerks. He wasn't responsible for teaching them the errors of their ways when they crossed the line. Throwing a punch to defend Brooke's honor was something the old Flash would've done. The new-and-hopefully-improved Flash settled for glaring in the direction of the whistler.

Besides, causing a scene didn't serve his goals. He wanted to get reacquainted with Brooke Bonner. He needed to find out if there was something worth chasing between them or if he just needed to man up and move on.

If he got lucky, then he'd get lucky. If not, well, he still had to win it all.

The All-Around All-Stars Rodeo was in Nashville this weekend and he'd been hoping to find a way to run into her. When she'd posted on social media she'd be at the Bluebird tonight, he'd driven like a bat out of hell to get to Tennessee five days early just to see her.

At the bare minimum, he needed to make things right between them. Starting a brawl less than two minutes into her set would pretty much guarantee he'd never get another shot. So he kept a lid on his temper and took another drink of his soda.

When the crowd settled down, Brooke leaned in close to the microphone and said, "I'm so glad to see so many people agree—it's my favorite piece of furniture, too!"

Flash let out a slow breath, grinning in spite of his nerves. He'd loved her snarky sense of humor last year, too. She hadn't fawned over him and he had done his best not to fawn over her. There'd been an…understanding between them, almost. And a woman with a sense of humor was surprisingly erotic.

Thank goodness that a year of superstardom hadn't changed that about her.

Then Brooke began to sing as she played her guitar, and something in Flash's chest let go as the sound of her voice washed over him. By God, he'd missed the hell out of her.

She might not remember him—although, given how her eyes had widened slightly when they'd made eye contact, he thought maybe she did. And she might not want to see him again. But for a little while, he could lose himself in her world.

Until he realized what she was singing.

"It's just a one-night stand,
No tomorrow, no plans."

Well, damn. Yeah, she remembered him. But it wasn't a good thing. Especially not when she got to the chorus.

"You weren't worth the fun.
My one-night stand."

And the hell of it was, it was a great song. She had the audience eating out of the palm of her hand.

"Don't want to hear your excuses,
I don't care about your plans.
Not waiting any longer.
Screw your demands.
It's time I made my one-night stand."

Chills raced down his back as she held the last note, strong and powerful. He hadn't even had the chance to say hello and she was already shutting him down.

When the song ended, she did not look at him. She didn't sneak a peek out of the corner of her eye, didn't pivot in her chair, nothing. If she'd recognized him, it was clear she was ignoring him. "Whoo, y'all like that? That's just the beginning—I have a whole album of sass coming your way!"

Anger—an old, familiar feeling—began to push through his veins, but Flash refused to let it win. It was entirely possible that Brooke Bonner had forgotten all about him after her whirlwind breakout year. There was also a distinct possibility that, if she did remember him, she didn't hold him in any particularly high esteem.

He should've anticipated the song, though. He should've anticipated her anger. Anger was his second language. It came as naturally to him as breathing. But he hadn't seen this *attack* coming.

Okay, yeah, there'd been a superhot one-night stand. They'd hooked up in her dressing room before the show, which had made her late to go on because leather miniskirts weren't easy to work around. And it'd been good.

God, he still went hard just thinking about taking her against the wall in that tiny room, staring into her eyes as they both fought not to make a single sound. So damn *good*. And she had to have agreed, right? Because he'd hung around after the show, and when she'd seen him waiting for her, her entire face had lit up and she'd crooked her finger at him. They'd spent the rest of the night wrapped around each other in her hotel suite, having hot sex and ordering room service and, in between the seductions, making each other laugh.

They'd parted friends the next morning. He'd made damn sure to leave her with a smile on her face. He knew he hadn't stopped grinning for days. Weeks, even.

So how had they gotten from *that* to *this*?

"My next song—now just wait for it," she all but purred into the mike, "is called 'How Many Licks' because that was always the question, right?" The crowd hooted. "How many licks to get to the center of the sucker?"

"Three!" some jackass yelled.

"As many licks as it takes," a different ass yelled. Brooke wagged a scolding finger at him.

Flash had to close his eyes and focus on his breathing. Behind his eyelids, the world was red. They weren't disrespecting her. She'd chosen that title to get that exact reaction. She knew what she was doing and it wasn't his job to defend her from every slight. He'd already tried that once and had the criminal record—and nemesis—to prove it. He'd busted Tex McGraw up pretty damn good because the man had dared to put Brooke's name in his mouth.

Obviously, Flash understood why Tex hated him with a white-hot fury—Flash had knocked the man out of the All-Stars with a solid right hook. But Tex hadn't let up any with his online attacks since then, and he sure as hell hadn't accepted either of Flash's apologies—not the court-mandated one and not the more sincere one Flash had made after a few months of sobriety. But it was fine. Flash had gotten to a place in his life where he could handle online swipes from Tex without being driven to fits of rage. That was how far Flash had come in a year.

Brooke launched into the song, which cut off any other outbursts. The red haze behind his eyes faded, and he was able to breathe without feeling like punching someone.

Not surprisingly, this song felt personal, too. The double entendres flew fast and furious, but the core of the song was about a guy who couldn't take his licks and bailed.

A lot of people didn't like Flash. He'd never made it particularly easy for anyone to like him, but at least he knew it. However, he'd never inspired such strong feelings that someone could write an entire album based on how much they hated him, for God's sake.

Right. Instead of being insulted and letting it get to him, he was going to focus on feeling…flattered. Yeah, flattered. Not just any rodeo rider had an entire album dedicated to him, officially or unofficially. And if she publicly acknowledged that he was the inspiration, well, Flash was sure that his sister, Chloe, would find a way to spin Brooke's new album as a positive for Flash and the All-Around All-Stars Rodeo. Probably.

Besides, Brooke had said herself the album wouldn't be out for a few more months. She was still fine-tuning some of the material, still recording. Forewarned was forearmed. It was a good thing he was here tonight. He could work with Chloe to plan for a couple of different contingencies.

His sister had already basically figured out that Flash was crushing hard on Brooke.

Although…she'd want to know why Brooke was so furious with him. And he did not have an answer for that. Brooke had kissed him goodbye. Thanked him for the amazing night. Told him to take care.

And that was *it*.

At least she hadn't forgotten him, right? If there was one word that described Flash Lawrence, it was *memorable*.

When Brooke started the next song—titled "Not Going Down (Without a Fight)"—Flash almost couldn't take it. What the hell? If it'd been any other club or dive bar in Nashville, he would've bailed. But when a songwriter or a singer started their set at the Bluebird, no one moved and no one talked—house rules. So he had no choice but to sit there and listen.

He'd spent a year trying to make sense of the fact that Brooke Bonner was an itch he hadn't finished scratching. Before her, he'd bounced around bars and rodeos for four, maybe five years, picking up buckle bunnies and beautiful women in every town from Phoenix to Peoria while riding on the All-Stars circuit. Brooke Bonner should've been just one more woman. It'd been a one-night. Meaningless. Satisfying.

Except that that night had meant something to him and he'd spent nearly thirteen months unsatisfied.

Coming here tonight hadn't been a good idea. But damn it, he needed to know if their night together had meant anything to her.

Something more than raw material.

Finally, her set ended and the crowd came back to life. Because she was the last act, she stayed in the center of the room and signed autographs and posed for pictures. Flash hung back at the bar, debating his next move. Should he wait for the crowd to thin and then approach her? Or would it be better if they didn't have an audience? In that case, he should head out to the parking lot and wait by her car. Or was that too creepy?

Brooke glanced at him, a frown wrinkling her forehead before she quickly looked away. Nothing about that said *invitation*.

But he didn't care about that little frown. He didn't care about the songs or the radio silence that had lasted over a year.

He wanted to look her in the eye, make his case and then hear whatever she needed to get off her chest in person—without losing his temper. He wanted to know how they'd gotten from that wild night to this.

And if he didn't get lucky…he'd walk.

But he wasn't playing this guessing game.

He paid his tab and headed outside. The Bluebird was in a nondescript strip mall, and it took some work for Flash to work his way around to the back of the building. There—that plain sand-colored sedan had to be hers. She'd told him that she drove a boring car because it blended in.

He took up residence against a wall a good ten feet from the door of the Bluebird, giving her plenty of room. Lying in wait for her was a terrible idea, especially after that window into her mind and most especially after that frown. Frankly, he wouldn't be surprised if she pulled a gun on him.

But that was a risk he was willing to take.

# Three

"Great set," Kyle said, a note of pride in his voice. "It's going to be a massive hit. The whole album. Very girl power. I wish I'd written half of it."

"Be sure to tell the record label that, okay?" Brooke said, her cheeks beginning to hurt with all the smiling she was doing. She valued Kyle's opinion and the crowd had seemed to enjoy the songs as well, so this was all great.

Except Flash Lawrence was here. What was she supposed to do now?

"I'm so proud of you," Kyle added, giving her an awkward hug.

She hugged him back but her mind was stuck on Flash. She'd almost, *almost* gone up to him out there. There were a lot of people milling around, so it wouldn't have been a big deal if she'd walked up to the bar and asked for something else to drink, right? People wouldn't have made any connection between her getting a drink and making small talk with a random cowboy, right? Then she could've at least figured out why he was here. The only two possibilities she could think of were—this was either a stunning coincidence or...

Or he'd come to see her.

And as she had only mentioned the Bluebird appearance on her Twitter feed two days ago...

She'd bet good money Flash was outside waiting for her. Which meant she had to talk to him. Which meant she had to tell him about Bean. Her son.

His son.

Oh *God*, this was going to suck.

"Hey," Kyle said, putting a hand on her arm. "You okay?"

"Fine," she said, working hard for that smile. She'd kept Bean a secret for a lot of good reasons, but none of them came to mind now that she knew she'd *have* to tell Flash. Because the alternative was to do exactly what her mother had done—keep on hiding and lying for the rest of her life—and Brooke couldn't do it. She was done hiding.

Or would be, just as soon as Flash knew. But to Kyle, she said, "Just relieved the new stuff is solid."

Kyle gave her a worried look. "You sure? I know you, Brooke. I know how you write. That stuff...it seemed kind of personal."

"We need to get going," Alex said, all but hip checking Kyle into a wall. Bless her heart. "Sorry, Morgan."

"Jeez, woman," Kyle said, rubbing his shoulder. "You should've stuck with football."

Brooke gave him another quick hug and made a not-exactly-quick stop in the ladies' room. Damn it, she was stalling.

*Not hiding anymore*, she repeated to herself as she picked up her guitar case. Alex opened the back door for her and, as she walked out into the humid Tennessee air, Brooke felt it again—that tingling at the base of her spine.

"Brooke."

That was all he had to say for her worst nightmares and her fondest dreams to come true at once because this was really happening.

Flash had come for her.

Oh, God—she wasn't going to be strong enough because even just the sound of her name on his lips was making her resolve weaken.

It didn't have the same effect on Alex. "Hey—back off," she rumbled, stepping in front of Brooke. "Show's over, buddy."

"Brooke?" Flash said again. "I just want to talk. Privately."

Yeah, she knew what happened when she and Flash had any privacy. At least the first time they'd hooked up, in her dressing room, she hadn't planned to have sex with him. At least, not right then. But Flash was that rare, dangerous creature—an irresistible man.

Okay, so not total privacy. But maybe semiprivate would work.

Brooke put a hand on Alex's shoulder. "It's okay," she said quietly as she stepped around her friend. "I know him."

Alex leaned down to whisper, "I don't like him." Of course, her whispering wasn't exactly quiet and, given Flash's smirk, it was clear he'd heard.

Yeah, neither would Crissy Bonner. The record label executives would love Flash, though—a showy pro-rodeo cowboy would be great for PR.

But she didn't want Flash to be a public relations bonanza. She wanted…hell. She didn't know what she wanted. Except for some privacy. She owed him that much.

"It's fine. Can you wait in the car?"

Alex glared at Flash and growled. But then she said, "Fine—but only for a few minutes," as she took the guitar case from Brooke.

Then he did the ballsy thing and approached Alex. "Hi. Flash Lawrence. And you are?"

Alex gave him a look that made lesser men turn tail and run, but Flash held his ground. He wasn't a coward, that much was for certain.

With a quick look at Brook, Alex said, "Alex Andrews.

Don't try anything funny." She jabbed a finger in Flash's direction and pointedly did *not* shake his hand.

"Wouldn't dream of it. As Brooke can tell you, I don't have a sense of humor." She couldn't help the smile that danced over her lips at that bold-faced lie. She remembered quite well how easily she'd laughed with Flash. It would've been one thing if he'd just been amazing between the sheets. But he'd been so dang easy to be with—kind and funny and tender and hot and...

He'd made her like him.

She'd liked him a good deal. Seeing all those news headlines about his violent temper and plea deals had felt like a betrayal, almost.

Because she'd been wrong about him.

Had any of it been real?

Flash stood his ground as Alex crowded into his personal space on her way to the car. The one with the baby bucket-seat base in the back seat. True, there was a blanket thrown over it because God forbid anyone should notice that Brooke Bonner had a child restraint system in her car, but still. Hard evidence of Bean was practically within line of sight.

How was she supposed to do this, damn it?

Because Flash looked so much better in person than he did in her dreams. Maybe it was just the jacket. But maybe it was him. There was something almost...calm about him.

With a huff, Alex slammed the driver's side door. It wasn't like Brooke and Flash were alone—the door to the Bluebird's kitchen was still propped open and Kyle might come out at any second. But for this brief moment, she and Flash had something resembling privacy.

"You look great," Flash began.

Brooke barely managed to avoid rolling her eyes even as the compliment sent a thrill through her. She was still at least one size above where she'd been before she'd gotten pregnant, and her mother was pushing her hard to lose the last of the baby weight so people wouldn't get suspicious. To know she looked okay was a relief.

No, no—she was not falling for superficial compliments. Because that was just the generic sort of statement that any man trying to get laid would open up with.

"What do you want, Flash?"

*Please don't say something romantic* ran through her mind in the key of G at the exact same moment *say something romantic* did the same thing in harmony. She'd have to write that down later—could be a good hook.

Flash whipped off his hat and launched the smile at her that had melted her heart—and other parts—so long ago. "I wanted to see you again, but I get the feeling that you're not exactly happy with me right now."

"You picked up on that, did you?"

"It was subtle," he replied, that easy grin on his lips, "but I did notice a little anger in those songs."

"Well, your powers of deduction are in fine form." She made a move to step around him, but he mirrored her movements. "What, Flash? I'm tired."

"I want to apologize," he said, moving closer.

She inhaled sharply. This sounded like a trap. "Oh? And what, exactly, are you apologizing for?"

"Don't know. But—" he went on when Brooke scoffed heartily "—clearly I hurt you and, judging by the songs I heard tonight—which were great—I hurt you badly. So let me apologize, Brooke."

Lord, did he have to sound so damned earnest about it? She almost wished he was cocky and overconfident. This would be so much easier if he was trying to talk his way into her panties again. This time, she'd be ready for him. This time, she wouldn't make a mistake.

But, no—the cocky cowboy she'd taken to bed was nowhere to be seen, and in his place stood a serious man staring at her with so much longing and tenderness that, if Brooke allowed herself to think about it at all, he might take her breath away. So she didn't think about it.

"Fine. Apology accepted. Good night, Flash."

"Brooke," he said, her name a whisper on his lips. "I've missed you so much and the hell of it is, I don't know why."

"Really?" she snapped at him. *Anger* was great. *Anger* was not being seduced by his sweet words or intense looks. *Anger* was reminding her exactly who he was—a smooth talker with a violent streak—and, more importantly, who she was. He'd gotten her pregnant and she'd had to deal with the fallout without him because she couldn't trust him. Her whole life had been upended because of this man because she'd fallen for his sweet words and right now, he wasn't even that smooth at the talking. "That's not an apology, Flash. That's an insult."

"Would you listen?" he said, a warning in his voice. But then the weirdest thing happened—he took a step back and drew in a deep breath before letting it out slowly. "What I mean to say is, you were amazing—gorgeous and funny and smart and so easy to be with, and I'd be a fool not to want more of that. With you," he added quickly.

She snorted again, crossing her arms in front of her chest as different harmonies for *don't say something romantic* played in her mind.

"We had one night. A one-night stand, as you so eloquently put it." He ran a hand through his hair and then looked at her again, and this time the need in his eyes really did take her breath away. "That was all it was supposed to be, damn it, and…and it wasn't. Not for me. I wanted more with you then and I want more with you now."

"That's all well and good, Flash, but it's not enough. Not for me."

She needed to tell him about Bean. It wasn't fair to him

to keep his son hidden away, and it wasn't fair to Bean to deprive him of his father when the man was right here.

But she couldn't.

Not until she knew what he wanted and not if all he wanted was another night. Because she couldn't make a mistake like Flash Lawrence again. She needed him to be a father to his son. She needed him to be a co-parent, at the very least.

She needed to know she could trust him. And right now? Not a lot of trust to go around.

Eyes closed, he took another one of those weirdly deep breaths and then he stepped up to her. Even though the night was warm and sticky, she felt the warmth from his body as if he'd shined the heat of the sun down upon her. And it only got worse when his hand came up to cup her face and his thumb stroked over her cheek. She knew she should push him away, but when he touched his forehead to hers she couldn't help leaning into his touch, breathing in the clean scent of him—leather and man and, Lord, it was wonderful.

"I followed your career, watched your climb up the charts. Celebrated your number-one hits and cheered your award-show wins. Saw your face every night I closed my eyes," he said, his voice soft as his breath brushed over her skin like a lover's kiss. Her body clenched in an involuntary response to his touch, his words. His *everything*. "I tried so hard to forget you, but I couldn't. And I'm so sorry."

He wasn't making any sense. He *wasn't*. But damn it all if he wasn't reminding her exactly why she'd taken him into her bed, because even when he was speaking in riddles he still made it sound so good—and feel even better. "Because you can't forget me?"

"No." He laughed a little. She looked deep into his eyes and saw unflinching honesty as he said, "I'll never be sorry for that. But I looked you up and I realized, what if you'd looked me up, too? What if you read about the arrest and trial and plea deals? So I'm sorry for how you must've felt when you read the headlines. I'm sorry you saw the worst of me, playing out in real time on the internet. I'm sorry I destroyed a perfect memory of a perfect night, because that's what you were to me. A perfect memory."

She inhaled sharply, her eyes stinging even as she squeezed them tight. That was a *very* good line, one that was already weaving its way into the chorus her brain was trying to write.

"I came here tonight not to tell you I wanted you—although I do," Flash went on. His other hand settled in the curve of her hip, gently pulling her into him and, weak as she was, she let him.

Her breasts brushed against his chest. "Then why?" she whispered, afraid of his answer even as she was desperate to hear it.

"I came here to tell you what happened after the headlines. After I got sentenced and suspended from the circuit, I did my community service and completed my anger management courses. I made a promise to myself and my family that I was going to rein in my anger and stop letting it rule me."

"You did?" Somehow, her hand was underneath his jacket on his chest—not pushing him away but resting right over his heart. She could feel it beating, strong and steady.

He turned his head ever so slightly, his lips brushing against her temple, then down her cheek. "I also quit drinking. I won't say I'm an alcoholic, but when I drank I couldn't keep a handle on my anger, and that's when I got into trouble. I've been sober for eight months and counting."

"Tonight?" Her voice came out breathy and tight, and the space between her legs felt warm and liquid with want because she hadn't had a man in her bed since him and she missed him.

No, no—she missed sex. Which was normal. She'd been cleared to resume her nonexistent sex life from the private OB/GYN—who her mother had made sign a nondisclosure form, HIPAA be damned—six weeks ago, as long as she used reliable birth control, and it had taken everything Brooke had not to laugh in the woman's face.

So she didn't necessarily miss this man. She just missed men in general.

Right.

"Ginger ale. In a beer glass." Then he brushed his lips against hers, and she was powerless to do anything but open her mouth for him. When he licked inside her, she tasted sugar and ginger, not beer.

Pop shouldn't be so seductive, but this was crazy. How did he know that was exactly what she needed to hear? How could he taste so good?

How could she still want him so damned much?

Because she did.

He broke the kiss but he didn't pull away. Somehow, they were closer now and she could feel the heat of his erection pulsing against her belly. She could feel her pulse matching his, beat for beat.

"I want to see you again," he murmured against her lips. Then his mouth was trailing over her cheek, toward her ear. "I need more than just one night, Brooke. But I won't ask you for anything else."

"Yes." The word slipped out before she could think better of it, before the logistics of another night in Flash's arms could rear their ugly head. She needed more from him, too.

"Where? Say the word and I'm there, babe. I'm anywhere you need me." As he spoke, he pressed his knee between her legs, putting pressure right where she needed it. She couldn't fight down the moan. God, it'd been so long since another person had touched her for pleasure. *Her* pleasure. "Just tell me you need me."

"My house. I need…"

But reality reared its head.

Her mother was at her house, babysitting her son. Mom didn't live with Brooke and Bean, but she did live in what the real estate agent had described as the mother-in-law house on the property, a completely separate building almost 250 yards away from the main house—close enough for baby emergencies, but not under the same roof.

However, if Brooke waltzed in with Flash on her arm, they'd never get to the bed. Mom and Flash—that was a scene Brooke wasn't ready to face tonight. Maybe not ever.

"I need half an hour before you come over." She could get Mom out of the house and give herself a chance to change her mind. Or at least make sure she had some condoms because she wasn't going to make the exact same mistake again.

A honking horn tore through the night. Flash and Brooke jerked apart just as Kyle Morgan emerged from the back of the Bluebird. Guiltily Brooke glanced at the car, where Alex glared at her, then at Flash, then back at her.

Right. They had an audience and Flash had just kissed her, and she'd probably been about twenty seconds from completely throwing herself at him.

"Hey, Brooke—everything okay?" Kyle asked, sounding meaner than she'd ever heard him. "Where's Alex?"

Flash took another step back. He looked at Brooke like he was waiting for her to lead here.

"In the car." Kyle stopped next to her, eyeing Flash with a healthy dose of warning. "This is a friend of mine."

"Great set tonight," Flash said, cutting through the awkwardness and stretching his hand toward Kyle. "Flash Lawrence. Sounds like you had some big hits waiting to happen in there. Eric Church, maybe? He could bring down stadiums with that one song about rebels."

Kyle glanced warily at Brooke before returning Flash's

handshake. "Thanks. Toby Keith was also eyeing 'My One, Her Only' for his next album."

Flash whistled appreciatively and Brooke felt Kyle relax. How did he do that? Flash Lawrence could charm his way into any situation. She'd fallen for that charm once.

She couldn't afford to fall again.

As Flash and Kyle made small talk about country singles and Flash offered his opinion on what played well at the rodeos, Brooke had to accept that somehow, Flash had known exactly what she needed to hear—that he wasn't the same man he'd been when he'd made all those awful headlines. He'd worked on being a better man.

Had he become the kind of man she'd want around her son?

Except she wasn't *just* a single mother thinking about dating again, and Bean wasn't *just* her son. He was Flash's son, too, and she couldn't keep his baby away from him, no matter what. She knew what it was like to grow up without a father. She couldn't do that to Bean. Not if Flash was willing to step up.

Was he?

"Well, it was great meeting you, Morgan," Flash said, shaking Kyle's hand again. "Looking forward to hearing your next big hit."

Kyle actually blushed at that. "Always great to hear from a fan. Will we be seeing you again soon?" He held out his hand to Flash.

Brooke didn't miss that *we*.

Flash heard it, too. He cut a glance at her as he shook Kyle's hand again. "That depends on Brooke."

Kyle leveled an intimidating look at Flash and didn't let go of his hand. Instead, he pulled Flash off balance. "You're damn right it does. Alex isn't the only one you'll have to go through if you hurt her." Then, just as quickly as it had appeared, the threat of violence dissipated into the night air.

Surprise registered on Flash's face but, after a beat, he broke out that smile Brooke saw every time Bean grinned at her. "Trust me, hurting Brooke is the last thing I'd ever want to do."

Then both men turned to her.

So this was the moment when she had to make a decision. Was letting Flash back into her life and her son's life a good idea, or was it another mistake waiting to happen?

Knowing her luck, both.

Just like Bean had been both the biggest mistake of her life and the best thing that had ever happened to her.

"Let me give you my info," she told Flash, holding out her hand for his phone. She would have preferred not to do this with Kyle standing right next to her, but this was still better than having Kyle catch them kissing.

Flash unlocked his phone and handed it to her. Her heart going a mile a minute, she put in her address and number and added the note, "half an hour" to give her enough time to get Mom out of the house and…and decide how she was going to handle Flash.

She was not bringing Flash home to have wild, crazy, *great* sex with him again. Absolutely not. This was about Bean. Her world began and ended with him now. That's all there was to it because a boy needed his father. Even if that boy was only three months old.

She handed the phone back and turned to Kyle with a studied casualness she definitely wasn't feeling. "Hey, if I need a little help on a few songs, you're interested?" Because everything on the *Roots* album was…energetic, to say the least, and Kyle was good for ballads.

Kyle's eyes lit up. "Hell, yeah, sweetheart. Just give me a call. Good meeting you, Lawrence."

But the man didn't move. He just stood there, watching her and Flash to see what was going to happen next.

"Morgan." Flash tipped his hat. "Brooke. I'll be seeing

you." He packed a hell of a lot into his gaze before he turned on his heel and strolled out of the parking lot.

She about broke out into a sweat as she watched him walk away. One thing was for sure—if anything, Flash's ass had only gotten better in the last year. A man who rode broncos and bulls for a living had the legs and backside to go with it. The first time they'd had sex—against the wall of her dressing room—he hadn't even taken his chaps off. She'd had a view of that ass in her dressing room mirror that even now threatened to make her melt.

She wasn't inviting him over for sex. She had a single-minded purpose here—informing him he was a father.

But Lord, that man made every part of her weak. Always had and, apparently, always would. She just needed to be strong enough to get through the next few hours.

Honestly, she wasn't sure she was *that* strong. Especially when he turned and tipped his hat to her, the model of the country gentleman.

"Honey," Kyle started when Flash was out of sight. "Did I just meet the inspiration for all those new songs?"

"It's not like that," she protested, and to her own ears, it sounded weak. "He's a friend."

Kyle gaped at her. Yeah, he wasn't buying it, either.

"The way he looked at you? No way. That's a man who wants a lot more than 'friendship,'" he said, throwing in air quotes for good measure. "And the way you're looking at him? Come *on*. I may be an old man, but I'm not blind."

Brooke didn't have a snappy comeback to that, but Alex saved her. "Are we going?" she all but shouted through the car window.

"Be careful!" Kyle called as Brooke climbed into the car. "And call me if you need backup!"

Yeah, like that was going to happen. She just waved as Alex sped off.

How would people like Kyle react when he found out

that she'd been sitting on the juiciest of details for months? She hoped people wouldn't be too hurt that they hadn't been important enough to be in the know, but, seriously, aside from the executives on her record label, the private OB/GYN and nurse who'd delivered Bean at Brooke's home, the equally private pediatrician and Alex—and Mom, of course—no one else knew.

But she couldn't hide her son forever. She wanted to take him to parks and the zoo and…and just out. She wanted to talk to other moms she knew about what was normal and what wasn't. Hell, she wanted to take some pictures with Bean, not just cell phone shots. She wanted to do all the normal stuff with her son.

She didn't want to hide. Not from her friends, not from her fans and not from Flash.

Worse, when she daydreamed about all those fun things, she wasn't alone. Flash was next to her.

In her perfect world, Flash was by her side during the day and in her bed at night. Her son didn't have to grow up without his father, like Brooke had. And she didn't have to feel so alone anymore.

But that fantasy was just that—fantasy. Instead of that perfect world, she'd invited him home to tell him about Bean and also to *not* have sex with him.

The tension rolling off Alex was palatable, which had to be the only reason Brooke heard herself repeating the lie, "He's just a friend."

"Uh-huh." Yeah, Alex wasn't buying any of that as she took off for the 440.

From there, they'd take 40 west to the house she'd bought with the money her uncle had managed not to embezzle. Her home was on five fenced-in acres. If she had another hit record and successful tour, she had plans to completely renovate the sprawling mid-century ranch house. She hadn't even been able to paint the rooms while she'd been pregnant because the smell of primer had made her sick.

"The show went well, don't you think?" Brooke tried again, desperate for a subject change.

"Hon," Alex said in her growly voice, "did you tell him about Bean?"

This was the problem with best friends. There was no hiding anything from them. Because of course Alex had figured out that the one show she'd missed was the rodeo in Texas.

"No," she said, because more lies would only be an insult to Alex's intelligence.

Alex thought that over as she began to weave through traffic like the devil himself was hot on their tail. Finally she asked, "Are you going to?"

Brooke had closed her eyes. Flash was the boy's father. She simply didn't have a choice.

"Yes," she admitted, wondering why it felt like such a defeat. "But…"

"Yeah, I know—don't tell your mother," Alex grumbled. "She'll find out sooner or later."

*Later*, Brooke prayed. Please let it be much, much later.

Her mother had sat on the secret of Brooke's paternity for twenty-some-odd years. Brooke could keep Flash a secret for just a little bit longer.

She was going to tell Flash about Bean and hope all he'd said about not letting his anger rule him was the truth. But…

God, it was selfish and wrong, but she wanted just one more time with him before she told him she was the mother of his child.

One last grasp at the woman she'd been a year ago. A lifetime ago.

Humming a melody that built itself around the words, she had to wonder—was bringing Flash to her home another huge mistake or the making of another perfect memory?

# Four

At exactly eleven forty-five, Flash walked up the front walk to Brooke's house, which was a long rancher that looked a bit shabby around the edges. The whole thing was set almost half a mile back from the road, creating the appearance of privacy. Flash didn't see any other lights and the night was hushed. He did his best to tread quietly, afraid to disturb the quiet.

Clearly, Brooke didn't want anyone to see him coming or going and he respected that—after their night together, she'd become the subject of a lot of media scrutiny.

The temptation to whistle was strong, but he tamped it down. It was a nice night and Brooke had kissed him. Sure, her new music was a broadside attack on him, but she was stunningly talented and she'd kissed him. He'd said what he needed to say and then *she'd kissed him.* She needed him and, by God, being needed was freaking amazing. This had all the markings of another amazing night.

All in all, things were looking up.

But doubt was trying to crowd out his good mood. Why did she need so much time to get ready? Possibly she just needed to pick up—as if he gave a flying rat's ass if there were dishes in the sink or clothes on the floor.

Another possibility bugged him. Because what if she needed the extra time to get rid of someone?

The thought of her being married or hustling some dude out of the house made his stomach tighten, but he breathed through the pressure. He was not the boss of Brooke. He had no claim on her whatsoever, and it'd been over a year since they'd been together.

He wanted her but not enough to ask her to cheat with him. The bonds of marriage were unbreakable. Hell, his own father still deeply mourned the loss of Flash's mother and that'd been fourteen years ago. Trixie Lawrence was still Milt's wife. Not even death would change that.

Flash would do damn near anything for another night with Brooke. But he wouldn't wreck a marriage.

Everything else, though...

Kissing Brooke Bonner again had brought it all back to him. The feel of her body flush against his, the taste of her singing on his tongue. She was honey sweet and he wanted to sip her. Just thinking about her hand on his chest, how her fingers had curled into his shirt to hold him close while he'd done his damnedest to show her how good he could be for her—he was downright giddy.

A long, painful year of "self-improvement" and "introspection" was behind him. All that time without women to relieve the pressure, without beer to dull the frustration. Months of reining himself in, no matter how much some jackasses deserved a punch to the mouth. Thirteen freaking months of watching Brooke from a distance, wondering if he haunted her dreams like she haunted his—and now he was so close to having her again that it was physically painful to walk.

The need to bury himself in her body beat a steady rhythm through his veins, all because she'd kissed him.

Flash had to stop just outside the circle of light cast by the porch lights and wait for his blood to cool. He wasn't expecting anything from this...*visit*. There was no way six songs worth of percolating rage had been erased with some good groveling and a kiss.

But...best case, they'd be naked at some point before dawn broke and stay that way until at least lunch tomorrow. He had a pack of condoms in his back pocket, purchased in a fit of optimism after discovering she'd be at the Bluebird. He didn't have to report in at the Bridgestone Arena before Friday afternoon. He could happily spend a few days wrapped up in Brooke.

But that was best case. Hope for the best, plan for the worst, and the worst case was Brooke taking advantage of what seemed like acres of privacy to read him the freaking riot act. Just because she'd molded her body to his and whispered, "I need you," in his ear didn't mean Flash was about to get lucky.

*Failure to plan is planning to fail.* He'd learned that the hard way over the last year.

So this was the plan. If she got mad, he wasn't going to get mad back. This wasn't a screaming contest and he didn't have to win. Yeah, it would suck, but he deserved to be put in his place, as his brother Oliver and brother-in-law Pete loved to remind him. He would grit his teeth, focus on breathing, take a walk if he started to lose his cool and hopefully figure out what, exactly, he'd done to inspire such passionate songwriting. Then he'd make his apologies—again—and do what he could to make things right and...

And then he'd walk away.

If that's what she wanted, that's what he'd do.

And if he had to walk away, he wouldn't go to a bar and pick a fight. He'd go pound out a few miles on a treadmill at his hotel workout room until he couldn't move.

There. That was a plan.

With his emotions firmly under control, Flash strode up the front steps.

Before he could knock, the door swung open and there she was.

"Brooke," he said, his body tightening at the sight of her.

She'd lost the vest thing and the belt, as well as the heavy jewelry that'd been around her neck. Which gave him a hell of an unobstructed view of her cleavage. But the worst thing of all was she'd lost her boots. The sight of her bare toes slammed into his gut, and he went hard when she placed one delicate little foot on top of the other. Her toes were painted a deep, sultry red, and he wanted to suck on each one until she screamed.

The space between them sparked with electricity, just like it had the first time he'd clapped eyes on this woman. There was something about her that lit him up, and he was tired of trying to ignore that elemental reaction.

She needed him. She'd asked him here. He wanted her. Simple.

He realized he was still staring at her toes. He jerked his eyes up.

Brooke stared up at him, her mouth forming a round little O. Then she dropped her gaze, blushing furiously. "Flash. You're on time."

"I would never disappoint a lady."

She tucked her lower lip under her teeth and he fought back a groan. Was she trying to torture him?

He desperately wanted to believe her hesitation was because she didn't know how to ask for what she wanted. She hadn't had any problem telling him where and how to touch her last time, and he'd done his best to give her what she'd needed. Because he wanted to give her anything she wanted. *Everything* she wanted.

And he couldn't do that outside the house, so he stepped

inside. Into her. Her head popped up, her eyes wide and dark with what he prayed was desire.

"I missed you," he said, cupping her cheeks in his hands and lifting her face to his. He didn't kiss her, but they were right back to where they'd been earlier, before they'd been interrupted. Brooke was in his arms and he didn't know how he'd get her out of his system.

"You said that."

"Well, it's true. I've never missed anyone like I missed you."

Her hand snaked up behind his neck, holding him against her. It was the sweetest thing he'd ever felt, that touch of possession. "How much?" Her voice was whisper soft as she backed up, pulling him with her.

He slid one hand down her neck, tracing the valley between her breasts before he settled it on her hip and pulled her into him. The last time he'd held her like this, she'd looped her arms around his neck and her legs around his waist and begged him to make her come. He'd done exactly as she'd asked. Twice.

"So much, babe. I'll do anything you want—you know that, right?"

Her eyelashes fluttered, the blush spreading down her neck and across her magnificent chest. He leaned down and pressed his lips against her pink skin, the warmth of her body setting his blood on fire. The last time he'd seen her breasts, he'd sucked on her rosy nipples until she'd moaned and thrashed beneath him.

Her chest heaved at his touch as her fingers curled around his neck, pulling him closer. "Anything?"

*Yes*—it was right there in her voice, waiting for him to come get it. Brushing his lips against her cheek, he slid both hands down her waist, around to her backside. He filled his hands with her, lifting her and pulling her against his erection. She gasped and he thought he might come right then. "*Anything.* You want me to stop, I'll stop," he murmured, pressing kisses that trailed over her skin until he could whisper in her ear. "You want me to leave, I'll leave. Just say the word."

Then he waited, the lobe of her ear resting against his lips, her bottom firm in his hands, the warmth of her breasts heating him up. This might be the last moment he could walk away from her, and it sure as hell wouldn't be a dignified walk. Every square inch of his body—a few inches in particular—throbbed to be closer to her, to pull her into his arms and hold her for as long as he could.

He felt her inhale, then let the air out slowly, her honey-sweet breath caressing over his cheek. Each second that ticked by was an eternity of torture, but he forced himself to be patient.

"Don't leave, Flash," she whispered, her lips touching his cheek. He shuddered as she leaned forward, bringing her body completely flush with his, and kissed his neck. "Stay."

Then she bit him—not hard, but with enough pressure to take everything that was already throbbing in his body and kick it into overdrive.

She didn't have to ask twice. He kicked the door shut behind him and spun her around. Her back hit the door with a muffled thud and then Flash was kissing her, her sweetness overwhelming his senses, her body erasing everything but this moment.

He squeezed her ass and ground his aching erection against her, and, God help him, he couldn't get enough. He closed a hand around one of her breasts, letting the heavy weight fill his palm.

She sank one hand into his hair, knocking his hat off. With the other, she grabbed his hand and jerked it away from her breast at the same time she pulled his head back.

"Shh!" she hissed, real fear in her eyes. "Quiet!"

"What is it, babe? What's wrong?" He swallowed and, holding himself in check, did the right thing. "We can stop. We don't…"

Shaking her head *no*, Brooke released his hand and stroked her thumb over his cheek. "I don't want to stop but…it's complicated, that's all."

"Just so we're clear—you're not married?" She shook her head *no* again and he almost sagged in relief. "Engaged?"

She gave him the saddest of smiles, one that did some mighty funny things to his heart. "No. Just… I need you, Flash. Like before." Her voice was barely a whisper, something he felt more than he heard. "But you have to be quiet and don't touch my breasts."

He gave her a strange look—if he was remembering correctly, she'd absolutely loved it when he'd played with her breasts.

"Please," she said softly, pulling him back down to her. "Just one more time, like it used to be. And afterwards… I'll understand, no matter what happens."

He stared at her. What the hell was going on? He was missing something, and he couldn't tell if it was *bad* or *really bad*.

"Babe," he said, hoping to reassure her, and he made damn sure to do it quietly. "If another night—or another weekend is what you need—that's what I want, too." He touched his forehead to hers. "Just tell me."

Breathing hard, she didn't reply right away. Then her beautiful green eyes fluttered open, and even before she spoke, Flash knew what her answer would be.

*Yes.*

He covered her mouth with a hard kiss, stuck in between this exact moment right now and an almost identical one last year. This is what he wanted—Brooke pressed against him, her mouth opening for his, her teeth scraping his lip.

She dug her fingernails into his scalp, the flash of pain burning bright into pleasure.

Oh, yeah—she pushed him and tormented him like no other woman ever had and he loved it.

Then she jerked her head away from his. "Condoms," she hissed, her voice soft but serious. *"Now."*

"Bed?" he asked, reaching to get the packet from his back pocket.

"No—can't wait." While he struggled with the foil wrapper on the condom, she went to work on his belt buckle.

God, she really couldn't wait.

He groaned as her fingers closed around him, and he almost dropped the condom when she stroked up, then down.

"I missed you too, Flash," she said, her mouth at his neck again. "No one makes me feel the way you do."

Then her teeth scraped over his skin and she squeezed him, and if he had been able to think right now, he might pause to break that statement down. But he couldn't think, couldn't do anything but feel her hands on him, feel the warmth of her breasts pressing against his chest.

She needed him. It was a hell of a thing.

Somehow, he got the condom on and got her skirt lifted. Thank goodness she had on a thin pair of panties. Flash didn't even bother to pull them down. He just shoved them aside and positioned himself at her entrance. The smell of her sex hit his nose like a bomb going off, and he groaned again.

"Now," Brooke breathed in his ear, hitching one leg over his hip. "Now, Flash. Now, now *now...*"

He slid his hands under her ass to lift her and then, with one thrust, he sank into her wet heat.

*"Oh,"* she moaned, and he swallowed that sound with another kiss.

For a moment, he couldn't do anything but stand there as sensations swamped him.

For a year he'd been trying to forget how right she felt surrounding him, how perfectly they fit together.

It hadn't worked.

He couldn't forget what they had together, this electric physical connection.

"Brooke," he said, his words coming out a strangled whisper. He touched his forehead to hers and stared down into her eyes. He desperately wanted to believe he saw his own desire reflected back at him. "Oh, *Brooke*."

"Shh." Then she was kissing him with all the passion he remembered from last year, all the pent-up desire that had been driving him slowly mad.

He began to rock into her, each thrust threatening to destroy him anew—especially when she whispered, "More," in his ear before she bit down on his lobe.

"Yes, ma'am," he whispered back.

It'd been like this in her dressing room, hard and fast and quiet against the door because people were right out in the hallway. It'd been exciting then. It was still exciting.

He paused long enough to shift his grip on her bottom, lifting her up and bracing his feet so he could support her with one hand. With the other, he reached down between their bodies to where they were joined. Brooke's head dropped back, her chest heaving as Flash pinched the folds of skin right above where he was buried inside of her.

Beneath his touch, her body shuddered. Her head thrashed against the door and he felt the spasms of her orgasm begin to move around him, clenching him so, *so* tight. A low roaring sound filled the air around them as he came and she came, too. It was only after that he realized the roaring was him, groaning in pure bliss.

He collapsed against her body, pinning her to the door, still inside of her. Breathing hard, he couldn't think, couldn't talk.

*Home.*

That was the only word he had, one that repeated itself over and over again when Brooke kissed his neck, then his mouth.

This was what coming home felt like.

Which was wrong. She wasn't home. He followed the rodeo. This was just…one of those things. A good night. Maybe a great week.

He pulled free of her body but not her arms. "Babe," he murmured against her hair, but then he stopped because he wasn't sure what was going to come out of his mouth next.

"I'm so sorry," Brooke whispered, and he heard the catch in her voice.

He reared back, staring down at her. No, he wasn't imagining things—she was on the verge of tears. "Don't apologize to me, Brooke. You and I…"

But that was when a new sound reached his ears—something high-pitched, almost a whine. Something that sent a shiver of real fear racing down his back.

A single tear spilled over and ran down Brooke's cheek. "So, *so* sorry," she whispered, slipping out from under his arm and leaving him hanging—literally. "I didn't want it to be this way."

"Brooke?" He turned but she was already halfway up the stairs. Her skirt had already fallen back down and she didn't look like she'd just changed his world.

And she didn't stop.

"Brooke!" he said as the noise got louder, grating over his nerves like sandpaper. "What—"

"We woke the baby," she said, choking on the words.

"The baby? What *baby*?" Flash stared up at her, the hairs on his arms standing at full attention, like lightning was about to strike.

Someone else's baby. That was the only thing that made sense. Not hers. Not…

Oh, God.

She made it to the top of the stairs and still hadn't answered.

"Brooke," he shouted. *"Whose baby?"*

"Mine." She turned around then and looked down at him, crying hard. "And yours. Our baby, Flash. *Our son.*"

Then she turned and ran.

# Five

"Oh, Bean," Brooke murmured, scooping the baby into her arms. "Momma needed just a few more minutes." Five more minutes to break it to Flash that his son was upstairs. Five more minutes to untangle her body from his.

But it wasn't meant to be.

The baby howled his displeasure, and Brooke quickly realized what the problem was. He was soaking wet and probably hungry, too. He'd already been asleep when she'd gotten home.

Everything was wrong. That wasn't how she'd wanted to tell Flash. It wasn't fair to just drop that bomb on him. Not mere seconds after he'd been inside of her. Not when her legs were still shaking with the force of the orgasm he'd unleashed.

She hadn't planned to have sex with him again. No, that was a lie because obviously, she *had*—God, he was still so good—but she'd resolved to do the right thing and tell him about Bean first. And that resolve had lasted all of thirty-seven seconds. Right until he'd touched her.

She handed Bean his rattle shaped like a frog that croaked when he shook it. He only got to play with that toy when she was changing him and Bean was endlessly fascinated with it. Thankfully, it worked and the baby quieted down as she got him cleaned up.

That was when she realized the house was silent. Too quiet.

Was Flash still here? Or had he opened that door and walked out of her house and her life? Oh, Lord. Not that she would blame him for that, because she couldn't. She'd hidden Bean from him. An entire pregnancy, a birth, *a baby*—and she hadn't breathed a word of it to him. Really, that was unforgivable.

If Flash walked, that didn't change anything. She was still responsible for Bean, just like she'd always been. But now that Flash knew, she wasn't going to hide the baby anymore. It was time to show the world she had an amazing little boy. She'd tell her mother and her record label that she was going public and that was *that*. Her next album would get some extra PR, so everyone would win.

Brooke focused on the job before her. One day at a time and, when that didn't work, one hour at a time.

The sound of heavy tread on steps ricocheted through her body like a gunshot, and she gasped. The baby began to fuss again.

Flash hadn't left. Instead, he was coming upstairs. Somehow, that was worse.

*Breathe.* She had to breathe. It was good Flash hadn't left. Yay, he wasn't abandoning them! That was great, right?

Then he was standing in the doorway, staring at her with his mouth open and his eyes bugging out of his head, white as a ghost. He didn't say anything. She wasn't sure he was breathing.

This felt like something out of a nightmare, the reoccurring one she'd had after she'd realized she was pregnant, had looked Flash up and seen all those news stories. A shiver of panic raced down her back as she remembered everything she'd read—the drunken bar fights, the criminal charges for assault.

But as she stared at Flash staring at her, she knew she wanted more than just a fight-or-flight reaction out of Flash, more than sex against the door.

Well. The show had to go on, didn't it? She picked up Bean and turned to Flash. "Can you hold him?"

His mouth shut, then opened. "What?" The word sounded like she'd tortured it out of him.

"Here." She held Bean out to Flash. "This is Bean." She swallowed. "James Frasier Bonner, but I call him Bean."

She wouldn't have thought it possible, but Flash got even paler as he stared at the baby in her arms.

"He's yours," she said. "Please, Flash. I have to change his sheets and wash my hands. Can you hold him? For just a minute?"

Bean seemed to notice Flash for the first time. His little body went stiff and he made a noise of concern. On instinct, Brooke tucked her son into her arms. "It's okay," she murmured, watching Flash over the top of Bean's head. "It's…" she swallowed. "That's Daddy, baby. That's your father."

"You… I…" Flash stuttered. Then, without another word, he spun on his heel and was gone.

It felt like a punch to the gut, but before Brooke could do anything but stiffen in pain, he returned, his eyes blazing. "I am coming back," he said, his voice quiet and level and, somehow, all the more unsettling for it. Then he was gone again. This time, she heard his footsteps thundering down the stairs.

She hurried to the doorway. "Flash?" she called after him. Was it a good thing that he was coming back?

He stopped when he got to the bottom of the stairs, his back to her. His hands were definitely clenching and unclenching. He looked like he'd just been bucked off a bronco a half second too early to win it all.

"I need a minute," he said. The look he shot her over his shoulder made her stumble back, it was that intense. "Just give me a damned minute, Brooke."

He straightened and walked out the front door. At least he didn't slam it. That had to count for something, right?

Brooke had a baby.

Brooke had *his* baby.

*He* had a baby.

Flash paced relentlessly around his truck, struggling to breathe. The old Flash would've probably already punched the side of the truck a few times, breaking his hand and denting the metal. It was a pointless, destructive way of coping with a problem, striking out like that.

He'd thought she'd been giving him the gift of forgiveness with her kiss, her touch, her body.

And the whole time, the baby had been upstairs.

Jesus, he and Brooke had a baby *together*.

How old?

Flash did the math and, oddly, counting months helped him breathe. Thirteen months. Babies took nine months, right? No, wait—Renee, his sister-in-law, had been pregnant for ten months. So thirteen minus nine and a half, just to be safe, meant that baby boy was...

Three, maybe four months old.

Flash's knees threatened to buckle, and he had to hang on to the side of the truck bed just to keep from collapsing. He had a son who was almost four months old already and he hadn't known.

Because Brooke hadn't told him.

The world went a deep, crimson red at the edges again at what he'd missed—the first heartbeat, the labor and delivery, his son's first breath, first smile, first *everything*. All those moments, gone. He'd never get them back. All because Brooke hadn't told him, goddammit.

That was unforgivable.

But the moment the thought crossed his mind, Flash pushed back at it. He had to reframe this right *now*, because he was many things but he didn't like to think *stupid* was one of them.

He was angry, yes. Flash let the anger flow but he didn't try to hold on to it. He let it pass him by and forced himself to look underneath. Before he'd started court-mandated anger management therapy, he never would have thought there was more to anger than good old-fashioned rage, but he knew better now.

For starters, he was surprised. Not that *surprised* was a strong enough word, but it'd have to do. Brooke hadn't told him and then the baby had been crying, and Flash had been *stunned*—and that was a perfectly normal reaction to discovering a one-night stand had a child that was his.

What the hell did he know about being a father?

He'd gone over to his brother Oliver's house and played with his niece, Trixie, but that didn't mean he was qualified to be a father. He rode bulls and wild broncos for a living and did stupid stuff like having one-night stands. Not exactly the kind of thing a good dad did.

He didn't know how long he paced in circles, but eventually the world went back to being plain old dark.

He paused and looked up at Brooke's house. One light was on in what might be the baby's room. No, Flash couldn't keep thinking of that child as "the baby." That boy had a name. He was James Frasier Bonner, which was a good, strong name—even if she had given the boy Flash's real, awful name. James could be a Jim or a Jimmy or even a Jamie—*never* a Frasier.

What had Brooke called him? Bean? What the hell kind of nickname was that, anyway?

He took comfort in the fact that he must have been right—she'd tried to look him up and found those headlines and seen the pictures and decided it was safer for her and her child if Flash wasn't around. That was the only thing that made sense. He understood that on a rational level. It was a good thing that she'd do anything to protect their son.

But that didn't change the fact that *she hadn't told him.* She'd kept his son away from him. She'd never even given Flash a chance to show he had what it took to be a good father.

He would not let his anger get the better of him, but, by God, he had no idea how he was supposed to forgive her for what she'd done.

Forgiveness could come later. Right now, he had to make sure that Brooke never again managed to hide his son from him. That boy was his just as much as he was hers.

Brooke was the mother of his child.

He knew what he had to do.

He pulled out his phone. Brooke probably wasn't going to like this, but that was too damn bad, wasn't it? He wasn't about to try to handle a situation of this magnitude by himself. God only knew that'd be a disaster. Something like this required finesse and PR skills, not to mention a sensitive touch. None of those things would ever describe Flash, in this life or the next.

But they did describe his sister, Chloe.

He got voice mail and, scowling, hit Redial. He knew Chloe and her husband, Pete, were already in Nashville. They always got in a few days early to get everything set up for the All-Around All-Stars Rodeo. Finally, on the third try, Chloe answered and said in a breathless voice, "This better be important, Flash."

He cringed, trying not to think about what he'd interrupted. "Sis," he began, but the words, *I have a son with Brooke* got stuck in his throat.

Not that Chloe would've listened anyway. "I swear to

God, if you're in jail, I'm going to leave you to rot this time," she snapped.

In the background, Flash heard Chloe's husband, Pete Wellington, growl, "Now what's he done?"

Well, sometimes she had finesse. "Go to hell," Flash muttered. "I am having a legitimate problem and I thought I could count on you, but if you both are going to treat me like I'm a child, I'll do this myself." He hung up and then had to walk around the damn truck a few more times.

Yeah, he'd done more than enough to screw up his own life in the past. He knew that. Hell, everyone knew that. But since he'd started therapy, he would've thought he'd demonstrated that he was serious about being a better man. But maybe Chloe would always see a failure when she looked at him and, frankly, Flash didn't have the time or space to deal with that. Especially not right now.

He hadn't gotten far when his phone rang. Chloe. If he wasn't desperate he'd ignore her, but…

"Sorry," he gritted out. Chloe had always been the one to bail him out before, and he knew she hated it. "I'm not in jail or drunk. Not in a bar."

"What's wrong?" At least now she sounded concerned. And, oddly, that was what Flash needed.

"If I send you an address—a house—can you and Pete be here in…" He mentally calculated how long it'd take them to get from the hotel next to the Bridgestone arena in downtown Nashville to Brooke's house. "In twenty minutes? Quietly, without attracting any attention?"

After all, Flash hadn't known about his son because no one did. James Frasier Bonner hadn't shown up on any social media or paparazzi site. Brooke had gone dark months ago. Probably about the time she'd been unable to hide her pregnancy anymore.

"Flash," Chloe said, and finally she sounded about

right for this situation—worried, a little scared. "What's going on?"

He looked up at that lit window, where the one woman he couldn't forget was holding a son he hadn't known he had. This was how it had to be.

"I have a baby."

Chloe gasped, a noise of pure pain. Flash could hear Pete in the background saying, "Hon? You okay?" Belatedly, Flash remembered that Chloe had been trying to get pregnant for months now with no luck.

"Sorry, sis. I just found out. And I need help."

"Yes." He could hear her pulling herself back together. "Yes, of course we'll help. Who's…" She swallowed nervously. "Who's the mother?"

He looked up at the window again. Brooke was standing there, James Frasier Bonner in her arms. She'd always been the most beautiful woman he'd ever seen, but there was something about the image she presented, his son resting his head against her breast, her arms holding the baby tight—there was something right about it.

Why hadn't she told him? Damn it all to hell.

"It's Brooke. Brooke Bonner had my son."

He exhaled slowly. He was going to make things right, starting *now*.

# Six

What was he doing out there?

Flash appeared to be pacing around his truck, which was hopefully an improvement over the way he'd all but bolted out of the house like the hounds of hell were nipping at his heels.

It was a good sign, she decided as she quickly washed up. He hadn't driven off in a blind fury, and even though he'd obviously been upset—what a pitifully weak word *that* was—he hadn't done anything...scary.

God, this was a freaking mess. She was nauseous with worry. For crying out loud, she could face down an arena filled with fifty thousand screaming fans with little more than a few butterflies in her stomach, but one man was going to be her undoing.

As if he could sense her panic, Bean looked up at her from where she'd set him down on the rug and smiled like he was trying to reassure her. He had his father's charm, but Bean's drooly grin was all sweetness and innocence, whereas Flash's grins promised wonderful, dangerous things. Things like long nights in hotels and hot sex against the door.

Brooke clung to that innocent baby grin. "Oh, you're having a grand time, aren't you?" she cooed to him as she swept him into her arms. "All sorts of excitement happening here tonight, and none of it involves sleeping."

Bean gurgled appreciatively and Brooke kissed his little head. At least someone was having fun.

Bean in her arms, she peeked out the window. Flash was still out there, leaning against the side of the truck. Wait—was he on his phone? Oh, hell.

Just then Flash glanced up, and even through the dark and distance, she *felt* the moment their gazes locked.

Who was he talking to? This could be a disaster. Of course there was a contingency plan for when she announced Bean's existence and, knowing her publicist, there was one for if the information leaked. She didn't want Bean to be gossip. She wanted to be the one controlling the information. She wanted to introduce her son to the world.

She could still get in front of this. She was supposed to meet with the publicist about tonight's show and approve a series of small shows on Music Row in downtown Nashville until the album officially dropped. Then there was a tour that was already set up, even though it hadn't been announced yet. She had to go over the album the final time with the producers. And then there were the interviews—so far, all by phone.

They might have to spend all that time talking about her one big mistake instead of her album, but she was going to control this narrative, by God.

With or without Flash.

Would he acknowledge the baby publicly? Would he sign off on the inevitable PR that would go along with introducing Bean to the world?

Or was this about to be a fight?

She didn't want a fight. She didn't want to be on opposite sides of Flash, stuck in a tug-of-war with the baby as the rope. She wanted Flash on her side.

Especially since Brooke was going to have to tell her mother about him. At the rate things were going, Brooke would have to tell her soon. Like, in a day or two. God help her, Brooke didn't want to.

Flash Lawrence was the sum total of things Crissy Bonner hated and Brooke knew it. Crissy would do the exact same thing Brooke had done—she'd start by researching Flash, and the moment those headlines came up it'd be all over.

It wouldn't matter how much Flash would claim he'd changed. Crissy Bonner would see only the irresponsible, immature ass who'd knocked her daughter up and abandoned her to brawl in bars and ride bulls—all of which put the carefully crafted career Crissy had been arranging since Brooke had turned five in danger of collapsing under the weight of scandal. Brooke didn't know anything about her father, who Mom claimed had split when Brooke was still crawling. But, needless to say, Crissy Bonner was not a big fan of any man who abandoned a woman and a child.

Nope. None of that was *for the best*.

Cuddling Bean to her chest, Brooke settled into the rocker. No matter what, her son came first. She and Flash would…work something out. Shared custody, maybe. Brooke wouldn't allow her mother or her record label or anyone—not even Flash himself—to hurt her child.

But what if there could be something more? For the first time since Bean had announced himself to Flash, Brooke's thoughts turned not to what'd happened months ago or what was going to happen tomorrow, but to those last few moments before it'd all gone to hell.

Flash, pressing her back against the door. Flash, kissing her even better than she'd remembered. Flash, bringing her to orgasm like no time at all had passed between this night and the one thirteen months ago.

Flash, reminding her who she'd been before she'd become a mother.

She shuddered, her body tightening almost painfully with need. She didn't know how this would work—would they date? Be co-parents? It seemed pretty obvious that she couldn't spend any time with Flash without having hot, *great* sex. She was too aware of him, too needy for him. So could they be co-parents with benefits, maybe? She'd be okay with that. Bean could spend time with his father, and she could keep Flash in her bed.

Anything more seemed unlikely—he'd be chasing the rodeo and she was supposed to go on tour. They'd rarely be in the same town at the same time, much less in the same state.

Of course, that all depended on if he was calling his lawyer or the press or, hell, his girlfriend, didn't it?

She stared down at Bean, his eyes already half closed as he held on to her thumb with his tiny fingers, nursing happily. She'd never been away from her son for longer than a few hours, recording her album in between nursing him. She wanted her son to know his father, she really did. It pained her to think of him missing that part of his life, his history. She had no idea who her father's people were. Her mom had erased any trace of that man from the record.

She wouldn't allow that to happen for Bean. She was *not* going to turn into her mother.

But she couldn't bear the thought of a custody battle with Flash, couldn't even consider the idea that she might lose her son.

Brooke made her decision.

She wouldn't ask for anything more from Flash than he was willing to give, and she wouldn't let him reject his son. And there was no way in hell she would let him take the boy away from her.

She might have dozed, she couldn't tell. The next thing she knew, Flash was sitting on the footstool before her, staring at where Bean was still barely latched on.

Flash didn't look mad. If anything, he looked...focused. He wasn't pale and that wild look was gone from his eyes. When he glanced up at her, that ghost of a smile played over his lips, and she felt a smile of her own answer his.

"I'll put him down, then we can talk," she whispered. Flash nodded. She moved Bean to her shoulder and gently patted his back. Flash studied her every move with an intensity that sent little shivers down her back. When she pushed to her feet, he stood with her.

She put Bean on his back in the crib and stared down at her perfect little boy, clinging to what might be the last moment of peace for a while. The moment she left this room, things would change—quickly.

Then Flash stepped up next to her, shoulders touching, his hip warm against hers, his fingers brushing hers on the crib rail. She fought the urge to wrap her arm around his waist and lean into him.

This was what she wanted, this closeness. This feeling of being part of a team. Yeah, she had Alex and her mother, but it wasn't the same. Only Flash could seduce her with that smile, make her feel like he did.

But it was an illusion, one shattered when he leaned over and said against her ear, "We need talk. *Now*."

She nodded and, after leaning over to brush her fingers over the baby's forehead, headed down to the library. At least, that's what she called the room, because it's where all the books were, as well as her piano. It was mostly where she went when she needed a little peace and quiet to write, because the library was on the complete opposite side of the house from Bean's room. If there had to be shouting, hopefully they wouldn't wake the baby back up.

Flash didn't follow her at first. She turned back to see him lean over the crib, a look of what she hoped was adoration on his face as he touched Bean's forehead almost the exact same way Brooke had.

"Sleep for Mommy, little man," he whispered, and if it were possible to fall in love with him in a moment, she might have done so because Flash was going to love Bean, and the baby would know his father and everything would work out.

A vision of a happy family assembled itself in her mind's eye, one where Flash got up with Bean when he fussed at night and kissed her awake in the morning. A lifetime of teaching Bean to walk and swim and ride horses, of singing along to her songs when they came on the radio and watching Flash ride from the bleachers at the rodeo. She wanted it all with him, everything that went into being a family—first steps and first words, first *everything*.

And when Bean went to bed, she wanted Flash waiting up for her after a show or coming home to her after a rodeo, celebrating his win and her hits with hot kisses and hotter sex. A lifetime of losing themselves in each other, where the sex only got better and Flash was a man she could count on, through good times and bad. Where she was the only woman he needed or wanted.

Then Flash turned to her and another icy shiver raced down her back. That intensity was still there, but anything sweet or adoring was long gone.

*Say something romantic.* She didn't miss that the other chorus line—*Don't say something romantic*—had disappeared completely. She couldn't stop the melody from running through her head, couldn't stop wishing Flash would hear the same song.

But it wasn't meant to be because even if Flash wasn't

throw-things-against-the-wall mad, it was obvious he was still freaking furious.

Right. Best get this over with.

She headed down the stairs, determined to hash this out. She could like him and she could want him, but she wasn't going to torpedo her career or risk her son's happiness to soothe over Flash's ruffled feathers. He could just be mad. She would protect her family.

By the time she reached the bottom of the stairs, Flash caught up with her. He grabbed her hand, as if he were afraid she might bolt. "How old?" he asked softly, even as his fingers were as hard as steel around hers.

He was hard and soft all at once, intense and gentle. She wanted to lean into him, but she wasn't entirely sure she could trust that he wouldn't push her away.

"He'll be four months next Wednesday. In here," she replied, leading him into the library. "I was in labor the night of the Grammys. I had him at three in the morning."

"Ah. I wondered why you weren't there." Flash guided her to the long blue couch arranged in front of the fireplace, but instead of sitting next to her he moved to the mantel. "Did everything go okay? Any..." He swallowed, looking ill. "Any problems for you or him?"

"No. Labor was long and not fun, but everyone was fine. Seven pounds, six ounces, all his fingers and toes. The doctors say he's right where he should be."

Flash slumped against the mantel in relief. "Good. That's good. I wish I'd been there for you."

"I wish you had been, too."

Flash stared down at the floor. "Was I right earlier? You looked me up and found the headlines?"

Her cheeks blazed with heat, but the hell of it was, she had no idea why she was embarrassed. "I did. I'm sorry, Flash. I—"

"Don't apologize." His voice was harder now. "I brought

that on myself, as my sister is so fond of reminding me." He closed his eyes and another few moments passed. Was this normal for him? She should know—but she didn't because every time she was around him, they wound up having sex instead of deep, meaningful conversations.

"Just for the record," he began suddenly in a low voice, "if I walk out of the room, it's because I don't want to lose my temper, not because I'm walking away from you. I'll come back when I'm in control because we are nowhere *near* done, Brooke."

Honest to God, she had no idea if that was a threat or a promise. "All right." She shifted nervously, trying to find something to do with her hands. She wished she could go sit at her baby grand piano and let her fingers work out a melody. She thought better when she let the music carry away her anxiety.

"Are you mad at me?" she asked. As if that answer wasn't obvious.

"I am extremely upset," he said, his voice oddly level. His eyes closed again, and he exhaled for a long moment before going on, "I am mad at you because you didn't tell me about my son. I am mad at myself because I know we used protection, but obviously it failed and I failed you. Repeatedly. I obviously wasn't as careful with your health as I should've been, and I wasn't the kind of person who you thought you could trust."

Wait—was he not throwing her under the bus here? Was he taking *responsibility*? At least some of it? "I don't blame you for this, Flash. We used condoms, but it takes two to tango."

He nodded curtly, which was the only way she knew he'd heard her. "I've learned that, for me, anger is a catch-all for my emotions, and it takes work to understand the other things I'm feeling. I am *damned* hurt right now. And surprised and a little scared and...*mad*. Because how could you hide him from me, Brooke? How could you not even give me a chance?"

His voice had begun to approach a shout, but he checked himself and began to pace in a tight circle in front of the mantel. She was reminded of an unbroken horse in a corral, running back and forth and trying to decide if it was going to charge the fence or not.

Would he bolt? Or would he settle?

"I was going to tell you," she explained.

"When?" he snapped. "Because that baby's well past newborn, Brooke."

She winced. She hated this guilt, but he was right. "I always meant to tell you, but it was easy to put off contacting you until tomorrow and tomorrow and tomorrow, and the longer I didn't tell you, the more I was afraid that you'd…"

"That I'd punch a wall or wrap my truck around a light pole?"

She winced at the truth of that. "No one else knows about him except Alex, my mother and a few medical professionals, all of whom signed nondisclosure agreements in addition to their legal obligations to keep my medical history private. Oh, and a few record executives, all who had a vested interest in keeping the news quiet."

Confusion flitted across his face. "Why, though? Are you ashamed of him?"

"Of course not." Brooke slumped back against the couch. Suddenly she was tired. She'd done a show tonight and hooked up with Flash, and now had to defend the choices she'd made during the most stressful moments of the last year. Of her *life*. "It's because I wouldn't tell anyone who you were. Not a single person knows you're Bean's father— or knew. Alex figured it out tonight. I never wanted to keep this a secret, but I got overruled by literally everyone else, all because I didn't want to bring you into it."

His eyes bugged out. "You didn't tell anyone about me?"

"You were my secret. Those headlines..." She shuddered. "Because I wouldn't identify you, my mother and my record label decided to keep the pregnancy quiet."

"Damn it," he growled, but at least he growled quietly. "I was following your career and you suddenly fell off the map and I had no idea. If I'd known, I..." He stopped and suddenly paced to the doorway, but he didn't walk out. Instead, he turned back around. He looked tortured and it hurt her.

She'd made the best of a bad situation, but she'd never stopped second-guessing herself. And the fact that he wasn't screaming and blaming her for getting pregnant in the first place—that was what she'd feared. And what she'd expected, to be honest, after reading all those headlines.

His response gave her hope. Maybe this could work. Somehow.

She went to him, resting her hand on his arm. His eyes softened as he cupped her cheek with his hand and stroked her skin with his thumb. "I wish it'd been different," she whispered, leaning into his touch. "I'm so sorry, Flash. I'd change the past if I could but..."

"Neither of us can."

Somehow, she and Flash were getting closer. His arm slid around her waist and her head rested on his shoulder. God, it felt so damn good. This was who she wanted—Flash at his best.

"He's such a great baby, Flash. I want him to know his whole family—your family."

"I called my sister," he told her. "Chloe—remember meeting her at the Fort Worth rodeo?" Brooke nodded and Flash went on, his arms tightening around her waist. "She and her husband Pete run the All-Stars and they're in town. They're heading over."

"That's fine. Chloe seemed nice."

Actually, Chloe had been more than a little upset with

Brooke because hooking up with Flash had made Brooke late to start her show. But Brooke couldn't hold that against the woman. The show had to go on, after all. If someone had to be the first to find out about Bean, it was probably for the best that it was family.

Flash snorted. "She's a bossy know-it-all, but she's saved my butt more times than I can count. And she loves babies."

"That's nice. I…" Swallowing nervously, she tilted her head back and stared up at Flash. It was wonderful that this conversation about the past wasn't a fight, but that didn't mean a discussion of the future would be easy. Especially as his fingers stroked over her skin again, warm and encouraging. Brooke got the words out before his touch distracted her. Again. "I want to make this right. I don't know if you realize this, but to this day my own mother won't tell me who my father is, and I refuse to let my own son grow up like I did. I want us do this parenting thing together."

He took several long breaths, but he didn't close his eyes, didn't walk out of the room and he wasn't yelling—so this was all progress, right? Instead, he pulled her closer, her chest flush against his. Languid heat began to build in her body because even though she was exhausted and relieved and so, *so* thankful that Flash was finally here and it was all going to be okay, she'd had all of one orgasm in months and she selfishly wanted more. With this man—no one else.

*Say something romantic*, she silently begged him as she molded her body against his. Something sweet and hot that would let her know it would all work out just fine. Something that would take this perfect melody between them and make it into a song.

He didn't. He didn't kiss her or offer to hold her for the few short hours of sleep she might get before Bean woke up hungry. Instead, something in his eyes hardened as his arms crushed her against him. When he spoke, his voice was silky smooth and it sent a chill down her spine.

"We're absolutely in this together from now on. That's why we'll get married as soon as possible."

# Seven

"*What?*"

Flash didn't miss the way Brooke's body went stiff in his arms. "Married," he repeated, feeling his blood pressure rise. "As soon as possible. That boy is a Lawrence by blood and by right."

Brooke moved but, instead of curling into him, she twisted out of his grasp. "Flash—what are you *talking* about?"

Not that he expected Brooke to start jumping for joy or anything, but hadn't she just said they were in this together?

"We need to get hitched," he said. "Quickly. Tomorrow, even."

Brooke stared at him with a look of horror on her face. "No. Absolutely not."

No? *No?*

Obviously, they needed to make this legal, especially if she was going to announce *their* baby to the world at large.

"This is nonnegotiable, Brooke. You can't keep pretending that I don't exist because it's convenient for you. That's my son, by God, and I won't let you keep him from me. You *will* marry me!" he yelled.

"I have no intention of keeping your son from you," she shouted back.

Oh, if that didn't just take the cake. "More than you already have, you mean?"

A little of the shock bled into fury as her eyes flashed with righteousness. "We are *not* getting married, Flash. Under *any* circumstance."

She couldn't have hit him harder if she'd actually punched him. He had to grab on to the door frame to hold himself up.

"The hell we aren't," he snapped. "That's my son and we're good in bed—against the door—together. Why wouldn't we get married?"

Dimly, he was aware that probably wasn't the best way to phrase it but, damn it, he was *pissed*. This was not complicated. Brooke was the mother of his child and he liked her. Simple.

Her cheeks blazing, her mouth opened for what looked like a blistering response, but just then headlights flashed through the parlor, cutting her off. They both turned toward the windows as the sound of doors slamming filled the air.

Brooke went to push past him but he grabbed her arm. "This conversation isn't over," he said, trying to make it sound nice and gentle.

But the way her eyes flashed a warning and the way she jerked out of his touch made it plenty clear he hadn't succeeded. "I will *not* be forced into anything I don't want," she said, her tone icy.

Then the doorbell pealed through the house. "Oh, no— the baby!" she said, making a break for the door. "Come inside—quietly," she said to Chloe and Pete, but it was too late because that was when James Frasier Bonner decided he needed to be part of the festivities.

"Oh, I'm so sorry," Chloe Lawrence said in a quiet voice,

even though they were way past whispering. James began to wail. "We didn't mean to wake him!"

"My bad," Pete Wellington said, whipping his hat off his head. "I rang the bell. Didn't think."

Brooke heaved a mighty sigh even as she launched a forgiving smile at Chloe and Pete. "It's okay. Things haven't been exactly *quiet* here tonight," she added, shooting a look at Flash that was part challenge, part scold and all mad.

Was she going to blame this on him? He hadn't been the only one yelling! "With good reason," he shot back, crossing his arms over his chest and trying not to glare. Given the way Pete frowned at him, Flash was pretty sure he hadn't succeeded with that whole not-glaring thing.

But then again, neither had Brooke. "You'll excuse me," she said, her voice tight. "I need to go see to *my* son."

"*Our* son," Flash snapped.

Chloe and Pete took in the tension, shared a look and then moved like a calf-roping team with years of competitions under their belts. "I'll come with you, if that's okay? I can't wait to meet this little guy, even if he's grumpy," Chloe said gently, putting an arm around Brooke's shoulders and turning her toward the stairs. "I'm sure it's been a long night—for all of you."

"You have *no* idea," Brooke said, almost sagging into Chloe. Even through the haze of emotions he was barely keeping in check, Flash heard the sheer exhaustion in her voice.

Well, if that wasn't enough to make a man feel like crap.

But before he could open his mouth—regardless of what was going to come out of it—Pete advanced on him, crowding him back into the room where Flash and Brooke had ended up before.

"How's it going?" the man had the nerve to ask, his hands up as if he were ready to give Flash a hard shove should the need arise.

"Great. Freaking great. Thanks for asking," Flash said. Okay, *snarled*.

He turned and began to pace around the couch. The one where Brooke had sat and said things about understanding and co-parenting, and why, for the love of everything holy, was she so hell-bent on not getting married? Was it marriage in general? Or was it just *him*?

It wasn't like he wanted to get married. He rode the rodeo. He lived out of his suitcase ten months out of the year and rarely saw his own home. That wasn't a lifestyle that lent itself to raising an infant. And this was the year he would win it all. He was off his suspension for fighting, he was sober and focused, and he did not have time to settle down. He'd make time, damn it, because that's what family did. But if he wasn't extremely careful about how this played out, he could kiss his championship year goodbye.

Damn it all to hell. If Brooke had told him about the baby months ago, he could've spent the off season getting to know his son and making plans. Now he had to scramble—and rely on Pete Wellington, of all people, to help him out.

Flash hadn't punched a single person in months—not since he'd gotten into a brawl with his father, his brother Oliver and Pete over Pete's underhanded tactics to win the All-Stars and Chloe away from the Lawrence family. And even then, Flash hadn't been as mad as he was right now. The last time he'd felt this dangerous had been...

It'd been when Tex McGraw had said those things about Brooke and Flash had been booted off the All-Stars as a result of the fight.

"What happened?" Pete kept his voice calm and level, but he wasn't inspiring anything calm or levelheaded in Flash.

"She had my baby and didn't tell me! Come on, Wellington—keep up!" Flash realized his hands were fists now, swinging loosely at his sides as he stalked Pete around the room. He was primed to throw a punch. God, it'd feel so good to just let go...

But Pete had been around Flash long enough that this outburst didn't faze him. "You need to hit something?"

"You volunteering?"

"Jackass," Pete said easily, dancing just out of reach. "Here." He bent over, grabbing the cushions from the seat of the couch. When he had two of them stacked, he held them in front of his stomach and stood in front of Flash. "Go."

"Seriously?" Was the man actually giving Flash permission to punch him?

Pete smiled. Not a big thing, but it was there. "Afraid a cushion will bruise your tiny little—oof! Damn, man— you've got a hell of a kick," Pete wheezed out, stumbling back a step.

A minute passed with nothing but the muffled sounds of Flash punching light blue couch cushions and Pete grunting as he absorbed the blows.

"I told her we had to get married immediately, if not sooner, and she said no, and that's when you showed up." He finished this off with a quick three punches. "This is *supposed* to be my year to win it all. She was *supposed* to be a one-night stand. And we have to get married because I'm not going to let her keep that boy from me, even though it'll screw up all my plans. But she said *no*."

Now that he'd hit something, he felt his anger going from a roiling boil to a low simmer. He punched the cushions one more time and sagged forward, his forehead resting on the top.

He had a son. The enormity of that fact still made him see stars. A healthy little boy who Brooke obviously loved and...

And she hadn't told him.

"Better?" Pete asked, sounding winded.

Flash nodded. He was breathing hard and his hands hurt, but the throbbing pain was good, anchoring him to his body.

Pete shifted, one arm coming up and lying over top of Flash's shoulder. Not that Flash needed a hug and not that this was a hug—but there was something comforting about it, all the same. "I guess I'm not as calm as I thought I was," he mumbled into the cushions.

"Did you hit anyone?" Pete asked, patting Flash on the back.

"Do you count?"

"Not today."

Flash shook his head. "Walked away when I needed to. Called you guys for backup when I realized I couldn't handle this myself."

"Didn't punch me in the face, either. All things considered, you're doing real well."

Flash snorted. It didn't feel like he was doing anything but losing it.

"You said you told her you were getting married?"

"Yeah." The thought left him uneasy. Marriage was… forever. Lawrence men—and Pete by extension—were one and done. If Flash married Brooke, that was it. He was *done*.

He'd do it. He'd do it in a heartbeat because that's what a father did for his son and, honestly, the sex was great. People throughout time had gotten married for less.

But…*marriage*.

To a woman who had no problem keeping secrets from him.

It was a recipe for disaster. And that was if she agreed. Huge *if*.

Pete was silent long enough that Flash lifted his head. When he'd been a hotheaded kid, he'd looked up to Pete

Wellington. The older man was a hell of a good rodeo rider, one Flash had aspired to be like. But for ten years, they'd been on opposite sides of a feud about the ownership of the All-Stars Rodeo. They'd made their peace, mostly, but it was still hard to think of this man as a friend.

Even if Flash suspected that's what Pete was. Who else would take a cushioned pummeling for Flash?

And now Pete was staring at Flash with a look of incredulous amusement on his face. "Where's the charm, Lawrence? I thought—*ow*—you were this legendary ladies' man. You could talk your way into any woman's bed and—*ugh*—make her feel like she was the only woman in the world."

"I am," Flash said, throwing another punch. He was going to owe Brooke a new couch, probably. "I was," he corrected.

He hadn't been that man since, well, since Brooke.

*Maybe it wouldn't be so bad*, a traitorous voice whispered in the back of his head. Great sex, yeah—but Brooke had gotten under his skin well before infants had come into play. Hell, he'd never looked up a one-night stand before, much less a year later. It might even be good...

But he'd have to trust her for that to happen, and she'd have to believe he wasn't the same asshole he'd been before he cleaned up his act, and, yeah, that felt like an impossible mountain to climb.

"You told her," Pete said yet again. "You *told* that woman to marry you, you giant jackass."

"Do you have a point?" Flash punctuated this with another combo punch. "Or are you just going to repeat yourself until the end of time?"

"What did you think would happen, issuing orders like that—to Brooke Bonner, of all people?" Flash paused midswing to stare at Pete, who rolled his eyes. "Next time, try *asking* her." Then he shoved Flash with the cushions.

Stumbling back, Flash gaped at Pete, who shook his head tauntingly.

*Ask* her?

Ask her to marry him. Like, down on one knee, with a ring and a promise.

*Not* an order. A proposal.

Like he cared about her.

Oh, hell—what had Flash done?

# Eight

"I'm so sorry about this," Brooke said, leading Chloe Lawrence upstairs into the nursery, where Bean was screaming.

She felt like screaming, too. The nerve of that man, demanding that she rearrange her entire life—again—to get *married*.

Married! She had a comeback to orchestrate, a record to release, a tour to get through and a baby to announce to the world. Not to mention the whole mom thing, which was a full-time job all by itself. Who the hell had time for a wedding? Maybe in a few years…

Besides—Flash wasn't exactly making his case.

Yes, the sex was as amazing as ever, but she was not going to permanently tie herself to any man, much less one with an arrest record and a penchant for issuing orders. She had enough people in her life telling her what to do and when to do it, treating her as if she couldn't possibly make her own decisions about her life and her career. And now she had to deal with his sister because, of course, Flash had called in reinforcements to try and wear her down, no doubt.

She was more than tempted to call Alex for backup, but

that would undoubtedly lead to a brawl. And calling Crissy Bonner was out of the question—that'd be a brawl *and* a police report. For a brief second, Brooke debated calling Kyle Morgan, but that wouldn't work either, because Kyle would be just as stunned to find out about Bean as Flash had been.

No, Brooke was on her own here.

Then Chloe said, "Do not apologize for anything involving my brother," in a way that made it seem like she might consider Flash to be a butthead or something. When Brooke gave her a funny look, Chloe merely shrugged. "Look, I know he's got it bad for you and I also know I don't currently have all the facts, but just because he *wants* you doesn't mean he *deserves* you."

Brooke gaped at the woman in surprise because that was the thing she'd needed to hear right then. The second part, anyway.

What did she mean, Flash had it bad for Brooke?

"Thank you."

But Chloe wasn't listening. Instead, she'd moved to stand next to the crib, staring down at Bean with absolute adoration in her eyes. "Oh my. Oh, my *goodness*," she whispered, clutching her hands to her chest. "Look at you, sweetie. Hi, honey—I'm your aunt Chloe."

Brooke stepped around Chloe and picked Bean up. Chloe gasped, "Oh, he's *perfect*," her eyes filling with tears. "What's his name?"

"James Frasier Bonner, but I call him Bean," Brooke said.

"Can I hold him?" Chloe was already reaching out for the baby, but she stopped before actually plucking Bean from Brooke's arms. "I'm sorry. I'm just—this is such a surprise and I love babies so much and it's Flash's baby. You even gave him Flash's name!" She gave Brooke a watery smile.

"Sure. Here, take the rocker and we'll see if Bean is feeling sociable."

"Do you want to tell me what's happened?" Chloe said. "I gather that Flash didn't know about that little angel before a few hours ago?"

"No, he didn't. No one knows, really." She nestled Bean in Chloe's arms.

"Oh, goodness," the other woman whispered as Bean stared up at her. Then he turned on his father's charm and smiled at his aunt, who promptly began crying. That startled Bean and made him cry. Frankly, Brooke had no hope of holding herself together. It'd been *such* a long night.

"I'm so sorry," Chloe said again as Brooke took Bean back. "We've been trying to have a baby and…"

"It's okay." Brooke snatched the tissues and everyone took a moment to calm down. She felt terrible for Chloe—Brooke couldn't imagine dealing with infertility and then discovering a sibling had accidentally had a child despite taking precautions? Brooke couldn't fight the guilt that swamped her.

"I'm fine," Chloe said, and her gaze shifted to Brooke. "So how did my brother stick his foot into it this time?"

The story spilled out of Brooke. She tried to keep to just the facts, but then Chloe would say something like "Those headlines must have *horrified* you," or "He did *what*?" It probably wasn't smart to pour her heart out to this woman she barely knew and only in a professional capacity because Brooke had no idea what might be splashed across the internet tomorrow, but, God, it felt so good to talk to someone besides her mother and Alex. The isolation of the last few months caught up with her all at once, and, before she knew it, she was crying into a tissue and Chloe was rocking the baby and everything was still a huge mess. Amazingly, Brooke felt better.

As Brooke finished the story, Chloe gazed down on

Bean, who was playing with an expensive-looking necklace, his eyes drowsy. If Brooke was lucky, Chloe would be able to get the baby back to sleep, and if she was very lucky, no one would shout or slam a door or anything.

Brooke wasn't feeling that lucky.

"So let me see if I've got this right," Chloe said gently. "He told you that you had to marry him? He didn't even *ask?*"

"No!" Brooke said as quietly as she could. Thank God, Chloe got it. "And that's when you walked in."

"Such a jackass. Whoops, sorry, sweetie," she cooed to Bean, who blinked up at her and then launched another charming smile at his aunt. "But he didn't lose his temper?"

"I guess not?" Brooke swallowed. "I mean, he's got a right to be upset. But it was nothing like what those headlines described."

Chloe smirked. "Did he tell you what the fight was about?"

"No?" That didn't sound good.

But Chloe didn't see fit to expand on that comment. Instead, she looked at Brooke. A shiver went down Brooke's back because there was a calculating gleam in the woman's eyes that hadn't been there a moment ago.

"Here's the thing, though—he's not wrong." Brooke inhaled sharply as Chloe went on, "From a public relations point of view, I mean. If you two are married, we could spin this as a secret long-distance relationship instead of a wayward one-night stand. We could make it sound highly romantic while we release little teases of this supposed relationship without revealing too much, while we build up to exclusive interviews and magazine covers. We'd have both your audience and ours *hooked*. The press would be fantastic."

A pit of disquiet began to yawn open in Brooke's stomach. That was probably exactly what the record company would tell her to do, but…

Yes, she wanted to go public with her son. Yes, it made sense to have a plan. And the PR would probably be great.

But was it asking too much for it to be on her terms?

To try to keep some part of her private life private?

"I don't know if I like the sound of that," she told Chloe, trying to be diplomatic about it.

"It's a shame we can't retroactively get last year's date on the wedding certificate," Chloe mused, all of her attention on the baby. Brooke wasn't even sure Chloe had heard her. "But a lie you can prove wrong with a simple records search is a bad lie. Always lie as close to the truth as possible."

Brooke definitely did not like the sound of that. "I don't want to lie anymore."

"Not lie," Chloe went on. "We just want to bend the truth a little. You guys met, had an instant connection, but you couldn't get your schedules lined up…hmm. No, that won't work—Flash was kicked off the rodeo for half the season last year. He could have followed you around easily. No, you were hot and heavy until his arrest, and then you gave him an ultimatum to shape up, which he did."

"Can we slow down for a second here?" Brooke asked, because this was exactly what she was afraid of—Chloe was still going to strong-arm Brooke into doing what Flash wanted, just like Flash had tried to do. The only difference was that Chloe would do it while being all sympathetic and understanding instead of yelling. "There's no way my mother would approve of someone like Flash."

But there was no slowing Chloe. "So he straightened up and you guys have been secretly dating for…five months seems about right. And now that he's passed your tests with flying colors, you guys decided to get married! Yes, I like this. Flash gets his redemption story and you get a huge PR boost for your new album and—"

"I am *not* getting married right now," Brooke burst out.

"I understand your reluctance," Chloe said, not quite as sympathetic as she'd been before. "Flash has that effect on people. But here's the problem—beyond a redemption story or a marketing blitz, what if something happens to you, God forbid?" Before Brooke could panic at this statement—was this a *threat*?—Chloe went on. "Without the legal protection of marriage, would Flash be able to take custody of his own son? Or would your mother keep this perfect little angel away from his own father? Not that we wouldn't fight it in court," Chloe went on, smiling at Bean. "After all, what's the point in being billionaires if you can't buy the best lawyers?"

Billionaires? Brooke inhaled sharply. This *was* a threat.

"But it'd be a long, messy legal battle, one where Flash might not get to see his own son for a long time. I don't know what kind of person your mother is, but if you're concerned about her choices now…" She let the words trail off, her implication clear.

A churning panic took hold of Brooke's stomach because she was not going to get married so Flash could be redeemed and she was not going to marry anyone for the PR, but making sure Flash could care for his own son?

Because Chloe wasn't wrong.

Crissy Bonner might be disappointed that Brooke had gotten knocked up and she would definitely hate Flash, but she loved Bean. She loved being a grandmother and keeping Bean all to herself.

Brooke realized she didn't know how far Crissy would go to keep things that way—all while proclaiming it was *for the best*, no doubt.

"Is that a risk you're willing to take?" Chloe finished softly. "I wouldn't."

"I'm not on death's doorstep," Brooke said, surprised to hear her voice shake. She surged to her feet and plucked

Bean out of Chloe's arms. "I don't have to marry your brother to make sure he gets to see his child, and if you're only here to be the good cop to Flash's bad cop, then you can leave. *Now.*"

She didn't wait for an answer as she stormed from the room and headed downstairs. She was done talking, done with the entire Lawrence family. God, she felt like a fool. Nothing had changed. She and Flash were electric together, but sexual chemistry only got a girl so far. She was not going to let a little lust blind her to the big picture.

She got to the bottom of the stairs and glanced at the front door. Had it only been—what, an hour since Flash had pressed her back against the door and made her feel exactly like the girl she used to be?

Less than an hour. Less than an evening for Flash Lawrence to blow into her life like a twister, leaving a wake of destruction in his path.

And who had to clean up after the storm had passed? She did. Again.

Starting right now, she and Flash were on a no-touching basis. She couldn't afford to be selfish anymore. She had to be a mother, and if that meant it was her against Flash, the Lawrence family, her own family, her record label and, hell, the whole world, then that's the battle Brooke would fight.

She was done hiding and done apologizing. As much as she might miss the girl she'd been before, she was a different woman now. There was no going back.

She strode into the library, her mouth open to tell everyone to get the hell out—but what she saw made her stumble to a stop. Flash had Pete Wellington pinned against the far wall and was punching him in the stomach again and again as Pete grunted in pain, like something out of her nightmares.

"What are you doing?" she cried out in horror.

# Nine

Flash spun midpunch, stumbled and almost lost his balance. "Brooke?"

Bean began to cry and Pete said, "Oh, hell."

Damn it.

"It's not what it looks like," he said in what he hoped was a calm voice. He'd just figured out how he'd screwed up. He couldn't afford to make this worse.

"He's not hurting me," Pete called over his shoulder, although the slightly pained tone of his voice made it seem like a lie.

"That's not what it looks like?" Brooke edged toward the door, tucking the baby so Flash couldn't even see the kid.

Oh, God—if she ran now, he had no idea when he'd get to see his son again, and that was a risk he wasn't willing to take. So he said, "It's not. I'm hitting cushions."

"Cushions?" Brooke's eyes bugged out of her head.

"It's okay. No one's in any danger," he said.

It hurt, the look in her eyes. She was furious and scared and exhausted, and Flash wasn't making anything better. God, he never should've ordered her to marry him. Pete had been exactly right. Obviously Brooke felt backed into a corner.

"What's wrong?" Chloe said, running into the room. "Who's hurt?"

"No one," Flash said as calmly as he could—which, all things considered, actually did come out calmly. He owed one to Pete for helping him get to this point because if the man hadn't had the idea to punch a couch, Flash knew he wouldn't be able to think, much less act rationally.

What a mess.

"Brooke? I was hitting cushions."

"Cushions," Pete confirmed. He stepped around Flash, holding the cushions up. "From the couch. See?"

"It's okay," Chloe said softly, reaching out to pat Bean, who was not having a great night, either. None of them were.

"Why would you do that?" Brooke said, looking completely bewildered.

Aw, hell. He'd never wanted a do-over so badly in his entire life. He'd hit the chute at the start of the ride but, unlike in the rodeo, he wasn't going to get a reride. The night had started so well, but then she'd dropped the bomb about the baby, and since then he had not handled things well. He needed to get back to where she was in his arms and he remembered how to be the charming guy she wanted and they weren't on opposite sides.

"Like primal scream therapy, you know? Just blowing off steam so I could think. It was a controlled release. It's okay," he repeated.

"Don't you dare try that—*charm*, Flash Lawrence," Brooke said, her voice cracking as she backed away from Chloe's touch. "Nothing about this is okay!"

"I know," Flash said through gritted teeth, holding his hands out in the sign of surrender. He kept plenty of distance between him and Brooke and shot a look at Chloe that said, *Back off.* Which, to her credit, she did. Crowding Brooke right now would only make the fight-or-flight reaction worse.

"It'll be okay." He lied because he didn't trust her, she clearly didn't trust him, and neither of those facts changed reality—in this case, the baby boy who was making pitifully sad noises.

Brooke looked from worried face to worried face. Chloe helped Pete put the cushions back on the couch, leaving the exit open. Brooke eyed them warily, but she didn't bolt, and for that Flash was thankful.

"You weren't attacking him," she said, dropping her gaze as her cheeks shot scarlet.

Flash had the overwhelming urge to sweep her into his arms, take her upstairs and tuck her in. Then, in the morning, they'd have a good laugh about this. Ha-ha-ha.

"No."

"He really wasn't," Pete added, thankfully no longer sounding winded. Flash glanced back to see Chloe and Pete standing side by side, his arm around her shoulders as she leaned into him, her gaze fastened on Brooke and the baby. Flash got the feeling that Pete was holding Chloe back. He caught Flash's gaze and nodded encouragingly. "Miss Bonner, I know you don't know me from Adam, but I've known Flash for almost eleven years now and I'd swear on a Bible in a court of law that he's not the same immature, hotheaded jerk he used to be."

"Thanks, Pete, but I got it from here," Flash grumbled.

"It was my idea for him to hit the cushions," Pete went on. "I was just holding them."

"Oh, my God, I'm such a fool," Brooke blurted out, shifting Bean so she could swipe the back of her hand over her eyes.

More than her hard *no* to his terrible proposal, more than the surprise of the baby, it was the sight of Brooke

trying not to cry that did him in. He was so mad at her—
that wasn't going away. But he also wanted to take care
of her and those two things weren't playing nicely inside
his head.

"No, you're not," Flash said quickly. "Nothing tonight
has been normal." There had to be a way to fix this, damn
it. But how? Well, an apology was a good place to start.
"I'm sorry, babe."

She made a noise that was halfway between a sob and
a laugh. "Do you even know what you're apologizing for
this time, or are you just guessing again?"

"It's a long list," he agreed, managing to put a good smile
into it. "But top of the list is that I shouldn't have told you
we had to get married. Even if it's a good idea."

"No," Brooke said, her voice shaky and her eyes huge,
"you shouldn't have. No one should've." She cut a glance
at Chloe. Flash didn't follow Brooke's gaze, but he heard
Chloe sigh. "I don't want to be forced into anything."

*That* Flash understood completely. He'd always been
the kind of guy who'd get a direct order and do the exact
opposite just to prove he could. God, why hadn't he seen
her reaction coming? He'd just been so convinced of the
rightness of him and Brooke being together that he'd stam-
peded right over her.

Brooke sniffed again, dashing more tears off her cheeks.
Flash wanted to fold Brooke into his arms and make everything okay again. But it was clear that doing anything like
that would just make Brooke dig in her heels even deeper.
Sometimes, a man had to call a tactical retreat if he wanted
to live to fight another day.

Figuratively speaking, of course.

"It's been a long night and you've got to be exhausted
from the show," he said, trying to give her a nice smile.
"I'm truly sorry how this evening has gone down. I think
it's time for us to leave so you and James can get some

sleep." And he could figure out what Chloe had said that had thrown Brooke into such a panic.

He wanted her. He didn't trust her. He needed to marry her.

God, what a freaking *mess*.

Brooke stared down at the baby. Even Flash could tell the boy was uncomfortable, squirming in his mother's arms. "We can try, anyway."

He came damn close to offering to stay the night so she could sleep and he could rock his son in his arms and get to know the boy. And then he'd be here in the morning when Brooke woke up and they could...

Well, the odds of them having great sex again seemed so small right now as to be nonexistent. But they could talk, hopefully without panic or bitterness.

But discretion was the better part of valor, damn it. And he needed to regroup in a serious way. So, instead, he said, "I'd like to see you again so we can try this whole talking thing. I'm in town through..." He thought quickly. He didn't have to be in Lexington, Kentucky, for ten days, which didn't seem like enough time to get this situation resolved peacefully.

Crud. His lead in the rankings was tenuous. Skipping a rodeo would knock him down several places and might ultimately cost him the Cowboy of the Year championship.

But then he looked at Brooke again and sighed. Missing one rodeo wouldn't be the end of the world. Just so long as it didn't become a habit. Surely, in a week or two they could get some sort of custody plan or visitation schedule set up, and he could come right back to Nashville after the rodeo.

"For as long as you need me to be," he corrected. "We can meet here or in public, wherever you want. Bring Alex."

He didn't want Alex there because Alex would probably beat the ever-loving hell out of him, and Flash would have no choice but to take it.

"You're being charming again," she mumbled, but he caught the way she tucked her lower lip under her teeth and peeked at him.

"Trying to," he agreed with an easy smile. That little flash of normalcy was encouraging. If everything could just calm down, he was sure he could talk sense into Brooke. He truly did want what was best for her and for their son. Brooke in his life was what he wanted. And if that included her being in his bed, well that was just icing on the cake.

"Flash, we need to have a plan—" Chloe started to say.

Flash held up a hand, cutting her off. "Nothing needs to be decided tonight. The only thing that needs to happen right now is Brooke needs to take care of herself and the baby. That's it." And he needed to get a grip on his priorities.

The look Brooke shot him was full of worry and hope and maybe just a little appreciation. At least, he hoped it was appreciation. "I have a meeting at one tomorrow to discuss the Bluebird show. I suppose we could meet after that? Maybe for coffee?" She glanced back at Chloe and Pete again. "Just the two of us. No offense."

It was Pete who answered. "None taken."

Flash worked real hard not to show his disappointment. Because he *wasn't* disappointed that she wasn't asking him to stay. He was happy that she wasn't insisting they bring their seconds to the meeting. Really, it was great news that Brooke was still willing to talk to him at all. "You name the place and I'll be there. Just text me."

She nodded and then looked toward the door. Right. They were leaving—now.

Chloe and Pete got the hint. They stepped forward, Chloe's gaze locked on to the baby. "My deepest apologies for coming on too strong," Chloe said, regret filling her voice. She reached out and, when Brooke didn't shy away, Chloe rubbed James's back. "I hope we can see this special little guy again soon?"

"I'll set it up with Flash." Brooke didn't sound too sure about it, though.

"Thank you," Chloe said, her voice cracking. "He's such a beautiful baby."

Pete held her tight and said, "Miss Bonner, we love your music. Can't wait for the new stuff. And no matter what, welcome to the family." Then he led his wife away.

As the front door opened, Flash heard Chloe almost whimper, "Oh Pete—that baby!"

"I know, hon. I know," Pete replied, his voice choked with emotion.

Then they were gone and Flash was alone with Brooke. "I'm sorry about that. I thought they were going to help," he said quietly.

"Did they?" She didn't move back, didn't shield the baby with her body.

"Pete did. This was—*is* a lot. For both of us." He closed the distance between them and lifted James out of her arms. Thank goodness she didn't resist. He tucked the baby under his chin. This, at least, he was pretty good at. He'd had plenty of practice holding Trixie, after all. He should probably thank Oliver for that—right after Oliver got done tearing him a new one for getting Brooke pregnant in the first place.

Man, this was one of the bigger messes he'd ever been in.

"I don't think I've ever apologized *for* my sister before," he went on. "Usually it's the other way around."

Brooke looked at him, her eyes huge and tired. But despite the toll the night had taken on her—on them all—Flash was pretty damn sure he'd never seen anyone as beautiful as she was. "It's fine, Flash," she said. He couldn't tell if she was being honest or not. "I suspect that you Lawrences are a hardheaded lot."

"Guilty as charged," he said with a good-natured grin. He patted James's back. "Thank you for this—for *him*. I don't know if I said that earlier or not."

"No, you didn't." Her face softened as she looked at the two of them. Wildly, Flash hoped she liked what she saw. Because he wasn't going to give this kid up. Hell, no. Whether she married him or not, whether he forgave her or not, they were in this together.

It'd be so much easier if they were really together, though. There had to be a way.

Flash pressed a tender kiss to the top of James's head. "Sleep for your mom, okay, sweetie?" Then he turned his attention back to Brooke. "Is there anything else I can do for you tonight?"

He knew she wasn't going to ask him to stay, not after he'd made a royal ass of himself tonight. But that didn't change things.

Damn it. He needed to marry her to make things legal for the baby. But did he seriously want to marry her?

He'd dreamed of this woman for a year. He thought he'd been dreaming of the sex, the easy jokes. What if he'd really been dreaming of something more?

*Something more* had to wait.

He had to man up and make things right. Any potential feelings he had for Brooke would come later, if they came at all.

"I'll… I'll see you tomorrow?" she said softly, taking a sleepy James back from Flash. Then her gaze dropped to his lips.

This wasn't Flash's first rodeo. "Tomorrow," he agreed, his voice barely a whisper. Then he leaned forward and brushed his lips against hers.

He didn't linger, didn't press the issue. "Call me for any reason. I can be right back out here in under twenty minutes." He'd have to see about getting a different hotel room closer to her house.

She nodded, looking breathless. Flash was sorely tempted to lean in for another kiss, something longer and hotter and...

Yeah, no. He backed away before he let his dick do the thinking. That's what had gotten them into this mess in the first place. "Good night, Brooke."

He was almost out of the room when she spoke. "Flash?"

*Yes*. But he didn't cheer. He turned and asked, "What, babe?"

"This can't get out yet. I can't have my mother finding out about you. Not..." Even across the room in the dark, he saw her swallow nervously. "Not yet."

Hadn't she mentioned her mother earlier? Brooke's record company and mother had all decided that she had to keep her pregnancy and baby a secret because Brooke wouldn't name him as the father? And now Brooke wasn't necessarily afraid of the press finding out about the baby, but she was clearly worried about her mother.

That bothered him. Damn it. He wished his own mother was still here. She'd be able to tell Flash if that was a normal mother-daughter thing or not. But maybe his sister-in-law Renee could shine a little light on how tense mother-daughter relationships worked. He'd have to ask, after Oliver got done chewing him out.

"I won't. No one outside of Chloe and Pete will know until you're ready to tell them. Well," he quickly corrected, "Chloe and Pete and my older brother, Oliver, and his wife, who's Chloe's best friend. It doesn't go farther than that."

They'd all wait to tell Milt Lawrence for a little bit. If Dad found out he had another grandbaby, life would get very complicated very fast.

"Your brother and his wife? Will they keep it quiet?"

"Absolutely. But outside of them, no one will know. You can hold me to that, Brooke."

She sagged in what he hoped was relief. "Okay. Good. Um, good night."

"Night, babe." Then, moving as quickly as he could, he walked his butt right out of that house and started thinking hard about tomorrow.

How did a man propose a marriage of convenience the second time after completely botching the first time?

# Ten

"So you'll think about it?" Kari Stockard said, trailing after Brooke as she walked out of the conference room. "The press we'd get from the baby pictures alone could put your album sales over the top, Brooke. You know that."

"Yes, you said as much in the meeting." Repeatedly. Kari was a fine PR manager, but Brooke could take only so much browbeating, and what should've been a quick check-in about the Bluebird performance had instead been Brooke on one side of a conference table and seven— seven!—executives, managers and other people wearing suits on the other side, all trying to tell her what to do with her personal life. And they didn't even know about Flash yet.

Brooke had done a thorough internet check before she'd walked into that meeting this morning, and there was nothing connecting her and Flash. Bless Kyle Morgan's heart, he'd kept his mouth shut.

Brooke wished she'd brought Alex as backup today— but this was supposed to have been a short meeting, not the full-court press, so she'd told her best friend to take the day off because she wasn't up to the conversation Alex would want to have about Flash. Brooke hadn't even brought Mom, who was technically her manager. Instead, Mom was at home with Bean. Not that Mom would've been much help, anyway. She would've agreed to everything the label wanted, as evidenced by her parting shot this morning, which had been, "Sweetheart, don't you think that, with the album release coming up, you're going to want to tell the world about Jimmy?" No one called Bean that except for Crissy Bonner.

"The timing is perfect," Kari went on, still trailing Brooke. "Think of the buzz!"

So, yeah, Brooke was on her own here and it was exhausting. Was it wrong to want someone in her court? She picked up the pace. If she could make it to her car…well, then she could go meet with Flash and fight a completely different battle.

She didn't want it to be a battle, though. She wanted… to feel like she was in control of something. Anything.

Kari wasn't giving up anytime soon. She matched Brooke's pace. "We wouldn't even have to name the father. We could say you'd done in vitro! From a sperm bank?"

"Nope." She was practically jogging at this point. "When I'm ready to take him public, I'll let you know." She made the door.

"Before the album drops?" Kari yelled after her.

"You, too!" Brooke called over her shoulder, intentionally mishearing Kari's question. Her head hurt. Kari didn't know who Flash was so there'd been no discussion of a redemption arc or marriage, but, otherwise, Kari's plan was practically identical to what Chloe had outlined last night.

Brooke got to her car and paused long enough to make sure Kari hadn't trailed her before she slumped back in the seat. The day of public reckoning was coming, that much was certain. But would it involve a wedding or just a baby?

She just wanted to write her songs and perform, and,

yeah, she wanted to make a lot of money—money she controlled, not her mother or her uncle, the rat bastard. Being raised by a single mother meant that Brooke hadn't grown up rich. But everything else that went with being famous? It was all a huge pain in the ass, frankly.

She sat for a moment, trying to get her thoughts in order. Which, of course, took the shape of a melody. Somewhere in the middle of the night, dozing in the chair with Bean, the song in her head had shifted to something darker, something more raw. *Don't say something romantic* was still there, but another song was lurking at the edge of her subconscious.

The stripped-down acoustics of the new melody ran through her mind, full of anguish. A song about being stuck in an impossible situation with no right answers. She opened the notes program on her phone and dictated the lyrics. If nothing else, art imitating her life made for good inspiration.

God, this was a mess.

Because the fact was that everything Chloe Lawrence had said last night hadn't been wrong. Legally, Flash was a persona non grata when it came to Bean. He wasn't on the birth certificate and, until paternity tests happened, he couldn't prove that he was Bean's father, although all anyone had to do was look at the way those two smiled to see the truth.

It didn't matter how Chloe or Kari promised to spin it to her advantage—the simple truth was that for a few weeks, the press would be brutal. All the more so because she'd had the nerve to hide her pregnancy and child this long. Maybe it was selfish or cowardly, but she didn't want to face it alone.

Part of hitting it big last year had been the public perception that Brooke Bonner didn't screw around, do drugs or drink. She might write some saucy songs, but she was a role model to girls—play by the rules and you'll go far. Shattering that mostly true image with an out-of-wedlock baby would cost her fans.

Getting married to Flash—and quickly—meant that she wouldn't have to face the press on her own. It'd also mean she wouldn't have to hide the fact that she was sleeping with him. Assuming she was going to keep sleeping with him.

Was she assuming that?

Just thinking about the orgasm last night kicked her pulse up a notch. But that perfect moment, like the one in Fort Worth over a year ago, was completely overshadowed by what came afterward.

How was marrying Flash the smart thing to do?

The words *but how could I say no?* popped into her mind. Frankly, after that meeting, Brooke could use a drink. *I could use a shot of something stronger,* she dictated, letting the words flow, feeling her way toward what came next.

*Can't afford the mistake the whiskey would help me make?*

Yeah, it needed work. And she was stalling. She'd told Mom she had a coffee date planned with Kyle Morgan to go over a song. And she was, technically, thinking about lyrics, so it wasn't a total lie. But she had an afternoon to decide the direction of her life for the immediate future before everything spun out of control for her again.

She knew what she had to do. She needed to ask Flash to meet her at a coffee shop. Where are you? she texted.

He answered back in seconds. My hotel. Where do you want to meet? Clearly, he'd been waiting on her. The thought made her relax just a bit.

The responsible thing to do would be to name a bar or restaurant or coffee shop. They needed to stay in public, as part of a crowd, so they could have a mature, rational discussion about parenting and not getting married like adults. That certainly would be the smart course of action.

But all the logic in the world didn't seem to apply when it came to her and Flash. She wanted to feel like she had a choice. And, damn it all, she wanted him. In a bed, this time. Yeah, she was apparently going to keep sleeping with him. What's your room number?

The replay came immediately: 623—you want to meet here?

She wanted a do-over of last night, before it'd all blown up in her face. Just him and her and no big surprises, waiting to ruin everything, lurking in the wings this time. Brooke wanted more than fifteen minutes of satisfaction in Flash's arms. It was selfish, sure. And after last night, it was clearly a mistake of epic proportions.

But, apparently, when it came to Flash, she'd just willfully keep making that mistake.

I'm still not marrying you, she typed, hitting the letters with extra force. Just FYI.

Noted, he replied.

It was so hard to tell if he was looking forward to her showing up or if he was bracing himself for the worst or what. Well, he could just brace. She needed a little more from him. Just for her. Then they could go back to being co-parents or whatever.

I'm coming to you, she texted, and then started the car.

Just as she pulled out of the parking lot, he texted back, Thank God.

Brooke knocked on the door, at least 73 percent sure she was making a mistake. But before she could bail, it swung open and Flash was there.

Damn, he made rugged look *so* good.

He wore a black All-Stars T-shirt, which showed off his muscled forearms. But the funny thing was his feet were bare. No boots, no socks. He gave her that look that she'd always been powerless to resist. "Hey, come in. Thanks for making it."

"No problem."

A memory pushed to the forefront of her mind, of the last time she'd been alone in a hotel room with this man. Of Flash pressing her against the door and whispering in her ear, "Tell me what you want," as he'd ground his erection against her, her entire body humming with need for him. "I'm going to give it to you, Brooke," he'd all but growled in her ear. "But be honest."

She shuddered and shoved the memory away. Now was *so* not the time for erotic flashbacks. God, meeting in his room really was an awful idea, wasn't it? She hadn't even been alone with him for thirty seconds and she was already thinking about sex.

Flash shut the door behind her and, dang it, she startled. He had a knowing smirk on his face. "You sure you want to meet here?"

"No." She didn't like this awkwardness between them and she liked it even less that she was the only one feeling it.

Once upon a time, she had promised him honesty. She'd done a terrible job of that when it came to Bean. Being upfront with Flash now was the very least she could do for him. So she took a deep breath and said, "I don't think I should be alone with you."

He chuckled, not looking the least insulted. God, Brooke just wanted to curl into him but, no, she couldn't. She had to remember why she was here and, more importantly, how she'd gotten to this point. Neither of them would be in this position if she and Flash had been able to keep their hands to themselves.

"If you're not supposed to be alone with me," he asked slowly, "what are you doing here?"

"If we met in public, we'd run the risk of being spotted." It wasn't a great excuse.

And Flash knew it. His gaze sharpened. "Are you saying you've decided to keep *this*," he said, motioning between them, "a secret?"

"No. I'm saying I don't want public perception to force our hand." She turned away from him because it was hard to think with him like that. He looked so damn good in this hotel room.

Wow, she hadn't realized he had a corner suite instead of a regular room. This place was bigger—and nicer—than the apartment she and her mom had shared for most of her adolescence. She certainly hadn't been able to afford rooms this nice when she'd been touring—especially not after her uncle embezzled all her earnings.

This was a *very* nice room. Huge windows behind a dining room table set for eight showed her the view of Music Row and the Cumberland River. She was standing in a living room that not only had a couch and matching accent chairs and tasteful lamps—not industrial light fixtures, but real lamps with stylish shades—but the whole thing was arranged on top of an expensive-looking Persian rug. An office area backed up to a full wet bar. Next to the dining room table, to the left, there was what looked like a full kitchen and a set of doors to the right where, she assumed, there was a bathroom and a bedroom. With a bed. Probably a nice one.

Nope. Not thinking about the bed Flash slept in.

She turned her back on those doorways and walked toward the window overlooking Music Row. Even though this was probably one of the nicer hotel rooms she'd ever been in, she could still tell that Flash had settled in. Behind one of the accent chairs was a duffel bag with a protective vest and ropes spilling out—his bull ropes, no doubt. Chaps were draped over one of the dining room chairs and his black hat was tossed onto the granite countertop. Coffee cups were scattered around the coffeepot on the wet bar, along with a few plastic grocery bags.

Okay, so Flash wasn't the neatest of guys. Somehow, that made him seem more…real. More normal, anyway. He wasn't just this perfect fantasy she'd created or this thug the headlines had painted him to be. He was a flesh-and-blood man.

One who could afford the best room in the hotel, apparently. Rodeo riders weren't known for their tastes for the finer things in life. Half of them lived out of their cars during the summer or crashed on floors because the money from rodeos was only good if one was winning. Hadn't Chloe said something about the Lawrence family being billionaires? It'd been couched in a vaguely threatening statement about affording the best lawyers, but…

Was Flash actually rich?

"I got you some tea," he said, startling her out of her thoughts. "I didn't know which kind, so there's a few sample packs. The concierge found an electric kettle so you wouldn't have coffee-flavored tea to drink."

Oh no—thoughtfulness. This was terrible—if Flash was going to be both charming *and* thoughtful, she was doomed. "Any green tea?"

"Jasmine or peach?" She heard the sound of him rustling through the bags. "Oh—there's a plain green in here, too."

"Jasmine, please." She couldn't let herself be sweet-talked. She had to remember why she was here, and it wasn't because she'd missed Flash or he'd missed her or even that they'd been great in bed together and would probably get even better.

She was here because Bean was almost four months old and had spent a whopping twenty minutes with his father. She was here to ensure that Flash was a man of his word and really had turned his life around. That everyone last night had been telling the truth when they'd said Flash was just hitting pillows and that his whole family and their possible billions of dollars wouldn't be used to cower her into submission. She was here to make sure her son would be safe with Flash.

That *she* was safe with Flash. She wanted to know that he wouldn't make her fall in love with him and then rip her heart right out of her chest. That he wouldn't force her into a marriage and then force her to choose between her child and her career. She needed to believe that he wouldn't abandon her to deal with the hard realities of parenthood alone while he chased the rodeo once the naked lust between them cooled.

Because it would cool, right?

Flash wasn't the kind of guy who settled down. He played the field, kept his options open and never met a woman he didn't love.

Except…was that him? He sure as hell had been that a year ago when she'd taken him up on everything he'd had to offer.

But he'd been waiting for her outside the Bluebird. He'd come to her house. He'd said repeatedly that he hadn't looked at another woman since their night together, and his sister had casually mentioned that she knew Flash had it bad for Brooke. Would he be faithful to her—even if they didn't get hitched? Was she even being fair to ask that of him if she kept telling him no?

The fact was that she wanted it all—great sex with a perfect man who made her feel wonderful *and* her career *and* an equal partner to raise Bean.

But she knew if she asked for that, he'd be hustling her down the aisle before she could do anything else and there'd be no guarantee she'd get anything on her wish list. No matter how much charm Flash wielded right now, he wouldn't be in a big hurry to drop the rodeo and be a stay-at-home dad. The rodeo was in his blood, just like the music was in hers.

She couldn't have it all. There simply weren't enough hours in the day. Which meant she couldn't have Flash. She had to put her son first. Her selfish wants and physical needs came last.

No, not last. Marketing plans and press releases and, *ugh*, magazine covers with exclusive interviews and redemption arcs and record sales—all of those things were dead last on her to-do list. But that didn't mean she could ignore them.

Lord, what a mess. She rubbed her eyes.

"Did you get some sleep?" he asked behind her. She could just make out his reflection in the glass window. He was leaning against the wet bar, watching her. "You look better."

So much for that legendary charm. She knew exactly what she looked like—cutoff shorts, a loose-fitting black tee and a Nashville Predators ball cap pulled over an extremely messy ponytail. She looked exactly like a woman who'd had a terrible night. "That's the best you've got?"

Flash came to stand beside her, grinning wildly. He traced his fingers over her shoulder and down her arm until he laced his fingers with hers. She shivered at the touch and fought the urge to rest her head on his shoulder. "I could say that I've never seen you look more beautiful than you do right now, but we're past flattery, don't you think?" Leaning closer, his voice dropped to a deep whisper. "Here's the thing, babe—I'm not going to lie to you. Never have and I'm not about to start."

She blushed because she realized he was right. He'd told her up front about his arrest record. She was the one who'd kept secrets. "Okay. Yes. I, uh, I apologize again for not telling you about the baby." When he didn't answer right away, she asked, "Are you still mad at me?"

He squeezed her hand—and took his sweet time answering. The longer he was silent, the more her stomach sank. How was this going to work?

Finally, he said, "I'm still working on it. I want to trust you but..." He went on before she could interrupt, "I get that you did the best you could with the information you had." He cleared his throat. "And I'm sorry I didn't handle last night well. I won't attempt to make decisions for you again."

This was the Flash who'd been waiting for her behind the Bluebird Cafe, the one who said all the right things at all the right times. This was the Flash who made her want him.

This was not the Flash who had to walk out of a room before he lost his temper or hit cushions to keep control. This wasn't the Flash who issued life-changing orders and just expected her to go along with them, no questions asked.

Which one was the real Flash Lawrence?

"Seriously, though—did you sleep?" The way he asked made it clear he really wanted to know. He wasn't just making polite small talk.

At least, she hoped he wasn't. "A few hours. No one sleeps well with a fussy four-month-old on their chest. Mom thinks he might be teething. Which is super early, but not unheard-of, apparently."

He winced. "That's going to suck. My niece is teething and it's rough for all of them. I don't want you to have to deal with that on your own."

How was she supposed to interpret that? She'd made it clear she wasn't marrying him—but was he implying that he'd be around to help share the load? Or he'd take Bean back to his place? Which was, presumably... Texas, maybe? Or did he mean he'd hire a nanny or something?

Before she could ask, the kettle beeped and he left her side to get the water. She absolutely wasn't going to miss his warmth, for heaven's sake. He was all of five feet away. It's not like she couldn't go five minutes without touching him. She'd managed a whole year without him!

But then he asked, "How much honey do you take with your tea?" and she knew she was in trouble because, seriously, this level of thoughtfulness was dangerous.

"You remembered I like honey?"

Flash paused midstride and then spun back to her, an almost predatory gleam in his eye. "Do you know," he said, his voice suddenly that much lower and that much deeper, and her traitorous body vibrated like a tuning fork at exactly the right pitch, "that every time I kiss you, I taste honey on your sweet lips?"

"No," she said breathlessly as he backed her against the window, his hard body making her soft with need.

"I do." His breath caressed her lips as his hands came to her hips, pulling her against him. The hot length of his erection pushed against her and she couldn't help the moan that escaped her. "I could get drunk on your kiss and never want for water again."

Oh. Oh, *my*.

"Good line," she whispered, tilting her head up for him.

"You can have it." But he didn't take the kiss she offered. He held himself back, which was probably a sign of maturity or something ridiculous like that. "Not gonna lie, Brooke—I want you so bad." He thrust against her and she moaned. He made a matching sound of need, and she couldn't think, couldn't do anything but feel him against her, want him inside her.

Then he cruelly pulled away. Not far, but enough that he wasn't pressing against her anymore. "Right now, we don't have to do anything except talk." His hand trailed up her side, over her ribs, skimming the edge of her breast before his fingers spread across her throat, and then he cupped her cheek in his palm, his thumb stroking over her skin. Her eyes fluttered closed and she let herself just *feel*.

No one else made her feel like Flash did.

"That's why you're here, isn't it?"

Was it? That's what she'd told herself last night, and then he'd given her an amazing orgasm against the door. She hadn't been able to think until they'd gotten the sex out of the way.

She could've met him in public today, could've insisted on a chaperone. She could've made him come back out to the house and subjected him to her mother, made him change Bean's diapers.

Instead, she'd come straight to his hotel room. He hadn't had to convince her of anything. She was here willingly.

She was *his* willingly.

"No," she whispered, lacing her fingers through his hair and pulling him down to her. "It's not."

# Eleven

*Hers*. That's the word that crossed her mind when she crushed her lips against his.

This man was hers.

He always had been, since the very first moment he'd taken her hand and bowed over it like some lordly duke. If nothing else, they had this.

"Bed?" Flash asked against her mouth, his hands skimming down her back, over her bottom.

"Bed," she agreed.

She loved the hot, heavy sex against the door, but a window wasn't quite as reassuring. Besides, she wanted the luxury of limbs twining together, his bare skin against hers.

The next thing she knew, Flash had bent over and swept her legs out from underneath her. "Whoa!" she squeaked, throwing her arms around his neck for balance.

"I've got you, babe." Oh, she'd needed to hear that. "Do you have any idea what I want to do to you?"

She leaned forward and kissed the side of his neck. His pulse beat wildly against her lips. "Tell me."

"I want to feast on your body and make you scream my name when you come, and then I want to hold you afterwards until you've come back down to earth, and then I want to bury myself in your body until you break again, until I can't take it anymore. I want to lay you out and spend the next two days making love to you," he growled against her ear. Then he wrapped his lips around her lobe and tugged gently as he carried her back through the suite. "Then I want to do it again."

Every muscle in her body clenched at his charged words and, given the wolfish grin he shot her, she knew he'd felt it, too. She'd done that once with him, that glorious night in Fort Worth when he'd swept her off her feet.

Once a year wasn't enough.

Sadly, though, reality wasn't on their side. "We—oh, *Flash*," she moaned as he kissed her neck, "we don't have that kind of time." But Lord, it sounded wonderful, didn't it? A few days to explore how deep this connection went. A few days to selfishly enjoy this man and his tremendous skills.

Because the man had *skills*.

"Then I'll take the time I get with you." He kicked open the door to the bedroom and then kicked it shut, all without missing a single stride.

"Another good line," she murmured as he set her down on the bed and pulled her hat from her head.

"I'm full of them." Her hair tumbled wildly around her shoulders, the ponytail a distant memory. He paused, sucking in air. "God, Brooke—do you have any idea what you do to me?"

She leaned forward, stroking a hand over his obvious erection through his jeans. "I'm getting one."

"You…" He swallowed as she rested her head against his stomach and began to work the buttons on his fly loose.

She shoved his jeans down, then hooked her fingers into the waistband of his blue boxer briefs, which hugged his narrow hips, his ass, his *everything*. Then she pulled and he sprung free.

"If you don't want me to taste you, you let me know."

Flash groaned, his fingers finding her hair as her hands found his hot length. "Please," he got out through gritted teeth as she stroked him. "I want you to do what you want, Brooke," he moaned when she gave him a little squeeze. "I won't tell you what to do."

"You did last night."

There was something powerful about this moment. She had him in the palm of her hand—literally—and she could do what she wanted with him. She looked up at him through her eyelashes and then, slowly, pressed her lips to his tip. He shuddered, but before his hips could flex, she'd pulled away and ran the pad of her thumb over the area she'd kissed.

"A mistake. A huge one," he groaned, his head falling back. "You're killing me, babe."

"Don't mess up again," she said, knowing it sounded like an order. But it wasn't, not really. She was all but begging him.

She'd given him a second chance last night when he'd told her he'd sobered up and straightened himself out, only to have him struggle when she told him about Bean. Yeah, that was partly her fault because she'd broken the news in the absolute worst way possible. But she hadn't forgotten the hard edge to his voice when he'd informed her that they were getting married as soon as possible. And that didn't even take into account the awful moment when she'd thought he'd been attacking his brother-in-law.

She didn't need a domineering, immature jerk in her life. She needed a man, one who did right by her and her son, one who stood up for her, not to her.

She needed Flash to be that man.

"You get one more chance," she told him in all seriousness.

"I won't fail you again." His grip on her hair loosened and then was gone entirely as he tilted her head back. "You can count on me, Brooke—now and forever. No matter what we decide, we're in this together." Even through the haze of lust, she could see how serious he was.

"I know," she whispered, emotion clogging up her throat.

He leaned down and kissed her, the kind of kiss that said as much as his words had. It wasn't a kiss of frenzied passion, but one of heat and something richer, deeper.

Something that might even be love.

No, no—she wasn't going to let love get hopelessly mixed up with lust. Especially not right now. This time with him right now—this was about satisfaction and then about planning. Neither of those two things had a damn thing to do with love.

They'd had so little time together that she hardly knew what this man looked like nude. One night together and a few stolen moments—plus several hard, awkward conversations.

"Take these all the way off," she demanded, releasing her grip on him. "I want you naked."

"God, yes." He stumbled back, kicking out of his pants and yanking his shirt over his head. "I'll always give you what you want. You know that, right?"

She nodded as she did away with what was left of her ponytail and started to pull her shirt off. Flash stopped her. "Just be honest with me, Brooke. Not just about sex—about everything. Be honest with yourself."

Then he grabbed the hem of her shirt and lifted it over her head. She'd gone with the pretty teal bra today, one of the only non-nursing bras she owned that still fit. Her boobs looked *huge* in it.

"Okay to touch?" he asked, stroking a finger down her chest.

She started to nod but then stopped. Last night had been

about reclaiming a part of the girl she'd been before she'd become a mother. But this?

This was the first time Brooke felt like she was having sex as the woman she was now. And he had said he expected complete honesty, so… "Not right now. Let's leave the bra on."

Flash grinned widely as his hands skimmed up her skin and came to a rest on her shoulders, where he kneaded at the tight muscles there. Clearly, the request didn't bother him in the least. "Can do."

She reached for him again, gripping him firmly as she slid her tongue over his tip and took him into her mouth.

He groaned, a noise of pure desire that traveled down her body to where they were connected. She stroked him with her hands, licked him with her tongue. Suddenly, he pulled away.

"Nope," he growled as he pushed her over.

"Nope?" She flung her hands out for balance as she rolled. His hands pressed between her shoulder blades, firm but not hard. "Did I do something wrong?"

He laughed, a noise that sounded almost unhinged as he gently pushed her onto her stomach. "Wrong? Hell, woman. I've never felt anything so right in my life. But you're about to break me and I'm not going down like that. Not until…"

He stripped her shorts and panties off and Brooke let him. She grabbed handfuls of bedding as he nudged her legs apart and then his hands were between her legs, opening her.

"Woman," he growled again, palming her bottom.

She propped herself up on her elbows and looked back at him. "Not until what?"

"Not until you come first." He trailed his hands over the small of her back, but instead of reaching for that space between her legs that was already hot and heavy for him, he knelt on the bed and rested his hands on her shoulders. His strong hands began to massage her shoulders and she let her head drop as her muscles began to relax. "How much time do we have?"

"An hour, maybe." Bean would wake up from his nap and he'd be hungry and she'd need to nurse him. And then there was dealing with Mom...

"Then we'll make that hour count. Don't think, babe," he said, working at a particularly painful knot. "Just let me take care of you."

His hands moved lower, smoothing over her ribs even as he skipped right over her bra strap. The calluses on his hands chafed at her skin, heightening the sensations, making her more and more aware of his every move, his every touch. She stiffened when he ran his hands over her hips. But then he said, "You are *so* beautiful," in a voice that didn't contain a trace of mockery or teasing in it.

"I'm not back to where I was before," she said, cringing as he traced the stretch marks she'd earned with Bean. "So?"

She half rolled and shot him a look. "Seriously? Do you know how many people tell me I need to get back to my prebaby weight? My mother, the record execs—they all say the same thing." Her voice cracked a little on the end.

Flash's eyes—well, they flashed. "Let's get one thing straight," he said, rolling her on to her back and pinning her to the bed. "I loved your body last year. I love your body now. But if you think all you are to me is your body and that any variation in your appearance is going to send me running, then you have sorely misjudged how much I need you. All of you."

God, he really was going to make her cry. She tried to wiggle free, but he held her fast.

"So you're not the same person you were then?" he went on, his erection hot and heavy against her thigh, "Well I'm not, either. We've both grown the hell up, Brooke. And, I think, we've both gotten better." Then he released her wrists and moved lower until she felt his lips pressing against those stretch marks, reverently kissing each and every stripe. "You *are* beautiful," he repeated.

Brooke was glad he wasn't staring into her eyes anymore because it wasn't just the compliments. This wasn't Flash being smooth or charming. This was Flash being fierce and proud—of her. This was the man she wanted in her corner, by her side, when record execs tried to railroad her. This was a man who'd fight for her, for their son, for their family.

How had she failed to realize that romance wasn't just pretty words or a sweet song? Because *this* was romance. It was strong and determined and intense. Just like Flash.

Flash looked up from where he was between her legs. "I wanted you a year ago when we were wild kids looking for a good time," he told her. "I want you now when you've had my son and made me a father. A year from now, five years from now, you won't be the same person you are at this exact moment and *I'll still want you.*"

Oh, Jesus, that was a hell of a good line, one that fit right into *Don't say something romantic*. He rolled her over again, and this time she let herself relax into his touch. Then one hand slid between her legs, stroking over her sensitive flesh, and the lyrics fell away, only the melody drifting through her mind.

"Yeah, just like that," he said, his voice husky as he touched her, rubbed her, kissed her back. "Don't think. Just feel what I do to you." With his other hand, he pushed her hair to the side and then gripped her neck, gently holding her down while he nipped at her shoulder with his teeth, his stubble scraping over her skin.

Then one finger was inside her and she shuddered at the touch. "Yeah, babe," he breathed in her ear as he worked her body with more patience than she'd ever imagined. Until right now, every time with Flash had been hot and heavy, and neither of them had ever been able to hold back.

But now? Now he was holding himself back, overwhelming her senses and demanding her full attention. She gave it willingly. There was no room for PR plans or redemption stories or albums or should haves, could haves, would haves. There was only him and her and the music that wove their lives together.

Because she'd swear Flash could hear the song, too. With two fingers now, he thrust inside of her in rhythm with the melody as he bit into the skin between her shoulder and her neck. The orgasm began to build and she tried to reach back for him, but he didn't let her go. "You want more?" he growled in her ear, and she heard the raw desire in his voice, felt it in the way his body covered hers, the way her body covered his.

Whimpering, she nodded, and then his hand was gone from her neck, his fingers pulled free of her body. "One sec, babe. Do you have any idea what you do to me?" She peered over her shoulder to see him rolling on the condom. Then he lifted her by the hips and she scooted forward on the bed. "This okay?" he asked, kneeling back on the bed and running his hands over her bottom. "Because I've got to tell you, the view is *amazing.*"

She laughed and widened her pose, bracing herself on her elbows. "I seem to recall this was better than okay a year ago." Actually, she remembered the shattering orgasm that had hit her so hard it'd knocked her completely off her knees. She'd been unable to do anything but shake while he'd held her for long, glorious minutes.

No one else had ever made her feel the way Flash did. There were reasons she needed to be careful about him— good reasons, no doubt—but right now, as he fit himself against her, his body strong, she couldn't remember what those reasons were. All she knew was that he was going to make her feel wonderful.

"God, woman," he said, giving her backside a light smack before he thrust into her.

*"Oh,"* she moaned in sheer pleasure as he filled her. Even now, she could feel her orgasm straining against him.

"God, I missed you," he murmured, withdrawing and thrusting back in.

"Yes," she got out, dropping her head onto her forearms on the bed, which gave Flash even more access. He squeezed her bottom and teased her delicate flesh with the softest of touches while he drove into her and she lost herself to the rhythm of their bodies. He'd always been so damn good at this, at making her body react at his mere touch. This was why she couldn't keep her hands off him, couldn't kick him to the curb. She simply needed him too much.

He shifted, reaching around and rubbing her in time with his thrusts, and the pressure built and built, and then he wrapped her hair around his fist and pulled her into him until he could bite down on her shoulder.

The climax hit and crescendoed, her body tightening around his as a cry of satisfaction ripped itself from her chest.

"That's it," he murmured against her skin. "Come for me, babe. Just like… Oh, *God.*"

He reared back, grabbing her hips and thrusting with such force that she couldn't keep her knees underneath her as the sensations completely overwhelmed her. The orgasm went on, strengthening until she cried out again.

Seconds later, Flash made a noise of raw lust and collapsed onto her back, driving her into the bed. He managed to roll off to one side, his arm and leg still draped over her. She didn't know how long they lay there, panting, but soon enough the heat from their bodies dissipated and she shivered.

"Oh, babe," Flash sighed, wrapping himself around her and holding on tight. "I…"

She didn't know how he was going to finish that sentence. *Say something romantic.* This time, her brain modulated the key up to A.

No, no—she didn't want him to say something romantic. She didn't want him to make her fall for him all over again, didn't want him to propose when she was weak for him because, after sex like that, she might just say yes.

She just wanted to enjoy him while she could, which she had. Now she needed to focus on reality.

She rolled away from him and out of bed. "I'm still not marrying you," she tossed over her shoulder as she walked—okay, hurried—to the bathroom.

She shut the door before he could answer.

# Twelve

She wasn't going to make this easy on him, that much was clear.

While Brooke got cleaned up, Flash flopped across the bed, trying to get his thoughts in order. He wanted nothing more than to pull her right back into bed, curl around her body and nap the rest of the afternoon away, but they didn't have that much time. Not yet, anyway.

Okay, he could do this. He was calm, cool and collected and, thanks to the amazing sex, he could think without getting distracted by her body or his dick. Probably.

First things first—tea.

Just because he wanted her in ways that continually surprised him didn't mean she was his. And it especially didn't mean that he was over her hiding James from him. All it meant was they were…exploring areas of consensus or some such BS.

He launched himself out of bed, disposed of the condom and hurriedly washed his hands in the kitchen. Then he assembled her tea. The water had cooled a little, but it was still hot enough, he hoped. Then he squeezed in a dollop of honey. There.

She still didn't want to get married. She'd made it crystal clear before she'd come over here that she wasn't going to marry him. What he needed to figure out was if she was digging in her heels because he'd pushed too far, too fast or if, when she said she wasn't going to marry him, she was really saying *not right now*. And the sooner he figured that out, the better off they'd all be.

He made it back to the bedroom just as the bathroom door opened. Brooke walked into the bedroom in all her glory, and he was so stunned by her that he damn near dropped the mug. "Babe," he all but groaned, his body straining to muster a response.

She crossed her arms in front of her breasts, still teasingly contained by that pretty bra. "Focus, Flash. We have to talk."

"Right, right." He let his gaze travel down her body, taking in every curve and dip. "Are we talking with or without clothes? I vote without."

"Of course you do." She sighed, but she smiled while she said it. "Is that tea?"

"Jasmine green tea with honey." He held out the tea, making sure not to touch her.

Which was harder than anticipated when she took the mug from him, that satisfied smile on her lips. He'd put that smile there, and he'd do whatever it took to replace it with another one. If she'd let him, he'd make sure she smiled like that every day for the rest of their lives.

Then she frowned and he realized that she wasn't scowling at the tea, but at his hands. His swollen, red hands. "Is that from hitting couch cushions?"

Flash flexed his fingers, wincing. He didn't like that note of doubt in her voice. "Nope. This morning I found a boxing club that let me punch a bag for an hour." He'd had to buy a year's membership, but that hadn't bothered him a bit. Nashville was where Brooke was—her family, her career, her life. He'd be back in town. Often.

Luckily, the boxing club had been three blocks from a jeweler's shop, so he'd been able to kill two birds with one stone, so to speak. The ring itself had seven stones. God, he hoped she liked it.

Brooke looked worried. "And that helps?"

"Absolutely. I have a bag at home, too," he added. "Like I said last night—it's a controlled release. I haven't been in a fight in months."

"Do you remember what it was about?" Clearly, she expected the answer to be *no*.

But he did. "I got into it with Pete right before he and Chloe got hitched—and I was stone-cold sober when I did it. I thought I was protecting my sister, but Chloe let me know in no uncertain terms that she did not need my protection and that I was a jackass for thinking she'd ever want my help." He chuckled, rubbing a hand over his jaw. "Pete'll never let me forget that he broke my jaw. Of course, my face is pretty hard. I broke his hand, so we were even."

She gaped at him. "Seriously?"

"Seriously. I went cold turkey after that—had to. My hands were a mess and my jaw was wired shut for a while. But that was the wake-up call I needed. I almost cost my sister everything she loves, almost ruined my entire career and came damn close to destroying the All-Stars—not to mention risking jail time—all because I couldn't get a handle on my temper."

The thing that still boggled his mind was how damned sure he'd been at the time. When he'd overheard Tex McGraw making horribly crude comments about Brooke, Flash had known he'd needed to defend her honor. That had gotten him arrested and nearly sent to prison. And when he'd gone after Pete, he'd been convinced that the man was taking advantage of Chloe. He'd been positive he'd been right both times.

Now? Now he could see that neither woman had needed his protection. Brooke probably didn't even know Tex existed, much less that he was a sexist jerk. Chloe had been able to handle Pete and the All-Stars just fine on her own. The only thing Flash had ever done was make things worse.

It'd been a hell of a hard lesson to learn but he was learning it. Yeah, last night he'd been 100 percent sure that Brooke needed to marry him immediately, and because of that he'd almost destroyed any chance at a real relationship with her.

"And you're telling me you have a handle on that anger now? That you and Pete are...friends?" Skepticism dripped off every word.

Flash took a deep breath. It was all right if she was skeptical. She'd had months with those headlines eating at her. It would be unreasonable for her to nod and smile and pretend his past didn't bother her at all, especially after last night.

"We get by. And he treats my sister right." He cleared his throat. "Just so you know, I called Oliver, my brother. I told him about James, but not who you were." Although Oliver had figured it out, no doubt. He wasn't the one running the family's energy company by accident.

"I met him, right?"

"I think so, at the Fort Worth rodeo. Oliver's the oldest. He runs Lawrence Energies, which is the family business. He's married to Renee and they have an eight-month-old daughter, Trixie. My dad doesn't run the company anymore."

"Are you really a billionaire?"

"Me, personally? Probably not. Why?"

Brooke's eyes about bugged out of her head. "*Probably not? You're not sure?*"

"I sold my stake in Lawrence Energies when I started riding in the All-Stars to avoid the conflicts of interest. Invested most of it, blew some of it on cars and horses. Bought a nice piece of land a few hours south of Dallas with a big ol' house on it—plenty of room for a boy to have a good time," he added. "I get statements from the brokers, but I don't really read them."

Brooke clutched her tea like it was a life preserver and she was trying not to drown. "You don't even know…" she said quietly.

Flash took advantage of this to climb into bed behind her. He sat in the middle and pulled the sheets up over his waist.

He wasn't going to win the fight to not touch her. As softly as he could, he skimmed his hand over her back. She didn't lean away from him, so that had to count for something. "Is it a problem?"

"No, no. It's just… I didn't grow up rich, and then my uncle stole most of my money or lost it, and…" Her voice trailed off as she focused on him. "And, in the interests of honesty, part of what set me off last night was your sister implying that your family had the money to take me to court and bleed me dry if I didn't cooperate."

Flash groaned. "Yeah, I can see how that'd be upsetting," he said, closing his eyes and pushing back against the frustration. The whole point of calling his sister was so she would *help*, not freak Brooke the hell out! "Sorry about that. The point she should've made was that if you have any outstanding bills for his care or if he needs anything else—diapers or, uh, strollers?" Honestly, he had no idea what a baby would need. "Definitely a pony when he gets old enough."

Brooke grinned at his cluelessness although at least she was trying to hide it behind the mug.

"Or whatever—it's covered," Flash went on. "If there's

anything *you* need, just let me know." He tried to think—what would she want? Then it hit him. "Aside from all the tea you could drink, if you want a recording studio at my place, I'll get one built. If you decide you want a different house, one we share, I'll get it—with your name on the title. I'll start a trust fund for James, too, for college or whatever."

She blinked at him. "You'd build me a studio?"

"Hell, yeah." Actually, the more he thought about it, the better he liked that idea. Brooke could stay for weeks or even months. She could work on her music while Flash taught James how to ride and take care of his pony or took him to a rodeo. Then she wouldn't be tied to Nashville. Although they'd maintain a residence here because obviously Brooke would need to come back here on a regular basis. "I can get contractors started on it next week." He didn't actually know what went into a recording studio, but, hell, money wasn't an object. He'd hire someone who did know and tell them to get top-of-the-line equipment. Problem solved.

"That…" She actually blushed. "That would be lovely."

Yeah, that was exactly how he would show her he was good for her. "But the point is, you've already done the hard part. I want to make things easy for you from here on out, and I don't want the money differences to be a wedge between us."

"I appreciate that." She took a long drink. "Anything else I should know about your family?"

He shrugged. "You've met Chloe, who runs the All-Stars, which used to be part of Lawrence Energies, but now she owns it outright. And me." He launched a self-deprecating grin at her. "I don't run anything."

"But you're one of the best all-around rodeo riders in the world," she said, which had him puffing out his chest a little.

"I try. We haven't told Dad yet because subtlety isn't his strong suit, especially when it comes to grandbabies." Point of fact, the man had gone hog-wild for Trixie, all the more so because Oliver and Renee had named the baby after his beloved wife. It's not like that little girl wanted for any-thing—Oliver was much better at the whole money thing than Flash would ever be. But every time Milt Lawrence saw his granddaughter, he had another toy, another frilly dress, another keepsake present just for her. The man was over the moon.

"What about your mom? Is she still in the picture?"

Flash swallowed hard as he stroked her back. "She died when I was eleven."

Brooke gasped. "I'm so sorry. I hadn't realized."

"It's okay," he said with the casual shrug he always used when talking about his mom. He was used to her being gone, anyway. That was practically the same thing as it being okay. "I know now that everyone did a lot to shield me from the chaos, but, obviously, everything changed when she lost her fight with cancer."

Mom would've loved Brooke. And there would've been no getting her away from James. She would've known if Flash was doing the right thing. She would've loved her grandson, would've protected Brooke as if she were her own daughter. Trixie Lawrence would've made everything about this better. Flash didn't often miss her—she'd been gone more than half his life—but right now, he missed his mom.

"I'm sorry to hear that," she sniffed, wrapping her arms around his chest and hugging him back.

"It's okay. It was a long time ago. Right after that, Dad won the All-Stars in a poker game and relocated the entire family to Dallas. He couldn't stay in New York where we'd lived with Mom, so we all moved. He started going to ro-deos and hanging out with cowboys, and he took me with him. And I learned real quick that there were two kinds of guys at those things—those who were quick with a wink and a joke and those who were quick with their fists."

Dad would disappear to go play cards with his buddies, shooting the breeze and drinking, leaving Flash to run wild. Chloe was usually at the rodeos with them, and she been charged with keeping an eye on him, but Flash had insisted that he hadn't needed a babysitter and had ditched her whenever he could.

"That's where I got my nickname," he told Brooke. "I was small and quick, and I could get into trouble and then disappear—" he snapped his fingers for emphasis "—in a *flash*."

He'd always looked back at his childhood with such fondness. What kid didn't love doing whatever he damn well pleased? But now Flash wondered how things might have been different if Milt Lawrence hadn't been in the grips of a midlife crisis and deep depression following the loss of his beloved wife. Would Flash be a different man today if his father had shown him how to be a different man then?

Brooke sniffed again. "I don't know that I realized you hadn't grown up on a ranch somewhere. You're such a quintessential cowboy."

"I'll take that as a compliment, but I was a city slicker kid from New York."

She curled against his side, and it only made sense for him to drape his arm around her shoulder and hug her close. This was…nice.

"But my point is, for most of my life, I only knew how to be one of two people—a ladies' man who sweet-talked all the pretty girls or a fighter who refused to back down. But when I'm with you, I don't have to stay stuck in those two extremes. I can be someone else."

"Oh, *Flash*," she whispered, looking up at him. He wiped a lingering tear from her cheek.

"I need to be in my son's life on a regular basis," he told her. "And I think it's pretty clear that sex between you and me is gonna be a thing."

"A *good* thing," she murmured, not sounding happy about it. "It'd be easier if it wasn't."

Yeah, if he could keep his hands off her, it'd make what was supposed to be a negotiation more cut-and-dried.

But he couldn't keep his hands off her, as evidenced by the way he stroked her back. "What about your family?"

She shrugged, but he felt the tension ripple through her body. "It's me and Mom. I don't know who my dad was—Mom refuses to talk about him."

"Really?"

"Oh, yeah," she said, slumping back against the bed. "She won't tell me a damn thing about my father, but yet she's been pushing me to sign off on a big baby reveal. Plus, she refuses to see how much of a hypocrite she's being about it. All she can say is it isn't the same—because why? Because I've got a music career? It's BS. Mom is very… focused," she explained. "She pushed me into a singing career from when I was in kindergarten. Which wasn't bad," she added, maybe a little too quickly.

Flash was getting a mental image of her mother that was anything but flattering. The woman sounded domineering, controlling and more than just a little mean. "Are you sure about that?"

She nodded. "I love what I do and I've had some great friends."

"Like Kyle Morgan?" Flash hadn't forgotten the way the older man had given Flash a mean look.

"Yeah, Kyle's been a great mentor. But even the best mentor isn't a replacement for a father. I don't even know if my dad knows I exist and I *hate* it. I've always hated it.

I can't help wondering if he didn't want me." She leaned against him as she said it.

Flash's mind reeled even as he held her tight. True, he'd always butted heads with his father—but he'd always known how much he was loved. His heart hurt for Brooke, for the pain in her voice.

"That's on him," Flash said, furious with this random sperm donor. "Not you, babe. And I would never do that to my child. Even if *this* doesn't work out between you and me, I'm not abandoning my kid. He's a Lawrence no matter what."

She exhaled heavily. "Good. That's good. You know, I'd made peace with it, with her and with him," Brooke went on, her voice small. "Or I thought I had. Then you happened and I got pregnant and it brought it all home—how much Mom kept hidden from me. I love her, but I don't know if I can ever forgive her. Does that make sense?"

Flash felt like she'd punched him. "Yeah," he got out in a strangled voice. "I understand completely."

Because he felt exactly the same way. He cared for Brooke, more than he probably should. And he felt such a powerful, instinctual love for James that he couldn't even put it into words.

But how would he get past the fact that Brooke had kept that baby boy a secret from Flash? Was forgiveness even possible?

"And it was so hard not to call you up and tell you then," she went on, seemingly unaware that she'd just blown Flash's mind. "You've got to believe me, Flash—I always meant to tell you. I never intended to keep you from Bean or him from you. Because I know it's not right. I was just…"

"Waiting for the right time," he said softly after she'd trailed off.

"Yeah." She swallowed. "I wish I'd realized that the right time was actually a few months ago."

That made two of them.

"I'm not going to be like her," she said, her voice stronger as she sat up straighter. "I want Bean to know you and your family. I want us to get to a point where we can make some version of *this* work."

Flash had to swallow a few times. "Yeah, me too."

She tapped a pattern on the tea mug. "The question is, how do we make that happen?"

He scratched a hand through his hair. "The general consensus is that me telling you we *had* to get hitched was the dumbest thing I've done in a long, long time."

"So why did you do it?"

He kept his gaze locked on her face. "*Because.* Which—" he added with a chuckle when her lips twisted off to the side in disapproval "—is a bad answer. I've learned that. But the truth is, you mean something to me, Brooke."

He felt, more than saw, the eye roll. He tried again. "From the moment I laid eyes on you, I haven't looked at another woman—and that's not just a figure of speech. There's something between us, and it's got the potential to be something good. Something great, even. But," he went on before she could tell him where he could shove all his *potential*, "that doesn't mean we make sense married. We both have careers that require near-constant travel, and there's a lot riding on us doing our jobs well."

"That's true," she admitted, sounding almost regretful about it. "I'm not giving up my music."

"Which is absolutely fair. You've been the front line for a year. More than a year," he said. "Have you done it alone?"

She didn't meet his gaze. Instead, her fingers continued to tap out a rhythm on her mug. "I've got Alex. And my mother. She's with Bean now. I may not agree with all of her *choices*, as you put it, but she loves him completely." She winced, her fingers stilling as she shot him an apologetic look. "She'll like you even less than Alex does."

Every single time, Brooke's statements about her mother had been couched in worry and maybe a little bit of fear. If Mrs. Bonner was James's primary babysitter, that probably meant Brooke had needed the time between when she'd left the Bluebird and when Flash had shown up at her house to get her mother out of her house.

Mrs. Bonner was a problem.

Oliver had made it clear why Flash needed to establish paternity immediately, if not sooner. For once, Flash and Oliver had been in agreement about something—marriage would make everything smoother.

Smoother for the Lawrences, yeah. But for Brooke? She needed more than that and, by God, Flash wanted to be the one to give it to her.

"I'm not worried about your mom. I'm worried about *you*." He stroked his thumb over her cheek. Unexpectedly, her eyes began to water. "You impress the hell out of me, you know? You toured while pregnant and had our baby and still wrote a bunch of kick-ass songs. You've done such an amazing job, and I couldn't ask for a better mother for my son."

"Damn it," she sniffed, pulling away from his touch and swiping at her eyes. "Don't be charming, Flash. I'm too tired to cope with you being perfect."

"I'm not being charming," he told her as he put her almost empty mug on the nightstand and then lifted her into his lap. "I'm being honest. I'll always be honest with you. Just be honest with me, too. That's all I ask."

Crying, she settled into his lap, her arms around his neck. This wasn't sexual, although there was no missing the fact that there was little more than a sheet between their nude bodies.

No, this was him taking care of her. He wrapped his arms around her, and relief coursed through him when she rested her head on his shoulder. Leaning back against the headboard, he let his body take her weight while he stroked her back and kissed her forehead and let her get it all out.

Long minutes passed, and he didn't think about her mother or his family or songs or rodeos or anything but this woman.

He wanted her.

It really didn't make sense, except it did. He'd wanted her a year ago and he wanted her now. Would he still want her in another year?

Would she still want him?

It was a huge risk. But, hell, he was Flash Lawrence. Everything he did was a risk.

"Anything between us has to start from trust, and I..." He swallowed hard. "I understand why you did what you did. But I don't trust you as much as I need to right now, and you probably don't trust me as much as you need to, either." She gasped, but he didn't stop. He couldn't. "I'm not going to get it right all the time. I didn't last night. But that doesn't mean I'm going to stop trying."

Another tear trickled down her cheek and he wiped this one away, too. "You're being perfect again," she said in what might have been a scolding voice if it hadn't been so choked with emotion.

"Trying to be, anyway," he said. She laughed, and she was so beautiful, a smile on her face even as tears clung to her eyelashes, that he kissed her. His body surged to attention as he held her tight.

He could get lost in the honeyed sweetness of this woman, and that thought made him realize something—he did want to marry her. It might be a disaster and it'd definitely be messy but...

His father still talked about how he'd taken one look at Trixie Cunningham and that'd been it for him. In the years since her death, he'd never dated, never taken a lover. He was still in love with his wife. She'd been the only woman for him.

How was that different from how Flash had reacted to Brooke? He'd laid eyes on her at the All-Stars Rodeo in Fort Worth and he hadn't stopped thinking about Brooke, hadn't touched another woman, since then.

What if this was the same thing?

What if this was forever?

# Thirteen

She pulled away, resting her head on his shoulder again. "We don't have much time."

"Right." Damn it. He tried to get his mind back on track. "Okay. We need a plan."

"Yes. Definitely a plan." But then she gave him a dreamy smile and kissed him again.

She was absolutely *killing* him, but what a way to go. "First things first—what do *you* want to do?"

That dreaminess faded, replaced by a worried furrow between her brows. "You know, I don't think anyone's ever asked."

Flash winced. Yeah, he'd skipped that step last night. "We need to find a workable solution. And that may or may not involve marriage. So be honest."

She was quiet for a long time, but Flash held himself still, and finally she began to talk. "I don't want to use my child as leverage. I want people to see him as a person in his own right instead of a marketing tool. I want to take him to parks and the zoo and introduce him to my friends—who'll all be mad that I've lied to them for the last year. I don't want to lie anymore. I want to feel like I'm in control of at least some part of my own life."

"That all sounds good to me," he said softly. He didn't want to interrupt her.

"I don't want to be forced into anything, like I was when my mother and my record company made the executive decision to hide my pregnancy," she went on. "I don't want to be made to feel ashamed of who I am or who Bean is. I want my new album to do well, and I want to do a smaller, more manageable tour that won't be so exhausting. I want to keep my son with me and I want…" Her gaze cut to him and he hoped like hell he saw desire there.

He leaned forward, hoping to catch that last word, hoping it was *you*.

As her words trailed off, she rolled onto her side and stared at him. "I want to be friends with you, because I like you, too." Her tone was suddenly diplomatic. Was she being honest? "I want to know you better, and you're right—I want to trust you more than I do now. I want Bean to know his whole family. I want everything to be perfect."

She didn't say *not like this*, but Flash heard it anyway.

"That's quite a list."

She swiped at her eyes again. "Yeah. Not going to apologize for any of it."

He could sense the frustration underneath every request—the long nights, the loneliness, the worry that underscored her every moment, and it wrecked him that he hadn't been here for her.

The truth was that he'd nearly ruined his entire life because he'd had some dumb-ass idea that attacking another guy for daring to talk about her was protecting her, but it wasn't. Truly protecting her would've been standing by her side for the last year, backing her up when she'd needed to push against her mother or her record label, holding her hand during labor, being there for the sleepless nights.

He couldn't change the past. The important thing was that she didn't see herself on opposite sides of him or his family. Everything else, he could work with. He wanted her to keep writing, keep singing, and if she wanted to tour, he'd make it work.

Mrs. Bonner was *definitely* going to be a problem, though. Because if there was one thing Flash understood, it was being an adult who everyone still treated like a kid.

He leaned over and pulled the ring box out of the drawer where he'd stashed it when she'd called. "Brooke."

Her eyes went wide as she scrambled into a sitting position—one where she wasn't touching him. "Flash, don't do this."

"I'm not proposing—promise," he corrected quickly. He set the box down in the no-man's land between them. "Let's call it a…business partnership."

She eyed him warily. He hated that look, hated that she still felt she had to guard herself against him. "What kind of partnership?"

"Several things need to happen." Things he'd discussed with Chloe and Pete last night and again with Oliver this morning. At least Oliver had only yelled for a few minutes, although there had been that threat of permanent dismemberment…

"We need a paternity test, for starters. Not because I doubt you," he said, which made her roll her eyes. "Anyone who looks at that boy knows he's mine." Chloe had said as much.

"You do have the same smile," she said quietly, giving him a grin that was almost shy.

"We need the test, because I'm not on the birth certificate and I don't want anyone else to question the fact that he's my son." Anyone like her mother, specifically.

Brooke blew out a long breath. "Yes, of course. There's no question about that."

"Good." The next part, however, was trickier. Chloe had told him what she and Brooke had talked about—including how Chloe had gotten distracted by the baby and started thinking out loud about how they were going to sell this to the public. Flash had called her because he wasn't good at big-picture thinking like that, but he also completely understood why it'd overwhelmed Brooke.

"Have you thought about what Chloe mentioned last night? Before the cushion incident?"

Brooke slumped back onto the bed, her fingers tapping a rhythm only she could hear. Flash was sure she didn't know she was doing it.

"Yes," she said quietly, not looking at him. "It's not a bad plan. It's definitely the kind of thing the record label will sign off on, especially when your name gets out there. But I don't want to get married, you know?"

"Okay. Got that." He'd have to be dead to miss it.

"So what is this?" she asked, nudging the box. "How is a ring—it is a ring, right?" Flash nodded. "How is a ring a business proposal?"

He thought back to that list of things she wanted out of their relationship. The good news was she wanted to be friends with him. Friends spent time together. They hung out, went out, called and texted and sent pictures. Sometimes, friends even stripped each other naked and had extremely satisfying sex.

But she'd also didn't want her choices taken away, and she didn't want to feel ashamed. "Chloe said she could spin our relationship so you're in the driver's seat. We were dating and you got pregnant and then I screwed up and you gave me an ultimatum to shape up or ship out, which I did. Right?"

"Basically…" She crossed her arms and stared at the jeweler's box as if it held the Ring of Sauron or something.

"So we could get engaged." He opened the box, the huge diamond surrounded by sapphires, all catching the light. Brooke gasped in what he hoped was approval.

"Holy crap—look at the size of that rock!" she whispered. Then she looked up at him, her eyes huge. "Engaged? Are you asking me to marry you again?"

Flash took that to be a sign that he'd chosen well. "Nope." She snorted, but her gaze fell back to the ring. "We don't have to set a date, much less book the band and send out invitations. Chloe said we'd tell people we'd be keeping it quiet, like our whole relationship. Then, in a year or whenever, we could break up, ask for privacy during our difficult time, and promise that we would continue to put our child first. And none of that would be a lie, necessarily." Although the thought of her moving on, falling in love with someone else who'd get to spend time raising his son—yeah, that rankled.

"You're serious," she said, sounding breathless. She stretched out a finger toward the ring before she snatched it back, like the ring might burn her.

"Yep." Months of a friendly fake engagement gave Flash room to work. He could take her—and James, of course—out. He could demonstrate he had the chops to be a good father and, most importantly, that he was trustworthy—all without screwing up his big championship year.

Hopefully, during that time, he could get to a point where he could trust her, too. He knew that was a ways off, but he didn't want to spend the rest of his life questioning her every statement or action, either.

And if they were together, it only made sense that they might spend some time in bed, right?

"You can tour for your new album, I can still ride the rodeo on the weekends and, when we can, we make time to work on this parenting thing." He laughed nervously. "I need more work than you do, I reckon."

"And I could call it off whenever I wanted?" she asked softly. This time, she did pick up the ring, studying the huge round-cut diamond.

Yeah, he'd made the right choice. "Of course. You could do that even if it were a real engagement."

"You won't ask me to marry you again?"

He chuckled. "Nope. The offer stands, though." He took the ring from her. "I guessed on the size." He held out his hand for hers.

She made him wait for it, which he probably deserved. "This is the last moment before everything changes. *Again*," she murmured. "After this, it'll be out of our hands."

"No, it won't," he promised, pulling her into a hug. "I won't let anyone run you down. We're in this together."

"What about sex?" she murmured against his bare shoulder.

His pulse stuttered at the thought. "I'm not about to step out on you. The only thing I ask is that you do the same. And…" He had to dig deep to get the words out. "And if we go our separate ways, I want to meet whoever you date before you introduce him to our son."

She nodded against him and said, "Like I have time to date, anyway."

"Yeah," he agreed, letting his hands roam down her back. "I'm going to be busy for the foreseeable future." He had a championship to win, a kid to father and Brooke…

Yeah, he was going to have his hands *full*. "If you want sex to be a part of this *whatever* it is we're going to do, then I'm okay with that." That was the freaking understatement of the century. Just having this conversation was making him hard for her all over again. "If you don't want to be physical, that's okay, too. I still won't sleep with anyone else."

She sighed. "I think…no, I *know* that if we're going to be around each other, we're going to wind up just like this, whether we plan on it or not."

She pulled away and Flash managed not to groan in frustration, so score one for maturity. Damned maturity.

"If we're engaged," she went on, finality in her voice. "I wouldn't want to say it's fake, because I like you, and *this*," she said, motioning between their bodies, "is very, *very* good."

"Happy to hear," he replied, waggling his eyebrows suggestively.

Was she agreeing?

She was.

Taking a deep breath, she squared her shoulders and held out her left hand, palm down. "Okay," she said, sounding for all the world like she was gearing up for battle, not accepting his ring. "Let's do this. For Bean."

"For *us*." Flash didn't realize his own hands were shaking until he slid the diamond onto her finger. "Whatever happens," he told her, his voice low and serious, "we're in this together. Trust me."

The ring fit.

A part of his mind wanted to say it was fate, that she was meant to be his and he would always be hers.

She stared at his ring on her finger. "Trust…" She sighed heavily. A little too heavily. "Because nothing says *trustworthy* like an only sort-of-real engagement, right?"

"It's a challenge," he told her. One that involved working together as a team, developing a physical connection and, *far* down the line, the chance to win it all.

Being almost really engaged to Brooke Bonner was not unlike riding in a rodeo, frankly.

This was Flash's year, and Brooke Bonner was the biggest challenge of his life.

# Fourteen

Things happened very quickly after Brooke managed to pull herself out of Flash's arms and out of his bed.

First, she called Alex and updated her friend on the new plan. Not unsurprisingly, Alex wasn't a huge fan of the plan. Or of Flash. "*Engaged?* Seriously? I'm not sure this is the best idea."

"You got a better one?" Brooke shot back. "I can't keep hiding, Alex. You know I can't. It's not right. And, yes, it's going to suck for a while, but it was always going to suck. We just delayed the suckiness."

"Yeah, yeah, I know." Another longish pause. "You going to marry him?"

"We're *engaged.*" Which wasn't really an answer to that question, but it was the only one she was going to give to Alex, to her mother, to the press. They were engaged. Period. End of discussion.

"I'll break him if he hurts you," she growled into the phone.

Brooke laughed it off because how else was she supposed to respond to what was probably a serious threat?

"I'll fill you in on all the details later." Alex made what

sounded a lot like a retching noise. "But the main thing right now is that we're going to bring Bean to the All-Stars Rodeo Friday night and I hope you'll be able to be there. It'd mean a lot to me." Flash gave her a thumbs-up. "To both of us."

Alex, however, was in no mood to be charmed. "I'm not gonna like him, so quit trying," she snapped, but, in true Alex form, she softened immediately. "Okay, fine. We're all going to the rodeo. Have you told your mom yet?"

"No, that's next. We're going out to the house after this," Brooke said.

"Well, good luck with *that*." She hung up.

Some of Flash's good humor faded. "That didn't sound good."

"It's not." There were no words to describe how little Brooke was looking forward to this introduction.

Flash kissed her forehead before saying, "However you want to handle it is how we'll handle it. I'm here to back you up."

She couldn't help the sigh of relief that escaped her. This was the Flash she wanted. Perfect and charming and thoughtful and beside her. Not out in front, not trying to take over, but supporting her. "Just…maybe focus on demonstrating you're a good father? For all our issues, she does love Bean."

If he tried to charm Mom outright, it'd be a disaster. But if he could convince Crissy Bonner that he'd take good care of her grandson, then maybe it wouldn't be too bad.

"That I can do," he promised, pulling her to her feet and brushing a kiss over her lips, then her cheek. "And then afterwards?"

The next kiss was anything but soft or sweet, and maybe it wasn't the smartest thing to do, but Brooke let herself be swept away by his heat, his taste.

"Will you stay tonight?" she whispered against his

mouth. She could sleep in his arms and maybe he could at least get up with Bean, even if she'd still have to nurse him. And if they were already sharing a bed... "Will you stay with me?"

He touched his forehead to hers, his thumbs stroking over her cheeks. "For as long as you'll let me, babe."

She chose not to think about what he was really saying.

Forty minutes later, Brooke was pretty sure she'd made a tactical error bringing Flash home with her unannounced.

"*Who* is this?" Mom demanded, clutching Bean to her chest as she eyed Flash suspiciously. The look in her eyes promised a storm was about to be unleashed.

But Brooke wasn't going to back down. Not this time. Not ever again.

Mother might know best, but Brooke was a mother now, too. And she knew what was best for her family.

She glanced at Flash. He was family now, especially when he gave her hand an encouraging squeeze and shot her a little wink. Then he turned the full power of his charming smile back to her mother and said, "Mrs. Bonner, I'm Frasier Lawrence. My family owns Lawrence Energies in Dallas." Then, because he was Flash, he threw in a little bow. "I'm Bean's father and," he continued smoothly over Mom's gasp of horror, "I've asked your daughter to marry me." He lifted Brooke's hand and kissed her knuckle, right above the simply huge diamond engagement ring.

She noted that Flash carefully avoided the lie that Brooke had agreed to be his wife. He simply let the jewelry and his real name do the talking for him.

The noise Mom made was barely human. "You *what*? Who the hell *is* this?"

She startled poor Bean, who definitely hadn't recovered from all the excitement the night before. He promptly melted down.

"Now look what you've done!" Mom yelled at Flash over the baby's wails. Bean cried louder.

Brooke tensed because if Flash was going to lose his temper, this would be the moment when it happened.

He didn't. Instead, Flash simply squeezed Brooke's hand and focused on Mom. "Ma'am, I think my son is hungry. Let me check his diaper before I give him to Brooke." He plucked the baby out of Mom's stunned arms. "Hey, honey. I heard you let Mommy sleep a little last night," he cooed to the baby as he headed for the stairs. He shifted so Bean was tucked against his shoulder. "Maybe we'll let her get some more sleep tonight. Won't that be great? Yeah, that's my good boy."

Bean, bless his heart, managed a wobbly grin, even as he gave Brooke a worried look. But he let Flash carry him upstairs.

Brooke's heart clenched with a fierce need because, yeah, he was putting on a show for Mom, but, God, the sight of him cuddling his son, of Bean responding to him—that was what she needed from him. *She* needed to know he'd be a good father.

"You're getting married?" Mom asked, not bothering to wait until Flash and Bean were out of earshot.

"Not today," Brooke replied. "But Flash—that's Frasier's nickname—and I are going to—"

"Wait—that's *Flash* Lawrence?" Mom interrupted, the blood draining from her face. "The criminal?"

"Actually, he's a rodeo rider." Brooke took a cue from Flash and counted her breaths for a moment until she was sure she had her temper under control. "I don't expect you to understand or approve, Mom."

"You're damn right I don't," she fired back. "Do you have any idea what he's capable of? He will destroy your career." With great physical effort, Mom attempted to look caring. She didn't come close. "Honey, let's think about this. I'm just not sure this *marriage*," she said, like the word tasted bad in her mouth, "is for the best, you know? We've kept his…contribution quiet for this long. There's no reason to break that silence right now." She shot Brooke the look that normally had her dropping her gaze, unwilling to risk further angering Crissy Bonner. But then her mother added, "You know I just want what's best for your career," in what was probably supposed to be a gentle voice, except it came out as an order.

Right. If Mom was truly worried about Flash's "criminal" history, she'd be worried about Brooke or about Bean. But it always came back to the career with Crissy Bonner.

Brooke ignored the sting of rejection layered within her mother's words. "He can't be any worse for my career than your brother was when he stole all my money and disappeared to Mexico," Brooke shot back. "But you convinced me that hiring Uncle Brantley was 'for the best' because it kept my career in the family, right?"

"He's my brother," Mom snapped. "I trusted him, too. It's not my fault he made poor choices. Just like it's not my fault you made poor choices!"

"Do *not* call my child a poor choice," Brooke seethed.

"All I'm trying to do is contain the damage," Mom went on. "And until we know what that man's motivations are, it's for the best to keep him out of the picture. That doesn't make me the bad guy here!"

"Oh? Just like you kept my father out of the picture?"

Mom had already opened her mouth to fire back another excuse, but at Brooke's words, her jaw snapped shut. "You have no idea what you're talking about," she said in a dangerous whisper.

"Of course I don't—because you won't tell me!" Brooke was shouting now, but she didn't care. Years of resentments bubbled up and poured out. "For God's sake, Mom, I'm not a little girl anymore! I'm a woman, and I'm more than capable of deciding what I need to be protected from. Or were you just protecting yourself?" The words came flying out of her mouth before she could stop them. "Maybe you were just afraid that, if I knew my father, I'd choose him over you!"

True hurt flashed over her mother's face, but it was gone in an instant. "After all I've done for you, this is how you repay me?"

That line might've worked on Brooke when she was a teenager, but she wasn't about to fall for that guilt trip now. "Who was he, Mom?"

Everything about Crissy Bonner screamed, *Not telling*, from the tight line of her mouth to the way she'd crossed her arms in front of her.

"Don't you think I deserve to know? At least for Bean's sake. What if there are medical issues we should know about?"

"This discussion is over," Mom snapped. She made a move toward the door.

Brooke blocked her. Somehow, she knew that if Mom walked out that door, she'd never get answers. "I've let you keep your secrets for years, but you owe me this. You made sure I grew up without knowing anything about my father. If you think I'm going to let you do the exact same thing to Bean, then you've underestimated how far I'll go to protect him!"

"You foolish girl—did you ever consider the fact that maybe *he* didn't want you to know who he was?"

"Of course I did." It didn't take a big mental leap to figure that her father simply didn't want her, because if he did, he'd have found a way to be with her. "But does that justify lying to me my entire life?"

Mom tried to push past her, but Brooke wasn't having any of it. She grabbed her mom by her shoulders and demanded, "Who was he?"

"This is a mistake," Mom hissed. She twisted out of Brooke's grasp and made a turn, probably heading for the back door.

Brooke snatched her hand and held tight. "Mom, please. It won't make me love you any less." Who knew, maybe it'd help her understand her mother's *unique* kind of love even more. "Promise."

"You really think I haven't told you just because I'm embarrassed or something? Fine. But you take this up with him. I wash my hands of this whole mess."

"Fine?" Was Crissy Bonner actually going to tell the truth? And Brooke wasn't entirely sure what Mom meant with that *mess* comment. "Who?"

"Kyle Morgan," she snapped. "There. Happy?"

"Kyle? *Kyle?*" Brooke's old friend? The man who'd taught her how to write a song, who'd given her a guitar for her eleventh birthday? Who'd been there the night of her first show at the Bluebird and helped her land her record deal? The man who'd threatened Flash behind the Bluebird?

Kyle Morgan was her father.

And he'd never told her.

"Does he...does he know? Who I am?"

"Of course he does, not that it ever mattered to him. But just because Kyle cut and ran doesn't mean you have to marry *that* man," Mom went on, wrenching her hand away from Brooke and pointing to the second floor. "You've already made one mistake. Two wrongs don't make a right. Trust me on *that*, Brooke."

Numbly, Brooke looked up to see Flash standing at the top of the stairs, Bean in his arms. "Brooke?" he said softly into the eerie silence that settled in the space between Brooke and her mother. "We're ready for you."

She was not going to cry in front of her mother. She was not going to rant and rave and demand to know what the hell Mom and Kyle had been thinking. She was not going to lose it completely. She simply wasn't.

Suddenly she understood why Flash had been punching couch cushions.

"I will cut you out of Bean's life if you ever refer to him as a mistake again," Brooke said, her voice unnaturally calm. "Flash and I are engaged. He's Bean's father and we're together now. And I think it'd be best if I found a manager who understood the difference between managing my career and managing me. I love you, Mom, but I don't know how I'm going to forgive you for this. Or Kyle."

A muscle twitched on Mom's forehead. "Fine. You're on your own."

"Fine." Actually, it was a relief. She was zero-for-two with family members as managers. "Thank you for watching Bean today."

"His name is Jimmy," Mom shot back. "I hate that nickname."

"His name is *James*," Brooke replied, stepping to the side. "James Frasier Lawrence."

Mom stormed past her, slamming the door with all her might.

Brooke stood there for a long moment—okay, several long moments—trying to process everything that had just happened. She'd expected a fight about Flash. She'd considered Mom quitting as her manager a possibility, maybe.

But… Kyle Morgan was her father?

"Babe?" Flash called down softly.

Right.

"Did…" Brooke's voice broke. "Did you hear?"

Flash practically flew down the stairs to stand next to her, close enough to bump her shoulder with his. "Impossible not to."

"Yeah."

"Yeah," he agreed.

The silence stretched but it didn't feel painful. She realized Flash had laced his fingers with hers.

"I…" She cleared her throat and tried again. "I need you to stay. With me. Tonight. I…" Tears began to drip off her chin. "I don't want to be alone right now."

"You won't be."

# Fifteen

"Everyone, this is Brooke Bonner, my fiancée, and our son, James Frasier," Flash announced.

Brooke cringed, although she tried not to show it. After so many months of holding her secrets close to her heart, it felt really weird to just announce Bean to four people in this room. She wasn't ready for this. She might never be ready.

But then, she'd be just as bad as her mother and she wasn't having that. So Brooke straightened her spine and lifted her chin. Really, this was no different than walking out onto a stage. Except this wasn't a stage—it was a private luxury suite in the Bridgestone Arena, where the All-Stars Rodeo would happen in a few hours. She was here to put on a show, except instead of singing her heart out, she was putting herself out there as Flash's bride-to-be.

"And this is Alex Andrews, a close friend of Brooke's," Flash went on, launching that charming grin around the room. Thank God, Alex was here. Between her oldest friend's unwavering support and Flash's dogged protectiveness, Brooke was sure she could do this.

Reasonably sure. She still had to give a convincing performance, one that had nothing to do with the last two days of Flash basically living with her, making her dinner and rocking Bean to sleep at naptime so she could lie down, too, and holding her when she cried about her mom and Kyle and the whole mess.

No, this evening had nothing to do with that glimpse into what married life could be like with Flash. It had everything to do with damage control and redemption arcs.

From a far corner, Chloe Lawrence looked up and smiled in welcome. Brooke and Flash had agreed that, for the time being, Kyle's contribution to her life was completely off-limits to anyone outside of the two of them and Alex because Brooke wasn't ready to have that part of her life implode, too.

Unfortunately, Chloe was also on the phone, so the first person Brooke got introduced to was...

"Oliver, this is Brooke," Flash said, leading Brooke over to an imposing-looking man who was clearly Flash's brother, a little taller and broader, with silver shot through his hair. Otherwise, they had practically the same eyes, the same chin. But not the same smile—that much was clear when Oliver grimaced. In an undertone, Flash added, "Be nice or *else*."

If Oliver heard the threat, he didn't react. Instead, in a deeply professional voice, he said, "Ms. Bonner, a pleasure to see you again."

Brooke notched an eyebrow at that. Flash had warned her that his brother could be a bit stiff. She'd barely met the eldest Lawrence sibling at the Fort Worth rodeo before she'd disappeared with Flash. But she remembered someone who'd been very...overwhelming, especially when compared to Flash's easygoing nature. That, at least, hadn't changed.

"Don't worry," the blonde woman next to him said, handing Oliver the baby girl she was struggling to hold on to. "The awkwardness won't last. Welcome to the Law-rence family!"

"This is Renee, Oliver's wife," Flash said, leaning over and giving Renee a kiss on the cheek. Then he mock-whispered to Brooke, "Don't believe a word she says about what we did as kids. It's lies, all lies, I say!"

Renee laughed and stuck out her hand. "I never thought I'd meet the woman who could rein Flash in, but I'm glad I finally have." Renee had a wide smile that seemed vaguely familiar. She patted the little girl. "This is our daughter, Trixie. She's almost nine months old." Trixie barely looked at Brooke before burying her head in her father's neck. "I'm so glad she has a cousin!"

Brooke exhaled in relief. Another mom, another baby—she felt less out to sea already. She only hoped Renee would prove to be as friendly as her smile.

Renee leaned forward, staring at Bean with open adoration. "Look at you," she whispered. "I know tests have to be done, but Oliver, do you see the resemblance?"

Bean chose that moment to launch one of his daddy's smiles into the room, and Renee gasped at the same time Oliver said, "Well, that settles *that*."

"Yeah," Brooke agreed. "We're all in trouble, aren't we?"

Oliver gaped and Brooke was sure she'd screwed up. But then, unexpectedly, Oliver burst out laughing. "You're going to be very good for my brother, aren't you?" he said, slugging Flash on the shoulder.

Apparently, the awkwardness didn't last long. "The better question is, how good will he be for me?"

Oliver beamed, which was sort of unsettling because when he wasn't scowling, he was almost as charming as Flash. "He better be great for you—or else."

*"Boys,"* Renee scolded as she held out her arms. "May I?" Brooke handed over Bean, who immediately gurgled in what sounded like approval. "I practically grew up with

Flash—although he was still Frasier then. Oh, the stories I could tell you!" She fixed him with a piercing gaze. "Remember the elevator incident?"

Next to Brooke, Flash groaned. "You're killing me, Renee."

"It's good for you to be brought down a peg or two," she replied with an easy grin, and it was clear these two had a long history of teasing each other.

"I think discovering fatherhood has run me right out of pegs," Flash countered. "Come on," he said to Oliver, taking Trixie from his big brother's arms, "I could use a drink. A *ginger ale*," he said, meeting Oliver's scowl head-on. "Sheesh, man. Even when I drank, I never drank before a rodeo. Babe, you want green tea? I had them get some just for you."

Brooke's cheeks heated. "That would be wonderful. Thank you."

Flash winked at her, and then the brothers headed off to the side of the suite where a variety of nonalcoholic beverages were displayed on a sideboard.

"I remember when Trixie was this little," Renee said, bouncing Bean in her arms. The baby trilled in delight. She eyed Brooke sympathetically. "How are you holding up?"

"Okay, I guess." Sure, she hadn't seen or spoken to her mother in two days, nor had she decided what to do about Kyle Morgan.

At least Alex was here. Brooke glanced over to see that Flash had somehow gotten Alex over to the drinks and was introducing her to Trixie. It was sweet of Flash to make sure Alex was a part of what was, essentially, a family gathering. And despite all her protestations that she wasn't going to like Flash, Brooke could tell her friend was relieved Flash was including her.

"I understand Chloe has a whole plan in place," Renee said.

Brooke felt awkward standing in the middle of the room,

so she moved to the huge picture windows that overlooked the arena. Renee followed. Below, she saw someone who might be Pete Wellington making the final preparations. In a few minutes, the doors would open and the stands would begin to fill. And once the crowd was in place…

It was just another performance, one where she wouldn't have a guitar in her hands. Just a baby. "Yes. I ran it through the record label's PR department and they signed off on it, as well. I think Chloe's got a job at the label if she ever gets tired of the rodeo."

"Trust me, that'll never happen. The only one who's tired of the rodeo is Oliver."

Redemption arcs for everyone, apparently. Chloe was probably on the phone with Kari right now, coordinating the Big Reveal, as Brooke had started to think of it.

Right before Flash's first event, she and Bean, who had his own set of baby-sized noise-canceling headphones, would go behind the chutes where she would very publicly give Flash a kiss for good luck. The cameras would zoom in to capture the moment. Alex would be right behind her, just in case.

The announcers would draw everyone's attention to her and Flash, at which point Flash would lift Bean out of Brooke's arms and cuddle him. If Bean was cooperative, he would smile, and Brooke would put her head on Flash's shoulder and it would be perfect.

Brooke looked at her son, who was currently attempting to stuff his whole fist in his drooly mouth. Life was so rarely perfect. "It's going to be very messy for a while, though," she said, and sighed.

To Brooke's surprise, Renee wrapped an arm around her shoulders and gave Brooke an awkward hug. "You'll get through this," she said. "No matter what happens, you and this special little guy are family now and family is everything to the Lawrences."

"It is?" Brooke was horrified to hear her voice catch. Family had done nothing but let her down for the last few days. Weeks. Lifetimes, it seemed.

Renee nodded. "It absolutely is. Even when Flash had a rough few years there—which he mostly brought upon himself," she quickly added, "his family stood by him. I don't know your history, aside from your official bio. But my own family was—" she shrugged and turned her attention to Bean "—less than ideal. Having the Lawrences stand with me when everyone else bailed? It's *everything*."

Brooke blinked hard. "I don't really have anyone else but Alex. My mother stopped speaking to me when she found out about Flash." That was a gross simplification of the situation, but it was all she could cop to without crying.

At least with Flash in the house, she'd been able to get some more sleep. She wouldn't have had a prayer of getting through this night otherwise.

Renee handed Bean back to Brooke and then gave her another sideways hug. "I'll be honest—the Lawrences can be overbearing, overwhelming and completely over-the-top. But they'll fight for you and this little guy until the very end, if you let them."

Bean launched his daddy's smile at Brooke. "I just want things to work out," she said softly, hugging her baby tight.

"They will," Renee promised. "Just maybe not the way you thought they would."

Flash stood off to the side, making Trixie giggle as he blew bubbles on her tummy. The whole time, he watched Brooke, who was deep in conversation with Renee.

Chloe came up and topped off her water. "It seems to be going well," she said, nodding toward the two women.

Flash introduced Chloe to Alex. "She's nervous," Alex announced. "Excuse me."

"I'd be worried if she weren't," Chloe agreed. Once Alex had joined Renee and Brooke, Chloe turned her full attention to Flash. "All the pieces are in place. You know what you need to do, right?"

"Yes. I knew the last three times you asked, too."

He was not going to let everyone's nervousness get to him, though. The situation was under control. The babies were happy, the tea was steeping and Brooke's introduction to his family was going well. Really, really well.

He still couldn't get over the fight between Brooke and her mother, though. Meeting Crissy Bonner had made sense of a lot of stuff. He could see how Brooke had been completely overruled by her mother, how Brooke keeping Flash's contribution to their son quiet hadn't necessarily been a selfish act but one of quiet rebellion.

Oh, he was still plenty mad at Crissy Bonner. But between that fight and everything Brooke had told him since then, it was getting a lot harder to hold on to his anger at Brooke herself. He'd always understood on a logical level that she hadn't told him about the baby because she'd seen those headlines and panicked. But when he counted how Brooke's mom had been manipulating her...

Brooke had stood up for Flash. More than that, she'd stood up for herself.

God, she was amazing. And, better than that, she was wearing his ring.

Oliver rumbled, "You *are* going to marry her, aren't you?" while snatching Trixie from Flash's arms.

"That is the literal definition of *engaged*," Flash said, refusing to allow any resentment to take hold at the note of doubt in Oliver's voice. "But I'm not going to drag her down the aisle tomorrow. That was the deal."

"Of course I'm not saying that." This serious declaration was interrupted by Oliver spinning in a circle with his daughter, making the baby shriek with glee. "I'm saying, make it legal."

"Working on it," Flash said through gritted teeth as he squeezed the honey into Brooke's tea.

Chloe slapped Oliver on the arm. "It's been four days, dude. Give the man some room to work. We have a plan." She turned back to Flash. Any gratitude he might have felt toward her for standing up for him evaporated when she added, "You remember your part, right?"

"Would you two back off?" Flash was really proud of the way he kept his voice calm. "I'm not going to blow up and I'm not going to lash out. I know why I'm here and what I'm supposed to do, so stop acting like I'm still nineteen, got it?"

Chloe and Oliver exchanged a look. It did not inspire a great deal of confidence.

"Got it?" Flash said more forcefully.

His phone buzzed—a message from Dad. Good luck tonight—and bring that girl and that baby home on Monday! I want to meet my grandson!

Flash grinned. At least they'd convinced Dad to stay home for this night. Things tended to go haywire when he showed up at rodeos. Besides, Flash hadn't wanted to overwhelm Brooke with relatives and if Milt Lawrence was anything, it was overwhelming.

Will do. Thanks, Dad, he texted back.

"You need to head down," Chloe said after listening to the earpiece. Pete was no doubt on the other end. "Hey— about the Cowboy of the Year championship…"

"Listen," he told his siblings. "I'm still in it to win it, okay? Tomorrow we'll work on setting up visitation schedules around the All-Stars and her concert dates. But that's tomorrow. Tonight, I'm counting on you to keep Brooke and James safe and happy. Do *not* upset her. No mentioning lawyers or money or anything that starts with the phrase 'you should.' Can you handle that?"

"Of course," Oliver scoffed, as if he hadn't spent a few decades telling Flash what he should or should not be doing.

"Promise," Chloe added, looking about as chastised as Flash had ever seen her. "The situation is under control."

"The more you say that, the more worried I get," Flash muttered as he cut around them and headed toward Brooke, tea in hand.

Awkward family meetings aside, this was the sort of thing he could get used to. Brooke and James were looking out at the arena. They'd watch him ride and then they'd head back to her place for the night. James would probably exercise his lungs at some point in the wee hours and Flash would get up with him, letting Brooke sleep as long as possible. Then they'd flop back in bed together, taking comfort in each other's bodies.

He hadn't been lying—tomorrow would bring schedules and negotiations and complications. But tonight was his. This was his rodeo and she was…

She might just be his forever.

Because if he married her, there was no going back on that. Lawrence men—and women—were one-and-done people.

"Hey, I've got to head down," he said, slipping his arm around her waist and pulling her back against his chest. Renee shot him a wink and excused herself. Alex did the same, giving him and Brooke as much privacy as possible in the crowded suite. "Your tea. Doing okay?"

"Your sister-in-law is nice," she said, and he was thankful to hear relief in her voice. "I didn't tell her everything, but I got the feeling she'd understand."

"She would. She's one of the nicest people I've ever known, but—and I mean this—don't ever trust her when she's holding water balloons."

Brooke chuckled, which made Bean look up from where he was gumming a rattle.

"You up for this, little man?" Flash asked, stroking his son's soft hair. A week ago, he'd been a single man, pining for the woman of his dreams. Now?

Now he was so much more.

James grinned around his rattle.

"That's my boy." Flash leaned his chin onto Brooke's shoulder. "We're going to get through this, babe. Just a few hours and then we'll be back home. You can do it."

She blew a hard breath. "Trust me, no one knows that the show must go on like I do. Now get going."

"I'm going—but I'm coming back," he said with a grin, kissing her on the neck. "See you soon." When he turned around, he found the attention of every single person in the room on him. Oliver almost smiled, which was the same as a normal person jumping for joy. Chloe gave Flash a thumbs-up, and he could tell that was exactly the sort of display she wanted to see in an hour. Renee beamed a huge smile at him, and even Alex nodded in approval.

So far, so good. Now they just had to get through the rodeo without tanking his place in the standings, and then he could have Brooke all to himself again.

Yup, he was feeling lucky tonight.

# Sixteen

"Ready?" Alex muttered.

"Yes."

This was just ten minutes out of Brooke's life. She'd basically handed over the reins of her social media to Chloe and Kari so she wouldn't have to deal with the notifications for a few days. So really, this was no big deal.

Brooke did a final check on Bean's headphones to make sure the baby hadn't knocked them off in the last three minutes. Then she squared her shoulders and put her game face on.

"And Dan Jones makes the time!" an announcer yelled over the roar of the crowd.

Dan was their cue.

"It's time," Chloe said, guiding them out from the tiny alcove created underneath the chutes that had been blocked off from public view by promotional banners. Brooke followed and Alex brought up the rear.

They climbed the rickety metal stairs to the top of the chutes where Flash was waiting. He turned to her just as the announcer said, "Up next is Flash Lawrence, who's having a heck of a comeback year."

"Hey babe," Flash said over the roar of the crowd as he stepped into her. "You okay?"

She knew it was for the show, that they were both playing to the cameras; still, the obvious concern in his eyes was touching. "Holding steady," she said as he lowered her head to hers.

"Good girl," he murmured against her lips.

"That's right," the other announcer said. "After a rough...uh, Jimbo? Who's Flash kissing?"

Brooke kept her eyes closed because she didn't really want to see Flash kissing her blown up on a jumbotron.

"Is that Nashville's own Brooke Bonner, the country superstar?" Jimbo asked. "Larry, is there something going on we didn't know about?"

A hush fell over the arena, and Brooke knew everyone was staring and asking the same questions.

"Almost there," Flash whispered as he lifted Bean out of her arms. "Being good for Mommy?" he asked as he pressed a kiss to the one small section of Bean's head the headphones weren't covering. And, bless his little heart, Bean smiled.

Brooke exhaled in relief and remembered to smile. Hopefully, it looked real and not like she was having a low-grade panic attack, because there was no going back now. Bean was officially public knowledge.

"Jimbo—is that a *baby*? Did you know Flash Lawrence had a baby?"

The crowd gasped in complete unison as Brooke flattened her palm high on Flash's chest so the massive diamond he'd bought her was right next to Bean's back.

"Larry, is that an *engagement* ring?" Jimbo asked.

"Look at the size of that rock!" Larry was clearly impressed.

Seconds later, the crowd erupted into cheers so deafening that even with his protective headphones, Bean flinched.

"Flash, you're up!" Pete said. "Good job, everyone!"

Brooke took Bean back and gave Flash a kiss for luck while the crowd cheered. So far, so good. She'd been in front of enough audiences to know they had the arena eating out of the palms of their hands. This might be a show, but it was a good one.

And Flash knew it.

"Proud of you, Brooke," he said, his satisfied smile almost enough to make her forget they were being watched by thousands.

"Jimbo, I bet there's more to this story—I hope we'll be able to get a word with Flash after the show?" Larry asked.

"Boy, me too," Jimbo agreed. "But first, he's got to make the time on this bronco!" Thankfully, they turned the conversation back to the horse's stats.

"Have a good ride," she told him, digging deep for that smile.

With a nod, he turned and climbed down into the chute onto the bronco's back. Brooke edged away from the chute so Pete could help Flash get his ropes adjusted.

"Damn near perfect," Alex muttered behind Brooke.

She nodded but didn't look away from Flash. The gate opened and his horse spun out, bucking high into the air while Flash held on for dear life.

"That's Daddy, sweetie," she murmured to Bean, shifting the baby so he could watch. "Look at him go!"

Seconds ticked by slowly as Flash clung to the horse's back. The buzzer sounded just as Flash lost his fight with gravity and he went tumbling to the dirt. Brooke gasped and held her breath, but Flash popped right back up again, pumping his fist into the air.

"Looks like it's Flash's lucky night," Jimbo said. "That ride's going to earn him first in the rankings!"

Brooke cheered along with the crowd. She'd almost made it. Now she just had to wait for Flash to get back to the chute, and then he'd escort her backstage, where he'd hand her off to Chloe, who'd take her back to the family's suite for the rest of the rodeo.

"Well, well, well—this explains everything, doesn't it?" a silky voice said, cutting through the crowd noise and the announcers.

Brooke spun just as Alex snarled, "Hey, back off."

The cowboy staring at Brooke wasn't wearing a vest or a rider's number, but he looked vaguely familiar. Had she met him before? Or just seen his picture somewhere?

"Easy, honey," the cowboy said to Alex, which made the big woman growl. "I'm an...old friend of Flash's." He gave Brooke the once-over, and a burst of apprehension shot down her back.

"Explains what?" she asked, looking around for Pete or Chloe or *anyone*. She did not like the look in this guy's eyes.

"He was screwing you the entire time. How about that?" The cowboy laughed but when Alex went to shove him back, he spun gracefully past her, and suddenly only a foot separated Brooke from him.

Oh, hell. She couldn't back up because there was no room and she couldn't get to the stairs without getting past him. "Leave us alone," she ordered.

"Hey!" Flash shouted from the arena floor. How close was he? Where was Pete? Why couldn't Alex catch this guy? "Tex, back off! Pete! Alex! Get him away from her!"

"You know your little boy toy beat the ever-loving shit out of me?" the cowboy apparently named Tex all but purred. Another hush fell over the arena, but Brooke could feel the difference between this one and the way the crowd had quieted at the reveal of the baby and the ring. "Broke my jaw and my leg, all because I hoped you'd be a good fuck. He ended my career, all for a little piece like you!"

Behind Tex, Alex lunged but the man had catlike reflexes, apparently, because he easily danced out of her way—which only brought him closer to Brooke.

"I had nothing to do with that," she told him, curling around Bean. That's why she recognized him—his picture had been in the articles about Flash's arrest and trial. Had the fight been about her? Because this creep made some creepy comments?

Someone in the crowd shrieked. "Larry, what's Tex McGraw doing here?" Jimbo asked.

"He quit the All-Stars, didn't he?" Larry responded, sounding worried. "After that fight with Flash?"

"The bastard took away everything I love," Tex said, charging forward, his hand clamping around her arm with so much force that it took her breath away. "It's time I returned the favor."

Brooke tried to yell, but her throat wasn't working as Tex twisted her arm hard enough that she saw stars. The baby! She spun, trying to keep hold of Bean, who began to scream bloody murder.

"Brooke!" A body slammed into Tex—oh, thank God, it was Flash.

Brooke stumbled before Tex's grip on her arm gave, and then Flash and Tex crashed off the top of the chute, landing in the dirt with a thud. Flash came up swinging.

"Jesus," Alex said, grabbing Brooke and hustling her down the stairs. "Is Bean okay?"

Brooke stumbled to a stop, staring in horror as Flash threw a punch and then another one. His fists were a blur. "You touch her again and I'll *end* you," he roared as blood flew off his knuckles.

"Move, Bonner," Alex bellowed, shoving Brooke past the fight and into the tunnel under the stands. *"Move!"*

Brooke looked back over her shoulder as Alex pushed her away from the arena. Complete pandemonium had broken out—Pete and a bunch of cowboys were trying to get Flash off Tex, who was throwing a few punches of his own.

The last thing Brooke saw before Alex dragged her through a pair of doors was Flash's head snap back as Tex's fist connected with his jaw and Flash turning a bloody grin on Tex, letting his fist fly.

Brooke's stomach turned and she began to run.

God help her, that man was enjoying the fight.

# Seventeen

"The *good* news," Chloe said in the tone of voice that made it clear there wasn't a whole lot to go around, "is that, despite your record and your history with Tex, the prosecutors are declining to press charges on assault for you. The whole fight was caught on camera. You were clearly defending your family. Oliver's talking to them now."

*That* was the good news? Flash moved the ice off his face and squinted at Chloe. "The bad news?"

Wincing at his black eyes, Chloe held her phone out for Flash to read. Which was a challenge. The words drifted before him like they were floating down a lazy river, but he managed to get one eye to focus.

What he saw chilled him colder than any ice pack ever could. Brooke had sent a group text to Chloe, Oliver and Flash: Thank you for welcoming me and James into the Lawrence family. We will be in touch to set up a visitation schedule. No mention of Flash coming back to her house tonight, no mention of engagements—nothing.

His vision narrowed to those few lines of text. He forgot how to count, how to breathe.

*We will be in touch.*

If it were possible for five words to break him, those five might just do the trick.

She'd promised. *Promised!* They were in this together now! They were a team! She'd sworn she wouldn't keep him from his son—not again!

No. He refused to accept this.

He had to make this right. He struggled up, which made the room spin. "I need to go," he said, except his jaw wasn't moving right—again. If people could stop breaking the damn thing, that'd be great. He couldn't talk to Brooke with a broken jaw and he definitely couldn't ride.

"No," Pete said, putting a firm hand on Flash's shoulder, "you don't. You show up looking like someone flattened your face with a steamroller and it'll only scare her more."

"Worse than the cushion incident in the library," Chloe agreed, picking up the ice and putting it back on Flash's face.

He tried to bat it away because, yeah, he probably looked horrifying, but he couldn't let Brooke hide behind that cold text. "Tomorrow, then," he managed to get out.

"Shit, man—is your jaw busted again?" Pete said, crouching before Flash and studying his face.

"You should see the other guy," Flash tried to say but that was way too much talking. Crap.

"Buddy, you're done for the season," Pete said. "Chloe, we've got to get him to a hospital."

"On it," she said, and sighed.

His championship season…gone. Just like that.

But the moment self-pity tried to crowd into his head, it was pushed aside by the look of terror on Brooke's face when Tex had grabbed her. In that moment, she'd been more important than anything else—his jaw, the rodeo… none of it mattered. What had mattered was making sure she was okay and Bean was safe.

He couldn't wait until tomorrow.

He needed to see with his own eyes that she was fine, that the baby was okay, that Brooke understood he'd do anything to protect her.

*We will be in touch.*

He needed her to have some faith in him. Instead, she was pulling back, locking him out.

He wasn't going to stand for it.

"I will knock your ass out if you try to stand up again," Pete warned, shoving him back into the chair. "I've done it before and I'll do it again."

The room spun. Flash might have blacked out, he wasn't sure. Maybe Pete really had tagged him. The next thing he knew, he was being loaded into the back of an ambulance and Oliver was next to him, looking as worried as hell.

"It's going to be okay," Oliver said, his voice sounding strained.

"Brooke," Flash moaned. The ambulance began to move and the world got spinny again.

"It'll be okay," Oliver repeated, holding on to Flash's arm.

As Flash slipped back into the darkness, he was pretty sure it wouldn't be okay. Not until he could get to Brooke.

Thankfully, Bean was fine. Once Brooke settled in the rocker with the baby on her lap, he was out like a light.

Brooke, however, was not fine.

She had forgotten what *fine* felt like. Every one of her nightmares had played out in real time—Flash Lawrence, out of control.

"You're still shaking," Alex said, sounding as close to crying as Brooke had ever heard her.

"Am I?" Brooke laughed, a high-pitched noise that startled Bean. Brooke adjusted him to the other side. "Sorry."

"I sent that text you wanted," Alex said, sitting down on the footstool.

"What text?"

The worry lines deepened on Alex's face. She pulled out a phone—Brooke's phone, she recognized it—and read the text. "You told me to send it when we got home, so I did."

"Then I must have wanted you to." She didn't remember telling Alex that, but who knew. She was pretty sure she was in a state of shock.

She'd been nearly assaulted and then her fiancé had snapped, and none of that took into account the situation with her mother and Kyle or the press...

It was safe to say she was *not* coping well. Nope.

"Brooke? If he shows up, do you want to see him?"

"I don't..." She cleared her throat. A part of her wished that Flash would stroll into the nursery, a mug of hot tea with honey in his hand and a charming smile on his face. That he'd bring the music back with him and they'd write the ending to their song together.

But how could she trust him? How could she trust that she'd make the right decision this time?

Thank God she hadn't married him.

She held up her left hand, where his enormous ring was heavy on her finger. It hadn't been real. That was a comfort, right? No one would blame her for breaking it off with him, not after what had happened tonight.

"I don't think so," she said softly.

"Are you sure that's the right thing to do?" Alex asked, her voice gruff.

"I thought you didn't like him."

"I don't. But Brooke, he was defending you. Because I missed." Tears overflowed Alex's eyes. Brooke stared in shock. Had Alex ever cried? "I wasn't quick enough to catch that guy, but Flash was faster. If I'd done my job..." A sob racked her big body. "I'm so sorry I let you down. But don't hold it against Flash. He was *protecting* you."

Was Alex right? After all, hadn't Brooke been up there

on that chute, praying he'd get to her in time? And he had. He had!

Someone rang the damned doorbell and Bean startled, mewling in displeasure.

"I'll get it," Alex growled, rubbing at her watery eyes.

Sighing, Brooke began to pat the baby's back. "If it's Flash, I'm not home." Maybe Alex was right, maybe she wasn't. But Brooke wasn't going to deal with any of that tonight. No way, no how.

Being around Flash was too intoxicating. He made her forget things, like how Bean was her first priority and how she didn't need someone who was good in bed—she could go whole years without sex. She had after she'd met him, hadn't she? But the moment he got within ten feet of her, she craved him like a junkie craved a hit.

That wasn't healthy.

Two sets of footsteps echoed on the stairs. Oh, no—Alex had decided to let Flash in after all, hadn't she? "I told you, I didn't want to see…"

But it wasn't Flash who followed Alex into the room—it was Kyle Morgan. Of course. Because Brooke didn't have enough going on today.

"What do you want?"

Kyle had the decency to look embarrassed. "Caught the rodeo on TV tonight."

"So? What do you care?"

Kyle blushed. "Didn't know you'd had a baby. Sorry I missed that."

"Are you?" She knew she was being a total witch, but she couldn't help it. Anyone who was expecting her to go along to get along was in for a hell of a surprise. "Are you my father?"

Kyle dropped his gaze, scrubbing his hand through his short silver hair. "She finally told you, huh?"

"I will never let you see your grandson ever again if

you don't cut the crap, Morgan. I've had a shitty evening and you're not helping. You've been my friend for years and never once even hinted that you were my damned father, so *spill it*."

"Look, I got your mother pregnant. We had a couple of wild nights and…"

Alex growled menacingly behind him.

"And I didn't want to be a father. I was too young and I'll be honest—I was doing a lot of drugs. I wasn't fit to be around a baby. Told your mother as much. Told her I wasn't going to be a father to any child she had. She made the choice to keep you."

"Oh. Okay. So you really didn't want me. Sure."

If this night got any worse, Brooke was going to lose her mind. She couldn't take another shock.

"Morgan, that's the crappiest excuse I've ever heard," Alex rumbled.

"Yeah, I know," he shot back, but he kept his attention on Brooke. "By the time you were a kid, I'd gotten clean and my songs started selling and you had so much talent…" He cleared his throat. "I'm not father material. Never was. But a mentor? I could do that. Your mother saw the same thing I did—you had what it took to be a star. And I could help make it happen."

Brooke let her head fall back against the chair. This man was her father. And in his screwed-up way, he'd done his part to look after her. It hadn't been enough, but it'd been something.

"Look, I may have messed up," Kyle began.

"You think?" Brooke shot back.

"But I did the best I could. I didn't have anything else to give, especially before I stopped using. It's been the joy of my life, being a part of your music." He stared at Bean. "Wish your mother had told me you were going to have a baby, though. Sorry I missed that," he repeated.

Brooke couldn't look at him. She closed her eyes and her mind immediately turned to Flash. What would he do, if he were here? Would he throw Kyle out on his rear? Get into another fight? Or would he stand next to Brooke, holding her hand and ready to back her up, no matter what she decided?

Kyle had had a fling with Crissy Bonner and left her high and dry. When he'd found out about Brooke, he'd cut and run.

Flash hadn't done that, though.

Instead, he'd offered her and Bean the protection of his name and his family's power and wealth. He'd done it in a crappy way at first, but one thing had been clear from the very moment he'd found out about Bean—he'd move heaven and earth to be a father to his son.

Was that still true?

"Why is my name Bonner?"

"Morgan is a stage name." She cracked open one eye to glare at him. "What? I had a lot of kids calling me Bonnie when I was growing up. I married your mother to give you a name and then we got a quiet, quick divorce."

Of all the damn things…insisting that he give her his real name but not anything else took the cake. "I am going to hate you for a while." Which was a lie. She was going to hate him for as long as she damn well wanted. And she wasn't going to think too kindly about Mom, either. The level of deception they'd sunk to was mind-boggling. And for what?

She was so tired of lies wrapped in lies and buried under more lies.

Kyle looked hurt but he nodded grimly. "That's fine." He stood to leave. "I've always cared about you, honey. That doesn't mean I haven't been the world's worst father," he said over the combined sounds of Brooke and Alex scoffing in unison, "but I still care. If you let me, I'll care about that boy of yours, too."

"Don't push your luck, *Kyle*." Because she wasn't calling him Dad. He definitely hadn't earned that right.

He nodded in resignation again and turned to go. "One last thing—that fiancé of yours?"

"I don't think we're engaged anymore," Brooke mumbled.

"Yeah, I looked him up after the Bluebird. Those headlines must have pissed your mother off in a major way—too close to what happened to her and me, I think."

Brooke scowled at him again. "You got a point? I've had a long night and I want James to get some sleep." She might not get any, but someone in this house should.

"James. Good name. Fits him." He leaned forward and Brooke let him brush a kiss against her forehead. "I walked away from you and your mother. It's always been my biggest regret, that I threw away the love of my life and my family just because it got hard. Don't make the same mistakes I did."

"That supposed to be fatherly advice?" she snipped, because it was either be snippy or start bawling.

Kyle gave her a sad smile as he turned to go. "Just… think about it. Let me know when you want to talk." He straightened. "I'm not going to throw away a second chance to be a part of your life. You have always been my greatest hit, honey."

Alex showed him out, leaving Brooke alone with her tumbled thoughts and her sleeping son. Now that some of the shock of the attack and fight was wearing off, she was more confused than ever.

Kyle Morgan was her father, but he'd completely abdicated any responsibility for her, choosing to be a friend instead of a parent. He'd abandoned Mom, but had helped Brooke as she'd worked her way up in country music. But he hadn't wanted her unless she was easy and talented. He was a selfish, egotistical asshole, and forgiveness would be a long time coming, if ever.

Flash, on the other hand, wanted to marry her and make it legal—not just in name only, like Kyle and Crissy had, but as a real family. He wanted to be a part of Bean's life. He'd talked about building her a studio on his ranch in Texas and buying Bean a pony. He'd introduced her to his family and staked his claim in front of what felt like the whole world.

Was what happened tonight a deal breaker? Or was she overreacting? If she walked away from Flash, was she doing the same thing Kyle had done? Pushing Flash out of her life because it was easier?

She simply didn't know what the right answer was.

Probably because there wasn't one.

# Eighteen

Flash woke up in the hospital to find Milt Lawrence sitting next to the bed, watching baseball. That seemed off. Dad was supposed to be in Texas. Texas was a long way from Nashville. Or was Flash in Texas?

"What time is it?" Flash asked groggily. Or tried to. Damn it, his jaw had been wired shut again.

"High time you woke up," Dad replied, clicking off the television. "That was a hell of a concussion that ass gave you. But don't worry," he went on, and Flash thought the old man winked, but it was hard to tell because one of Flash's eyes was swollen. "You did a hell of a lot more damage."

That sounded bad. "Didn't kill him?"

"Naw, he's alive and pissed. You've bested him twice. His pride is never going to recover and Oliver's working to have him brought up on charges. Plus, your sister has banned him from ever entering an All-Stars event again and I believe she's gotten him kicked off the Total Bull Challenge, too. She can be very persuasive when she wants to be." Dad chuckled. "Mighty proud of that girl, going to the mat for her family like that."

Flash grunted.

Dad stood on bow legs and peered down at Flash's face. It took Flash's eyes a second to focus. "Never known anyone who had such a glass jaw but could keep fighting."

"Thanks, Dad," he slurred. He didn't care about his jaw at the moment. He only cared about two things. "Brooke? Baby?"

Dad's smile cracked a little and he sat back down. "They're fine. Not really in the mood to deal with your brother and sister. That friend of hers has been sending updates, though."

Flash tried to think, but he could tell he was on painkillers. His brain was muddy and he couldn't see through the silt. Dad couldn't be saying what Flash was afraid he was saying. "Need her."

"Not sure that's the best idea at the moment," Dad said, sounding sad about it. "You gave her quite a fright. But, hell, I saw the tape. I'd have done the exact same thing. When someone threatens the woman you love, you step up and throw down to protect her. You did the right thing."

"Don't *love* her." Funny, those words really hurt to say.

Thankfully, Dad was having no trouble understanding Flash's slurring. "That's not what it looked like to me, boy."

"Like her. Lots." Protecting her had been the most important thing he'd ever done and, if he had to, he'd beat the hell out of Tex again. Anything to take care of her and James. "Need her."

"Son," Dad began in that tone that signaled Flash was in for a hell of a lecture, "I don't know who you think you're trying to fool, but I've got eyes and I've loved my Trixie far longer than you've been walking on this planet."

"She doesn't trust me," Flash said, or tried to say. "She hid the baby from me."

"So?"

Flash managed to roll his eyes at that, although it hurt like hell.

"I'm serious," Dad said, leaning forward to meet Flash's gaze. "No, I don't think she should've kept that kid from you—but I can count, son. I did the math. I'm betting she saw those headlines, just like everyone else did. And your sister says that Brooke's mother is a problem."

"Huge problem," Flash agreed. His father was making sense. Never a good sign.

"So she had her reasons. And you have yours. But if you're waiting for the stars to line up and everything to be perfect in a relationship, then you're gonna spend the rest of your life alone, pining for the girl that got away from you. You're in love with her, and don't even try to deny it—I *know* you, boy. She's pretty crazy for you, too, from what I can tell. But everything that comes after that, including faith and trust and love, is a choice. Every day you have to choose to do what it takes to be in love, to stay in love and then? Then you've got to do the work."

Flash blinked at his old man in confusion. "But...you and Mom?"

Milt Lawrence snorted. "There were times your mother, bless her soul, didn't like me very much. More than once she almost strung me up by my toes and I'm not too proud to admit I deserved it. And, as much as it pains me to say, there were days when she drove me up a wall. We had our fights, although we made sure you kids didn't know. But the next day, we'd choose to love each other all over again and *do the work*. Every single day, I made it my job to show her not just that I loved her and needed her and trusted her, but that I was the man she could love, trust and need, come hell or high water." He snorted again. "I never cheated. I made time for her. I put her needs first and I was there for you kids. And let me tell you, flowers never hurt a thing."

Was Flash hearing this right? His parents' marriage had always seemed so perfect—a love story for the ages. At no point had it looked like *work*.

"A year ago…" Dad rubbed his chin thoughtfully. "A year ago, I don't think you would've been capable of it. I sure as hell wouldn't have told you to go get your girl. Wouldn't have been fair to the girl," he added with a chuckle.

"Thanks, Dad," Flash slurred. His head was spinning and he had no idea if it was the drugs or the concussion or the jaw or…

The truth.

He and Brooke hadn't chosen each other after their one-night stand. But doing the work…that sounded a lot like proving Brooke could trust him.

Would she choose to prove he could trust her? Or would she bail?

Dad kept going. "But you got your act together. You did the work on yourself and, Lord knows, I've never been prouder of you. So now? Now I know you can do the right thing. I know you've got it in you, Flash."

A warm feeling spread through Flash's chest. He had, hadn't he? That year of sobriety and anger management and, yes, celibacy had been the longest, hardest year of his life. Every single day he'd had to get up and choose to stay on the straight and narrow, even when it sucked.

There wasn't just one thing he could do or say that would prove to Brooke he was worthy of her. He had to show her, day in and day out. It'd take a lifetime to prove it, but it'd be a lifetime with her.

Because he loved her.

Damn it, he hated when his dad was right. Made the man insufferable.

"So give her a few days to cool off. You don't have a choice—you're being held for observation for that concussion." He sighed heavily. "Flash, you're not gonna want to hear this, but…"

For a panicked second, Flash thought Brooke had called

in lawyers. But then Dad wouldn't be giving him that pep talk if Brooke was done with him, right?

"Your jaw can't take another break," Dad said, his voice…sad, almost. "This one is going to take a few more surgeries before it's all said and done." He cleared his throat, a sound like a tractor engine turning over. "Might not be best for you to compete anymore."

That sounded like… *the end*. The end of a career.

Like his body couldn't take the jarring from bucking broncos and bulls, like steer wrestling was completely off the table. Maybe he could still do calf roping?

Oh, hell—was he done? *Done* done?

No.

No! This was his year! Cowboy of the Year was his for the taking! He'd finally earned his place at the table and he was the best in the world! Hell, he'd been chasing the rodeo for over half his life. If he wasn't chasing the buckle, what was he doing?

But the moment the question crossed his fuzzy mind, the answer followed it. He'd known it since he'd seen Brooke up there, trying to protect their son from Tex.

Nothing mattered more than she did.

Brooke and Bean were everything to him. The rodeo was…just a job.

He'd be a husband and a father. He'd be there to read bedtime stories to his son and travel with Brooke when she toured. Maybe there'd be more children, babies he'd be able to hold the moment they came into the world. Brooke would test her songs out for him, and he'd be by her side when she did things like walk the red carpet at the Grammys or the Country Music Awards.

A family of love and laughter, for the rest of his life. That was his future. Not another buckle or another brawl.

Or another broken jaw.

He'd show up and do the work because Brooke was worth it.

One problem with that plan.

He needed to get to Brooke right *now*.

Dad grabbed his hand away from the IV before Flash could pull it out. "Knock that off, son. You're no good to anyone all busted up."

"How long?" He had hazy memories of time passing, but clearly he'd been sedated so the doctors could work on his jaw. Stupid head injuries.

"Day and a half. Oliver sent the company jet to get me." His phone chimed. "Hey, listen to this—your sister forwarded this to me. Know what the press is saying? Here. 'Flash Lawrence Defends Fiancée Brooke Bonner in All-Stars Brawl.' You're a hero, son."

Yeah, a hero to everyone. Did that include Brooke?

"Need her," he mumbled to his father.

"I know you do. Lawrence men fall hard and fast and forever. It was the same with your mother, God rest her soul."

A hush settled in the hospital room, except for all the beeping. Hey, he'd noticed the beeping! Maybe his head was starting to clear.

Then it came to him. Flowers were great, but he needed to show Brooke that he knew her and cared for her.

"Tea," Flash managed to say. Yeah, his head was definitely clearing because his jaw was starting to throb. But the pain was good. It centered him and gave him something to fight against.

"What was that?" Dad leaned in closer.

"Send her tea. And honey. Good honey. From me."

Dad leaned into Flash's line of sight, a crafty grin on his face. "That," he said, "I can do."

# Nineteen

"Just so we're all operating on the same page, let's look at the footage," Kari Stockard, the PR exec, said as the footage of the All-Stars Rodeo from two weeks ago began to run. "As you can see, we arranged for Brooke and the baby to be behind the chutes for a touching moment with Flash Lawrence."

Two weeks since Brooke had last seen Flash. It felt like a lifetime. She kept telling herself she was still making up her mind about him, but that was a lie.

She was doing the exact same thing she'd done after she'd discovered she was pregnant. She was hiding.

And she hated it.

Brooke stared in horrified fascination as her life played out on the screen in a conference room at her record label's executive offices, surrounded by men in suits and her new manager, Janet Worthington. Bean trilled in delight when the camera zoomed in on Brooke's face. Because Bean went everywhere with her now. She didn't have to hide him anymore. And also, because Mom was no longer his primary babysitter.

She didn't want to watch the exact moment she'd lost

control of her life again. She was still having nightmares about living it.

But she was seeing it now while Kari talked over the video. Brooke watched as Flash kissed her and then cuddled Bean, and it took Brooke's breath away because it'd all been for show, right?

But that's not what she saw. What she saw was *real*. Real adoration in Flash's eyes when he'd looked at her, real tenderness as he'd held his son.

She saw real love in her eyes when she'd kissed him for good luck.

It was as plain as day that Flash Lawrence loved her.

It was all over his face, in every single movement he made, in every touch between them. He was head over heels in love with her. And she…

The camera caught her touching her lips as Flash walked away from her, a happy smile lighting up her face. She didn't even remember doing that, but apparently she had.

Oh, God—it hadn't been for show.

It'd been real. All of it.

The camera cut back to Brooke and Bean, still on top of the chute. This time, that terrible Tex McGraw started advancing on her.

Brooke gasped in shock to see the horror that'd been on her face. She watched helplessly as Alex lunged but missed and suddenly Tex had hold of Brooke, his hand digging into her arm and then…

Then Flash had been there, moving so fast he was little more than a blur. He'd gotten Tex off her and she had to swallow back tears as she watched herself stumble, struggling to hold on to her son. Then Alex rushed her down from the chutes, and that was when the video clicked off and a graph came up on the screen.

Kari was talking again but Brooke couldn't listen. She had to keep her gaze on the top of Bean's head while she struggled for control. The incident was every bit as bad as she remembered and yet…not as bad, either.

Because Flash loved her. It was *so* obvious.

Why hadn't she seen it at the time?

What would Tex McGraw have done if Flash hadn't been there?

Alex had been right. Brooke hadn't been able to separate her terror at the attack from her feelings for Flash. All those emotions had sloshed around, mixing together.

She looked down at Flash's ring glinting brightly on her finger.

It'd been real to Flash. She remembered him saying he wouldn't ask her to marry him again, but the offer was on the table. She'd thought he'd been asking her out of duty or a concern about custody.

But had he really been asking her to marry him?

"As you can see from this chart, the number of social media hits from the last two weeks has been tremendous and the reception has been overwhelmingly positive," Kari explained to the bored-looking suits. "People are not only excited for Brooke's new album, but they can't get enough of Brooke and Flash!"

He had. He'd been asking Brooke to marry him because he wanted her. Not just her body or a quickie against the door but her, Brooke Bonner. Hadn't he said as much?

And what had she done?

The one thing Kyle Morgan had told her not to do because it'd be the regret of her life. She was perilously close to walking away.

What was she *doing*?

"Brooke?"

Brooke startled. Everyone in the room was staring at her, expecting an answer, maybe? "Yes?"

Kari's smile tightened. "When can we schedule an in-

terview and photo shoot with you, Flash and that beautiful
baby boy?" Clearly, she'd already asked once.

How could Brooke schedule interviews and photo
shoots? She hadn't spoken to Flash since that awful night!
She'd ignored his gifts, his notes.

Brooke looked helplessly at Janet Worthington, her new
manager. Janet had heard the whole messy story, mostly so
she could successfully run interference in situations like
this.

"Who did you have in mind?" Janet asked, keeping her
tone cool.

"*People* is our first choice, but we've had offers…" Kari
launched into the pros and cons of the print publications.

Brooke tuned it all out because it was nothing but noise.

Because Flash had sent the most thoughtful, charming,
*perfect* gifts, starting with a box of jasmine green tea and
local clover honey with a note that read, "I will never stop
fighting for you and Bean."

The next day, a sampler of black teas and a different
honey—wildflower—had been delivered. "I have faith in
you," the note had said.

Every day since, different flavors of tea and honey and
occasionally delicate teacups or thermal mugs and, once,
even a plastic toy tea set for Bean had shown up, each with
a short note written in Flash's scrawl. He missed her. He
hoped Bean was letting her sleep and having fun getting
out and about. He asked about how the plans for her album
were going. Was she doing okay with Kyle and her mother?
Did she need anything from him? He'd be there for her.

The last note—the one from yesterday—had said, "I
choose you. I want to do the work. You're worth it."

Flash loved her.

He hadn't said the words—it was true—but his love
was in every cup of tea she drank, in every bit of honey
sweetness.

He wasn't backing her into a corner and he wasn't forcing her to make a choice. Instead, he'd spent the last two weeks showing her how much he cared, and she hadn't responded. Not even to check on him.

Bean fussed. Brooke took the chance to escape. "Is there anything else you need me for?"

Janet got the hint immediately. "We'll get back to you on dates."

Brooke slipped out while Janet settled the details. For two danged weeks, Brooke had been hemming and hawing, asking herself how she could trust him when, really, she'd been trying to figure out how she could trust herself.

She couldn't do it. She couldn't walk away.

All she needed to do was make a leap of faith.

She texted Flash, Where are you?

My hotel room, was the immediate reply. In Nashville.

Relief coursed through her. Still here?

Never left, babe. I might walk away from you and you might walk away from me when we need to calm down, but I will always come back for you. Been hoping you'll come back to me, too.

Dear God, he really did love her. I need to talk to you.

Where?

She was more than half tempted to ask for his room number, but she had a drowsy infant in the back seat. Meet me at my house in half an hour.

Just as she pulled out of the parking lot, Flash texted back, Thank God.

Flash hadn't waited half an hour. He was on Brooke's doorstep less than fifteen minutes later, waiting. Dad hadn't been happy about Flash driving himself, but a man had to do what a man had to do.

Finally.

It'd taken two weeks of every kind of tea and tea accessory known to mankind, but she'd reached out to him.

*Please let this be good*, he prayed.

Of course, she needed to talk to him, which was kind of a problem because right now, Flash wasn't doing a whole lot of talking. And kissing—good, deep kissing, the kind that led to clothing-optional activities—was also off the table. Nibbling was strictly forbidden.

Stupid busted jaw.

It felt like an eternity before Brooke drove up, and Flash was thrilled to see she was alone except for the baby.

He hurried to open Brooke's door but the next thing he knew, she was in his arms and he was struggling to hold back the tears because for two long, awful weeks he'd been afraid he'd lost her, and Brooke Bonner wasn't the kind of woman a man just got over.

"Missed you," he mumbled into her hair as best he could.

"Missed you, too. Let me put the baby down and then we'll talk?"

Reluctantly he let her go. He held the door for her as she pulled a napping James Frasier out of the back seat and then got the front door for her as she carried the baby inside.

They got Bean into the crib without waking him. Flash wrapped his arm around Brooke's shoulders and held her as they stared at their son.

Yep. This was right. This was where he belonged.

Now he just had to convince Brooke of that.

Silently she led him back down to the library where he'd nearly ruined everything. "God, I'm so sorry," she said, basically launching herself at him. "Your face!"

Flash grunted at the impact but, hell, he could play with the pain. The bruises had mostly faded to sickly greens and yellows, except where he'd had more work done on his jaw. But he knew he still looked terrible.

He picked her up and carried her to the couch—with its now-lumpy cushions. Then he pulled out his tablet and began typing.

"Are you okay?"

She read the message and then stared at him. "What's wrong with your mouth?"

"Broken jaw. Wired shut. Won't be able to do much talking or anything for a few more weeks. I'm officially retired from the rodeo. Doctors say I'm done—can't risk any more damage."

She went pale. "Oh, my God! Flash! I'm so sorry!"

"It's okay, babe," he typed. "Everything's okay as long as I'm with you."

Her eyes got all watery again. "It was all real, wasn't it? The proposals and this huge ring and all that tea and honey and…it's all real, isn't it?"

He nodded and touched his forehead to hers. "Love you," he tried to say.

"Don't talk, babe. You…" She sniffed and he wiped the tears off her cheeks. "You said so much in all your notes. I was just too confused to see it."

He kissed her then, *gently*, before he tucked her against his chest so he could type. "I love you. I think I always have, ever since that first night. But I didn't fight for you then. I let you go and I've regretted it ever since. I don't want to let you go again. I'm going to fight for you and for our family every day of my life."

"Oh, Flash," she whispered through her tears. "I'm so, so sorry because I was doing the same thing I did last time. I shut you out because I was scared. I was doing the exact same thing my mom and Kyle did, and I was wrong. I know you were protecting me, but everything got so screwed up in my mind that…"

"You had to walk away for a little bit," he typed quickly, his heart pounding. "Just to calm down. I understand. I had faith you'd fight for me, too." He swallowed, a raspy sound, and then added, "You are, right?"

Because it'd about kill him if she said no. He could let the rodeo go and the world would keep right on spinning.

But life without Brooke...no, he wasn't about to let her go.

Lawrence men fell hard and fast and forever.

That's what this was. *Forever.*

"I understand now," she told him. "I didn't before. But I talked with my...with Kyle, and he told me he didn't fight for me, didn't try to get right with my mom. He only wanted me when I was easy and talented. But that's not life, is it? It's hard work. That's what I want—someone who's willing to fight for me, who'll stick it out when it gets hard and help make things better. And that's you."

"That's you, too," he typed back, his hands shaking.

She shook her head, tears dripping down her face. "Not enough. I need to fight harder. Not just for you, but for myself. For us."

"We'll work on it," he typed back. He couldn't wait until he could talk to her again. It was damn near impossible to whisper sweet nothings into a girl's ear on a tablet. "Together. We're a team. Today, tomorrow, every day." When she gasped, he gritted his teeth and made the one concession he was willing to make. "We don't have to get married, but the offer stands. It'll always stand. I'm not giving up on you or on us. I want this to work. Every day, I'll prove it to you. That's a promise."

She took the tablet from his hands and tossed it aside. "But...what if I want to get married? Is that something you still want?"

Flash groaned. "Yes," he said out loud, although it sounded like a tire deflating. "God, yes."

"How will it work?" she asked, stroking her fingertips over his busted jaw.

He picked up the tablet again. "I'm done with chasing the rodeo. It's time I did the stay-at-home-dad thing. Go with you on tour. Be there for you. For our family."

"Oh, Flash," she whispered, carefully throwing her arms around his neck. "That's what I want. You and me and our family. With less broken bones, though."

"Working on it," he got out, holding her tight.

Then he set her aside and got to one knee next to the couch, taking her hands in his. She still had on his ring, thank God. She'd worn it this whole time.

"Brooke, would you marry me?" Although it didn't come out exactly right.

"For real?" she asked, her eyes shimmering with tears.

"For real," he replied, kissing her hands.

"Yes, Flash. Because I am always coming back for you, too," she sobbed.

Flash surged to his feet and pulled her into a hug. This was home. Brooke was home. "Thank God," he mumbled.

Thank God, he'd never have to get over Brooke Bonner.

\* \* \* \* \*

# WYOMING COWBOY BODYGUARD

## NICOLE HELM

For the female songwriters in country music whose songs make up the bulk of my book soundtracks, thank you for the inspiration.

## Chapter One

Tom was dead. She'd been ushered away from his lifeless body and open, empty brown eyes thirty minutes ago and still, that was all she saw. Tom sprawled on the floor, limbs at an unnatural angle, eyes open and unseeing.

Blood.

She was in the back of a police cruiser, moving through Austin at a steady clip. Daisy Delaney. America's favorite country bad girl. Until she'd filed for divorce from country's golden child, Jordan Jones. Now everyone hated her, and someone wanted her dead.

But they'd killed Tom first.

She wanted to close her eyes, but she was afraid the vision of Tom would only intensify if she did. So she focused on the world out the window. Pearly dawn. Green suburban lawns.

She was holding it together. Even though Tom's lifeless eyes haunted her. And all that blood. The smell of it. She was queasy and desperately wanted to cry, but she was holding on. *Gotta save face, Daisy girl. No matter what. Never let them see they got to you.*

It didn't matter the name her mother had given her was Lucy Cooper. Daddy had always used her stage name—the name *he'd* given her. Daisy Delaney, after his dearly departed grandmother, who'd given him his first guitar.

She'd relished that once upon a time, no matter how much her mother and brother had disapproved. Today, for the first time in her life, she wondered where she might be if she hadn't followed in her famous father's footsteps.

She couldn't change the past so she held it together. Didn't let anyone see she was devastated, shaken or scared.

Until the car pulled up in front of her brother's house. He was standing outside. She'd expected to see him in his Texas Rangers uniform of pressed khakis, a button-up shirt and that shiny star she knew he took such pride in.

Instead, he was in sweats, a baby cradled in his arms.

"You shouldn't have brought me here," she whispered to the police officer as he shifted into Park.

"Ranger Cooper asked me to, ma'am."

She let out a breath. Asked. While her brother was a Texas Ranger and this man was Austin PD, Daisy was under no illusions her brother hadn't interfered enough to make sure it was an order, not a request.

When the officer opened the door for her, she managed a smile and a thank-you. The officer shook hands with Vaughn, then gave her a sympathetic look. "We'll have more questions for you, Ms. Delaney, but the ones you answered at the scene will do for now."

She smiled thinly. "Thank you. And if there's any break in the case—"

"We'll let you and your brother know."

The officer nodded and left. Daisy turned to Vaughn.

"You shouldn't have brought me here," she said, peeking into the bundle of blankets. She brushed her fingers over her niece's cheek. "It isn't safe having me around you guys."

"Safety's my middle name," Vaughn said, and there wasn't an ounce of concern or fear in his voice, but she could feel it nonetheless. Her straitlaced brother had never understood her need to follow their father's spotlight, but he'd always been her protector. "You didn't tell me you'd come back to Austin."

She'd thought she could keep it from him. Keep him and Nat from worrying when they had this gorgeous little family they were building.

Daisy had been stupid and foolish to think she'd be able to keep anything from Vaughn. She couldn't afford to be stupid and foolish anymore. Though she'd lived in fear for almost a year now, she'd believed it would remain a nonviolent threat. Her stalker had never hurt her or anyone she'd been connected to.

Now he'd killed Tom. The man Vaughn had hired to protect her. It wasn't her own failure. Rationally, she knew that, but kind, funny Tom, who'd done everything in his power to protect her, was dead.

"Come inside, Lucy." Vaughn slid his free arm around her shoulders and the first tear fell over onto her cheek. She couldn't let more fall, and yet her brother's steadiness, and the name only he and Mom called her, was one of the few things that could undo her.

Well, that and murder, she supposed. "Tom…"

"We'll handle the arrangements," Vaughn said, squeezing her shoulders as baby Nora gurgled happily in her daddy's arms. "He was a good man."

"He shouldn't have died protecting me."

"But he did. He signed up for that job. You'll have time to mourn that. We all will, but right now we need to focus on getting you somewhere safe."

She wanted to say something snotty. Vaughn could be so cold, and though she knew it was his law-enforcement training, it grated. Except he held his baby like the precious gift she was, and Daisy had watched years ago as his voice had broken when he'd made his vows to his wife.

Vaughn wasn't cold or heartless. He just had control down to an art form. And his concern was her. Daisy felt like such a burden to him, and yet there was no way to convince him this wasn't his problem.

"Nat's got coffee on and Jaime is on his way over," Vaughn said, locking the door behind her then leading her up the stairs of his split-level ranch.

"What's Jaime got to do with this?" Daisy asked warily. "You can't get the FBI involved. I—"

"I'm not getting the FBI involved. I'm using my FBI connections to find a safe place for you while we let the professionals investigate."

"And by professionals you mean you."

"I mean anyone and everyone I can get on this case. With our connection, I'm not legally allowed to be part of the official investigation."

Which meant he'd launch his own unofficial one. No matter how by-the-book Vaughn was, he'd always break rules for his loved ones.

Nat came out of the kitchen as they crested the stairs. She pulled Daisy into a hard hug. "How are you?" she asked, brown eyes full of compassion.

Daisy had no questions about how Vaughn had

fallen for Natalie, but she did have some questions about the reverse.

"Unscathed."

Natalie pursed her lips. "Physically. Which wasn't all I meant." She eyed her husband. "Coopers," she muttered with some disgust, though Daisy knew—for as little time as she managed to spend with her family here due to her crazy touring schedule—Nat spoke with love.

The doorbell rang, Nora fussed and Nat and Vaughn exchanged the baby and words with the choreographed practice of marriage. It caused a multitude of pangs in Daisy.

Her divorce had started the press's character assassination—thanks to Jordan's team, who were desperate to keep his star on the rise.

Then the stalking had started, and everything had become a numb kind of blank.

But she could still remember marrying Jordan with the hope she'd have something like Nat and Vaughn had. That had been a joke.

"Sit down. You want to hold Nora for me? I've got to go check on Miranda." Nat was maneuvering her onto the couch, placing tiny Nora into her arms and hurrying off to check on their other daughter as Vaughn and his brother-in-law ascended the stairs.

"Ah, the cavalry," Daisy said with a wry twist of her lips.

"Good to see you again, Daisy," Jaime Alessandro greeted. An FBI agent, married to Natalie's sister, Daisy had met him on a few occasions. He was more personable than Vaughn, but the whole FBI thing made Daisy uneasy.

"Let's get straight to it, then," Vaughn said, taking a

seat next to Daisy on the couch. Jaime settled himself on an armchair across from them.

"I'm sure you know how concerned Vaughn's been even before the murder."

Daisy eyed her brother. "No. You don't say."

Jaime smiled. Vaughn didn't.

"We've been looking into some options, along with the investigation. As long as the stalker continues to evade police, the prime goal is keeping you safe. To that end, I have an idea."

"That sounds ominous coming from an FBI agent."

"How do you feel about Wyoming?"

"Cold," Daisy replied dryly.

"I have a friend I was in Quantico with. He has a security business. I talked to him about your situation and he came up with a plan. It involves isolating you."

"I was isolated before. The cabin—"

"Is isolated, but not completely off the grid," Vaughn said of their old family cabin that had been vandalized during her last hiding stint. "It was traceable, and you've been easy to follow. We're going to take extra precautions to make sure you aren't followed to Wyoming."

Daisy wanted to close her eyes, but she shifted Nora in her arms and looked down at the baby instead. "So you want me to secretly jet off to Wyoming and then what?"

"And then you're safe while we find this guy. This is murder now. Things are escalating, which means everyone else's investigation is going to escalate."

"We can have you there by tomorrow afternoon," Jaime said. "They'll be ready for you."

Part of her wanted to argue, but Tom's lifeless body flashed into her mind. She didn't want to die. Not like that. And more, so much more, she didn't want Vaughn or his precious family in the crosshairs.

"Just tell me what I need to do."

ZACH SIMMONS SURVEYED the town. It looked like every picture of a ghost town he'd ever seen. Empty, window-less buildings. Dusty dirt road that would have once been a bustling Main Street. You could feel the history, and the utter emptiness.

It was perfect.

He grinned over at his soon-to-be brother-in-law and business partner. "Still worried about the investment?"

Cam Delaney eyed him. "Hell yes, I'm still worried." He scanned the dilapidated buildings and the way the mountains jutted out in the distance, like sentries, in Zach's mind. This would be a place of protection. Of safety.

"This job's a big one for your first."

Zach nodded. He was under no illusions this wasn't a giant challenge. Tricky and messy and complicated. He couldn't explain to Cam, or anyone really, how thrilling it was to be out of the confines of the FBI's rules and regulations. He wouldn't take his time back as an agent for anything, but it had been stifling in the end.

So stifling he'd ended up getting himself kicked out.

This was better. Even if the first job was with some spoiled country singer star who'd gotten herself in a mess of trouble. Probably her own doing. But she was in trouble, and Zach and Cam's security company was getting paid, seriously paid, to keep her safe.

"Laurel come up with any connection to you guys?" Zach asked, hoping Daisy Delaney's last name was a coincidence. Not that he'd tell anyone, but all the Carson and Delaney coupling worried him a little.

He was technically a Carson, though his mother had run away from her family at eighteen and only started reconnecting this year. He told himself he didn't believe in curses or the Carson-Delaney feud the town of Bent, Wyoming, was so invested in.

So invested, Main Street was practically split down the middle—Carson businesses on one side, Delaney businesses on the other. Then there was the curse talk, which said if a Carson and Delaney were ever friendly, or God forbid, romantic, only bad things would befall Bent.

But over the course of the past year Carsons and Delaneys had been falling for each other left and right, and while there'd been a certain uptick in trouble in Bent, everything and everyone was fine.

Which his cousins and their significant others had turned into believing it was all meant to be, and went on and on about love solving things.

Zach didn't buy an inch of either belief—but still, the idea of a Delaney under his protection gave him a bit of a worried itch.

"She's still researching. It's giving her something to do now that she's on maternity leave. Baby should come any day, though, so I'm not sure she'll come up with any answers one way or another. You can always ask the woman."

Zach shrugged. "Doesn't matter either way."

Cam chuckled. "Sure. You're not worried about what might happen if she's some long-lost cousin of mine?"

"No, I'm not. I'm worried about keeping Daisy Delaney safe from her stalker, assuming there really is one." Because the Daisy Delaney case would set the tone for what he wanted to offer here. On the surface it would look like a ghost town. But below the surface it could be a place for people to find safety, security and hope while the slow wheels of justice handled things legally.

If he believed in life callings, and these days he was starting to, his was this. He'd been a part of the slow wheels of justice. He'd failed at protecting because of it. Now he'd do all he could to keep those entrusted to him safe.

"I should head off to the airport. You'll do the double check?"

Cam nodded. "Is turndown service offered as part of the package?"

"Up to you, boss," Zach said with a grin, slapping Cam on the back.

Cam eyed him, but Zach ignored the perceptive look and headed for his car. He didn't need Cam giving him another lecture about taking things slow, having reasonable expectations for a fledgling business.

Zach had endured a bad year. Really bad. His brother had been admitted to a psychiatric ward, and his long-lost sister had forgiven the man who'd murdered their father and kidnapped her. He'd been kicked out of the FBI—which meant no hope of ever getting back into legitimate law enforcement. And then he'd tried to help one of his cousins outwit a stalker-murderer and been hurt in the process.

In some ways all that hardship had brought him everything he'd ever wanted—his long-lost sister back in his life, a job that didn't seem to choke the very life out of him and some closure over the murder of his father.

Then there was this project. Ghost Town. He couldn't tamp down his enthusiasm, his excitement. He had to grab on to the rightness he finally felt and hold on to it with everything he had.

He didn't want to go back. He wanted to move forward.

Daisy Delaney was going to be the way to do that. He drove down deserted Wyoming roads to the highway, then to the regional airport in Dubois where his first client would be landing any minute.

Zach parked and entered the small airport, all the excitement of a new job still buzzing inside him.

He'd facilitated crisscrossing flights with his former FBI buddy, and only Zach knew the disguise she'd be wearing. Though he wondered how much a wig and sunglasses would do for a famous singer.

Zach liked country music as much as the next guy, so it was impossible not to know Daisy Delaney's music. She'd somehow eclipsed even her father's outlaw country reputation with wild songs about drinking, cheating and revenge. Country fans either loved her or loved to complain about her.

Of course, since her divorce from all-American sweetheart Jordan Jones, the complainers had gotten more vocal. Zach hadn't followed it all, but he'd read up on it once this assignment had come along. She'd been eviscerated in the press, even when the stalking started. Many thought it was a publicity ploy to get people to feel sorry for her.

It had *not* worked.

Zach couldn't deny it was a possibility, even if a man was dead—the security guard. A shame. But that didn't mean it wasn't a ploy. You never knew with the rich and famous.

Still, Zach was determined to make his own conclusions about Daisy Delaney and what might be going on with her stalker, or fictional stalker as the case may be.

The small crowd walked through the security gates. He'd been told to look for black hair and clothes, a red bag and purple cowboy boots. He spotted her immediately.

In person, she was surprisingly petite. She didn't exactly look like a woman who'd burn your house down if you looked at another woman the wrong way, but looks could be deceiving.

He'd done enough undercover work to know that well.

He adjusted his hat, gave the signal he'd told her people to expect and she nodded and walked over to him.

"You must be Mr. Hughes." She used the fake name Jaime had chosen and held out a hand. The sunglasses she wore hid her eyes, and the mass of black hair hid most of her face. Whatever her emotions were, they were well hidden. Which was good. It wouldn't do to have nerves radiating off her.

He took her outstretched hand and shook it. "And you must be Ms. Bravo." Fake names, but soon enough they wouldn't need to bother with that. "Any more bags?" he asked, nodding to the lone duffel bag she carried.

She shook her head.

"Follow me."

She eyed everyone in the airport as they walked outside, but her shoulders and stride were relaxed as she kept up with him. She didn't fidget or dart. If she was fearing her life, she knew how to hide it.

He opened the passenger-side door to his car. She slid inside. Still no sign of concern over getting into a car with a stranger. Zach frowned as he skirted the car to the driver's side.

But he wiped the frown into a placid expression as he slid into his seat. "We have about a thirty-minute drive ahead of us." He pushed the car into Drive and pulled out of the airport parking lot. "You could take your wig off," he offered. "Get comfortable."

"I'd prefer to wait."

He nodded as he drove. Tough case. A hint of nerves here and there, but overall a very cool customer. Cautious, though, so she clearly took the threat of danger seriously.

He drove in silence through the middle of nowhere Wyoming. He flicked a few glances her way, though it was hard to discern anything. He didn't get the impression she was impressed, but he hadn't expected her to be. He imagined she preferred, if not the glitz and glam of the city, the slow ease of wealthy Southern life she was probably used to.

Wyoming wouldn't offer that, but it would offer her security. He drove down the main street that was now his domain, this ghost town he and Cam had bought outright.

At some point they'd all be safe houses. Or maybe even a functioning town behind the facade of desertion and decay.

For right now, though, it was just the main house. He pulled up in front of the giant showpiece.

It had been built over a century ago by some railroad executive. From the outside the windows were all knocked out, the wood was faded and peeling paint hung off. Everything sagged, and it had the faint air of haunted house.

It made him grin every time. "Well, here we are."

For the first time he could read her expression. Pure, unadulterated horror. He'd be lying if he said he didn't get a little kick out of that. "I promise it's not as bad as it looks."

She wrenched her gaze away from the large house, then stared at him through the dark sunglasses. "Can I see your ID or something?" she demanded.

He shifted and pulled his wallet out of his pocket and handed it to her. "Have at it." He pushed open the door and got out of the car. "When you're ready, I'll show you where you'll be staying."

## Chapter Two

What Daisy really wanted to do was call her brother and ask him if he'd lost his mind. Call Jaime and ask if she was sure this guy was sane. Call anyone to take her home.

But inside the wallet the man had so casually handed her was a driver's license with the name Jaime had given her. The picture matched the man currently standing in front of the horror-movie house outside the car. There were also all sorts of security licenses and weapon certifications.

Vaughn had said this place was isolated, even more isolated than their old family cabin in the Guadalupe Mountains. But she hadn't been able to picture how that was possible.

*Oh*, was it possible. Possible and horrifying.

She flipped the wallet closed and then looked at the giant, falling-apart building. If she didn't die because a stalker was after her, she'd die because this building was going to fall in on her.

It had to be infested with rats. And probably all other manner of vermin.

She couldn't get her body to move from the safety of this car, and still, the man whom she'd been assured would keep her safe stood outside, grinning at the dilapidated building in front of him.

He wasn't sane. He couldn't be. She was stuck in the middle of nowhere Wyoming with an insane person.

But Vaughn would never let that happen. So she forced herself to get out of the car and slung the duffel bag over her shoulder. She tried not to mourn that she hadn't been able to bring her guitar. This wasn't a musical writing escape. It was literally running for her life.

She stepped next to Zach. She still didn't trust him, but she trusted her brother. She looked up at the building like Zach Simmons did, though not with nearly the amount of reverence he had in his expression.

"I know it looks intimidating from the outside, but that's kind of the point."

"The point?" Daisy asked, studying a board that hung haphazardly from a bent nail.

"From the outside, no one would guess anyone's been here for decades."

"Try centuries," she muttered.

He motioned her forward and she followed him up a cracked and sunken rock pathway to the front door.

"Watch the hole," he announced cheerfully, pointing at the gaping hole in the floorboards of the porch. He shoved a key into the front door and pushed open the creaky, uneven entry. "Even if someone started poking around, all they'd see is decay."

*Yes, that is all I see.* She looked around. She had to admit that although everything appeared to be in a state of decay, there were some important things missing. She didn't see any dust or spiderwebs. Debris, sure. Peeling wallpaper and warped floorboards, check, but it didn't smell like she'd expected it to. There was the faint hint of paint on the air.

He led her over the uneven flooring, then pushed a key into another lock. When this door opened she actually gasped.

The room on the other side was beautiful. Clean and furnished, and though there were no windows, somehow the light he switched on bounced off the colors of the walls and filled the room enough that it didn't feel dank and interior.

"This is the common area," Zach said. And maybe he wasn't totally insane. "Then over there past the sitting area is the kitchen. You're free to use it and anything inside as much as you like. Once we ascertain that you weren't followed on any leg of your trip, you'll be able to venture out more freely, but for now you'll have to stay put."

Daisy could only nod dumbly. Was this real? Maybe *she'd* gone insane. A break with reality following a stressful tragedy.

He locked the door behind them, which was enough to jolt Daisy back to the reality of being in a strange ghost town with a man she didn't know.

But he simply moved forward to a set of two doors. "Your bedroom and bathroom are through here." He unlocked the one on the right.

"What's that one?" she asked, pointing to the door on the left as he pushed the unlocked door open.

"That's where I'll stay."

"You'll… Right." He'd be right next door. This stranger. Hired to protect her, and yet she didn't know him. Even Vaughn didn't know him, and Jaime hadn't known him since they'd trained together in the FBI. Why were they all so trusting?

He handed her the key he'd just used to unlock the door. "This is yours. I don't have a copy. The outside doors are always locked up in multiple places, so how and when you want to lock your room is up to you."

She knew he was trying to set her at ease, but she could only think of a million ways he could get into the room even without a key. Or anyone could.

People could always get to you if they wanted to badly enough.

He studied her for a moment, then gestured her inside. "You can settle in. Make yourself at home however you need to. Rest, if you'd like."

"Is it that obvious?"

"You've been through an ordeal. Take your time to get acquainted with the place. I'm going to do a routine double check to make sure you weren't followed from Austin. If you need me…" He moved over to the wall, motioned her over.

Hesitantly, she stepped closer, still clutching her bag on her shoulder. He tapped a spot on the wallpaper. "See how this flower has a green bloom and a green stem instead of a blue flower like the rest?"

She nodded wearily.

He pushed on the green flower and a little panel popped out of the wall. Inside was a speaker with a button below it. "Simple speaker to speaker. You need something, you can just buzz me through here. I can either answer, or come over, depending."

He closed the panel and it snapped shut, seamless with the wallpaper once again. How on earth had her life become some kind of…spy movie? "You've thought of everything, haven't you?"

He smiled briefly—something like pride and affection lighting up the blank, bland expression. Just a little flash of personality, and for one surprising moment all she could really think was *gee, he's hot*.

"That's what they pay me for." Then the blankness was back and whatever had sparkled in his blue eyes was gone. Everything about him screamed *cop* again, or, she supposed in his case, *FBI*. It was all the same to her. Law and order didn't suit her the way it had her brother, but she'd be grateful for it in the midst of her current situation.

She studied the room around her. Gleaming hardwood with pretty blue rugs here and there. Floral wallpaper and shabby-chic fixtures. The furniture looked antique—old and a little scarred but well polished. The quilt over the bed looked like it belonged in a pretty farmhouse with billowing lace curtains.

It was calming and comforting, and in a better state of mind she might even be able to ignore all the facades and locks and intercoms and the lack of windows. But she wasn't in the state of mind to forget that Tom, who'd been paid to protect her, was dead.

"Settle in, Ms. Delaney. You're safe here. I promise you that."

She carefully placed her duffel bag on the shiny hardwood floor. Exhaustion made her body feel as heavy as lead, and she went ahead and lowered herself onto the bed with its pretty quilt. "I'm not safe anywhere, Mr. Simmons."

He opened his mouth to argue, but she wasn't in the

mood, so she waved him toward the door. "But I feel safe enough to take a nice long nap, if you'll excuse me."

He raised an eyebrow, presumably at her regal tone and the way she waved him off, but she was too tired to care.

He moved to the door, twisted the lock on the interior knob, then closed the door behind him as he exited.

Daisy took off the wig and then let herself fall into sleep.

ZACH SPENT THE afternoon going over the information he'd been given about Daisy's stalking, and the information he'd gathered himself in anticipation of her arrival.

The murder of her bodyguard while she'd been on stage was certainly the tipping point. The formal investigation had been lax up to that point. Except for the private one her brother had launched.

Zach appreciated the detail of Ranger Cooper's intel, and since he knew too well the stress and helplessness of trying to keep a sibling safe, Zach was grateful for his willingness to share.

Still, there were things that had been missed—well, maybe not missed. Overlooked. Probably still not fair. One of the things that had allowed Zach to do so well in the FBI was his ability to work out patterns, to find threads and connect them in ways other people couldn't.

The stellar way he'd handled himself as an agent prior to his brother's involvement in a case and Zach going rogue was what had kept him from having a splashier, more painful termination from the FBI.

He shrugged away the tension in his shoulders. He hated that it still bothered him, because even if he could rewind time, he'd do most things the same.

Daisy's doorknob turned, and she took one tentative step out. She'd finally ditched the heavy black wig, and her straight blond hair was pulled back into a ponytail. She'd done something to her face—it'd take him a little more time to get to know her face well enough to know exactly what. If he had to guess, though, he'd say she'd freshened her makeup.

She'd changed out of the sleek black outfit into a long baggy shirt the color of a midsummer sky and black leggings. On her feet she wore thick bright purple socks.

She'd been in there for five hours, and from the looks of it, she'd spent most of the time sleeping—unless her makeup magically fixed the pallor of her skin and the dark circles under her eyes.

"Got any food in this joint?"

He stood and walked over to the side of the common area that acted as a kitchen. "Fully stocked kitchen, which of course you're welcome to. Tell me what you want to make and I'll show you where everything is and how to work everything."

"Coffee. Scratch that. Coffee hasn't been settling lately." She sighed, some of that weary exhaustion in her voice even if it didn't show in her face.

"My suggestion? Hot chocolate and a doughnut."

A smile twitched at the corner of her mouth. "That's enough sugar to fell a horse."

He scoffed. "Amateur hour."

She sighed. "It sounds good. I guess if I'm stuck with a crazed psychopath ready to kill those who protect me, I shouldn't worry about a few extra calories."

"I think you'll live."

She rolled her eyes. "You've never read the comments on photos of women online, have you? Still." She waved a hand to encompass the kitchen. "Lead the way."

"You sit. I'll make it. We'll go over where everything is in the kitchen tomorrow. You get a pass today."

"Gee, thanks." But she didn't argue. She sat and poked at his stacks of notes. "That's a lot of paperwork for keeping me out of trouble."

"Investigating things takes some paperwork," he returned, collecting ingredients for hot chocolate.

"I thought you were just supposed to keep me safe while Vaughn and the police figured it all out."

He slid the mug into the microwave hidden in a cabinet and put a doughnut onto a plate. "I could, but that's not what CD Corp is all about."

"CD Corp sounds like the lamest comic villain organization ever."

"It's meant to be bland, boring and inconspicuous." He walked over and set the plate in front of her.

She smiled up at him. "Mission accomplished."

"And this mission," he said, tapping the papers, "is keeping you safe by understanding the threat against you." Not noticing the little dimple that winked in her cheek or the way her blue eyes reminded him of summer. "Anything I can do to profile or find a pattern allows me to better keep you secure."

"Can I help?"

He turned away, back to hot chocolate prep and to shake off that weird and unfortunate bolt of attraction. Still, his voice was easy and bland when he spoke. "I'm counting on it." He stirred the hot chocolate and then set that next to her before taking his seat in front of his computer.

"Have you noticed the pattern of incidents?" he asked, studying her reaction to the question.

With a nap under her belt, she didn't seem as cold and detached as she had on the ride over. But she also didn't seem as ready to break as she had when he'd shown her her room hours ago. As they'd walked through the safe house earlier, he'd finally seen some signs of exhaustion, suspicion and fear.

Now all those things were still evident, but she seemed to have better control over them. He supposed singers, being performers, had to have a little actor in them, as well. She was good at it, but it had frayed at the edges when he'd told her she was safe.

She'd shored up those edges, but there was a wariness and an exhaustion, not sleep related, haunting her eyes.

"The pattern that they always happen when I'm on stage? Yes, my brother pointed that out, but as I pointed out to him, that's just means and opportunity or whatever phrase you guys use. They know exactly where I'll be and for how long."

"Sure, but I'm talking about the connection to your songs."

She frowned, taking a sip of the hot chocolate.

"The incidents, including the murder of your security guard, always crop up in the few weeks after one of your singles drops on the radio. Not all of them, but I compiled a list of titles."

"Let me guess. The drinking, cheating and swearing songs?"

"No. There's not a thematic connection that I can find." Though he'd look, and would keep considering that angle. "But the connection right now seems to be that things escalate when the songs you wrote your-self do well."

She put down the doughnut she'd lifted to her lips without taking a bite. "That doesn't make any sense."

"Not yet. I figure if we pull on it, it will."

"How did you…"

He shrugged. "I'm good with patterns."

"Good with or genius with?"

He smiled at her, couldn't help it. He'd been trained as an undercover FBI agent. Took on whatever role he had to. He'd learned to hide himself underneath a mil-lion masks, but his personal attachment to this job and the safe world he'd created made it hard to do here. "Hate to bandy a word like *genius* around."

She laughed and for a brief second her eyes lit with humor instead of worry. He wanted to be able to give that to her permanently, so she could laugh and relax and feel *safe* here.

Because that was his job, his duty, what he was good at. Completely irrelevant to the specific woman he was helping.

He looked down at his computer, frowning at the uncomfortable and unreasonable pull of emotion in-side him. Emotions were what had gotten him booted from the FBI in the first place. He didn't regret it—couldn't—but it was a dangerous line to walk when your emotions got involved.

"So, I think we can rule out crazed fan. It's more personal than that."

"Fans create a personal connection to you, though. They think they know you through your music—whether it was written by me or someone else doesn't matter to them."

"It matters to someone," Zach returned. "Or the incidents wouldn't align so perfectly with the songs you wrote."

She pushed out of her chair, doughnut untouched, only a few sips of the hot chocolate taken. She paced. He waited. When she seemed to accept he wasn't going to say anything, she whirled toward him.

"Look, I don't know how to do this."

"Do what?"

"Hide and cower and…" She gave the chair she'd popped out of a violent shove, then raked shaking hands through her hair. "A good man is dead because of me. I can't stand it."

The naked emotion, brief though it was, hit him a little hard, so he kept his tone brusque. "A good man is dead because good men die in the pursuit of doing good and because there are forces and people out there who aren't so good. Guilt's normal, but you'll need to work it out."

"Oh, will I?"

"I'd recommend therapy, once this is sorted."

"Therapy," she echoed, like he was speaking a foreign language.

"Stalking is basically a personal form of terrorism. You don't generally get through it unscathed. Right now the concern is your physical safety, but when it's over you can't overlook your emotional well-being."

"You spend a lot of time evaluating your emotional well-being, Zach?"

"Believe it or not, they don't let you in or out of the FBI without a psych eval. Same goes for in and out of undercover work—and a few of those messed me up enough to require some therapy. Talking to someone doesn't scare me, and it shouldn't scare you."

"That hardly scares me."

But the way she scoffed, he wasn't so sure. Still, it was none of his business. Her recovery was not part of keeping her safe, and the latter was all he was supposed to care about.

"Let's talk about the people on this list," Zach said, pushing the computer screen toward her. On the screen was a list of people she'd told her brother she thought might want to hurt her.

Daisy rubbed her temples. "Vaughn gave you this?"

He rose, retrieved some aspirin from the cabinet above the sink and set it next to her elbow. "Your brother gave me copies of everything pertaining to the stalking."

Daisy frowned at the aspirin bottle, then up at him. "Am I supposed to tip you?"

"Full service security and investigation, Ms. Delaney. Speaking of that, Delaney's a stage name, isn't it?"

"What? You don't have a full dossier on my real name and everything else?" She smirked at him.

He shook his head. The Delaney connection wasn't important. As unimportant as the way that smirk made his gut tighten with a desire he would never, *ever* act on.

What was important was her take on the list and what kind of patterns and conclusions he could draw. So he turned the conversation back to the case and made sure it stayed there.

## Chapter Three

Sleep was a welcome relief from worry, except when the dreams came. They didn't always make sense, but Tom's lifeless body always appeared.

Even hiking up the mountains at sunset. It was peaceful, and Zach was with her, smiling. She liked his smile, and she liked the riot of sunset colors in the sky. She wanted to write a song, itched to.

Suddenly, she had a notebook and a pen, but when she started to write it became a picture of Tom, and then she tripped and it was Tom's body. She reached out for Zach's help, but it was only Tom's lifeless eyes staring back from Zach's face.

She didn't know whether she was screaming or crying, maybe it was both, and then she fell with a jolt. Her eyes flew open, face wet and breath coming so fast it hurt her lungs.

Somehow, she knew Zach was standing there. It didn't even give her a start. It seemed right and steadying that he was standing in her doorway in nothing but a pair of sweatpants, a dim glow from the room behind him.

Later, she'd give some considerable thought to just how

*cut* Zach was, all strong arms and abs. Something else he hid quite well, and she was sure quite purposefully.

"You screamed and you didn't lock your door," he offered, slowly lowering the gun to his side. He looked up at the ceiling, and gestured toward her. "You might want to…"

He trailed off and in her jumble of emotions and dream confusion, it took her a good minute to realize the strap of her tank top had fallen off her arm and she was all but flashing him.

She wasn't embarrassed so much as tired. Bone-deep tired of how this whole thing was ruining her life. "Sorry," she grumbled, fixing the shirt and pulling the sheet up around her.

"No. That's not…" He cleared his throat. "You should lock that door."

She wished she could find amusement in his obvious discomfort over being flashed a little breast, but she was too tired. "Lock the door to shield myself from lunatics with guns?" she asked, nodding at the pistol he carried.

"To take precautions," he said firmly.

"Are you telling me if I'd screamed and the door had been locked you wouldn't have busted in here, guns blazing?"

"They were hardly blazing," he returned, ignoring the question.

But she knew the answer. She might not know or understand Zach Simmons, but he had that same thing her brother did. A dedication to whatever he saw as his mission.

Currently, she was Zach Simmons's mission. She wished it gave her any comfort, but with Tom's dead face flashing in her mind, she didn't think anything could.

"You want a drink?" he asked, and despite that bland tone he used with such effectiveness, the offer was kind.

"Yes. Yes, I do."

He nodded. "I'll see what I can scrounge up. You can meet me out there."

She took that as a clear hint to put on some decent clothes. On a sigh, she got out of bed and rifled through her duffel bag. She pulled out her big, fluffy robe in bright yellow. It made her feel a little like Big Bird, which always made her smile.

Tonight was an exception, but it at least gave her something sunny to hold on to as she stepped out of the room. Zach was pouring whiskey into a shot glass. He'd pulled on a T-shirt, but it wasn't the kind of shirt he'd worn yesterday that hid all that surprisingly solid muscle. No, it fit him well, and allowed her another bolt of surprisingly intense attraction.

He set the shot glass on the table and gestured her into the seat. She slid into it, staring at the amber liquid somewhat dubiously. "Thanks." But she didn't shoot it. She just stared at it. "Got anything to put it in? I may love a song about shooting whiskey, but honestly shots make me gag."

His mouth quirked, but he nodded, pulling a can of pop out of the fridge.

"No diet?"

"I'll put it on the grocery list."

"And where does one get groceries in the middle of nowhere Wyoming?"

"Believe it or not, even Wyomingites need to eat. I've got an assistant who'll take care of errands. If you make a list, we'll supply."

She sipped the drink he put in front of her. The mix

of sugar and whiskey was a comforting familiarity in the midst of all this…upheaval.

"You don't shoot whiskey."

She quirked a smile at him. "Not all my songs are autobiographical, friend. Truth be told, I'd prefer a beer, but it doesn't give you quite the same buzz, does it?"

"No, but I'd think more things would rhyme with beer than whiskey."

"Songs also don't have to rhyme. Fancy yourself a country music expert? Or just a Daisy Delaney expert?"

"No expertise claimed. I studied up on your work, not that I hadn't heard it before. Some of your songs make a decent showing on the radio."

"Decent. Don't get that Jordan Jones airtime, but who does? Certainly no one with breasts." This time she didn't sip. She took a good, long pull. Silly thing to be peeved about Jordan's career taking off while hers seemed to level. Bigger things at hand. Nightmares, dead bodyguards, empty Wyoming towns.

"The police don't suspect him."

She took another long drink. "No, they don't."

"Do you?"

She stared at the bubbles popping at the surface of her soda. Did she think the man she'd married with vows of faith and love and certainty was now stalking her? That he killed the person in charge of keeping her safe?

"I don't want to."

"But you think he could be responsible?" Zach pressed. Clearly, he didn't care if he was pressing on an open, gaping wound.

"I doubt it. But I wouldn't put it past one of his people. After I filed for divorce they did a number on me.

Fake stories about cheating and drinking and unstable behavior, and before you point it out, no, my songs did not help me in that regard. Funny how my daddy was *revered* for those types of songs, even when he left Mama high and dry, but me? I'm a crazy floozy who deserves what she gets."

Zach's gaze was placid and blank, lacking all judgment. She didn't have a clue why that pissed her off, but it did. So she drank deeply, waiting for that warm tingle to spread. Hopefully slow down the whirring in her brain a little bit. "I don't want to have a debate about feminism or gender equality. I want to be safe home in my own bed. And I want Tom to be alive."

"I'm working on one of those. I'm sorry I can't fix the rest."

He said it so blankly. No emotion behind it at all, and yet this time it soothed her. Because she believed those words so much more without someone trying to *act* sincere.

"What did you dream about?" he asked as casual and devoid of emotion as he'd been this whole time.

Except when he'd been uncomfortable about her wandering breast. She held on to the fact that Mr. Ex-FBI man could be a little thrown off.

"Hiking. You. Tom. It's a jumble of nonsense, and not all that uncommon for me. I've always had vivid dreams, bad ones when I'm…well, bad. They've just never been so connected or relentless."

"I imagine your life has never been so relentless and threatening."

"Fair."

"The dreams aren't fun, but they'll be there. Meditation works for some. Alcohol for others, though I wouldn't make that one a habit. Exercise and wearing yourself out works, too."

"Let me guess, that's your trick?"

He shrugged. "I've done all three."

"Your job gave you dreams?"

"Yeah. Dreams are your subconscious, the things you often can't or don't deal with awake. It's your brain trying to work through it all when you can't outthink it."

"You've given brains a *lot* more thought than I ever have."

"There's a psychology to undercover work. Your work deals with the heart more than the brain."

Because he cut to the quick of her entire life's vocation a little too easily, and it smoothed over jagged edges in a way she didn't understand, she chose to focus on the other part of the sentence.

"You went undercover? Yeah, I can see that. Bring down any big guns?"

He shrugged. "Here and there."

"What's the point if you're not going to brag about it?"

He pondered that, then gave his answer with utter conviction. "Justice. Satisfaction."

She wrinkled her nose. "I'd prefer a little limelight."

"I suppose that's why I'm in security, and you're in entertainment."

"I suppose." She finished the drink. She wasn't really sure what had mellowed her mood more—the buzz or Zach's conversation. She had a sinking suspicion it was both, and that he was aware of that. "I guess I'll try to sleep now. I appreciate the…" She didn't know what to call it—from responding to her distress to a simple drink and conversation—it was more than she'd been given in…a long time.

Well, if she was fair, more than she'd allowed herself. And that had started a heck of a lot longer ago than the stalking.

She stood, never finishing her sentence. Zach stood, as well, cleaning up her mess. For some reason that didn't sit right, but she didn't do anything to remedy it. She opened the door to her bedroom, took one last glance back at him.

He was heading for his own door. A strange mystery of a man with a very good heart under all that blankness.

He paused at his door. He didn't look at her, but she had no doubt he knew she was looking at him.

"Daisy." It might have been the first time he'd said her name, or maybe it was just the first time he'd said her name where it sounded human to human. So she waited, breath held for who knew what reason.

"You've been through a lot. It isn't just losing someone you feel responsible for losing. You've uprooted your life, changed everything around you. You might be used to life on the road, but this is different. You don't have your singing outlet. So give yourself a break."

With that, he stepped into his room, the door closing and locking behind him.

ZACH DIDN'T NEED much sleep on a normal day, but even with the usual four hours under his belt, he felt a little rough around the edges the next morning. He supposed it had to do with them being interrupted by Daisy's screaming.

It had damn near scared a year off his life.

Any questions or doubts he'd had were gone, though. Someone or something was terrorizing her. Didn't mean he wouldn't look at cold, hard facts. Hadn't he learned what getting too emotionally involved in a case got you?

Yeah, he was susceptible to vulnerability. He could admit that now. Being plagued by dreams, by guilt over the man who'd died only for taking a job protecting her, it all added up to vulnerable.

And he was *not* thinking about the slip of her top because that had nothing to do with anything.

He grunted his way through push-ups, sit-ups, lunges and squats. He'd need to bring a few more things from home. Maybe just move it all. He wasn't planning on spending much time back in Cheyenne with his business here.

His room still needed a lot of work, and he'd get to it once this case was shored up—as long as he didn't immediately have another one. Still, he had a floor, a rudimentary bathroom and a bed. What more did a guy need?

He knew his mother worried about him throwing too much into his job, whether because she feared he'd suffer the same fate as his father—murdered in revenge for the work he'd done as an ATF agent—or because she just worried about him having more of a life than work, it didn't matter.

He liked his work. It fulfilled him. Besides, he had friends. Cousins, actually. Finding his long-lost sister meant finding his mother's family, and he might get along more with the people they'd married, but it was still camaraderie.

He had a full life.

But he sat there on the floor of a ramshackle room,

sweating from the brief workout, and wondered at the odd pang of longing for something he couldn't name. Something he'd never had until he'd met his sister—of course that had coincided with being officially fired from the FBI, so maybe it was more that than the other.

It didn't matter. Because not only was he *fine*, he also had a job to do.

He could hear Daisy stirring out in the common room. Coffee or breakfast or both, if he had to guess.

He'd hoped she'd sleep longer because there were some areas he wanted to press on today, and he'd likely back off if she looked tired.

Or he could suck it up and be a hard-ass, which was what this job called for, wasn't it? He knew what being soft got him, so he needed to steel his determination to be hard.

He ran through a cold shower, got dressed, grabbed his computer and stepped out to find Daisy in the kitchen.

She was dressed in tight jeans and a neon-pink T-shirt that read *Straight Shooter* in sparkly sequins on the back. On the sleeve of each arm was a revolver outline in more sequins. When she turned from the oven where she was scrambling some eggs, she flashed a smile.

Her hair was pulled back to reveal bright green cactus earrings, and she'd put on makeup. Dark eyes, bright lips.

The fact she'd made herself up, looked like she could step on stage in the snap of her fingers, he assumed she was hiding a rough night under all that polish.

But the polish helped him pretend, too.

"Want some?" she asked, tipping the pan toward him.

"Sure, if you've got enough." He dropped the laptop off on the table and then moved toward her to get plates, but she waved him away.

"You waited on me yesterday. My turn. Besides, I familiarized myself this morning. Thanks for making coffee, by the way. Good stuff."

"Programmable machine," he returned, not sure what to do with himself while she took care of breakfast. He opted for getting himself a cup of coffee.

He didn't want to loom behind her, so he took a seat at the table and opened his laptop. He booted up his email to see if there were any more reports from Ranger Cooper, but nothing.

She slid a plate in front of him, then took the seat opposite him with her own plate.

"So, what's the deal? Play house in here until they figure out who did it?" she asked with just a tad too much cheer in her voice—clearly trying to compensate for the edge she felt.

"Partially. We're working on a protected outdoor area, but staying inside for now is best." He tapped his computer. "It gives us time to work through who might be after you."

She wrinkled her nose. "Believe it or not, sifting through who might hate me enough to hurt me isn't high on my want-to-do list."

"But I assume going home, getting back to your family and your career is. Lesser of two evils."

She ate, frowning. But she didn't try to argue, and he was going to do his job today. Nightmares and vulnerability couldn't stop the job.

"I want to talk about your ex."

"So does everyone," she muttered.

"Your divorce was news?" he asked, even though he'd known it was. Much as he didn't keep up with pop culture, he'd seen enough magazines at the checkout counter with her face and her ex's.

"Yeah. I mean, maybe not if you don't pay attention to country music, but Jordan had really started to make a name for himself with crossovers. So the story got big. And I got crucified."

"Why didn't he?" Zach asked casually, taking a bite of the eggs, which were perfectly cooked.

"Because he's perfect?"

"You wanted to divorce him," he pointed out. "He can't be perfect. No one is."

"Or that's exactly why I wanted to divorce him."

He studied her. The lifted chin, the challenge in her eyes. "Yeah, I don't buy that."

Her shoulders slumped. "Yeah, our families didn't, either. Neither did he, for that matter. I don't know how to explain… Do we really have to discuss my very public divorce?"

"Yeah. We really do. The more I understand, the better I can find the pattern."

"And if it's not him?"

"Then the pattern won't say it is."

"People aren't patterns, Zach. They're not always rational, or sane."

"Yeah, I'm well aware, but routine stalkers are methodical. It's not a moment of rage. It's not knee-jerk or impulse. It's planned terrorizing. Murder of your bodyguard? There was no struggle. It was planned. This person is methodical, which means if I can figure out their methodology, I can figure this out."

She heaved out a sigh. "You believe that."

"I know that."

"Fine. Fine. Why did I file for divorce against Jordan? I don't know. It's complicated. It's all emotions and… Did your parents love each other?"

Unconcerned with the abrupt change, because every thread led him somewhere, he nodded. "Very much."

"Mine didn't. Or maybe they did, but it was warped. It hurt."

He thought about his brother, alone in a psych ward, still lost to whatever had taken a hold of his mind. "Love often does."

"You got someone?"

"Not romantically."

"Family, then?"

He nodded.

"I used to think loving my brother didn't hurt, not even a little—not the way loving my father did, or even my mom. Vaughn was perfect, and always did the right thing. He protected me and loved me unconditionally. But this hurts, thinking he could be in danger because of me."

"He's a Texas Ranger."

"That doesn't make him invincible. He also has a wife and two little girls and…" She swallowed, looking away from him. "I can't…"

"The best thing for 'I can't' is figuring this out. Looking at the patterns, and finding who's at the center."

"You really think you can do that?"

"I do. With your help."

She nodded. "Okay. Okay. Well, sit back and relax,

cowboy. The story of Daisy Delaney and Jordan Jones is a long one."

He lifted the coffee mug to his lips to try and hide his smile. "We've got nothing but time, Daisy."

## Chapter Four

"We met at a party." It was still so clear in Daisy's head. She'd stepped outside for air, and he'd followed. He'd complimented her on her music—never once mentioning her daddy.

She'd been a little too desperate for that kind of compliment at the time. She'd made a name for herself, but only when that name directly followed her father's.

"And this was before any of Jordan's success?"

Zach sat there, poised over his computer like he'd type it all out. Jot down her entire marriage in a few pithy lines and then find some magical *pattern* that either found Jordan culpable or...not.

"My brother looked into Jordan, you know."

"Yes, I know. I have all the information he gathered in regards to the...let's call it *external stuff*. But there's a lot of internal stuff I doubt you shared with your brother."

She laughed. "But you think I'll share it with a complete stranger?"

Zach blew out a breath, and though he had to be irritated with her, it didn't really show in the ways she was *used* to people being irritated with her.

"I know this is personal," Zach said, all calm and

even and perfectly civil. "It hurts to mine through all these old things you thought were normal parts of a normal life. I'm not trivializing what you might feel, Daisy. I'm trying to understand someone's motivation for stalking and terrorizing you, and murdering your bodyguard."

"So you can find your precious pattern?" she asked, her throat too tight to sound as callous as she wanted to sound.

"Yeah, the precious pattern that might save your life."

She wanted to lean her head against the table and weep. Somehow, she had no doubt Zach would be kind and discreet about it, and it made her perversely more determined to keep it together. "He was sweet, and attentive. We had a lot in common, though he'd grown up on some hoity-toity, well-to-do Georgia farm and I'd grown up on the road. Still, the way he talked about music and his career made sense to me. He made sense to me. He asked me to marry him assuring me that it didn't have to change my career—because he knew where my priorities were."

"So you married for love?"

"Isn't that why people get married?"

"People get married for all sorts of reasons, I think. In your case, you've got fame and money on your side."

"Are you suggesting Jordan married me for my fame and money?"

"No, I'm asking if he did."

"I didn't think so." Even after she'd asked for a divorce, she hadn't thought Jordan could be that cold and manipulative, but after everything that had happened since the divorce… "He was so careful about any work we did together. Had to make sure it was the right project. He didn't insinuate himself into my career. So it didn't seem that way…"

"But?"

She didn't like the way he seemed to understand where her thoughts were going. She was clearly telegraphing all her feelings, and Zach was too observant. She needed to pull her masks together.

"He didn't fight me on the divorce. We'd grown apart. He'd thrown everything into his tour, his album, and I was touring and… We were both sort of bitter with each other but couldn't talk about it. I said we should end it and he agreed. He agreed. So simple, so smooth. Everything that came after was…calculated. Careful. He wanted us to split award shows."

"Huh?"

"Like choose which award shows we'd attend. If he was going to be at one, I wouldn't be. Like they were holidays you split the kids between. I don't know. I remember when my parents got divorced, it was screaming matches and throwing things and drunkenness. Not…paperwork."

"So it was amicable?"

Daisy hesitated. She'd dug her own grave, so to speak, with some of her behavior after she'd asked for the divorce. Because when he'd politely accepted her request and immediately obtained the necessary paperwork, she'd been…

Sometimes she tried to convince herself her pride had been injured, but the truth was she'd been devastated. She'd thrown out divorce as an option to get some kind of reaction out of him, to ignite a spark like they'd had before they'd gotten married.

But he'd gone along. Agreed. Wanted custody agreements over *award shows*.

So she hadn't handled herself well. At all. She'd never imagined *this*. She'd only acted out her hurt and anger and betrayal the best way she knew how.

Breaking stuff and getting drunk.

"*He* was amicable, I guess you could say. I was… less so."

"But you were the one who asked for the divorce."

"Yes." As much as she didn't want to get into this with Zach, she supposed she'd end up giving him whatever information he thought might help with his precious patterns. What else was there to do? How else did she survive this?

"Yes, because I wanted him to fight for me, or be mad at me or react to me in some way. But he didn't. I started thinking he'd never loved me, because he was so calm. If there'd been love, it would have gone bitter. Mine did. I think he just used me for as long as I'd let him, then was happy to move on." As if it had been his plan all along.

Even now, a year later, the stab of pain that went along with that was hard to swallow down or rationalize away.

There were bigger tragedies in the world than a failed marriage, including her dead bodyguard.

"So maybe it could be Jordan, but if it is him, it's not because I divorced him. Trust me, he got everything he wanted and *more* out of that situation. I don't think he'd sully his precious reputation by slapping back at me, when the press did all the work eviscerating me for him."

"Okay. What about other exes?"

"Because only a jilted lover could be after me?"

"Because we're going through the rational options first. We'll move to the irrational crazed fan angle after—" The sound of a phone trilling cut him off.

He pulled his cell out of his pocket, glanced at the display, then answered. "Yeah?" His face changed. She couldn't have described how. A tensing, maybe? Suddenly, there was more of an edge to him. The blandness sharpened into something that made her stomach tighten with a little bit of fear, and just a touch of very inappropriate lust.

If only she knew how to be appropriate.

He fired off questions like *when?* and *description?* jotting down what she assumed were the answers on the back of one of the many pieces of paper in the file.

"Get what you can for me," he said tersely and hung up.

He jotted a few more things down then got to his feet like he was going to walk off to his room without saying anything.

"What was that?" Daisy demanded, hating the hint of hysteria in her voice.

"Just some updates. Nothing to worry about."

She fairly leaped out of her chair and grabbed his arm before he could disappear into his room.

He clearly didn't know her very well because he raised a condescending eyebrow, like that would have her moving her hand. But she'd be damned if she was letting go until she said what she had to say. "You want me safe? I have to know what's going on."

"That isn't necessarily true," he replied in that bland tone of his. "Knowing doesn't do much. All you have to do is stay put. I'll be back."

"You'll be back? You don't honestly expect me to—"

"I expect you to listen to the man currently keeping you safe. Do me a favor? Don't be cliché or stupid. Which means stay put. I'll be back." And then he walked out the front door.

And locked it from the outside.

ZACH HAD NO doubt he'd made all the wrong moves in there, but he didn't have time to make the right ones. He pocketed his keys, double-checked the gun holstered to his side and stepped out into daylight.

He took a deep breath of the fresh air, trying not to feel the prick of guilt at Daisy being locked inside for close to twenty-four hours. But it was for her safety, and Cam's phone call proved to him that he had to keep being excessively vigilant.

Which was why he scowled when Cam pulled up to the shack that disguised a garage behind the big house. Hilly was in the passenger seat so Zach tried to fix his expression into something neutral, but his sister being here complicated things.

Hilly was acting as their assistant. She ran the errands for groceries and the like, and she was helping with some of the paperwork while she went through nursing school.

Cam pulled his truck into the garage, then he and Hilly exited. Zach pushed the button himself to close the door so it went back to looking like a falling-down shack.

Cam's expression grave and Hilly's suspicious. "I still can't believe this place," she said with a little shudder. "It's so *creepy* from the outside."

Zach smiled thinly. "And, as you well know, perfectly livable from the inside. So what's the deal?"

"Is she in there?" Hilly asked with a frown.

"Yeah."

"Well, let's go inside."

Zach rocked back on his heels. "Not a great idea right now. Besides, she doesn't need to know about this."

Hilly's frown deepened. Zach wanted to scowl at Cam for bringing her, but that would only make Hilly angrier.

Truth be told, he didn't understand the way Hilly got angry at all. It was sneaky, and came at you in new and confusing ways. Like guilt. He didn't care for it.

She glanced back at Cam. "I thought I was here to see what Daisy needed."

"You are," Cam agreed. "I just have some things I need to discuss with Zach about the case privately. I thought maybe I could do that while you talk to Daisy about anything she might need."

She looked back at Zach, her lips pursed, surveying him. An expression he never knew how to fully read. Judgment? Disappointment?

"I still think we can go inside and talk. There are rooms. Or you can let me go inside while you two pow-wow out here."

"Aren't you going to demand to know what's going on?"

"No. Cam and I agreed that there were certain cases that required his confidentiality. I'm okay with that. So why don't you let me in?"

Zach nodded. He didn't particularly want to introduce anyone to Daisy, but she was likely tired of just *him* and walls for company. Hilly could talk to her about anything she needed, maybe make her feel a little more at home, and Cam could fill him in on the details in the privacy of his room.

They walked to the front of the house and Zach unlocked and relocked doors as they entered, and when he stepped into the common area he frowned at the absence of Daisy.

Then at the fact the door to his room was open. He stepped toward it, hand moving to his gun without fully thinking the move through.

He stopped short in the doorway, shock and irritation clawing through him at equal measure. "What the hell do you think you're doing?" Zach demanded from the doorway.

Daisy didn't even have the decency to jump as she sat there on his bed, rifling through his things.

"I can't say your room holds any deep, dark surprises, Zach. Bland guy. Bland... Oh, hello." Daisy leaned her head to the side to look around him.

"Get your hands off my stuff."

She blinked up at him oh so innocently. "Won't you be doing the same for me? Or have you already?" She got to her feet in a fluid movement and crossed to Hilly and Cam and held out her hand.

"Daisy Delaney," she offered with a sassy grin that likely served her well on stage.

"Hi, I'm Hilly," Hilly said eagerly, shaking Daisy's hand. "I'm Zach's sister."

"Zach's sister." Daisy looked at him and raised an eyebrow before her smile sharpened. "Well, Hilly, you might be my new best friend."

"Sorry, if you're looking for dirt we only kind of found out about each other last year."

"Okay, so you can't give me the Zach dirt. How about you tell me what the hell is going on? I'm presuming you know." She moved her gaze to Cam. "Or you do."

"I, uh…" Cam cleared his throat, looking shockingly ruffled and uncomfortable.

"He's a big fan," Hilly stage-whispered.

"I am not," Cam retorted, sounding downright strangled. "I mean, I *am*, but not… Oh, hell."

Hilly laughed, leaning into Cam. They were more of a unit than Zach would ever be with his own sister, and he was never quite sure what to do with that sick wave of jealousy that swamped him sometimes.

Hilly had been kidnapped and raised as someone else. What would he envy of her life?

But when she linked hands with Cam and talked excitedly to Daisy, he knew exactly what.

"Hilly, why don't you take Daisy out to the kitchen and get her list. Hilly's our assistant. She can run any errands you need."

"Oh, he's dismissing the womenfolk," Daisy said with a sweetness that went bitter at the edges.

Zach could tell Hilly was trying to suppress a smile. But she didn't fight him. "I'm sure there are some things you'd like to have, Ms. Delaney. I can get you whatever you need."

"Call me Daisy," she replied, heading for the door with Hilly.

Zach *knew* he should keep his mouth shut, let it go. But she downright needled him. "We'll talk about you going through my stuff later," he muttered as she passed.

"Ooh, shaking in my boots, baby cakes."

He sneered, as irritated with himself for letting her get to him as he was at her for being obnoxious as hell.

"Things are going well, then," Cam offered once Daisy and Hilly disappeared into the common room.

"Things are going fine. I want the full report."

"We didn't catch him at the airport, but a man was quizzing Jen at the General Store. Get many strangers, etc. She gave me a call and I ran him. Came in on a flight from Texas, but after Daisy's. No connections yet, but probably more than a coincidence. Someone's following her."

"I want to know *how*."

"Don't you want to know who?"

"Maybe. But if this is the stalker, they suddenly got so dumb they're sniffing around a small town thinking they won't make waves. My money's on a plant, or a hired hand. The *how* is more relevant than the *who*."

"He's rented a room in Fairmont, but I have some suspicions that's to throw us off."

"Does he know about *us*?"

"Unclear. As far as I can tell, he only has a vague idea of where she is. I assume he knows she's under some kind of protection, but he didn't make Hilly or me, and nobody followed us out here."

"We took every precaution." But something hadn't worked. Something had gotten through.

"It happens, Zach. Now we focus on protecting her. Jen's getting together her security footage and I'll work on an ID and any connections to Daisy. I'm sure you'll obsess over a pattern. Bottom line, we'll keep her safe."

Except hadn't he already failed at that? Maybe she was safe *now*, but the threat was at her door just like it had been back in Texas.

"Hey," Cam said. "Nothing's ever going to go according to plan. You know that."

Zach nodded at Cam. But a mistake had been made—plans or no plans—and that mistake had to be figured out before the consequences of his mistake started knocking.

## Chapter Five

Daisy liked Hilly. She hadn't thought she would when the young woman had ushered her out of Zach's room with only a mild display of amusement.

But Hilly was sweet, a little heavy on the earnestness, which Daisy could only find endearing. The fact she'd ask for Daisy's autograph to give to the man huddled in Zach's room appealed to both Daisy's ego and the idea that love didn't always have to be messy. Hilly clearly loved her boyfriend and wasn't miffed that he'd gone a little tongue-tied over Daisy.

"So you don't know what's going on with the caveman clutch in there?" Daisy asked, scowling at Zach's door as Hilly finished up the list. It would be nice to have some *real* food in this place.

Hilly smiled. "They aren't really. Cavemen, that is. They're just…serious."

Which didn't answer the question. "No offense, Hilly, but one's your brother and one's your…" She trailed off, glanced at the rock on Hilly's hand. Not bad taste for a caveman, but Hilly could have picked it out herself. "Fiancé. You're not an unbiased observer."

"I suppose not, but they're good men. They both helped save me from people who wanted to hurt me."

"Really?"

"Zach's saved a lot of people, and gotten himself hurt in the process more than once. He's a good man. That I can promise you."

Hilly smiled as Cam and Zach stepped out of Zach's room, looking just as Hilly had described them: serious.

"I'll tell you about it sometime. Or ask Zach."

"Ask me what?"

Hilly shook her head and stood, slipping the list into her pocket. "I should head out to get the supplies so I can get them back to you before dinner."

"I'll keep in touch," Cam said to Zach.

"Aren't you going to say goodbye to Daisy, Cam?" Hilly asked sweetly.

He glared at her but then offered Daisy a smile and a nod. "It was nice to meet you, Ms. Delaney," he offered stiffly.

"Call me Daisy, sweetheart."

Cam made a little noise that might have been a squeak if he wasn't so tall and broad. Hilly ushered him out and that left her with Zach.

She scowled at him. Truth be told, she should be used to overly serious men worrying a little too much about her safety, but she'd always managed to keep Vaughn on the fringe of all that. Travel and no real trouble had helped until the past year.

But regardless of Vaughn's interference in her life, she wasn't used to someone being all up in her business. She wasn't used to someone getting under her skin in such a short amount of time.

And none of it mattered, because at the end of the day, her irritation with Zach didn't matter. Getting through this mattered. "I want to know what's going on."

"And I want to know why you were rifling through my stuff," he retorted, a slash of temper barely leashed.

Was it wrong she liked temper on him? That he wasn't all Mr. Bland Stoic? Because *this* was a lot more enjoyable than his pat, crap answers. So she grinned at him, since it seemed to make him grind his teeth together. "Show me yours, I'll show you mine."

"Someone followed you."

It took any and all enjoyment out of the moment. She sank into the chair when her legs went a little wobbly. "What?"

"Someone followed you here," Zach said, his voice flat but his eyes flashing with anger.

Was it at her or whoever was here? She wasn't sure she wanted to know.

"So I need a list of everyone who knew you were coming."

"You know the list," she replied, trying to keep the tremor out of her voice. "You, Jaime and my brother. Hate to break it to you, but they're not high on my suspect list. Well, I don't know you. It could be you."

"You didn't tell anyone that you were going out of town, or post a picture from the airport or—"

Injured pride reignited her irritation. "Oh, screw you."

"Hey, someone is *here*, and now I have to keep you safe under an even bigger threat, so a little truthfulness would be nice."

"Because I'm such a liar?"

"Get it through your thick, obnoxious skull that your pride doesn't matter right now. One person, any person, who might have known you were leaving town, heading to the airport, anything. Because it matters. Clearly, if someone is here looking for you, it matters."

It was on the tip of her tongue to immediately dismiss him. But…it wouldn't be true, and she wanted to be safe more than she wanted to be righteous.

Just barely.

"I… I told my manager I was going to Wyoming, but—"

"Of all the idiotic bull—"

"I trust Stacy with my *life*," she shot back before he could finish. "I trust her with everything. It isn't her."

"Okay, great. So the three people who knew you were coming to Wyoming were your brother, an FBI agent and your manager. Who spilled the beans?"

"Maybe *you* did, jerk."

"Sure. I'm a security professional, but I bragged about bagging a big star client to someone who has a connection to you."

"I don't know you! You could have."

"But I know me, and I didn't. Stacy… Stacy Vine. That's your manager, right?"

"You cannot look into her."

"Can. Will."

She would not be so weak as to cry. She'd save that for when he couldn't see and lord it over her later. But her voice wasn't nearly strong enough. "You're asking me which of these people I *love* wants me dead."

He softened. She saw it all over his face and wanted to hate him for it. It would be easier if he was just the overbearing jerk, but he offered empathy far too often for it to be that simple.

God, she wanted something, anything, to be simple.

He took one of the chairs and moved it across from

her. He sat, facing her, so that their knees were almost touching. He leaned forward, and she found herself wanting to lean forward, too. Wanting to be touched, comforted.

Wasn't that a joke? She knew better on a good day, with a man who actually liked her. This was neither of those things.

"It doesn't have to be that cut-and-dried. She could have mentioned it to an assistant. Written it down and someone read it. This is why the *who* is important, Daisy. If it's someone who's got a personal tie to you, they might be stalking people you know and love, too."

"How many ways do you want to hurt me, Zach?" She held up a hand before he could answer. He wasn't trying to hurt her. He had a job to do, protection to see to. Anything that hurt was all hers. "Sorry. That wasn't fair."

"You don't have to be fair. I'm going to do my job no matter what you are. Be mad, be unfair, but I need the truth. Always. It's the only way we get you out of this."

*We.* Like they were some kind of team. Which was too much the story of her life. Thinking some man was in it for her—Dad, Jordan—only to find all they cared about was their own bottom line. She didn't know how to weather that again.

What other option was there? She could lie to him, not trust him, and where did it get her? Nowhere. She was in the hardest lose-lose situation of her entire life, and boy, was that saying something.

"She's the only one aside from Vaughn and Jaime that knows. Nat—that's Vaughn's wife—might know, but Vaughn's pretty by-the-book. Even if he told her, he'd swear her to secrecy, and Nat would listen. You could always ask them, but I doubt they'd be careless."

"So we'll look into your manager."

"Yeah, sure. Fantastic."

Zach sighed, then rested his hand over hers. Warm, strong, capable. She really wanted to hate him, and he made it so dang hard.

"One thing at a time, okay? And eventually, we'll get there."

It was a cliché, and stupid, and worst of all, it made her feel better.

ZACH SPENT MOST of his day looking into the manager, her connections and trying to figure out how anyone had followed Daisy here.

It couldn't be cut-and-dried because the person didn't know *exactly* where Daisy was, so that made any patterns sketchy at best. A frustrating point of fact Zach was having trouble accepting.

He also spent considerable time checking his security measures and watching the footage of the security cameras he had positioned on different places outside the house. When he was half convinced he saw a tumbleweed pass across his deserted Main Street he knew it was time to do something else.

Still, no matter what he did or how little he interacted with Daisy, he could practically feel the stir-crazy coming off her.

When Hilly returned with the groceries, and some updates on the tasks he'd asked her to accomplish, Zach thanked her and sent her away, though it was clear she wanted to stay and chat.

Much as Zach trusted Hilly and Cam to be aware of

anyone following them, he didn't want to take too many chances on comings and goings being noticed—whether by the wrong people or even by locals who might talk.

Armed with the special item he'd tasked Hilly to find, Zach went to Daisy's room. She'd been inside with the door closed for about an hour. He knew she wasn't sleeping because he could hear her moving around.

He knocked, feeling stupid and determined in equal measure. It wasn't his job to set Daisy at ease or make her comfortable, but it wasn't *not* his job, either.

She opened the door with that haughty, bad-girl smirk, though it couldn't hide the wariness in her gaze. Still, both smirk and wariness softened as she noticed what he held in his hands.

"A guitar," she breathed, like he was holding a leprechaun's pot of gold.

"I don't know much about music, but there's a music shop in Fairmont and Hilly stopped in and picked one up. Probably not the quality you're used to, but—"

"Hilly stopped in and picked one up or you asked her to?"

"Does it matter?"

She tilted her head, studying him. In the end, she didn't say anything. She took the offered guitar and slid her fingers over the wood, the strings, the body and the arm.

There was something a little too erotic about watching her do that so he moved into the kitchen. It wasn't quite dinnertime yet, but they could certainly eat. If only to keep him from embarrassing himself.

But he couldn't quite seem to keep his gaze off the way she stroked the instrument, which meant he had to say something. *Do* something. Anything to keep his mind out of places he couldn't let it wander.

"I get a free concert, right?"

She grinned, turning the guitar over in her hands. She slid the strap over her shoulder, picked at the strings, fiddled with the knobs and whatever else.

"Ain't nothing free in this life, sugar." She said it, and then she sang it, noodling into one of her father's songs. The relaxation in her was nearly immediate. She softened, eased and lost herself in the song.

It was...enchanting, which wasn't a word he'd ever used or probably even thought, but she was mesmerizing. Like a fairy. With a dark, mischievous side. She moved seamlessly from one of her father's raucous drinking songs to one of her newer ones—the one she'd had some success with right before her bodyguard had been killed.

Sadness crept into her features, but not fear. She moved into a song it took him a few chords to recognize as one of the few duets she'd ever recorded with her father.

She stopped abruptly halfway through the song. "Hell, I miss that old bastard," she muttered.

That was a sadness he understood, and it made it impossible not to try and soothe. "My father wasn't a bastard, but I know the feeling."

"Not around?"

"He was murdered."

"Well. Hell, Zach, ease me into it, why don't you. Murdered?"

Zach raised a shoulder, no idea what prompted him to share that information. Soothing was one thing, but volunteering details was another. Yet, they piled up and fell out of him at a rapid rate. "Risks of the job. He was in the ATF, investigating a dangerous group. A long time ago. It happens."

"It shouldn't."

Why that simple phrase touched him was more than beyond him. He'd had a lot of time to deal with his father's death, accepting it and the unfairness of life. He'd investigated his father's murder, made sure it didn't consume him like it had his brother. He'd come to terms. He'd dealt.

But it shouldn't happen. No. It shouldn't.

"Is that why you do this?" she asked, still fiddling with the guitar.

"No, but it's why I went into the FBI. I'm assuming your father is why you went into music."

"Yes and no." She played a few more chords, humming with them. "He pushed me into it, and I did it partly for him, because of him, but I did it partly because it's in me. The chords, the stories." She pinned him with a look. "I'd say the same is true for you. Your father's life pushed you into law enforcement, but there's something in you that fits it."

"You'd be surprised," he muttered. "What sounds good for dinner?"

"Whatever," she said, taking a seat at the table and still playing random chords on the guitar like they were a link to safety or comfort. "I guess you didn't find anything with Stacy."

"No. Cam's working on the identity of who's here, and I'll have a report tonight, along with some video I'll want you to take a look at."

"Who's here. Why do you say it like that?"

"Like what?"

"Like who's behind this and who's here might be two separate people."

Her worry was back. She gripped the guitar hard enough her knuckles went white.

Part of him wanted to lie to her, but that wouldn't do. That was letting himself get too emotionally invested. "It's certainly a possibility."

"So there could be two of them?"

"No, I'd say it's more likely someone hired."

"Like…a hit man?"

"Or just someone sent to find you. A lot of shady things are for hire out there. It'd be a way to ferret out your exact location without getting caught themselves."

"So even if you catch *this* guy, it won't mean you can connect them to the stalker?"

"Doesn't mean we can't, either. We don't know yet."

She rubbed at her chest. "I thought I knew how to deal with the unknown. You never know what's going to succeed or fail in music. I thought I would always just go with the flow, but if I hear you say we don't know one more time I might have a mental breakdown."

"Hey, this is the place for mental breakdowns. Creepy ghost town facade and all the modern comforts of home."

She laughed, but it faded quickly. "Home. Do you have a home?"

"I assume you mean home in the symbolic sense, not just four walls and a roof?"

"Bingo, cowboy."

Zach thought it over. Home to him was his grandparents' ranch they'd moved to after Dad had died. He'd never made one for himself. This place he was standing in meant something to him—bigger than just a building or a job—but it still wasn't...*home.*

"I guess not. I haven't really had anything permanent as an adult."

"I never had anything permanent."

"Do you ever wonder how you ended up the nomadic singer and your brother the stay-in-one-place Texas Ranger?"

"Are you just like your siblings?" she asked with one of her haughty raised eyebrows.

He sobered at the thought of his brother in a mental hospital, working through all the things that had twisted inside him since their father's death.

"You and Hilly seem similar," she offered as if *she* was trying to comfort *him.*

"Hilly and I only met just this year. I mean, I remember her when she was a baby, but—"

"She said the same thing. Add that to the murdered father and I'd say you've got quite the story, Zach."

"She was kidnapped by the men who murdered my father and raised under a different name."

Daisy blinked and opened her eyes wide. "I'm sorry, *what?*"

He shrugged, uncomfortable both with the subject and his idiocy for discussing it. "It's complicated, but... Well, it's all figured out now."

"Does the calm, bland, bored facade ever get exhausting?"

He didn't care for how easily she saw through him, so he did his best to raise his eyebrow condescendingly like she did. "Who says it's a facade?"

Her mouth quirked up at one side. "You weren't so bland or bored when I was rifling through your stuff."

Even now the reminder made his jaw clench, even more so when she full-on grinned and pointed at him. "See? Underneath all that robot exterior, there is a man with a living, breathing heart." She looked down at the guitar in her lap and frowned. "Believe it or not, Zach, I'd rather have a man with a heart on this case over a robot. That's why I was going through your things. I wanted to see if I could get to that heart."

"Believe it or not, Daisy, I do what I have to do to keep you safe. Robot exterior included."

She pursed her lips together as if she didn't quite believe him. As if she took it as some kind of challenge.

Lucky for him, he was not a man to back down from a challenge any more than he was a man to lose one.

# Chapter Six

Zach was dead. Lifeless blue eyes. Blood everywhere. Just like Tom.

She turned to run, to save herself, but she tripped over another body and gasped out a sob.

Vaughn. *No.*

But even as she wanted to reach out, grab her brother, breathe some life into him, she ran. She didn't know how, because her brain was telling her running into the dark was all wrong.

But she kept running into the black. Into the danger.

"Daisy. Come on. Daisy." Zach's voice. But he was dead.

Still, she ran.

"Daisy. Stop."

She tried to speak, but she couldn't. She could only run and Zach swore viciously, the words echoing in the dark around her.

"Let's try this."

Why was Zach's voice haunting her? He was dead. She was alone. No, not alone. Running from…from who?

"Lucy?"

It wasn't immediate, but slowly she realized it wasn't

totally pitch-black. A light glowed in the corner of the room. She smelled paint, not blood. And she could feel Zach there. Somehow she knew it was him, touching her shoulders.

"Lucy, wake up now."

Zach. Calling her by her real name. He was sitting on her bed. Twisted so that his hands gripped her shoulders, strong but gentle. He was using her real name and she was in Wyoming.

Dreaming.

"A dream," she muttered out loud.

"There now," he said, relief evident in his tone as he ran a hand down her spine. Weird to be comforted in a strange room with a man she barely knew touching her through the thin cotton of her pajamas.

But she *was* comforted. Enough that when he began to pull away she only leaned into him, ignoring the way his body stiffened. "You were dead. Vaughn was dead. And all I did was run."

His body softened against hers, and though his arms were more hesitant than take-control, he wrapped them around her.

A comfort hug. Maybe even a pity hug.

She didn't even care. She'd take comfort from pity if she had to. The images of that dream stuck with her, flashed in her head every time she closed her eyes. She focused on Zach instead.

He was warm with all that surprisingly hard muscle. He smelled like soap. She closed her eyes and breathed in deeply. She soaked in the warmth and rested her cheek against his chest, listening to his heartbeat.

A steady thump. As comforting as the rest of him.

She could feel his breath flutter the hair against her

cheek. When he breathed, her body moved with the movement of his. Underneath her hands, splayed against his broad, strong back, she could feel his warmth seep into her.

What would all that muscle feel like without the Henley between her palms and his skin? To have her cheek pressed against his naked chest instead of soft cotton? She'd seen him with his shirt off. She could almost picture it.

So much better than the other pictures in her head.

It took her a minute to realize the buzz along her skin was pure, unadulterated *want*. And another minute to roll her eyes at herself for being so stupid and simple. She straightened, pulling away from him. His arms easily fell off her and he got to his feet quickly.

It amused her, soothed her a little, to think he might feel that bolt of attraction, too. What would be going on in that regimented brain of his?

"How about some ice cream?" he asked.

It made her smile. "Is sugar your answer to all of life's crises?"

"I wouldn't say sugar is the answer. Sugar is the… comfort. Besides, you had Hilly buy you some low-cal fruit atrocity kind. I figured you might be up for it."

"I'll take it." She slid out of bed. She'd learned her lesson that first night and had worn something acceptable to be seen in to bed.

Though, if she was honest with herself, she now regretted it. Thinking about an attraction to Zach, and what could be done about it when they were stuck in a weird safe house together, was far better than thinking about her dream or even her reality.

So she tried to decide what kind of come-on Zach

Simmons, part robot, would respond to as she followed him out into the kitchen area. Nothing subtle. Being attracted to her was probably *very* against his personal code.

What would it take to make him break his personal code? She remembered the way he'd uncomfortably stared at the ceiling when her pajama top had been too revealing the other night. It made her laugh, which felt immeasurably good after the terror of that dream.

"Something funny?" he asked, looking at her with some concern—like maybe she'd lost it a little bit.

Maybe she had, but she figured she had a right to. "Just trying to think of things that make me laugh instead of cry or scream."

He frowned at that as he pulled out the carton of the frozen yogurt she'd requested. "I've been thinking about someone being here, and about what we can do."

"Thinking? Don't you sleep?"

He shrugged as he scooped the yogurt into the bowl. None for him, she noted. "When necessary."

When necessary. She had no idea why this man was such an endearing piece of work. Maybe it was because most of the men she knew pretended to have feelings when they really didn't, and Zach was the exact opposite.

"I think the leak is through your manager. It's what makes the most sense anyway. So we pull on that." He set the bowl in front of her, then went back to the freezer and pulled out a different carton.

She stared at the sad bowl of low-fat fro-yo that sometimes tasted good enough to make her forget about ice cream. Less so when someone wanted her dead or traumatized or whatever.

"What does *pull on that* mean in cop speak?"

Zach slid into the chair next to her. The bowl of dark chocolate, full-fat ice cream he set in front of him made Daisy's mouth water.

"Send a few fake messages, see which ones get followed. I haven't worked it all out yet, but that's my thought, and I'll need you to do it."

"You want me to lie to Stacy?" Daisy asked, her stomach turning at the thought. She was a decent enough liar, what with being a performer and storyteller and all, but the idea of lying to Stacy to prove someone she loved and trusted was part of this nightmare...

Yeah, fro-yo wasn't going to cut it.

"They don't have to be lies. They just have to be leads. Something we can follow and see who picks it up."

It still sounded like lying to her, and it sounded complicated. So she reached over and scooped a lump of his ice cream onto her spoon. Their eyes met as she slid the ice cream into her mouth.

It might have been funny if he didn't watch her so intently. If that direct eye contact didn't make her entire body simply *ignite*.

Under that stuffy exterior, Zach was proving to be a very, *very* dangerous variable in this whole mess. Because along with stalkers she didn't know what to do with, murder that scared her to her bones, and guilt that nearly ate her alive, she was still herself. Daisy Delaney. Lucy Cooper.

And she'd never been very good at pulling her hand out of the fire.

ZACH NEEDED MORE SLEEP. Clearly, a lack of it was the cause of his current lack of control.

Not that he'd done anything aside from watch her steal a scoop of his ice cream. And open her mouth around the spoon. And swallow the bite.

Then nearly spontaneously combust.

He looked down at his ice cream and tried to remember anything about what they were talking about. Anything that wasn't her mouth, or the way she'd leaned against him in the bedroom earlier.

He should cut himself a little slack. He was only human after all, and she was beautiful and engaging. She had that *thing* that made people want to watch her, get wrapped up in her orbit.

Maybe he'd like to be immune, but he was hardly a failure just because he wasn't.

But the one and only time he'd let his emotions get the best of him people had almost died. People he cared about. People he loved.

He couldn't—wouldn't—make that mistake again. No matter how tempting Daisy Delaney proved herself to be.

All his paperwork was in his room, as was his laptop. He had no shields to wield against her, and he had to think of this as its own version of war, even if it was only a war within himself.

"You could reach out and say you're willing to do a few shows," he said. He might not have his papers, but that didn't mean they couldn't talk through some options. When in doubt, focus on the task at hand. When tempted beyond reason, focus on what needed to be done.

"That'd go through my agent—the actual booking."

"Does your agent know you're here?"

"No. Not unless Stacy told him. I doubt she would have. She would have just told him I'm unavailable."

Maybe. The problem was, you never really knew what people told other people, and who those other people knew. There were so many fraying threads and he felt frayed himself. By her, by all this close proximity and by this damn dogged frustration that the case wasn't as simple as he might have thought.

"What about Jordan?"

She slumped, toying with her spoon. It amazed him the way she'd been mostly blamed and decimated in the press for being the instigator, the uncaring party, while Jordan poured his brokenhearted soul into his next album.

But every time Zach mentioned her ex-husband, she had a visceral reaction—in ways she didn't with other topics.

It twisted something inside him he refused to investigate, because emotions had to stay out of this. No more guitars. No more going into her room if she was having a nightmare. No more...

She took another bite of his ice cream.

Zach kept his gaze on his bowl. No more ice cream sharing, that was for sure.

"What *about* Jordan?" she asked, giving up on his ice cream and her own frozen yogurt.

"Would anyone have told him where you are? Does he have any connections to your manager or your agent?"

"He got a new agent when we got divorced. We never shared managers, though I guess Stacy was friends with

Doug. In the way two people who sometimes have to work together are friends. She knows… Look, she was there through the divorce. She wouldn't give Jordan any information, and I don't think my agent is a fan of Jordan's after the way he was treated."

*Or maybe he's not a fan of yours.* Zach made a mental note to look deeper into the agent. "I don't really understand the ins and outs of your…what would you call it, staff?"

"Team," she replied emphatically.

"Let's go over the hierarchy there."

She shook her head. "I think I'd rather go back to bed and take my chances with nightmares."

"That's fine."

She eyed him. "It's fine, but be prepared to do it in the morning?"

Zach shrugged. "I have to dig, Daisy."

"No, you actually don't. You just have to keep me alive."

It was true. He hadn't been hired to investigate. He'd been hired to protect. But that didn't mean he couldn't or wouldn't do both. He needed her cooperation, though, which meant he had to go about getting the information a little more…strategically.

"You're right," he said, doing his best to sound like he agreed with her. "I don't have to poke into this or you. It's not my job." He stood, taking both bowls and walking them to the sink. "I'll butt out."

He turned, ready to head to his room. If temper flared a little unsteadily inside him, he snuffed it out. Emotions weren't his job, either.

Not investigating wasn't an option for him. But if she didn't want him digging into it, he'd do it without her.

She stood and stepped very deliberately into his path to his door. She cocked her head, studying him in a way that reminded him of being back in the FBI Academy—constantly being sized up for his effectiveness and usefulness.

He hadn't minded it then. He'd been full of the utter certainty that he belonged there, and that he was more than fit to be an agent.

Now, here, it scraped along his skin, unearthing too many insecurities he'd much rather pretend didn't exist.

"You did one hell of a job undercover, didn't you?" she murmured.

He was surprised at the change in topic, but he didn't let any of his unaffected poise loosen. "I suppose."

"The problem now is that you aren't undercover, so when you put on the act it doesn't add up."

"I don't follow."

"You don't care if investigating isn't your job. You're going to do it anyway. You don't let things go, and one way or another, you'll keep poking at me. There's something under this…" She waved her fingers in front of his face. "I'd say I don't understand it, but I do. I may not have grown up with my brother, but I recognize that cop thing—truth and justice above all else."

"So I remind you of your brother," he said flatly.

Her mouth curved, slowly, and with way too much enjoyment. The move so slow and fluid and mesmerizing he watched it the entire time—from mouth quirk to full-on sultry smile.

"No, I can't say you do, Zach."

He wanted to shift, to clear his throat, to do *anything* that might loosen all this tightening inside him. But it would be a giveaway.

*Would it matter if you gave it away to her? She isn't your enemy.*

"But what I will say is that if it wasn't for my brother, I wouldn't believe in the existence of good men with an inner sense of right and wrong and a deep-seated need to protect."

He held still. He met her gaze with all the blankness he'd honed in his time undercover. You made eye contact, but you didn't fall into it. You didn't get conned into believing you could act so well that someone saw what you wanted them to see.

So you gave nothing. You counted eyelashes or recited the Gettysburg Address. You didn't think over your plan, and you didn't give in to trying to analyze their thoughts or feelings—because thoughts and feelings couldn't be analyzed or predicted. They couldn't be patterned out.

Which, unfortunately for Daisy, was why he thought this whole thing was *personal*. Someone who wanted to hurt her for something more than her music or her reputation.

"So you can keep poking at me, and I'll keep poking back, but that doesn't mean I don't understand what you're trying to do. It doesn't mean I don't want you to do it. It means I'm frustrated and you're an easy target. All that rational, factual thought is the rock I can toss my irrational emotion against. And isn't that nice?" She patted his chest. "Maybe we'll even get to the point where we enjoy all the...poking."

He might have risen to the bait. Laughed or coughed or fidgeted at her overt sexual innuendo, but he knew that no matter how smart or worried she was, she was hoping whoever was terrorizing her was a random stranger and his investigation was pointless.

He couldn't let her think that by getting distracted over her purposeful baiting. Because it didn't fit, in Zach's mind. Whoever was doing this *knew* her, and it was very possible Daisy trusted them.

He didn't have to tell her that. He didn't have to poke at her—in any way, shape or form—though he might have wanted to rest his hand over hers...*just* to offer a little comfort.

Instead, he held still. Unearthly still. He kept her gaze, until that easy, flirtatious grin of hers faded.

"Your safety is my primary concern. However, it isn't my job or my aim to cause you undue emotional distress. Therefore, if my method of questioning is problematic, I can easily engage in other avenues of investigation that don't require any..." He desperately wanted to say *poking*. Wanted to smile and make a joke and ease all of that sudden tension out of her.

But maybe it would be better for everyone if there was a little tension that kept them from being too friendly.

"That don't require any avenues of questioning that might feel problematic on either of our ends."

She blinked. "Primary concern," she echoed. "Emotional distress." She shook her head and took a few steps back. The look she gave him was one of suspicion.

Since it wasn't his job to have her *trust* him, such a look couldn't bother him at all.

At all.

"Yeah, I bet you were a *hell* of an undercover agent, Zach," she muttered, but she was gathering herself. She was sharpening all those tools she so effectively used against him—an insightfulness, a confidence that she lashed against him like a weapon. "But news flash. You aren't anymore. Keeping me safe, investigating this thing, you can be regular old Zach Simmons, and it'll be more than enough."

*How would that ever be enough?*

But he couldn't say that to anyone, could he? So he merely nodded. "Noted."

Then, with absolutely no warning, she stepped forward again. She reached out and touched his face—a gentle caress one might bestow upon a loved one. She held his gaze with a softness he couldn't possibly understand.

Then she did the most incomprehensible thing he had ever in his entire life witnessed or been on the receiving end of.

She lifted onto her toes and pressed her mouth to his.

## Chapter Seven

It was wrong. Daisy had been well aware of that when she'd done it. Maybe she'd even done it because it was wrong.

But he'd laid down a challenge—whether he'd known it or not. He'd tried to turn off his personality, his entire essence. He'd tried to use the robot on her and that had only spurred her on to try to short-circuit the robot.

She would never again be told she didn't really mean anything, that she could be easily moved aside and closed off in a room without a second thought. No. Not for a man she'd been married to and not for a man who'd been tasked to keep her safe.

She would show *him*. She would get to him. And what better way to do that than to use her mouth?

His initial stiffness was shock, obviously, but when she didn't move away, changing the angle of the kiss instead, something shuddered through him.

Or maybe something broke inside him. *She'd* broken something inside him, because he didn't just return the kiss—he started one of his own.

Not a challenge or some kind of attempt at one-upmanship. This was…just a kiss, except *just* didn't fit.

It was real. It was Zach. As if a few days under the

same roof could make you feel things for one another. But his mouth crushed against hers like they were long-time lovers, used to the act of kissing enough to have it practiced, but not so much that it didn't *melt*. A warmth that soaked into her bloodstream like alcohol, and a sudden weakness she knew she'd regret at some point.

But there was nothing to regret now with Zach's mouth on hers, his arms drawing her closer so that she was pressed against all that muscle and restraint.

Except there was nothing *restrained* about how he kissed her. It wasn't the explosion of lust she might have expected or understood. It was deeper, stronger. The kind of thing that didn't rock you for a moment, but forever. A kiss she'd remember *forever*.

Maybe because that thought horrified her enough to startle, Zach broke the kiss. He pulled his mouth from hers and nudged her back and away from him. Her knees might have been weak, but she saw a flicker of *something* in his gaze. Some kind of complicated emotion that disappeared before she could get a handle on what he might be feeling.

He fixed her with a gaze, and spoke with utter certainty. "This will never happen again."

She absolutely *hated* the way he said *never*, as if he were God himself and got to decree the way the world worked, the way *she* worked. So she smiled, all razor-edged sweetness. "Zach, don't you know better than to challenge me by now?"

"Do you want to *die*?" he asked with such a bald-faced certainty her insides turned to ice. Immediately.

"I don't know how a kiss is going to kill me," she managed, though she sounded shaken. She *was* shaken.

Even with the ice of fear shifting everything inside her, her limbs felt like jelly.

She could still feel Zach's mouth on hers. He'd wanted her, or was it all another act? A mask?

No, he might be blank now but there was a kind of anger radiating off him. One she didn't understand because it didn't show up in any of the ways anger usually did. No yelling, no fisted hands, no threats or furious gazes. Not even the condescending sigh Jordan had perfected during their short marriage.

"You are in a dangerous situation," Zach said, and his robot voice was back but it frayed along the edges. "Potentially a life-or-death situation, and you're adding…" He sucked in a breath and then slowly let it out. His next words were no more inflected, but they were softer. "Listen to me, as someone who's been in a few life-or-death situations myself. The only thing that happens when you tangle emotion into dangerous situations is catastrophe."

"It was just a kiss," she managed, wincing at how petulant she sounded.

"It was a complication. One you can't afford."

That stoked some of her irritation back to high. She lifted her chin. "Don't presume to tell me what I can afford."

"Are you always so damn difficult?" he demanded, the slightest hint of a snap to his tone.

"If you have to ask that, you haven't been paying attention."

He rolled his eyes, and she had no doubt she was about to be dismissed. Part of her wanted to throw a fit, make herself into more of a nuisance, but her surroundings were too much of a reminder of where her fits and anger and *feelings* had gotten her.

A failed marriage *everyone* got to have a say about. Isolation and loneliness that went deep because so many people were willing to believe the worst about her and think she deserved whatever she got.

Kissing Zach had been a mistake. She felt suddenly sick to her stomach at how much of one. Thoughtless reaction, plain and simple. When would she ever learn?

*Mr. Control kissed you, too.*

And since when did someone else's culpability matter to her end result?

His phone chimed in his pocket and he pulled it out, clicking a few things. His expression never changed.

But it was something like four in the morning. Who would be contacting him at four in the morning? Only someone with bad news, and since she was his current bad news...

"What is it? Is someone hurt? Is Vaughn—"

He shook his head sharply. "My cousin's wife had her baby."

Zach didn't exactly strike her as the type to receive middle of the night texts about a cousin's baby. "Don't lie to me about—"

He held out the phone and on the screen there was a picture of a red-faced baby wrapped in pink. Underneath the picture the text read:

Amelia Delaney Carson, 6 lbs 11 oz, 20 inches. Batten down the hatches.

It was *odd* that a pang could wallop her out of nowhere, when she'd convinced herself that she wasn't even sure she ever wanted babies. That she and Jordan had come to the conclusion they wouldn't rush bringing *children* into the world when they had careers to build.

But her career had already been built, and what she hadn't admitted to herself was that she'd been hoping marriage would be a transition of sorts.

What she'd really wanted out of marrying Jordan had been a home. Full of music and joy and no tours or constant travel. Stability. She'd dreamed of a peaceful life. Not one devoid of performing, of being *Daisy Delaney*, but one where she got to choose when and where to play the role.

Daisy *was* her, and she loved that persona. But it had been her whole childhood and adolescence, and the older she got the more she felt like she'd earned a little time for Lucy Cooper.

Why she thought she'd be able to build that with Jordan, in that distant future he always talked about, was beyond her.

She handed the phone back to Zach. "Cute," she managed to offer. "I like the middle name."

He made an odd face. "It's the mother's last name," he offered, studying her warily.

"A Wyoming Delaney?"

He very nearly *winced*, which she couldn't quite figure though she decided to enjoy his discomfort anyhow.

"Do you know… Wyoming Delaneys?" he asked, failing at the odd casual tone he was clearly trying to maintain. "I mean, Daisy Delaney is a stage name, though."

He seemed a little too desperate to believe it was true. "Yes and no. Why does that weird you out? Worried we're related or something?"

"Carsons and Delaneys aren't related."

"I thought you were a Simmons."

He shook his head. "Anyway. We should try to get some sleep. We'll come up with some things to tell your manager and see if we can't get a lead."

She studied him. There was something weird about his discomfort over the shared name. Since she was more than a little irritated with him, she wanted to poke at it. "My legal name might be Cooper, but my stage name was my grandmother's name before she got married. Daisy Delaney. She was born in some little town in Wyoming. Something with a B? I'd have to text Vaughn. He'd remember. Oh, wait, it was Bent. That's why Daddy always used to wear his hell bound and whiskey *bent* shirt."

"Jesus," Zach muttered, looking so downright horrified she nearly laughed.

"What?"

"Nothing," he said far too quickly.

"Are we close to there?"

"Kind of. Anyway. Bed."

"Maybe I'm related to your cousin's wife. Wouldn't that be a trip?"

"Yeah, a real trip. Goodnight, Daisy."

Zach was tired of women. Particularly opinionated ones. Pretty ones. Infuriating ones.

He really didn't need his sister to add to it, but here she was, trying to tell him what to do.

"You have to come," she said, her tone something closer to a demand than he was used to hearing from her. Still, it seemed every day Hilly got a little more confident, a little more situated to life outside the isolated cabin she'd been raised in.

He stood on the dilapidated porch of the building that usually gave him such satisfaction. After last night, not much did.

"I'm in the middle of a job. I can't just leave Daisy here locked up."

"You could bring her with you."

"Yes, that's genius. She has some kind of stalker snooping around Bent, so why don't I bring her to the hospital and potentially endanger every member of our family." *And hers, apparently.* Because Daisy Delaney's grandmother was from Bent, Wyoming.

He didn't believe in all the metaphysical nonsense spouted by his cousins—that the old Carson and Delaney feud had morphed into Carson and Delaney unions that were meant to be.

He didn't believe in meant-to-be.

"Are you okay?" Hilly asked.

The fact she even suspected he wasn't caused him to straighten, to remind himself he didn't have *time* for stupid worries over stupid nonsense.

"Of course I am. But this job is important. And we haven't found any solid leads. I can't leave her here, and I can't risk taking her somewhere else."

"She can't possibly still want to be cooped up in there."

"Hilly."

"I know. I know. Safety. Precautions. But…" She looked up at the dilapidated building. "How long can you feasibly keep her in this place? It's going to start to feel like a prison."

"Better a prison than a coffin, Hilly."

"Why do you have to be so *practical*?" she muttered.

"I believe it's in the job description."

"But your life isn't a job description, Zach. And neither is Daisy's."

Zach didn't know what other string of words would get her to stop this incessant merry-go-round. The flash of something far off in the distance put him on instant alert—enough so he no longer cared about words. Only getting her away.

"We're going to walk to your car. Once you're inside, I want you to call…" He racked his brain for someone who'd be able to help. Cam needed to watch the other guy. Most of his family was at the hospital with Laurel and Grady. Getting the cops involved would be tricky.

"What is it?" Hilly asked, her voice perfectly even, her expression still mildly bemused. But she understood.

He took her by the arm and they strolled back to her car. "Someone's out there."

He needed to make it look like he wasn't living here. He needed to lead the man somewhere else. And somehow, he had to get in contact with Daisy so she knew to stay the hell put.

"I couldn't have been followed. Cam's sitting on the guy." Hilly smiled brightly up at him as if he'd just said something hilarious.

"Well, then we have a second guy."

"All right. I'll call Cam and head his way. We'll come up with something. Don't worry about me. Keep Daisy safe."

"I don't want him following you."

"You can't want him staying here."

It was too close. Too dangerous. Unless he played all his cards right. "Go. Call Cam."

For the first time her cheerful, just-talking-to-my-brother facade faded. "I don't trust that tone, Zach."

"Trust the man who used to be the FBI agent, Hilly."

She hesitated, which cut like a knife even though she had every reason to doubt him. Hadn't Cam almost died because Zach had been too concerned about his brother's welfare to take care of business?

"I don't want you doing something on your own."

"I won't be on my own. I'll have you calling Cam for backup. But I need you to go on the chance he does follow you." Zach was counting on the former, but if it was the latter…

Well, he had a plan for that, too.

Eliminate the threat.

"Drive to Cam. Okay?"

"All right. Only because I can't think of a better plan. Do not do anything on your own, do you hear me?"

"I hear you."

She sighed disgustedly, presumably because she knew *I hear you* didn't mean he agreed to anything she'd said.

She reached out and took his hand, giving it a squeeze. She forced a smile for the sake of whoever might be watching them. "Just be careful. Because if you get hurt, I will have to end you." Her smile was a little more genuine at the end, and she turned and got in her car.

Zach couldn't spare a glance for the house, for Daisy. He stood exactly where he was and watched Hilly's car disappear.

Whoever was out there didn't follow.

Zach didn't head back into the house, and he didn't check on his sidearm or his phone, though he wanted to grab for both.

He didn't know who or what was out there. Someone could be watching, it could be a vehicle left behind as someone approached town on foot. It could be his eyes playing tricks on him, but the back of his neck prickled with foreboding.

Which meant taking every precaution necessary.

He walked down the dusty side of the road as if he didn't have a care in the world. He even forced himself to whistle. He turned down the alley, keeping up the act of unhurried unflappability.

Once he was around the corner, he sprang into action. He'd been keeping his car hidden since that first day, just so no one happened upon it. He popped open the hidden keypad on the garage hidden in the building. He entered his code and moved as quickly as he could, watching for anyone who might pop into view. There was the possibility whoever had been watching was trying to break in the house, but that would take time.

He'd use it.

He drove the car out and closed up the hidden garage. When he pulled out of the alley, there was no sign of anyone trying to get into the house. So he took the opposite way out of his town at a slow pace.

He caught the flash again. This time he could tell it was a small compact car half hidden behind one of the far buildings in town. He couldn't make out the license plate—number or state—only the black fender glinting in the sun.

He kept his breathing in check and drove on, remaining slow and unhurried and looking around, pretending to smile as he enjoyed the beautiful Wyoming landscape.

When the car didn't follow after several minutes, he swore.

They suspected someone besides him was in town, and that was absolutely no good. So he swerved off the road and ditched the car. Since he wasn't being followed, he didn't worry about hiding it. Time was more important.

He ran back the way he'd driven, darting behind buildings on the opposite side of the car and mostly tried to keep out of sight of the car.

He stopped for a second on the opposite side of the road as the house Daisy was in. He stilled and listened.

No motor running, so they wouldn't have a head start on him. But he didn't like their proximity to Daisy. Because he couldn't even be sure someone was in the car. Whoever was watching could have gotten out to start snooping around the house.

He wished he knew how long they'd been there and that he could be sure the car had followed Hilly. Because if they hadn't followed Hilly, they had more information than Zach liked to consider.

Either way, Daisy had a leak and now she was in the direct line of fire.

Which meant Zach had to move. And fast.

# *Chapter Eight*

Daisy impatiently tapped her fingers against the countertop. Where the hell was Zach? It wasn't like him to stay holed up in his room with the door closed, though she supposed he might have had a break in the case or was making phone calls he didn't want her to hear.

Since *she'd* been holed up in her room strumming on the guitar he'd gifted her, it was more than possible he'd left. She couldn't fathom him doing that without telling her, no matter how irritated he was about the kiss.

She smiled to herself. Oh, the moments after hadn't been any fun, but the in-the-moment had been something she'd willingly relive over and over again.

It was the first time in a while where she'd felt...normal. Like Lucy Cooper, or even the Daisy Delaney from years ago when she hadn't had anything normal outside the music. There had been a simplicity in that time.

Of course, there was nothing simple about being either version of herself now, and certainly nothing simple about the aftermath of kissing Zach.

Still, she gave herself permission, here alone, to enjoy the memory of something she could pretend was simple.

The slight creaking sound brought Daisy out of the

memory. She tried to shake away the wiggle of alarm. It was an old house—no matter what improvements Zach had made—of course it creaked.

But in the silence that ensued after, her heart beat harder until it became such a loud thud she knew she wouldn't hear the sound again even if it came from one of the walls.

She looked around, trying to remind herself she was safe. Locked and hidden away.

*But someone knows you're nearby.*

She marched over to Zach's door. She wouldn't tell him about the noise. She'd just insist he give her some information. Maybe she'd come on to him. Whatever it took so that he was around and making her feel safe.

She knocked. Harder than she should have.

He didn't answer.

Alarm went from a wiggle to a flop. She grabbed the knob and tried to turn it.

Locked.

The wiggles and flops turned into chains that restricted her breathing. "Zach," she croaked. She cursed herself for the nerves, the fear, the total ineffectuality of her voice. She breathed in and out, tried to use some of her old tricks for the occasional bout of stage fright.

"Zach," she repeated, louder this time but more firm. Surely, he'd hear it through the door.

Nothing happened.

She wouldn't panic. Couldn't. She pounded against the door for a while, but then she heard something else—a creak, a moan. Something definitely from the outside. Which meant if there was someone other than Zach outside, they could definitely hear the banging.

But he had to be in there. He was probably trying

to teach her a lesson or something. Scare her so she'd stop hitting on him. Yes, that had to be what this was.

Well, wouldn't he be sorry? She marched to the kitchen, ignoring the way her hands shook and her heart beat a painful, panicked cadence. She grabbed a butter knife and marched back to the door and got to work.

It took longer than she would have preferred as she had to wiggle the knife in the slot, then between the door and the frame. She was shaking at this point. Where *was* he? She thought for sure he'd pop out if she started trying to break into his room. Surely, he'd only locked it to keep her out.

The door finally gave and she swung it open. "Aha!" she yelled, pointing the knife into the room.

But it was empty. She moved around, searching every corner and under the bed, even the closet.

No one. Not a soul.

"Oh, God. God. Zach, if this is some kind of joke or test, I'm over it."

But he didn't appear, and those *noises* kept coming from outside this hellhole disguised as a safe place.

Panic bubbled through her, paralyzing her limbs and squeezing her throat. Her heart beat too hard in her ears and she desperately wanted to scream.

But she'd been through worse than being left alone. Seeing Tom dead was the worst. No one had a right to make it worse than that.

Then something rustled in the closet. Something big. But she'd just been in that closet. How could—

A figure stepped out and she screamed before her brain could accept that it was Zach *miraculously* showing up out of nowhere.

"How did you do that?" she whispered. He wasn't *magic*. There had to be an explanation.

"Tunnel. Shoes."

"Tunnel shoes? What does that—"

"Get some damn shoes, Daisy. Purse if it's handy. Ten seconds." Without further explanation he strode out of the room and into the kitchen. She scurried after him but stopped short when he pulled two guns out of the top cabinet above the refrigerator while she only stared.

Until he gave her a sharp look.

"Move," he ordered, snapping her out of her shock.

She had to move. Questions were clearly for later when he wasn't grabbing extra guns. She hurried into her room, shoved her feet into tennis shoes and looked around for her purse. Ten seconds. She had way less than ten seconds now and she was not the neatest person on the planet.

But she caught a glimpse of the strap under her duffel bag and lunged for it, tugged it from the haphazardly spilled-out bag and ran back to Zach. He held a laptop across one arm while he typed with the other, a huge backpack strapped over his back.

When she peered over his shoulder at the screen of the laptop—which had been full of pictures of the ghost town they were in—he snapped it shut. "The front is the best option. Follow me. *Stick* to me. Do whatever I say without question and everything will be fine. If something happens to me, no matter what, you run. You understand me?"

"Zach. I don't understand *anything*."

"We'll figure it out when we're safe." He took her by the hand and pulled her to the door.

Even as a million questions assaulted her, she understood Zach Simmons was not a man to overreact. If he wanted them to run, she'd run.

He pulled her out into the first room that looked as dilapidated as the outside. "Lock the locks," he said, handing her a key chain with three keys on it. They weren't labeled, but she didn't ask which one was for which—she just kept trying till she had all three locks locked.

He was peering at something through the wall. "See that picture frame on the ground?"

She looked down. There was an old, battered picture frame with a ripped piece of paper inside. "Uh, yeah."

"Hang it up on that rusty nail."

She did so, and blinked as it perfectly hid the key holes from view.

"Now, come hold my hand again."

She wanted to make a joke about hitting on her, but the words stuck in her throat. They were running, and that couldn't be good.

So she slid her hand into his and let him pull her along. He slid out the door, and she followed suit. He didn't lock this door, instead left a rusty-looking padlock hanging off the handle.

His gaze swept everywhere, and then he gave her hand a squeeze. "Now we run. I'm not going to be able to hold your hand without whacking you with the bag, so you'll just have to follow me. If you can't keep up—"

"I'll keep up." No matter what.

He nodded firmly. "Good. All right. Let's go."

He moved across the dusty road, and it was only then she realized he held the closed laptop in one hand and a gun in another. Still, she followed him, behind one building, and then through the alley between two even worse-off ones. Caved-in roofs, fire-scorched walls.

He reached the small ramshackle building at the end of the road and handed off his laptop to her while hanging on to his gun. With his free hand, he reached through a jagged break in the glass window of the back door, fiddling around until the door popped open.

He slowly pulled his arm out, and then opened the door just as slowly. It took her a minute to realize he was trying to mitigate the squeaking noise that echoed through the air as he opened it. When the opening was big enough, he gestured her inside.

Trying not to balk at the dark, or the spiderwebs, she stepped into the dank, smelly interior. Zach followed suit, pulling the door closed behind him before fishing a flashlight out of his pack.

He led her farther inside and she kept waiting for the nice part—the part that had been redone inside all the dilapidation.

But this one had no new pretty interior. No working kitchen. It was abandoned and untouched for years. "We're going to stay…here?"

Zach had put his pack on the floor and took his laptop back without a word. She was sure he wasn't paying any attention to her at all as he worked furiously.

When he finally spoke, she fairly jumped with adrenaline.

"*You're* going to stay here. I'm going to figure out what the hell is going on. You know how to shoot a gun?"

She blinked at the weapon he held out to her. Thanks to her brother, she'd had a few shooting lessons. She was even somewhat familiar with the kind Zach held out to her.

She nodded, and he handed the gun over.

"Anyone comes in here that isn't me or Cam, or doesn't say the code word *feud*, you shoot. Understood?"

She swallowed, and managed another nod.

With that, he got to his feet, strapped multiple guns to his person and strode for the door.

ZACH SLID OUT of the building, making sure no one was around to see him. It was painful to leave Daisy wide-eyed, scared and alone, but he couldn't hole up with her and hope the guys went away.

He'd learned, over and over again, that waiting in safety often caused more problems than it solved. Sometimes you had to act to keep people safe.

He hurried behind the buildings, keeping his body out of sight from as many angles as possible.

From what he'd been able to tell with his video surveillance, there were two men. One who'd been poking around the house, and the one who'd stayed in the car—presumably ready to drive off.

It turned his stomach to think he was ready to drive off with Daisy. Even more so that *two* men were here.

It had to be the manager leaking information to someone, whether maliciously or with an accidental slip to someone. He didn't have time to figure out the pattern, though. He had to stop those men before they had a chance to hurt Daisy.

He moved into a position where he knew he'd be able to see the driver of the car with minimal chance of being detected. He angled his body and his head, and managed to make out the car.

The driver was no longer in it, so Zach moved forward—until he saw both of them standing in front of the car, discussing something.

They had their backs to him, so descriptions would be hard, but it wouldn't matter. These weren't the masterminds trying to get to Daisy. Everything about them screamed hired muscle.

Which, again, in Zach's mind meant not a crazed fan, but someone with a personal connection. And someone with money.

Like Jordan Jones.

And if it *was* Jordan, he'd have endless funds to keep sending people just like this.

Zach moved back behind the building. Taking them out was only a temporary solution. More would come in their place. But if he could question them, he might be able to glean enough information to make the connection.

The only question was how to immobilize the threat of two men with guns who wanted the woman he was trying to protect.

He needed them to separate, and even then it would be risky. But it would be a risk he'd have to take. He examined the building he was hiding in. He needed somewhere he could isolate one man, without getting trapped by both.

He needed to get one headed in the other direction. He pulled the phone out of his pocket and pulled up the app he used to control security in the safe house. He poked around until he came up with an idea.

Have the back door alarm on the house go off. Once they started heading over, he'd make enough noise they'd feel like one of them had to come his way.

It took a few minutes—first the men headed toward the siren, alert and with hands on their weapons. Zach kicked at a board next to him, the hard crack of impact then splitting wood loud enough to hopefully get one's attention.

He couldn't watch for their approach. Instead, he had to stay hidden and hope he was about to fight only one man.

He saw the gun first and immediately moved. He kicked the gun out of the man's hand. The man leaped forward, but Zach had better vision and grabbed him from behind. Zach managed to get an arm around the other man's throat. Zach was taller, though the man was thicker.

"Who are you?" Zach demanded in a whisper as the man struggled against him.

The man didn't answer, and no one came to his rescue. Elsewhere, the alarm continued to beep, which was a good sound cover for the fight Zach was about to have here.

"Who sent you?" Zach asked, tightening his grip and dodging the man's attempt at backward blows.

The response was only a raspy laugh as he twisted and nearly got free before Zach strengthened the choke hold.

They grappled, but Zach kept the choke hold. He asked a few more questions, knowing he wouldn't get an answer but hoping he might get *something* that would ID the man or give him a hint.

Over the sound of his alarm, he heard something else. Something just as shrill. Sirens in the distance. It was unlikely to be coincidence that sirens were closing in on the empty ghost town. Cam and Hilly must have decided to call the cops. Hell. Zach sure hoped they'd sent more than one because he had no doubt that the other guy was now on his way back.

"You think the cops will help you? Or her, for that matter?" the man rasped.

"Guess we'll find out." Zach managed to jerk one of the man's arms behind his back, but it left him open to an elbow to the gut. His grip loosened just enough to have the man slip out of his grasp.

The man tried to take off on a run, but Zach lunged, tackling him to the ground. They tussled, landing blows. The other man was bigger but Zach figured he could hold his own until the cop car actually got here.

The next blow rattled his cage pretty good, so much so that he thought he heard a dog bark and growl.

But then there really was a dog, growling and leaping. Zach had a moment of fear before he recognized the dog, and it jumped at his attacker. The man screamed, and Zach managed to wrangle himself free of his grasp.

A cop appeared, gun held and trained on the man on the ground—the man who was clearly scared to death as the dog growled and snapped right next to his face.

"Free. Sit," Hilly's voice called.

The dog stopped growling, planted its butt on the ground and wagged its tail before turning his head toward Zach.

"Thanks for the assist." He gave the dog a rubdown, wincing only a little as his face throbbed. He glanced up as Hilly, who'd given her dog the command, came running. He was a little surprised when she kneeled next to him instead of her dog, Free.

"You're bleeding." She ran her hands over him as if checking for breaks or injuries, but he held her off.

"It's just a split lip. Please tell me Cam is here and you didn't try to white knight this yourself."

"It wasn't just me. I had Free. Plus the cops."

Zach swore, but he couldn't muster up much heat behind it. "I've got to get to Daisy." He glanced at the Bent County Sheriff's Deputy who was handcuffing the man who'd attacked him. Deputy Keenland efficiently did the job and read the man his rights.

"There's another one," Zach offered.

"We've already got him," the cop replied.

"I want to talk to them."

Keenland gave him a raised eyebrow. "We'll be transporting them to the station, where *we'll* question them. We'll take your report, as well."

He didn't have time for this. He glanced at Hilly. He didn't even have to ask. She nodded.

"Far building on this side," he said quietly so Keenland, busy pulling the arrested man to his feet, wouldn't hear.

He'd have to entrust Daisy to Hilly while he took care of this. It bugged him, but it had to be done. He pulled out his phone and turned off the security so Hilly could get into his apps, and then handed her his phone and his keys to the building.

"Be careful." They all needed to be a hell of a lot more careful.

## Chapter Nine

Back in the fake nice house inside an outside dilapidated old house, Daisy couldn't find any of the calm or resignation she'd had in the days leading up to this.

Someone had found her here. Maybe they hadn't gotten to her, but they'd tried. In this place that was supposed to be a secret from everyone.

Which meant someone she loved and trusted was either out to hurt her, or close enough to someone who did to slip the information to them.

God, her head hurt. Almost as much as her heart as she went back over so many interactions.

Could Jaime be the bad link? She didn't know him that well, even if he was Vaughn's brother-in-law. He could have told anyone, couldn't he? But Zach trusted him. Surely, Zach would know...

Except Zach wanted her to believe Stacy was responsible. Could her manager harbor some secret hatred of her? Was it as simple, and heartbreaking, as that?

Or was it deeper, messier, more complicated?

Worse than the riot of emotions and fear and questions pulsing inside her, Cam and Hilly were being obnoxiously and carefully tight-lipped about what exactly had gone down after Zach had left her in the abandoned house.

Only that he'd be back soon to explain everything. But time kept ticking by as she sat at the table, watching Cam and Hilly.

Which was actually the worst part of all. Hilly and Cam moved around the kitchen and common area acting like the perfect unit. A team. A partnership.

She felt so completely alone. The separation of the past few years echoing inside her like she'd been emptied out—of love and companionship and hope. There was only fear left.

She rested her forehead on the table and did everything she could to keep from crying. No one was going to see her cry. Nope. She would brazen through this like she'd brazened through everything else in her life.

Maybe she was tired. Maybe she wanted *normal* for a little bit. Maybe she wanted a little house in the country and a nice man she could trust to build a family with.

And maybe Daisy Delaney and Lucy Cooper weren't made for those things.

Her phone chimed and she nearly fell over lunging for it on the table. Surely, it would have to be Zach. Everyone else had stopped calling and texting and surely—

She stared at the text message from Jordan. The first sentence made her uneasy, so she clicked it to read the whole thing.

I just heard you're out of town for a few days. Someone told me it might be rehab. I really hope you get the help you need. Peace to you.

Peace. Peace? Anger surged through her, and while some of it was prompted by all the fear and things out of her control right now, most of it was prompted by that *ridiculous* send-off.

Peace to you.

*Peace.*

She'd like to give him some peace. Right up his—

"Is everything okay?" Hilly asked gently, but with concern.

Daisy smiled up at Hilly, though she knew it came out too sharp when Hilly took a step back. "Yes. Just a text from an annoying...acquaintance. Apparently, the rumor is I'm in rehab." She wanted to bash the phone into little bits. "How do I respond to a text like that?"

"You don't," Cam said in a voice that reminded Daisy of Zach.

Where *was* he?

"You'll have to excuse me if I don't want the world thinking I'm in rehab. My reputation is in enough tatters."

"But if people think you're in rehab, they won't think you're *here*," Cam replied reasonably. Apparently, whatever trouble had happened had cured him of his slight starstruck nature. Or he was just getting used to her.

Daisy couldn't say she cared for it. "Whoever is after me already knows I'm here."

"But the fewer people who know, the fewer people your stalker can use to get to you."

It was so reasonable, really unarguable, and now she wanted to bash her phone against Cam. She was tired of being reasonable in all these impossible situations. She wanted to act out. She wanted to *fight*.

She wanted to tell Jordan to go jump off a cliff. Or

write a song about lighting all his prized possessions on fire.

One by one.

But Cam was right and Daisy's only choice was sitting here, not responding, not reacting. Just waiting for someone to succeed in hurting her.

"Did Zach okay the cell phone use?" Cam asked, his attempt at casual almost fooling her into thinking it was a generic question.

"Yes, thank you very much. He did something to my phone to block traces or something. But he wanted me to be able to email my agent from my phone and a few other things. I don't know. Techie stuff. But it's perfectly Zach-approved." Because everything in her life now suddenly was Zach-approved.

Except herself. She could still rile him up to the best of her ability. Assuming he came back and didn't abandon her here.

She closed her eyes, nearly giving in to tears again. Oh, God. That was what she was *really* afraid of. Not that someone had found her, but now that they had, Zach would leave her.

Hilly pushed a mug and plate at her.

"Drink some tea. And eat some cookies."

"You Simmonses and your ungodly sugar addiction." An unexpected lump formed in her throat. "Where *is* he?" she asked, hating that the emotion leaked out in her scratchy voice.

Hilly patted her hand. "He's safe, and he'll be back soon."

She didn't need him to come back. She didn't *need* Zach Simmons. At *all*. He was a bodyguard, more or less.

But God, she wanted him here pushing cookies on

her, telling her what the next step would be, and reassuring her he'd take care of everything.

"FIVE MINUTES."

The deputy didn't move, didn't even spare him another condescending look. "We've taken your statement, Mr. Simmons. You're free to leave."

"I need five minutes. Hell, I'll settle for two questions."

"Simmons."

Zach turned around and sighed. Detective Thomas Hart stood, plain-clothed, in the doorway, and Zach knew he was officially done.

He followed Hart out of the building and into the parking lot. It was dark now, and Zach wasn't all that sure he knew how much time had passed. But he hadn't gotten what he wanted yet.

"There has to be something you can tell me."

"There isn't. Sincerely. He's not giving us answers."

"I want a name, Hart. A last known address."

Hart turned, crossed his arms over his chest. "You won't get one. Stop harassing the deputies. Go home. Deal with whatever business you've got going down on your own."

"I can hack into your system in five seconds flat," Zach returned disgustedly.

Hart held up a finger. "First, I didn't hear you say that. Second, be my guest. Because I can't give you that information. Zach, you know as well as I do, whatever they're after—however it connects to your mysterious business—these guys are hired muscle. They're not going to tell you or me anything you really need to know."

"But you'll investigate who's paying them."

"If it's pertinent."

Zach swore. "You're killing me."

"Hey, it's my day off. You're killing *me*. The only reason McCarthy called me is because he knows we're friends. You better know you'd have been arrested for disturbing the peace and interfering with an ongoing investigation if not for your connection to Laurel."

"I'm a Carson. Doesn't that mean your kind is always tossing mine in jail for no reason?"

"No real Carson was ever an FBI agent, that I can tell you." At Zach's scowl, Hart grinned. "Want to go play darts? Take your mind off it so you can work out the knots?"

Part of him did. It was something he and Hart did often when Hart was stuck on a difficult case and needed something mindless to do. Maybe it was exactly what Zach needed. Maybe he could get somewhere on this whole mess if he just separated himself from it for an hour or so.

But Daisy was back there and something had to be done. She couldn't spend the night there. Even with these two guys locked up, more would be coming. More might be on their way, and while Zach could lock them up in that building pretty tightly—anything could happen.

Damn, but he needed some answers. "Can't. Got work."

Hart nodded. "I'll leave you to it. Just leave the deputies alone."

"You going to pass along whatever information you find out?"

"Night, Simmons," Hart said, opening his car door and sliding inside.

Zach sighed but he dug his keys out of his pocket and walked to his car. He *could* keep pounding at the deputies, but they wouldn't budge. And the more he did, the less chance he had of sneaking some information out of Hart later.

He didn't have time for either, though. Action was required. Cam wouldn't approve of the idea forming, which meant Zach would need to be especially sneaky.

He drove back to the house, watching for tails, taking the long, winding way and missing the turn off the highway twice and doubling back before he was satisfied no one had followed him.

He parked his car back in the hidden garage, though he wondered if it should be easier to access.

Well, not if he could get his plan wheels turning ASAP. He'd need to get rid of Cam and Hilly first.

He texted Cam that he was disengaging the security from the outside and coming in. Then set about to do just that. When he finally stepped into the common room, Daisy jumped to her feet from where she'd been seated at the table.

"Oh, my God. You're hurt."

It startled him, the gentleness mixed with horror in her tone. Like she cared. She even rushed over to him and touched the corner of his mouth, which was a little swollen from the elbow he'd gotten there.

"I'm all right," he managed, his voice rusty. "Just a tussle." He ste/pped away from her too soft and too comforting hand. "I need to get the security systems—"

"I'll get them running," Cam said, holding up Zach's phone. He went to work and Zach turned back to Daisy.

She looked pale. Exhausted.

"Thanks for your help, guys, but you should head home," he said to Cam and Hilly, keeping his voice neutral. "We'll all sleep and reassess in the morning."

Cam studied him, and Zach did his best to look blank. Cam couldn't know what he was planning. Not yet.

Cam handed the phone back and looked at Hilly. Something passed between them because Hilly nodded.

He'd never been able to communicate with anyone like that, and he wasn't sure if that was just the nature of never having been in a serious, committed relationship the way Cam and Hilly were, or some fundamental lack inside him.

Right now was certainly not the time to wonder about it.

"Show him the text message," Hilly said, laying a comforting arm on Daisy's shoulder before she passed by.

"What text message?" Zach demanded.

Daisy glared at Hilly, but Hilly and Cam slid out the door, clearly leaving Zach to handle it.

"Daisy. Show me the text message."

"It's nothing," she replied, but she picked up her phone, tapped a few things, then slid it his way. "Just Jordan being oh so very concerned."

Zach read the text message, scowled at the screen. "Where did he hear you're out of town?"

"Zach. I'm sure any number of people are saying that about me since I'm not home or touring or anything else."

But Zach didn't like it. For a wide variety of reasons he'd parse later, once he got his plan off the ground.

"Does Jordan often contact you?" If this was out of the blue, it would give some credence to Jordan being involved.

"Not often. But a text message isn't out of the norm. Things like 'I'll be at x place on y date. I'd appreciate a lack of a scene.'"

Zach's mouth quirked, though he knew it shouldn't amuse him. "Let me guess. You caused three scenes."

She grinned at him, eyes sparkling. "How'd you know?" But she sighed. "I don't let anyone tell me what to do, most especially some *man* who thinks he has a right when he gave that up. And trust me, I want nothing more right now than to show up at his door drunk as a skunk. But I've learned not to give in to the impulse *every* time—because half the time it's a publicity stunt. He wants a scene from me so he can play the injured, horrified party."

A publicity stunt. "He wants to ruin you," Zach said flatly.

"He wants to make me look bad. I think there's a difference." She shrugged jerkily, pretending it didn't bother her. But he could see the bother written all over her tense posture and the way she gripped the phone. "The more I think about it, the more I can't pin him for this. He's too much of a narcissist. Nothing he does to me is trying to ruin me—he's just trying to help himself."

But a dead ex-wife could be helping himself, making him a sympathetic figure once again. And being a narcissist didn't make a person less likely to exact revenge if they felt they'd been wronged.

But he didn't need to argue with her or convince her of anything. Jordan was as high on his suspect list as her manager. He'd find out the truth and she'd deal with that one truth, instead of all the possible ones.

Weary, aching body, Zach lowered himself into one of the kitchen chairs. "Then your response should really stick it to him."

She looked at him sideways. "Go on."

"Verbal judo."

"What's verbal judo?"

"I won't give you the whole spiel, but basically it's a way of talking to people that neutralizes a confrontation."

"I don't want to neutralize it. I want to explode it."

"I know you do, sweetheart, but we're trying to give you a low profile."

"He expects me to explode. Shouldn't I give him what he expects? Just to keep him from looking too deeply into things? Or maybe even salvage some piece of my reputation."

Since Zach didn't believe Jordan was all that ignorant of what was going on, he merely shrugged. "You could, but he knows *something* is up. This is his version of fishing. So instead of giving him the reaction he wants, drive him crazy. Just say thank you for your concern. It gives away nothing. It harbors no ill will, and it admits no guilt. It'll probably eat him alive since he was clearly fishing for a reaction. It's *that* part I don't trust." Or the timing—reaching out just as two people trying to get to Daisy were taken into custody by police. Pretending he thought she was in rehab. Zach wasn't going to trust any coincidences.

Daisy stared at her phone, contemplating. "You really think a response like that will eat him alive?"

"He knows you, right? Understands that you'll do

the opposite of what he says, understands that any attempt at peace offerings will end with fiery explosions. So you don't give him what he wants."

"You make me sound like a shrew."

"No, I'm trying to make him sound like a jerk. Because he could just not. He doesn't need to reach out, doesn't need to poke at you. He could leave you be. But he's trying to piss you off, and so much worse than that, he's doing it under the guise of concern. Don't give him the satisfaction, because trust me, he's getting some satisfaction over that or he wouldn't be reaching out."

She contemplated her phone, then she picked it up and began to type.

Thanks for your concern!

She angled the screen toward him. "Is the exclamation point too much?"

"I think it works."

"Send," she said, tapping the screen with a flourish. Then she sighed and stared at him, her eyes lingering on the split lip and the bruising along his jaw. "I thought you were convinced Stacy was the culprit."

"I'm not convinced anyone is the culprit. We're looking into any possibility." And they needed to find them sooner or later.

He opened his mouth to tell her the rest of his plan, but she moved over to him and touched the part of his cheek that throbbed. Everything inside him tangled tight. She studied him, her fingers gently tracing over the line of his bruised jaw.

If he'd known what to expect, he might have been able to ward it off, but her gentleness undid him. Magnetized him. He couldn't remember anyone… His life was taking care of people, finding out the truth, saving people when he could.

No one ever asked if it was a burden. He'd never wanted or needed anyone to comfort that burden. It was his.

But Daisy's touching him was being given a gift so perfect, he wouldn't have ever thought to ask for it.

She slid into his lap. He held himself still, even if with all that stillness a desperate desire rioted inside him. It wasn't like the other night, her trying to prove something, defuse something, or just forget her circumstances.

There was a sweetness to this, even as close as their bodies were. Even though she made him want her in totally unsweet ways. She was gentle. She was…caring.

"Daisy." It was a croak, but he didn't have the wherewithal to feel self-conscious over it.

"Shh." She pressed her mouth to the side of his, just the gentlest, featherlight brush. "Someone's got to kiss the hurts."

A breath shuddered out of him, and even though it was the absolute last thing he should do, he closed his eyes as she gently kissed all along the bruised portion of his jaw. It was comfort and it was relief, and he had no business taking it from her when he was supposed to be keeping her safe.

*Safe.* Not hiding in abandoned buildings while someone prowled *this close* to being able to touch her.

No, today he'd failed. There could be no more failure. Only action.

"We don't have time for this." Which wasn't precisely true, but it was a hell of an excuse because his willpower was fading.

"I think we have all the time in the world," she replied, pressing her mouth to his neck.

His vision nearly grayed before he had a chance to slide her off his lap. Dear *Lord*, was that hard to do. Harder to let her go after he nudged her back a pace.

But he did it. "Pack your bags, Daisy. We're headed to Nashville."

## Chapter Ten

Daisy felt…strange leaving Zach's little ghost town. Like she'd miss it. Which was crazy since she'd been cooped up in that odd little house, not out enjoying the blue sky or mountains in the distance or in this very early morning's case, the stars out in their full and utter splendor.

Nothing had been good here, and yet she didn't want to leave. Didn't want to face Nashville or the people she knew, even with Zach at her side.

Because facing meant accepting that someone she loved and trusted might be behind this.

But she didn't argue. She'd packed her bags like Zach had said. She'd enjoyed maybe thirty seconds of looking up at the vast universe before Zach had whisked her into his car and started the drive.

He'd said nothing about the kisses, but for a few moments he'd relaxed under her.

She smiled a little to herself. Well, not *all* of him had relaxed.

She gave him a sideways glance. He was driving to some tiny independent airport in some other part of middle of nowhere Wyoming, where they'd fly in some tiny little plane to a few airports all the way to Nashville.

Nashville. It wasn't home, because she didn't particularly feel like she *had* a home. She'd been touring since she could remember, only ever staying with Mom and Vaughn for bits of time. As an adult she'd bought a house in Nashville, but she'd sold it when she'd married Jordan.

Then they'd sold the house they'd bought together. The house she'd thought she'd start a family in, have a life in.

"You know, I don't have a place in Nashville," she said after a while.

"I do."

"You have a place in Nashville?" she asked incredulously. She'd believed he knew enough people to take a small plane halfway across the country, but this seemed far-fetched. And yet, she trusted him implicitly, regardless of what seemed believable.

"I know people, Daisy. I found us a safe place to stay."

She kept staring at him, because something about the split lip and the bruising on his face—even with the dark five-o'clock shadow over it, made her feel safe even when she knew she wasn't.

But Zach would protect her, no matter the circumstances. Even though she knew Zach was human and that anyone could reach her if they wanted to badly enough, someone would fight to keep her safe.

Take blows. Give blows. For her.

He could push her away or insist they didn't have time for more than a kiss, but one thing Daisy knew was that Zach wasn't stoic or unaffected. He was worried about getting emotionally invested because he was already on his way to getting emotionally invested.

The thought cheered her enough that she dozed off, until Zack was waking her up with her real name again.

"Sleepy you doesn't seem to answer to the name Daisy," he offered, his voice rough with exhaustion and yet his lips curved.

"That's because Daisy Delaney doesn't sleep."

"All right, Lucy Cooper. You should really talk to that alter ego of yours, because you could both use some sleep." He gave her head a little pat and then slid out of the car.

She could only stare after him. There was something about the way he said her given name. It slithered through her, a not totally comfortable sensation—because it was too big for her skin. It made her heart swell and her eyes sting.

Jordan had never called her Lucy, even after she'd asked him to. Because she didn't want to be Daisy Delaney to her *family*. She'd wanted to separate it all out.

He hadn't understood.

Zach probably didn't, either, but he still used her name as though it didn't matter what he called her— she was the same. Not two identities fighting for space.

He opened the passenger door and looked at her expectantly. Right. She was supposed to get out of the car, not get teary over something so stupid.

"You haven't told me what the plan is," she said as she got out of the car. He grabbed their bags out of the trunk and headed for a squat little building.

The sun had risen, but it was still pearly morning light. And they had a long way to go to reach Nashville.

"Well, first we'll go see your manager."

"Together?"

He shrugged. "I don't see why not. You'll just tell people I'm your bodyguard." He walked to the building and knocked on the door, waiting for an answer.

When a scrawny young man answered he greeted Zach by name. They conversed for a while and then the young man led them through the office and out a back door.

Daisy felt like she was in a dream, complete with a tiny plane that made her breath catch in her lungs.

It didn't look safe, and if she'd been with anyone else she would have brought that up. But Zach would never take risks with her—that she knew. It had to be safe.

For a tin can hurtling through the air.

Zach helped her up the stairs and gave her hand a squeeze. "Afraid of flying?" he asked empathetically.

"I never have been before." She looked around the tiny cabin. "This plane changes things a bit."

"We'll be fine," Zach assured, and she was sure he thought so. She wasn't sure he was *right*, but she knew he believed he was. He gestured her into a seat and she took it.

"Why are we going to Nashville now?" Because if he talked maybe she wouldn't feel like running screaming in the opposite direction.

"Waiting isn't working. We're not getting closer—the trouble is only getting closer to you, and without warning. So we go straight to the potential leaks. We ferret them out. Besides, this way the rehab rumor can't really get anywhere."

He fastened her seat belt for her as she only stared, that same feeling from before—heart too big, skin too small.

She swallowed, trying to sound normal or just *feel* normal. "What does my reputation matter?"

"Jordan's taken enough from you, and whoever is behind this has taken even more. You don't need to give them pieces of yourself, too. We'll nip any rumors in the bud, and we'll find out the leak in one fell swoop."

No one had ever cared how many pieces she gave of herself as long as they got the pieces they wanted. Even Vaughn, for all his wonderful qualities, didn't understand her enough to do more than worry about her safety.

So she did the only thing she could think to do. She leaned over and pressed her mouth to his. She smiled against his mouth when he kissed her back for a brief second, then stiffened and eased her away.

Oh, he wanted her. She thought he might even *like* her.

"You have to stop doing that," he said sternly.

She did it again, a loud smack of a kiss, though this time he was tight-lipped and less than amused. Still, she flashed him a grin. "Stop kissing me back and maybe I will."

He didn't say anything to that, which made her settle back into her seat with a smile.

SHUTTLING ON AND off planes was exhausting. Add to that, Zach hadn't slept—not since the night before. But he drove the rental car through Nashville to the little farmhouse on the outskirts that one of his law-enforcement friends used as a safe house sometimes.

Daisy would like it. Somehow, he knew that. But he hadn't been prepared for the way her delight wound through him.

"Oh, my God! A chicken coop!" She jumped out of the car and practically ran over to it, leaning over the fence around the fancy little coop. He didn't see any chickens, but the gray, cloudy skies were spitting out a drizzle that probably kept the animals safe in shelter.

"My friend says there's a list of chores to do, if you're into that kind of thing."

She turned to look at him, eyes bright and smile wide. "Are you kidding? Why didn't you bring me *here* in the first place?"

He didn't mention it had been because he didn't trust most of the people in Nashville who had any connection to her. Her brother had wanted to isolate her to keep her safe.

It had been a failure of a plan—Zach's own fault for not seeing the holes in it.

He shook that failure off—had to until the job was done—and focused on the new plan. "I do want you to give your manager a call and tell her you're planning to come into town tomorrow. Tell her you want a meeting, morning or afternoon doesn't matter, but I want her to believe you're leaving in the evening."

"And are we keeping this meeting?"

"Of course."

Some of her simple joy over the chicken coop had faded, but she didn't argue with him. Didn't try to tell him for the hundredth time she trusted her manager. "And…"

She trailed off, turning her gaze back to the chickens. He couldn't read her feelings from just looking at her back, but he thought the fact she was hiding her face told him enough to gather she wasn't happy.

"You'll be with me, right?"

"You aren't going any damn where without me, sweetheart."

She turned to face him again, lifting an eyebrow. "Oh, is that so?"

"You're not going to be contrary over that. Not right now. This isn't about telling you what to do. It's about keeping you safe. You and me are stuck like glue."

She smiled sweetly—which should have been his first clue something was off, but he was dead on his feet. She sauntered over to him, chickens forgotten. She reached out, and he stiffened against the touch.

Not that it didn't shudder through him as she playfully walked her fingers up his chest. He tried to ward it off, but then she looked up at him under her lashes.

"Like glue? What kind of sleeping arrangements were you planning?"

Lust jolted through him so painfully it was a wonder he didn't simply keel over. Or give up…and in to her.

But he wouldn't. He couldn't. "We'll figure it out inside."

"Don't tease, Zach." She sighed heavily, lifting her palm to his cheek.

It was becoming too common, too much of a want to have her hands on him. Still, he couldn't move away, could barely hold himself back from leaning in.

"You need to sleep."

"Safety first."

She looked around the picturesque yard. Even with the drizzle falling, it had a cheerful quality to it. Green grass and trees, red chicken coop and barn bright and clean in the rain. It was the complete opposite to the desolate, decaying place he'd originally taken her to.

It felt weirdly symbolic, only he was so exhausted he didn't know if it was good or bad. He ushered her inside with the security information his friend had given him. He dropped the bags and followed the email instructions on how to set all the security measures for the house.

"What's the best way for you to contact your manager?"

She eyed him and he had to stifle a yawn, had to work to keep his eyes open.

"In this case I think I need to call her. She'll have to rearrange her schedule to see me, I'm sure. She'll do it, she'll want to, but we'll have to work out the when and where."

"Okay. So, you'll call and set up a meeting." There'd be security to worry about—if the leak was through her manager's office someone would know she was there and accessible. "Make sure she doesn't think you're getting in until tomorrow, and thinks you're leaving in the evening."

"Okay. Can I make the call in private or do you need to listen in and make sure I'm a good girl who follows instructions?"

He wasn't sure what that edge in her tone meant, so he decided to ignore it. He made sure he held her gaze and didn't yawn, though one was threatening. "I trust you. There are three bedrooms. Take your pick. Just give me the time when you're done."

She stared back at him for a few humming seconds. He thought about the plane, when she'd kissed him and he'd been stupid enough to kiss her back.

Even though intellectually he knew it was a failure

to get emotionally tangled with her, that it would put her in danger—put them both in danger. Though he never forgot how emotional entanglements had almost caused so much loss last year, he couldn't seem to help it. He was emotionally tangled.

There had to be a way to block it off. He knew better now. His brother was in a psych ward, and Cam had almost died. There were *costs* to an emotional connection—and if he couldn't control the connection, he had to find a way to keep it separate and make sure it didn't affect the case.

He knew better now, didn't he?

"You don't want a play-by-play of the phone conversation?" she asked after a while.

"The time will be enough." Because he had to focus on the facts of the case. The facts of what it would take to protect her. Enough with his precious patterns and trying to understand her and her life. He had to focus on the *facts*.

If he'd pulled her into more danger by bringing her closer to her stalker, he didn't have room for anything else.

Eventually, she nodded, picked her bag up off the floor and went in search of a room.

Zach picked up his own bag and pulled out his laptop. Before he could fall into blissful sleep, he had some work to do.

He'd been ignoring his phone for most of their travel, so he turned that on while he booted up his computer.

He winced a little at the ping of voice mails and text messages that sounded a few times. Yeah, a couple of people weren't too happy with him or his disappearing act.

He didn't bother to read all the text messages, and he deleted all the voice mails from Cam and Hilly without listening. But he did read the most recent text from Cam.

I hope you know what you're doing, because your client—you know, the guy paying us—isn't too thrilled.

So Zach would tell Daisy to contact her brother. Except, Texas Ranger or not, couldn't the leak just as easily be on his side?

Better to play this out as secretly as possible even if it meant everyone was angry with him. He'd suffer some ire to keep Daisy as safe as possible, and the best way to keep her safe was to test every possible leak in isolation.

So he didn't respond to Cam's text and went ahead and turned his phone back off. He needed to outline a plan for tomorrow.

He'd just close his eyes for a second, recalibrate the plan in his head, then formalize his hazy plan into something more specific. More…something.

The next thing he knew, someone was taking his hand. "Come on, sleeping beauty," an amused voice said.

He couldn't manage to open his eyes, but he was being pulled to his feet. Everything seemed kind of dim and ethereal. It was probably a dream.

Yes, he was dreaming Daisy was taking him somewhere, nudging him onto a bed, slipping the shoes off his feet.

He really was dreaming that after a while she curled up next to him, rested her hand on his heart and brushed a kiss across his cheek.

And since it was a dream, he let himself relax into it. Place his hand over hers, pull her curled-up body closer to his and settle into sleep.

## Chapter Eleven

Daisy wasn't sure what had compelled her to climb into bed next to Zach. He wouldn't appreciate it when he woke up. But she felt safer here, nuzzled against him, than anywhere else.

Talking to Stacy had been an exercise in torture. Daisy had wanted to tell her friend what was really going on, but all she'd been able to do was vaguely apologize for disappearing and ask for a private meeting, trying to evade Stacy's questions.

Daisy had read into every pause, every question. Was Stacy the one who wished her harm? Would this meeting end up being dangerous?

She swallowed against the lump in her throat and focused on Zach. The room was dark, but the glow from a bedside alarm clock was enough to illuminate his profile. His big hand over hers.

She felt safe with Zach. Not just the whole "in danger with a security expert and former FBI watching out for her" thing, but she felt…emotionally safe with him. Which was weird. She didn't even feel that with Vaughn or Mom. She felt she had to be careful around them, because she'd followed Dad's footsteps and they hadn't approved—even if they loved her, they didn't *understand* her.

She wasn't certain Zach did, but so far it sure felt that way.

*And are you really stupid enough to think Zach is different than all the other men who've let you down?*

Except she'd watched Vaughn fall in love with Nat, the way it had changed him, opened him up. Because good men existed. She just hadn't known very many. Could she really trust her own judgment that Zach was one?

Except here she was, curled up next to him, with none of those doubts that had plagued her with Jordan. She didn't doubt Zach. He didn't make her doubt.

She let that thought lull her to sleep. She awoke to the jerk of his body, and male cursing. She smiled before she opened her eyes.

"I fell asleep?" Zach demanded, practically leaping out of bed. Outrage and sleep roughened his voice. She tried to press her lips together so she didn't smile, but she failed.

"Yeah, you were kind of dead on your feet, cowboy," she offered, stretching lazily out across the bed. "I tried to wake you up, but the best I could do was half drag you to bed. I didn't take advantage, though."

He gave her a sidelong look. Then he scrubbed his hands over his face and through his hair. Her fingers itched to do the same to him, but she knew Zach would want to right himself and get to work.

And quite frankly her heart felt a little soft, waking up next to him—even with the jolting wake-up. She wanted to wake up next to someone, which was not a new dream or fantasy, but it was certainly even more compelling with Zach as that someone.

"The meeting with Stacy is at eleven."

"Eleven?" He swore again. "That only gives us about two hours to plan."

"Why don't you take a shower, and I'll make coffee. Then we can plan." She didn't wait for him to agree before she slid out of bed and started heading for the door. She needed…coffee. A little coffee would steady the fluttering feeling in her chest.

But Zach stopped her on her way out of the room—a hand to her shoulder—and the flutters only intensified. He stared at her for the longest time, his big, warm hand resting on her shoulder.

"Whoever is behind this is to blame for all of this, no matter how much you trusted them. You can worry about a lot of things, but I don't want you worrying that you should have seen through someone."

Was that the fear inside her? Maybe. Whether it was Jordan or Stacy, part of her didn't want to know because then it would mean she was wrong.

At least she already knew she'd been wrong about Jordan. Maybe she'd root for him to be the person who wanted to hurt her. Except… She'd still feel stupid. Stupid and guilty that Tom's life was lost over something so…

Zach pushed a strand of hair behind her ear, sending a shiver of delight down her spine. Easing some of that band around her lungs. "We're going to figure this out, and then you're going to go back to your life. I promise you that." He smiled, a small smile meant to reassure. "And now that I've actually slept, no one's about to stop me. Trust that."

"I do," she whispered with far too much emotion. More than the situation warranted. But he made her feel all of these things she'd yearned to feel her whole life. Only music had ever soothed her this way. Only music had ever given her a sense she deserved anything good.

Here was Zach. Good, through and through, standing there close enough to lean in to. To kiss. To believe in.

She cleared her throat and took a step away. It was one thing to kiss him when she was trying to get under his skin, or forget about all the things wrong with her life right now. It was another thing to kiss him when she felt this...vulnerable.

She turned and walked carefully to the kitchen. She poked around until she found the coffee. It was percolating when Zach came out of the room they'd slept in, showered and dressed. He'd shaved, and the ends of his hair glistened.

It wasn't just lust that slammed through her. It was something so much bigger than that. Which kept her from acting on the lust.

She cleared her throat and placed a full mug on the table. "Here. I already put way too much sugar in it."

"Thanks." He placed his laptop on the table, slid into the seat, drank a careful sip. "Perfect."

And this was far, far too domestic for her poor heart right now. "So what's the plan?" she asked, sliding into her own chair. She was in danger. *That* was a far more important, and in weird, emotional ways, safer, topic.

"We'll go into the meeting together. You can introduce me as your bodyguard. No names, that way we don't have to remember a fake one. You'll say you're worried about your safety, but you really think your reputation needs a few shows to prove you're not in rehab."

"Like I said before, that'd go through my booking agent."

"Right. We'll stick with a version of the truth. You don't trust anyone else right now. You want to work everything out through her. Maybe it's not her normal job, but she could do it with extenuating circumstances."

"I guess so."

"As casually as you can, mention how you're heading home tonight."

"I don't have a home," she returned, too soft to make a joke out of it.

But Zach didn't even blink. "Who knows that?"

"What do you mean?" she asked, trying to drink enough coffee to chase away her dogged exhaustion.

"I mean, who of our suspects would say you don't have a home? Would Jordan?"

"He'd probably say Nashville. Home is where the career is, after all."

"And Stacy?"

"She'd probably say Texas, since my brother is there and she knows how much he and his family mean to me."

"Okay, there's a flight to Austin at ten. So you mention you're heading home tonight. If Stacy or someone on her staff heads to Texas, we know it's her. If Jordan starts poking around Nashville, we have reason to suspect him."

"How will you know all that stuff?"

Zach shrugged, tapping away at his computer. "It's not a perfect plan, but I've got eyes and I've got ears." He took another sip of his coffee then looked over the table at her. "All you have to do is talk to her like you normally would."

"But I don't feel normal. The phone was bad enough. In person?"

"In person, I'll be there. I can talk for you if need be. Just pretend to be overwrought."

"I'm never overwrought," she replied, but she kind of wished she could be. Wished she could hand it all over to Zach and let him take care of it. But no matter what he'd said about it not being her fault, this was her doing. Some choice in her life had made this happen.

She had to stand on her own two feet to fight it.

ZACH KNEW DAISY was nervous. It radiated off her as they slid out of the rental car, three blocks away from Stacy's office building.

Still, Daisy had that chin-in-the-air determination pushing her forward, and she didn't hesitate to walk with him. She didn't let those nerves overcome her.

Zach scanned the sidewalks, the buildings, the people who walked in front of them, as they zigzagged their way to the office building. He kept close to Daisy, hand always ready to grab his concealed weapon if need be.

But he didn't see or sense a tail. He'd expected to. It was a relief, though, and sadly not just for Daisy's safety. If he could scratch her manager off the suspect list he knew it would take a weight off her shoulders.

Zach opened the front door to the office building and gestured Daisy inside. For the remainder of the time he didn't walk by her side, but at her back, as most body-guards would.

They rode the elevator in silence and walked down another hall without a word. Daisy's demeanor changed from vibrating nerves to cool determination, and that struck him as sadder somehow. How hard she was trying.

He noted every name on every door or sign, would write them all down after. Investigate any possible connections. Even though he shouldn't hope for any particular outcome because it would cloud his judgment, he hoped he could prove Stacy had nothing to do with anything.

As they entered the office labeled *Starshine Management*, a young woman behind a big desk immediately jumped to her feet with a bright smile. "Ms. Delaney! It's been so long."

"Hi, Cory. I've got a meeting with Stacy."

"Of course. Of course. Oh, my gosh, though, Ms. Delaney. I have to tell you, 'Put a Hex on My Ex' is getting me through a really tough breakup. I swear. I don't know what I'd do without your music."

Daisy smiled tightly. "You'd muscle through, but isn't it great we can have music to ease our hurts?"

"That's *exactly* right. I'll get Ms. Vine now." She grinned and bopped down the hallway before disappearing into an office with the blinds of the big glass front windows closed.

Daisy's expression melted into sadness. Worry.

"I'm not familiar with 'Put a Hex on My Ex.'"

Daisy's mouth quirked as he'd hoped it might. "Not many people are. It was on my first album after I stepped away from my dad's label and people didn't quite jump on the bandwagon right away. Not my most popular hour, though I love that song. Even more now."

He'd meant to change the subject, but it brought up

an interesting point he'd overlooked. "Did you write your own music with your dad's record label?"

Daisy rubbed a hand to her temple and closed her eyes. "A few songs, I guess. Though I had cowriters with all of them, I think."

It was an angle he hadn't looked into enough—that someone who might want to hurt her might have a connection not just to her, but to her father. "Did Stacy have any connection to your dad's label?"

"Yes. She was an assistant. I convinced her to leave and take me on as her first client."

Could that be the connection? But he didn't have time to press her for more details because a woman who didn't appear much older than Daisy stepped out with the perky secretary.

"Daisy! *God.* I've been worried sick." She engulfed Daisy in a hard hug before giving Zach a lifted eyebrow perusal.

"This is my bodyguard," Daisy said with a dismissive wave. "You know how my brother worries."

Stacy slipped her arm around Daisy's waist and started leading her down the hall. "Well, as he should. I'm so sorry this is happening to you, Daisy. What can I do?"

"I was hoping you'd ask that."

They were led back to Stacy's office, big and spacious, with a large window letting in a lot of light. Stacy didn't settle in behind the giant desk, instead taking an armchair that faced the one Daisy slid into.

They opened with small talk about mutual acquaintances, and Zach didn't notice anything odd about Stacy's demeanor. She acted like a friend, a concerned one, and a businesswoman invested in her client's career.

Daisy, to her credit, seemed perfectly relaxed, but there was just *something* about the way she held her purse in her lap that kept him from believing the act.

Daisy went through everything he'd tasked her with bringing up. The potential of a small, intimate concert with lots of security to promote her next single, the fact she was going to go home to relax for a few days. Asking Stacy to keep that last part secret.

"Daisy. Are you sure everything is okay? You don't seem like yourself."

"Would you seem like yourself if you'd found your bodyguard dead?"

Stacy winced. "I'm sorry. I'm just worried." Stacy gave Zach a cursory glance. "Not just for your safety, but for *you*. Are you sure you want to do any kind of performance with this going on? We can't exactly background check fans. I know you want to promote the album, but—"

"Wait. Why do you assume the person who killed Tom is a fan?" Daisy asked, and there was dismay clear as a bell in her voice.

Stacy blinked, all wide-eyed innocence Zach didn't know whether or not to believe. "Who else would it be?"

A loud siren interrupted the conversation, making all three of them jump at the jarring blast of sound.

Stacy frowned, glancing around the office. "What terrible timing for a fire drill," she called over the blaring noise.

Stacy looked uneasy, Daisy even more so. As for Zach himself, he didn't trust the timing at all.

"We should evacuate," he offered, holding out his hand for Daisy to take. "What route would you normally take for a fire drill?"

Stacy shrugged helplessly, getting to her feet. "I… I don't remember. The stairs, obviously. Outside the doors. Then out the front? Or is it the back? Cory would know."

Zach nodded grimly, keeping his grasp on Daisy firm as he led her to the door.

Cory was standing in the middle of the office's waiting area, a bunch of things in her hands. She glanced back at them, worry and confusion replacing her previously cheerful expression. "I don't know what to grab and what to leave and—"

"I'm sure it's just a drill…" But Stacy's words trailed off as Cory pointed to the hallway outside the glass doors of the office. Smoke snaked across the floor.

"Come on," Zach ordered, pulling Daisy for the door. "Keep low. Evacuate the building in the most efficient way possible."

"Someone should call 911," Cory said, her voice trembling as Zach opened the door and pointed Stacy and Cory out, keeping Daisy next to him.

"We'll call when we're out. The most important thing is getting outside right now."

Stacy and Cory seemed totally helpless in the hallway, staring at each other as smoke continued to snake around them.

"Follow us. Form a chain," Zach ordered, keeping Daisy's hand in his as he led them toward the staircase he remembered seeing.

The stairs were worse when it came to the smoke, but there was no heat—no flame that he could see. There weren't sprinklers going off, and Zach had a bad feeling it wasn't a fire so much as a distraction. Or a diversion.

Once they made it down the stairs, the lobby was filled with even more smoke, thick and acrid.

Daisy was tugging against his grip. He looked over his shoulder, but the smoke was thick enough he could only barely make her form out behind him. He didn't want to speak, trying to avoid inhaling as much as possible. But she kept pulling, harder and jerkier.

He nearly lost his grip on her, squeezing it tighter at the last moment and giving her a jerk toward him. "Stay with me," he ordered, and began pulling her through the smoke.

"Wait," she croaked.

But they were wading through smoke in a dangerous situation and he would most assuredly not wait.

He got them out of the building, milling crowds pushing at them the minute they stepped outside. Still, he kept pulling her, weaving through the crowd and away from the building.

"Zach! I lost my hold on Stacy. We have to go back," Daisy said desperately, her voice raspy from smoke.

Zach didn't stop moving or pulling her along. "They're fine. I don't think it's a fire. Now, what the hell was that stunt? Pulling on me that way? If I'd lost my grip on you—" He glanced back when she hacked out a cough.

Tears were streaming down her face, and his heart twisted painfully in his chest at her misery.

"It was Stacy," she offered weakly. "She kept grabbing and pulling at me in the opposite direction. I think she knew a better way out."

Zach nearly stopped cold, but the smoke and chaos reminded him to keep moving—with Daisy firmly in his grasp. "She did what now?" he demanded. It was easier to move faster out here where there was less of a crowd, so he hurried.

"I'm sure it was an accident. She was panicking and thought we needed to go in the other direction. But when you pulled on me, she lost her grip. She and Cory went out the back way, I think."

Zach shook his head, pulling her toward where they'd parked the car blocks away. He wanted to protect her from the truth, but he couldn't. It wasn't his job. "That doesn't look good for Stacy, Daisy. That wasn't a fire. It was smoke bombs, or something similar. Someone was trying to create a diversion. Someone knew you were coming and wanted to get to you, and it looks like Stacy was trying to help someone do just that."

## Chapter Twelve

Daisy didn't talk on the drive home. The pretty little farmhouse didn't cheer her up at all. She went straight to the bathroom and got into a steaming-hot shower and cried herself empty.

She'd trusted Stacy with her *life*. Everything Daisy had built for herself had been done with Stacy at her side.

She wanted to believe it was panic that had made Stacy try to pull her in the opposite direction of Zach. Maybe there was some explanation, but they hadn't stuck around to get it. Maybe she could still believe Stacy only *looked* guilty accidentally. Nothing was proven. Nothing was sure.

Except Zach, who was most definitely sure Stacy was involved.

Daisy half wished someone would just *do* something to her. At least it would be over then.

But that thought made her feel sick to her stomach. She didn't want to be harmed or worse, even if it ended this waiting game. Upset and alive was better than at peace and dead.

She got dressed in comfortable pajamas even though

it was only late afternoon. Part of her wanted to sleep until this whole thing was over. It wasn't possible, but maybe for tonight while she came to grips with how bad this looked for Stacy's connection to everything.

She stepped out of the bathroom, tempted to head into the room she'd put her stuff in yesterday. Which was not the room she'd spent the night in with Zach.

Zach. She couldn't shut him out even though she wanted to. He was trying to keep her safe, determined to. It wasn't his fault she apparently had terrible judgment when it came to people. It wasn't his fault the people she thought were trustworthy and honest were potentially wishing her harm.

So she forced herself to walk back out to the pretty little living room. It reminded her of something out of *Little House on the Prairie*, but there was a sheen of cleanliness and chicness to it. It was its own little fantasy world, and boy, could she use a fantasy world.

Complete with hot protector guy standing in the kitchen cooking. No doubt making her dinner. No doubt he'd watch like a hawk to make sure she ate.

When he turned to glance at her, there was sympathy there. It made her throat close up all over again. She didn't want to cry in front of him, though, much as she knew he'd comfort her and be perfectly sweet about it.

She wanted to be strong, not to prove something to him, but to herself. That a fleeting thought about wishing someone would just end things didn't mean she particularly wanted to be ended.

"So that was more eventful than I thought it would be." She settled herself onto a stool at the counter that separated the kitchen from the dining area.

"That it was. I know it's hard for you to think Stacy could be a part of this, but we have to accept that possibility."

Daisy nodded, spinning her phone in a little circle on the counter. "Yeah. I get that."

"If it helps, I don't think she's acting alone. The hired muscle back in Wyoming, smoke bombs. She doesn't strike me as someone who could run a demanding business and plan all this. I think she might be a pawn."

"Oh, gee, more people out to get me."

"She might be an unwitting one."

"Whatever she is, she's connected." Even saying the words made Daisy's stomach twist. She kept thinking she'd accepted it, and if she accepted it she could move forward.

Except she couldn't accept it. Even when Zach was calm and reasonable.

"All evidence points to yes." Zach drained pasta in the sink with a deft hand.

"Where'd you learn to cook?" she asked, wanting to talk about anything other than Stacy.

"My mother. She believed in raising boys who could take care of themselves." Something on his face changed.

"Boys. You have brothers?"

"A brother."

"You've only mentioned Hilly and your murdered father. I didn't know there was a brother."

He shrugged. "Did you want my life history?"

Because the honest question hurt her more than it should, she smiled sharply at him. "Well, we did sleep together, sugar."

His mouth quirked as if he almost found her funny. "Uh-huh. Well, I have a brother."

"Is he Mr. Protector guy, too? Or are you more like me and my brother?"

"What's you and your brother?"

"Opposites, through and through."

"But you love him."

"Of course I do. Vaughn was one of the very few uncomplicated relationships in my life. Well, mostly uncomplicated. I always knew he didn't really approve of me, but he supported me anyway." She hadn't always appreciated that support the way she should have, and she'd never thanked him for it.

Although he'd be horrified by a display of emotion, even if it was gratitude. The thought made her smile a little bit. But she realized, as Zach placed a bowl full of spaghetti in front of her, he'd very efficiently avoided the question.

"So what does your brother do?"

"He's done a lot of things."

She raised an eyebrow. "You know, when someone touches a sore subject with me I tell them to jump off a cliff."

"And I doubt it dims their curiosity regarding the sore subject," Zach replied.

"Avoiding the question doesn't dim my curiosity."

"Ethan's in a psych ward. He, in fact, nearly murdered Cam."

"Cam, your business partner, Cam? The man marrying your sister?"

"The very same."

He really, *really* never failed to surprise her. She might have thought him cold at the way he delivered that so emotionlessly, but his eyes didn't lie as well as the rest of him. The less sympathy she offered, though, the more he seemed to reveal to her. "Well. I can see why it's a sore subject."

"Dad's murder hit him particularly hard. He tried his hand at a lot of things, but the unsolved case was an obsession, one that became unhealthy and dangerous. I love my brother, even knowing his… I hesitate to call them faults. He's mentally ill. He's… Well, my attempts to protect him, to care for him, not only put the entire undercover FBI investigation I was a part of in jeopardy, but nearly got Cam killed, too. You learn from experiences like that. And, in my case, you get kicked out of the FBI."

"Which is why you shouldn't get emotionally involved," she said, remembering how seriously he'd asked her if she wanted to die after she'd kissed him that first time.

He tapped his nose, then focused on eating.

"It isn't the same," she said softly.

He raised an eyebrow, and somehow she'd known he'd give her that condescending look he thought hid all the turmoil inside him. Maybe he managed to hide it from other people, but not from her.

"You knew your brother had issues, and you kept protecting him until you didn't have a choice. That isn't the same as feeling something for me. Emotion didn't cause those mistakes. Underestimating your brother's illness and your power over it would have been the issue. It doesn't mean you'll make the same mistakes with me."

"Who says I won't?"

She blinked at that, more than a little irritated when

her phone trilled. Downright furious when it was Jordan's number calling her.

"Why can't that bastard leave well enough alone?" she grumbled, reaching for the phone to hit Ignore.

"Take it," Zach said in that leader-ordering-a-subordinate tone that would have angered her more if she wasn't so confused.

"Huh?"

"Take it. See what he wants. On speaker."

She didn't want to talk to Jordan, not when she was getting somewhere with Zach. Not when today was already in the toilet. But she did as Zach ordered her to do because she didn't know what else to do in the moment besides stomp her feet and throw a tantrum like a child.

"Jordan," she greeted as coolly as she could muster.

"Daisy. Thank God you're all right."

Fear snaked through her. While Zach had told her the smoke bombs at Stacy's office had made the news, people had been distracted enough not to notice she'd been in the building. So far. "Why wouldn't I be all right?" she asked, trying to keep her voice devoid of emotion.

"The attack on Stacy's office! They're claiming it was an innocent prank, but this is all too close for comfort. I'm worried about you, Daisy. What kind of trouble have you been getting yourself into?"

She glanced up at Zach, who had that icy law-enforcement scowl on his face. But again, in his eyes she could see the truth. Heat and fury.

"You know I'm in town?" she asked carefully.

"I keep tabs, Daisy. I've told you that before." He sounded so disdainful she wanted to punch him. "I have to know if you're going to show up and make one of your scenes."

"But you said you thought I was in rehab."

"No, I said that's what people were saying, and that I hoped you were getting help. You need help."

*And you need a knee to the balls.*

"We need to talk, Daisy. In private. No staff. No bodyguards. I have some important news for you and I need to make sure you're going to handle it the correct way."

She opened her mouth to say she'd show him the correct way to handle something, but Zach reached across the counter and tapped her hand. He scribbled something onto a piece of paper then angled it toward her.

*Take the meeting.*

She jerked the pen from his hand and wrote her own note back.

*Without you?*

"Daisy? Listen. Meet me at our old lunch place. What do you say, eight o'clock before your flight?"

Daisy stared at Zach, who nodded emphatically. She let out a sigh. "Fine, Jordan. I'll be there at eight. Goodbye." She hit End on the call before he could say any more.

"Stacy had to have told him you were here. She's the only one who knew about that flight," Zach said, scribbling more things onto a new piece of paper. "There has to be a connection there."

"Between Stacy and Jordan? They didn't like each other. Trust me. Cory could have told him, too."

"Cory didn't know about your flight unless she was eavesdropping. Besides, Jordan and Stacy disliking each other isn't valid enough to disregard the potential connection. Because it doesn't have to be a connection of friendship, does it? The enemy of my enemy is my friend and all that—and before you say anything, I know Stacy isn't your enemy, but sometimes people harbor resentments we don't know about. You said she was at your father's label with you."

"No, she was my father's manager's assistant. We used to sit around and complain about what a smarmy old codger he was, so when I finally got the guts to go out on my own, I asked if she wanted to come with. We'd been friends, dreaming about futures where we didn't have to answer to anyone. Might have been tough work those first few years, but I'm pretty sure Stacy has been amply rewarded."

Zach paced. "None of this adds up," he muttered. "We're missing something." He tilted his head, clearly working something out in that overactive brain of his. "Or someone. What about someone who would know both Jordan and Stacy separately. Someone who who knows you well enough to use them both against you? Who in your life would know both Jordan and Stacy enough to understand their relationship to you?"

"My agent. Jordan's staff—his manager, his assistant—basically anyone on his payroll who would have worked with Stacy during one of our joint ventures before the divorce."

"I looked into Jordan's staff before, but we'll go through them again. See if we can find a specific connection to Stacy. And then triangulate it to your father."

"And while you're doing all that?"

"You better get ready. Because you're going to have to hide some of your fury toward Jordan. Just long enough to get us through this meeting and get what we want out of it."

THE PATTERNS DIDN'T add up, but Zach was beginning to think he'd been looking at them all wrong. There were a lot of players, but no clear leader. No clear link.

If he could find the link, the pattern would fall into place.

Daisy didn't think anyone would have something against her writing her own songs, but Zach had to believe it was industry related. Jordan, the rising star. Stacy, the star's manager—who came from her father's record label.

"What about this manager? The one Stacy worked for."

"What about him?" Daisy asked, staring out the window as Zach drove through drizzly downtown traffic to the restaurant Jordan had picked out.

"Could he have been angry at you for stealing Stacy away?"

Daisy snorted. "He didn't care about Stacy. He cared about power."

"What does that mean?"

"Look, he'd be like…eighty now. I doubt he overpowered Tom and killed him. I doubt he'd have the wherewithal to follow me around the country."

"*He* isn't. Whoever is behind this is sending people, Daisy. What would this guy be angry about?" He didn't add *and why the hell didn't you tell me*, which he considered a great feat of control.

Daisy shifted in her seat. "Nothing. He got away with it all. There'd be nothing to be angry about."

"Got away with what exactly?"

She sighed heavily. "He just said some kind of inappropriate things and I told my dad about it. But it's not like… There was nothing to be angry about. Nothing happened to him."

Zach parked in the lot in front of the restaurant, then looked over at her. "*Said* some inappropriate things, or *did* some inappropriate things?"

She waved a hand and pushed the passenger door open. "Doesn't matter."

"It *does* matter," he insisted, but she got out of the car and started walking toward the door—which was not the plan they'd agreed on. He hopped out of the car, stopping her forward progress. "Follow the plan, Daisy. And tell me about it."

"It doesn't *matter*. Trust me. Nothing bad ever happened to him. If he's angry with me, it's not enough to want me hurt. Why would he be angry? He's old and rich and retired, I believe. Hell, he might even be dead. Whatever he is—he's fine, and not out to get me."

"Name."

"Oh, for God's sake, Zach. Can't you trust me?"

"I trust you implicitly. I don't trust anyone who would say or *do* inappropriate things to you when you were a teenager."

They couldn't keep having this conversation in public, even with her big sunglasses and baggy clothes.

"He grabbed me. I told him no. He grabbed me again. I said I was going to go tell my dad. He laughed and said Dad wouldn't do anything. And guess what? He was right. *Oh, Don's just old guard, Daisy girl. Don't be alone with him.* Problem solved, right?"

"The hell it is."

She shook her head, wrapping her arms around herself. "It was forever ago. It's ancient history."

It wasn't. He could tell it wasn't, but she didn't

want to discuss it and here wasn't the place. "What about Stacy?"

"What *about* Stacy?"

"Did he assault Stacy, too?"

"He didn't *assault* me, Zach."

"Grabbing is assault, Daisy," he returned forcefully. But he softened because even for all the difficult situations he'd been in, he'd never had to mine through his past. Never had to wonder who was against him. He placed his hands on her shoulders. "I know it hurts. I can't imagine how much it hurts to wonder about everyone you trust, or everyone you don't want to have to think about. I wish there was some other way, but we're missing a link and the sooner I can find it, the sooner whoever is torturing you can be brought to justice."

"I just want this to be over. I'm not even sure I care about justice," she said, looking teary.

He let her lean into him. Rubbed his hand up and down her back. "I know. I know. One link. I just need one link and then I can connect it all. I can make it over for you. Let me follow this lead. A name, and all you have to do is—"

She lifted her head off his shoulder, and nodded behind him. "Have dinner with my ex-husband?"

Zach didn't turn. Instead, he kept his arm around Daisy, kept looking down at her. "We're going to play this a little differently than we planned."

"Oh, really?"

He dropped his head and brushed his mouth against hers, inappropriately enjoying that for once he'd been the one to surprise her with a kiss. "Not your body-guard this time."

Her mouth quirked up. "Well, this should be interesting."

He slid his arm around her waist and turned to face Jordan Jones, who did *not* look happy to see them.

Zach grinned. "Indeed it will."

## *Chapter Thirteen*

Daisy's whole life, she'd prided herself on standing on her own two feet. Even when her father had been taking her from show to show as a little girl, she'd understood that it was necessary to prove a certain amount of independence so she didn't turn into her father's toy or trophy. If she hadn't inherently understood that, her mother had made sure to remind her.

Daisy had wanted to be a singer, and she'd become one. On her own terms. But there had been things that had undermined that independence, that certainty. Her father ignoring the fact his manager had—as much as she hated it, she'd use Zach's word—*assaulted* her. Jordan being…well, self-serving, she supposed.

Could she hate him for that?

"I thought we were going to have dinner, Daisy. I don't appreciate—" he trailed off, looking Zach up and down "—whatever stunt this is."

Turned out, she could hate Jordan for a lot of things. "No stunt. My boyfriend refused to let me out of his sight with everything going on." She patted Zach's chest. "He's very concerned about my well-being."

Jordan sighed, all long-suffering martyrdom. "If

that's supposed to be a dig against me, perhaps I should apologize for treating you like an independent woman?"

*Perhaps you should apologize for being an emotionally abusive jerk wad.* But she smiled sweetly. "Jordan Jones, this is my boyfriend…" She tried to come up with a fake name, but Zach intervened.

"Zach Simmons," he offered, holding out a hand for Jordan to shake. "I'm in law enforcement, so I understand just how dangerous this threat against Lucy is. Her going anywhere alone wasn't a great idea. I'm sure you understand her safety is paramount."

It…warmed her somehow that he was using her real name, and his. Jordan probably wouldn't notice or care, but it was…a gesture.

"Well." Jordan straightened his shoulders. "Of course. That's what I wanted to talk to Daisy about. Her safety."

"Great!" Zach said so genially Daisy wanted to laugh. "Let's head in." Zach kept his arm around her waist as he led them inside and told the hostess they had three in their party.

It was something to watch, how easily he could switch into someone else. A role. She understood that a little. After all, there was a certain amount of *role* she stepped into when she got on stage. Daisy Delaney was parts of Lucy Cooper carefully arranged into a different package.

But she'd really never expected too many other people to understand that. It had been part of the attraction of Jordan—that he understood the complications of being someone else at the same time you were yourself.

But she supposed there were all kinds of ways people put on masks every day, not just to go on stage.

The hostess led them to a dimly lit booth and Daisy had to fight the need to laugh hysterically. She was sitting in a restaurant with her ex-husband and her security expert slash fake boyfriend slash man she really wouldn't mind seeing naked.

While apparently, said man suspected both her manager and her ex-husband of stalking and murder.

Zach draped his arm over her shoulders easily, chatted with Jordan about the music industry. Daisy could hardly pay attention to Jordan's pretentious rambling about his career. Had she really been this *fooled*?

But she had been. Fooled or desperate or something. It made her feel sick and ashamed she hadn't seen through him—but he hadn't talked about himself back then. He'd talked about her. Flattered her—in just the ways she'd been desperate to be flattered.

A strange thought hit her sideways as Jordan nattered on. Could he have been coached? Told what would hit all her vulnerabilities, and then used them against her?

Oh, that was insane. Whatever was happening to her hadn't been going on for *years*. Her failed marriage was hardly some kind of convoluted plot to…hurt her or whatever. She was getting paranoid. Insane maybe.

"Which brings me to why I called," Jordan was saying, his gaze moving from Zach to Daisy. Pretty blue eyes the color of summer skies. She'd thought she'd seen love in them once, and she didn't know if she was just that delusional or if he had actually felt something for her and it had disappeared.

It made her unbearably sad. And then Jordan continued.

"The rumor *was* you'd disappeared to go into rehab,

and it got me thinking how great it would be if you just did that."

"What?" she replied, because surely he didn't mean what she *thought* he meant.

"You might want to work on your comedy, buddy. Because that isn't funny," Zach said, steel laced through his fake genial tone.

"Can I get y'all something to drink?" a perky waitress asked, clearly not reading the mood of the table.

They all ordered robotically, except Jordan, who smiled and flirted when the waitress recognized him and expressed her undying love for his music.

If she recognized Daisy, she didn't mention it.

When she disappeared to get the drinks, Jordan looked at them both with that patented *Jordan Jones* smile. It was charming, and he was handsome. She wanted to punch him in the nose, but Zach's arm around her shoulders had tightened as if keeping her seated.

"It seems to me a rehab facility would be safer than going around disappearing with—" he looked at Zach "—boyfriends. Especially the way your last one ended up."

"Tom was my bodyguard and he died trying to protect me, you inconsiderate—"

Jordan held up his hands, looking at Zach with a sigh as if to say, *What do you do with a problem like Daisy?* "I'm only suggesting a safe place for you, Daisy."

"You want me to fake going into rehab so I can be *safe*?"

The waitress put glasses in front of them, and this time she gave Daisy a much longer look. Though she was smart enough not to say anything.

Jordan sipped from his glass. "I mean, you could actually go."

"I'm not an alcoholic, Jordan. Contrary to your staff's attempts to make me out to be."

"Of course. Of course." He opened his mouth to speak, but the phone he held in his hand trilled. He glanced at the screen, a slight frown pulling at the corner of his lips. "I have to take this," he said, sliding out of the booth. "If you'll excuse me." He moved away from the table and Daisy couldn't hear what he was saying.

"I can't believe you married this joker," Zach muttered when Jordan was out of earshot.

"*That* is not the joker I married." No, Jordan knew how to slip into a role, too. Was she forever falling for men who acted one way, then turned out to be another? "You know a little bit about pretending to be someone else to get what you want, don't you?"

He looked at her, something like sympathy in his gaze that made her want to punch him, too. Or lean into his chest. She really wasn't sure.

He reached out and pushed a stray strand of hair behind her ear. "All I want right now is to keep you safe."

Which softened her up considerably.

"Which means I'm going to get my hands on his phone."

"Huh?"

"I don't trust this rehab thing."

"He's just trying to make me look bad, Zach. Ever since I asked for a divorce, that's his number one goal. Because if he can make *me* look bad, he can make himself look better."

"Maybe. Maybe that's all it is, but he doesn't strike

me as particularly smart. Manipulative, yes. A good actor? Sure. But someone is pulling his strings, Daisy. I'm going to find out who."

"It's got to be someone on his staff."

"I agree. His manager, maybe? Was there anyone he was particularly…deferential to?"

Daisy tried to think back over her time with Jordan. "I think he's been through something like three managers. He used to talk about some uncle who was in the industry, but I never met him. If he mentioned him by name, I don't remember him."

"I need his phone. So when I give you the signal, you're going to spill your drink on him. I'm going to palm his phone and head off to the bathroom to wash up."

"You're going to palm his phone? How?"

"Trust me." He smiled, tapping her nose. "If you do, maybe I'll teach you a few things about going undercover."

It amused her, even though all she really wanted was to have her life back. "You better be quick, though. His phone is like an arm. He'll notice it's missing."

"You just spill his drink. I'll handle the rest."

SHE DID SO, and beautifully. Perhaps with a little too much enjoyment as the dark soda splashed across Jordan's white shirt, but hell, Zach enjoyed Jordan's outrage a little too much himself.

Zach immediately jumped to his feet, calling for the waitress and shoving napkins at Jordan. It gave him ample time to slip the phone out of the sticky soda and pretend like he was going to run to the bathroom for more paper towels even though the waitress was hurrying over with a rag.

Zach moved quickly to the bathroom, locked himself into a stall and went to work on Jordan's phone.

Zach didn't have time to try and figure out Jordan's passcode, so he used a quick hack to bypass the code and get into Jordan's home screen.

He pulled up the contacts list. The first fishy thing was the lack of names. Everyone was labeled with letters and numbers rather than anything that helped Zach identify who they were. Pretty confusing for a guy who had tons of contacts in his phone.

And pretty damn suspicious. Zach pulled up the recent calls. With his own phone, Zach took a picture of the screen. Of the eight calls on top, two were repeated three times each. It might be nothing. It might mean everything. Now that he had the numbers, he'd go from there.

Text messages didn't reveal anything of importance, and his apps were as run of the mill as any. Zach didn't have time to dig further. Hopefully, the phone numbers would be something to go on.

He stepped out of the stall, wiped off the phone with a paper towel and turned it off, ready to head back to the table. If Jordan had noticed his phone missing, Zach would just explain he'd gone to wipe it down and Jordan would be none the wiser.

But when he stepped back into the restaurant, the few patrons had their noses and phones pressed to every available window, and Daisy stood next to an empty table, hand to her mouth.

"What's going on?"

She gestured faintly at the window, but there were so many people crowded around it he couldn't see anything.

"The cops came and arrested him." Daisy looked up at him, searching for some kind of answer, but he was as confused as she was.

"The cops came in and arrested Jordan?"

She nodded. "A-at first it was just… They asked if they could speak with him outside. He looked so confused, but wholly unconcerned. I think he even thought maybe they were going to ask for his autograph or something, but instead… I looked out the window and he was being handcuffed. *Handcuffed*. Zach, it doesn't make any sense, and it's already being uploaded onto the internet in three million ways."

Zach looked down at the phone in his hand. "I guess I should give the cops his phone."

"Did you find anything?"

"I took some pictures of his recent call numbers, but if he's being arrested for something, the police should have it." He led Daisy outside through the small crowds of people, pushing his way through to the female cop holding the curious onlookers as far back as she could.

"Excuse me, Officer? I have Jordan Jones's phone right here."

The officer looked at him with a raised eyebrow as he held out the phone, but she didn't say anything.

"We had a little drink spill," Zach explained. "I cleaned off his phone for him. But figured you might want it."

"And you are?" the cop asked with no small amount of distrust.

Zach explained who he was, and the cop managed to escort him and Daisy to a slightly private corner. Zach showed the police officer all his identification and permits to prove he was Daisy's security, and gave an account of the drink spill.

The cop took and bagged the phone. "I imagine our detectives will be in contact with you, Ms. Delaney."

"Can you tell me what he's being arrested for?"

The cop looked at Daisy, then him. "The murder of Tom Perelli."

Daisy audibly gasped, and Zach might have, too. *Jordan* as murderer? Even though he'd suspected Jordan was involved, it was hard to believe the man he'd just had dinner with was capable of murder.

But he didn't have time to dwell on that. Some people were beginning to look at Daisy and murmur among themselves. Phones began to move from the cop car where Jordan was now loaded up, to the dim corner where he and Daisy stood.

He moved his body to shield her from the prying eyes and phones, then discussed the best way to get out of the parking lot undetected. As the cop began to instruct the crowd to leave so she could back up the patrol car, Daisy and Zach slipped around the crowd and into Zach's car.

Daisy didn't say anything as they drove back. Zach couldn't read her mood, but he couldn't concentrate on it, either. He paid attention to every car on the road with them.

Quite frankly, he expected to be followed. He expected…something. Surely, this wasn't *it*. It was too easy, too neat. Something else had to be at work here.

But in the end they made it back to the farmhouse without any tail Zach could see. Once inside, he made as many calls as he could to weasel some information out of a few overly talkative individuals.

Daisy sat on the couch, staring at nothing. During one of his calls he'd fixed her some tea. She hadn't touched it.

After he'd gotten the answers he'd wanted, or at least *some* of the answers, he sat down next to Daisy. She didn't move. Didn't say anything. He supposed she was in shock.

"The police received an anonymous tip, which allowed them to obtain a search warrant for Jordan's place. They found the gun used to kill Tom in a hidden safe in his bedroom closet."

"Anonymous tip," Daisy echoed. "Someone else knew he… He couldn't have…" She swallowed. "Zach, I don't understand. I really don't. Maybe I could believe he stalked me, or even threatened me all those months, but to kill Tom? I can't…" She shook her head. "But it's over, isn't it? If Jordan is the murderer, and he's in jail, this is over."

Zach didn't know how to tell her he didn't think it was over, that this was all too easy. And maybe it *was* over. Maybe it wasn't his gut telling him things were too neat. Maybe it was his desperate desire to be with her.

"Zach?"

She looked up at him, and in all that confusion and despair there was hope. Hope that this meant she got to go back to her real life and feel safe again. Hope that this could all be put away as some ugly part of her past.

For her, he wished he could believe it. Even if it meant their time together was up. She deserved to go back to normal, instead of living in fear.

"It's possible it's over," he said carefully, not wanting to burden her with his doubts. "Obviously, we'll want to see if they give him a bond. I'd hope not, but we want to make sure he's going to stay in jail before it's...fully over."

Daisy nodded, wringing her hands together. "I can't... I didn't know him. I thought I did. I loved the version of himself he showed me, but it wasn't him. I can't imagine him *killing* someone, but I certainly can imagine him wanting to hurt me."

She popped to her feet, began to pace. "He wanted me to go to rehab. He wanted me swept away so I wouldn't be credible. That's why he wanted to meet."

It was possible, Zach supposed. But the timing struck him as odd, even more so with the arrest in front of Daisy. Zach had some research to do on those numbers from Jordan's phone before he fully accepted this version of events. And he'd want to read the police report and—

"What about you?"

He looked up at Daisy, his mind going over all the things he still needed to do to be *sure*. "What about me?"

"You'll have to go home, then, won't you?"

It felt like a slap, even as she watched him with wide, sad eyes. He cleared his throat. She might have kissed him a few times, he might have grown to like her quite a bit, but their odd relationship was a temporary one.

He pushed away all those conflicting emotions that were no doubt clouding his judgment about Jordan's guilt. "My job is to keep you safe. Until we're assured Jordan stays in jail, that means I'm still here."

She nodded, gave him a tremulous smile that just about cracked his heart in two. "Good." When she sat, she didn't sit next to him. Instead, she slid onto his lap, much like she had way back in Wyoming.

She cupped his face with her hands, looked right at him. "Then be with me. Really."

## *Chapter Fourteen*

Daisy poured everything inside her into the kiss. The pain, the uncertainty, the horrible sadness that swept through her at the idea Zach wouldn't be in her life anymore.

She wasn't sure if it was the kiss that finally broke through Zach's whole "emotions are distractions" thing—because it was one hell of a soul-searing kiss— or if it was as simple as he believed this was over.

She wished she could, but everything felt wrong and off. Maybe she couldn't believe Jordan was a murderer because it made her look like a fool, but there were all these wiggles of uncertainty inside her she couldn't quash—even with Jordan in jail.

Zach's kiss could eradicate it, and all the other painful things inside her. She could focus on pleasure and the absolute safety she found in him and leave everything else behind, even if only for a little bit.

She thought she'd have to convince him, but his arms banded around her and his mouth devoured hers as if he hadn't rejected her attempts at this *routinely*.

He maneuvered her onto her back on the couch, sprawling himself over her so that she sank into the cushions. She reveled in that feeling of being covered completely, safe and complete somehow—like being in Zach Simmons's arms was exactly where she needed to be.

He kissed her like she was the same to him—the place *he* needed to be.

There were so many ways she'd been made to feel small and insignificant in her life by the men who were supposed to love her. Zach had never mentioned love, but he made her feel cherished and important more so than anyone else. He believed her, he trusted her, and time and time again he'd put her above his own interests.

She pulled his shirt off quickly and efficiently. She sighed reverently, tracing her fingers down his abdomen. "I've been waiting for this since I saw you shirtless that first night."

He muttered a curse and then kissed her again, a fervency and an urgency she appreciated because it seared away everything else—all those awful things in the real world out there. It was only him and her, perfectly safe.

His hands streaked under her shirt and then pulled her up into a sitting position, his body straddling hers.

"If this is a curse, I'll damn well take it," he said, his eyes bright and lethal.

"Curse?"

"Carsons, Delaneys, long story." He closed his eyes and shook his head as if he couldn't believe he'd brought it up. "I'll tell you later." Then he lifted her shirt over her head and let it fall to the ground. His mouth streaked down her neck as his hands made quick work of her bra and she forgot her questions as he kissed her everywhere.

His groan of appreciation as he tugged the button

and zipper of her jeans made her feel like a goddess. "One favor. Don't call me Daisy."

He paused briefly, then met her gaze as he pulled her pants down her legs. "All right, Lucy."

It squirmed through her—somehow beautiful and uncomfortable at the same time. But she didn't want to be Daisy to him, not because she was ashamed of that part of her, but because Daisy had to keep people at arm's length from all the demands inside her—from her music, from her drive to succeed, from the chaos that sometimes existed in her head.

But if she was Lucy, just herself without the mantle of fame or curse of being a storyteller, then she could feel like she really belonged to *him*. Not something bigger than them. Just them.

Zach stopped suddenly, keeping his body ridiculously tense. "Wait. Condoms. We don't—"

She patted his cheek. "Never fear, sweetheart, condoms and booze are two things I never leave home without."

"Do I even want to know why?"

"Sometimes a girl has a rep to protect. Or destroy, as the case may be. I like to be prepared."

"Well, I won't look a gift bad girl in the mouth. Wow, that sounds wrong."

She laughed, and was surprised to find it made the moment that much more special. That she could want him and laugh with him and feel safe with him. She brushed her mouth against his as she slid off the couch. "Come to bed, Zach."

He followed her and she rummaged through her bag, in only her underwear and socks. She might have felt a little silly if Zach wasn't watching her as though he'd like to devour her from top to bottom, then bottom to top.

That made her feel powerful no matter what she had on. She found the old crumpled box of condoms, discreetly checked the expiration date and then pulled one out, holding it between her fingers. "Aren't you lucky?"

"Yes," he said reverently, so reverently her eyes actually stung. She tried to saunter over to him, keep it light—focused on the attraction and the laughter, not... not the way her heart felt squeezed so hard she could barely catch a breath.

But when she reached him, she didn't know how to keep it all together. All she could do was lean against the warmth of his chest. Try to find some strength of spirit against that strong, dependable frame.

"I don't want this part to be over. The us part," she whispered, listening to the steady beating of his heart. She'd never, ever revealed herself like that before, laid her emotions that bare.

But she'd never let herself be Lucy with anyone outside her brother and her mother, and even they still saw her as part Daisy. Why she thought Zach understood the dichotomy inside her, she wasn't sure. Maybe she was stupid—the kind of stupid who married a murderer and—

He swallowed and ran a hand over her hair. Sweet and full of care. "Lucy," he said raggedly.

She shook her head against that despair in his voice. "I know. It's impossible. And God knows I shouldn't trust my own instincts when it comes to men. Maybe you're a secret murderer, too. How would I know?"

She wanted to run away, but Zach pulled her back and took her face in his hands.

"Lucy," he repeated, quieting her. She still felt wound up and stupid, but his hands on her face were a balm.

She wanted to stay here—right here—forever. Safe with Zach, who was good, and understood her somehow. A man who cared, and not just for show. She kept trying to convince herself it was just her dumb brain fooling herself again, but looking at that steady gaze she knew. She *knew* Zach was different.

And she was head over heels in love with a man she couldn't have.

But she kissed him anyway, fell to bed with him anyway, and let the sensations overwhelm her so she didn't think about anything except pleasure. Except finding release with this man who meant everything.

This man she'd have to say goodbye to, and soon.

But he kissed her, filled her, and for sparkling minutes of ecstasy she forgot everything except them.

ZACH WASN'T SURE he'd ever slept so soundly, or so long. He woke up feeling like a new man.

Of course, that might have been the sex.

Which really shouldn't have relaxed him considering it added quite a few complications to his nagging worry that Jordan's arrest was too easy. How could he tell the difference between what was true, and what his feelings for Lucy made him *want* to be true?

But facts were facts, right? There was evidence Jordan had done it. Why was he letting emotion sway the facts again? Didn't he know how that ended up?

He was almost grateful for the pounding on the door. If it didn't worry him. He slid out of bed as Lucy grumbled complaints.

Lucy. It was funny how easy it was to vacillate between the names. She seemed like both women to him, but somehow it seemed more…meaningful that he'd gone to bed with Lucy.

Possibly he was losing his mind.

He pulled on his pants and grabbed his gun that he'd left in the nightstand. With the pounding continuing at increasing levels, he didn't have time to strap his holster on, so he simply held it behind his back as he made his way through the living room to the door.

He checked the security camera on his phone, but the man on the stoop wasn't familiar. He was about Zach's height, wearing jeans, an impeccably unwrinkled button-up shirt and a rather large cowboy hat.

Still, he was knocking. It could be information about Jordan. Zach eased the door open, weapon at the ready.

The man's cool blue eyes took in Zach's shirtless form and those eyes hardened.

"Can I help you?" Zach asked as he flipped the safety off behind his back.

"Vaughn!"

Zach glanced back at Lucy, who pulled the bright yellow robe she was wearing a little closer around her as she stepped forward.

Zach was glad he recognized the name as her brother's or the hot burn of jealousy at the pure delight in her tone might have had him acting stupidly and rashly.

"What are you doing here?" she asked, approaching them. She looked like she was about to lean in to hug her brother, but instead gripped her robe tighter. "I told you everything was fine."

Yeah, it wouldn't exactly be rocket science to figure out what they'd been doing together last night. And she certainly hadn't told him she'd contacted her brother.

"I came to take you home," Vaughn said, his voice cool and detached. But the words made Zach's blood run cold even as he set the gun back down on the counter.

"You didn't have to come collect me like I'm a sheep to be herded," Lucy countered. She glanced at Zach, but he couldn't read whatever was in her expression when she quickly looked away again.

"Maybe not," Vaughn countered. "But I thought Jordan being the suspect might hit you a little hard and you'd want—" he looked Zach up and down "—a friendly face."

"Uh, right. Well. Vaughn, this is Zach. I don't suppose you two have met, though you know of each other."

"Of each other, yes. Jaime spoke highly of you." After another moment of cold perusal, Vaughn offered his hand. "I was impressed by the detail in your reports."

Zach shook it. "Same goes. It's good to meet you," Zach offered, trying to sound businesslike despite the general lack of shirt, socks and shoes.

Vaughn did not return the sentiment, though it was hard to blame him. Zach hadn't had a normal brother-sister relationship with Hilly since they'd grown up apart, and she'd come into his life already connected to Cam, so there'd been no big-brother suspicion to be had.

But that didn't mean he couldn't understand Vaughn's. Especially considering Vaughn had arranged for Lucy's protection.

"Why don't you go get dressed?" Vaughn said to Lucy. He gave Zach a sharp smile. "Zach and I will chat."

Lucy rolled her eyes. "Yeah, you're a real chatterbox. But I'll go get dressed since I'll be more comfortable, and since I have no doubt Zach can stand up to the likes of you." She gave her brother a little poke, and then drifted her hand down Zach's arm as she sauntered away.

Zach thought he could probably handle her brother—Texas Ranger or not—but he didn't quite need her stirring the pot on the subject.

Especially when it gave him a quick few minutes alone with her brother, which meant, even though he still had his doubts, he had to tell Vaughn he didn't think this was over. Somehow, he had to convince her brother that it wasn't Zach's heart doing the talking.

"I don't think she should go back home with you," he said when Lucy disappeared into the room, firmly and sure, but with absolutely no transition or finesse. He *could* have eased into it, but Lucy could also only take a few seconds to change. Time was of the essence.

Vaughn merely raised an eyebrow, reminding Zach a little uncomfortably of Lucy.

"I'm not saying Jordan isn't involved, but…" Zach knew he'd be shot down, but the incessant worry in his gut meant he had to say it. "There was evidence he's the murderer—I can't refute that. What concerns me are the loose ends. I'm not convinced this is it, or that Jordan's arrest means the danger to Lucy is over."

Vaughn studied him, and Zach braced himself for some kind of condescending lecture about being stupid.

It didn't come.

"I'm not, either," Vaughn said. When Zach could only stare at him, openmouthed, Vaughn continued. "Which is why I came out here. I didn't want her alone thinking she was safe, any more than I wanted to have to tell her she wasn't."

"Join the club," Zach muttered. He had to tell her. *Had to.* And yet, she was just accepting her ex-husband was a murderer. How could he add the fact it didn't make Stacy or anyone else less potentially involved?

"Should I ask your intentions when it comes to my sister?" Vaughn asked with a wry twist of his lips.

"Why? Did we fall back in time a century? I'm pretty sure Lucy can handle my intentions." Not that he knew what they were, or why he suddenly wanted the curse to be true.

Vaughn didn't smile, but Zach didn't get the impression Vaughn was a particularly smiley guy. Still, his mouth loosened in what Zach would term *amusement*. Maybe.

"Lucy," Vaughn repeated as if surprised Zach was using her given name. "Well, that's new."

"Is it?"

Vaughn shrugged. "I don't make it a habit to poke into my sister's personal life, but she isn't keen on letting too many people call her by her real name."

It was funny how Vaughn said *real* and it didn't sit well with Zach. They were both real enough—Daisy and Lucy—they were both her. He shook his head. "So how do we break it to her?"

"I'd like to not. To protect her on the sly until we figure out the whole picture."

Zach snorted his derision, unable to stop himself.

"I said I'd *like* to, not that it would work." Vaughn sighed heavily and scrubbed a hand over his face. He didn't appear mussed by travel or beset by fatigue or worry, but that simple gesture told Zach he was all of those things. Sick to death worried about his sister's safety.

Vaughn gestured Zach to sit down on the couch, so Zach did so, Vaughn taking a seat next to him. "Quickest version you've got of the loose ends you think still exist?"

"Two main ones," Zach returned, keeping one eye on Lucy's bedroom door. "One, how Jordan had enough information to know Daisy was going to be with Stacy—which to me points to a potential connection with Stacy."

"What about other people in the office?"

"I laid a little bit of a trap. We gave information to Stacy and only Stacy—of course she might have slipped and told someone, but I'm willing to bet Stacy told Jordan, or someone who knows Jordan."

Vaughn shook his head. "That's going to hurt— worse than Jordan—if Stacy's involved."

"Yeah. And I'll be honest—the second thread? I think there's someone else. Someone from her past, or maybe your father's. Someone who is using Jordan and Stacy and whoever else to exact some kind of... revenge."

"Why do you think that?"

"Patterns. Hunches. The way it's all played out."

Vaughn sighed. "You got notes?"

"You wouldn't believe the notes I have."

"I'll want some time to go over them." He glanced back at Lucy's still-closed door. "We don't have time."

"No. We don't. Look, why don't you let me tell her? That way she can be mad at me instead of her brother. We don't have to go into details. We can just say we're taking precautions until we're sure Jordan worked alone."

"How good of a liar are you, Zach?"

Zach's mouth quirked. "I've worked any number of undercover jobs for the FBI. How good of a liar do you think I am?"

"To her," Vaughn replied simply, which made Zach's stomach lurch. "Believe it or not, I've…been where you're standing. At least, if my assumptions are correct—and they usually are. Protecting someone can lead to a lot of strong feelings."

"I don't think we're going to appreciate you warning me off. Grown adults. More important things at hand."

"The most important thing at hand is my sister's safety. Which you've been in charge of. Feelings—"

"Can complicate that. I'm well aware."

Vaughn gave him a look Zach couldn't read, then shifted uncomfortably in his seat. "Believe it or not, emotions aren't always the enemy when it comes to keeping the people you…care about safe."

"Not my experience, no offense."

"And yet in *mine*, I kept the woman safe, married her and have two amazing kids with her. So…you know. I guess it just depends."

Before Zach could say *anything* to that, because *marriage* and *kids* made his tongue stick to the roof of his mouth, Vaughn switched gears.

"Number one thing we should focus on?"

Zach forced himself to change gears, too. "Jordan was arrested over an anonymous tip, so someone out there knows something."

"It could be Stacy."

"It could be. No doubt."

But Zach was sure there was more, and that he was running out of time to find it.

## Chapter Fifteen

That was how Lucy found her brother and her lover, heads bent together going over the details of her case. She couldn't hear what they were saying in their low tones, but it made her realize Jordan had never really mingled with her family or her friends.

He'd never sat next to Vaughn on a couch and discussed anything with this kind of serious back and forth.

Of course, Zach and Vaughn weren't exactly arguing the finer points of the Cowboys' defense or the Astros' pitching staff. They were discussing Jordan or the case or something about her. Keeping her safe, while she wandered around wondering how many people in her life had betrayed her.

The second they noticed her there, Vaughn loudly mentioned something about the home value of a place like this. Lucy shook her head. "All right. Let's cut the crap."

Zach looked back at her, picture-perfect innocence. She couldn't understand why his ability to put on and take off masks with such ease didn't scare her, but it didn't. It was a part of who he was, and so far he hadn't used it for any negative reasons against her.

"Crap?" he asked cheerfully. But he watched her, steady and concerned, and maybe that was why she couldn't get uneasy about him. He never pretended about his emotions toward her. Oh, he might bottle them up, but he didn't try to fake any.

She moved into the living room, fidgety and desperately trying to hide it by perusing the books laid out on the coffee table. She wanted to be steady and calm like them, but she never could really get there.

"Did they give Jordan a bond?" she asked, hoping to sound casual and unaffected. Last night Zach had explained to her that when it came to murder most judges denied bond, but in cities like Nashville it wasn't unheard of to simply set the bond high.

And she knew no matter how high a bond, Jordan wouldn't just be able to pay it, he'd be certain to.

"No bond. He'll stay put in jail until the trial," Zach returned, watching her in that eagle-eye way of his. She might not have minded that too much, but her brother was doing the same thing.

It brought home how much she'd kept Vaughn at arm's length over the years, and how much he would have been there for her if she'd let him. She couldn't blame his stoicism or disapproval, because it had been she who hadn't wanted to give anyone that piece of her.

She hadn't even given Jordan any pieces of herself. She'd weaved dreams and fantasies about their future, but she'd never let Jordan in on any of them. He'd been more like a statue to build her fantasies around than a person to build a life with.

He might have manipulated her and taken advantage of her vulnerabilities, but he wasn't exactly the whole reason their marriage had fallen apart. Any more than she could really truly believe he was the full reason Tom was dead, no matter how much she desperately wanted it to be that easy.

"He's going to have himself a hell of a lawyer," Lucy replied, trying not to sound grim or resigned, but perfectly reasonable instead. "Money buys a lot. He could be out in no time."

"I imagine you're right," Vaughn agreed, devoid of emotion one way or another.

She wanted to scowl at the both of them, demand they *react* in some way, but they both looked at her. Concern and… Oh, she was stupid to think Zach was looking at her with love, but she'd already determined she was stupid, so why not just ride the wave?

"So when are we going to talk about the fact Jordan couldn't have known about the smoke bombs or to call to meet me without Stacy telling him?"

Vaughn sighed. "I'm sorry, Luce."

She tried to smile at Vaughn, though she knew it was weak at best. She perched herself on the arm of the couch on Zach's side. "I'm sorry, too, but…well, Jordan had a reason to hate me, I guess. Stacy didn't." No matter how many ways Lucy went back through the past few years, she couldn't even make up a reason.

Daisy Delaney could be prickly and difficult, but she'd always been those things with Stacy. Since those first days of stepping out of her father's shadow. Nothing about her behavior had changed. Except the addition of Jordan into her life and, in some ways, career. If this had happened while she was still married to Jordan, she might have been able to blame that, but she'd divorced him.

What reason did Stacy have to hate her now that she'd dropped the demanding weight around both their shoulders?

"I just can't understand why she'd want to hurt me. I know, I *know* there aren't other explanations for how Jordan got the info, but I can't understand it. That weighs on me."

"I've been pondering another angle," Zach said in that gentle way of his, which meant it would not be a gentle angle *at all*.

She saw the warning look Vaughn gave Zach and shook her head. She couldn't bury her head in the sand and let these two men handle things, though they would have gladly done it and it might be easier on her emotional well-being.

This whole time she'd been holding back, hoping things would right themselves. Hoping it would be taken care of by someone else, and it hadn't been. Oh, she'd thought about her past, who might hate her, but she hadn't tugged on old hurts or scars, because she'd thought surely all the people paid to keep her safe would figure it out.

But that just wasn't going to work. She needed to be present. She needed to revisit those scars so they could end this completely. Vaughn and Zach could only do so much—she was the real center of this problem—which meant she had to center herself in the solution.

Tom was dead. Jordan was in jail. She suspected one of her oldest, closest friends of being part of it.

Now was not the time to hide. It was time to be the woman in her songs—not just in name but in deed. The kind of woman who went after what she wanted and got it no matter the consequences, no matter what she had to sacrifice or lose.

She leveled Zach with an even stare. "What's the angle?"

"Your father."

She hadn't braced herself for that. The flinch that went through her had to be visible, and if only Zach had seen, that might have been okay, but Vaughn being here for this...

Vaughn hadn't had much of a relationship with Dad, and she knew that Dad's dying with no reconciliation weighed on him.

She stood back up and headed to the kitchen. She started the process of making coffee in the hopes that having something to do would ease her tightly wound insides. "Well, Stacy has a connection to Dad, sort of, as an assistant to Don. It's an awful long game for her to want to hurt me over something a dead guy did. Especially now after so many years of opportunity."

"I want to go back to the conversation we had before the whole Jordan debacle. Your father's manager— Stacy's boss."

She stiffened again. She should have known Zach would come back to this, no matter how it didn't connect. "I don't see how this connects to Don."

"I don't, either, but we have the fact that he hurt you, which caused you to leave your father's fledgling label. After which, that label fell apart—if my research is correct."

"Don hurt you?" Vaughn demanded.

Lucy gave Zach a warning look not to say more. "It fell apart because Dad didn't know what he was doing.

Excellent entertainer. Not so great on the business front. Everyone knew *he* was the reason for the failure, not me leaving."

"How did Don hurt you?" Vaughn demanded again.

"It was nothing," Lucy insisted. It bothered her to realize so many years later Vaughn would have supported her and protected her no matter what if she'd told him about the incident. But she'd known it would have come at the cost of the career she wanted…so she'd just kept quiet. Better to keep what she wanted and ignore the hurts, right?

"Lucy, you will tell me—"

"I don't need a big brother!" she shouted, slamming the can of coffee against the counter. So much for being calm and collected—but who said calm ever got a woman anywhere? Maybe she needed to be *angry* and let it out. Maybe she needed to rage and act.

"I need this to be over," she said a little more evenly but with just as much emotion. "So look into Don Levinson, who is probably *dead*." She flung a hand toward Zach. "Look into anyone who might have hated my father. I'll give you every name I can think of. I just need this to *end*."

Zach stood, moving over to the kitchen. He didn't touch her, though she desperately wanted him to. Wanted that anchor to something solid and true, because no matter how she told herself to be strong, all her foundations were shifting under her. Zach seemed to be the one thing left that wouldn't.

"We all want it over, because we all want you safe," he said gravely.

She wanted to tell him she didn't know how to *deal* with that. Who had ever protected her? But that wasn't fair to Vaughn, who would have if she'd have let him. Because the real issue was, who had she ever *let* protect her?

*Zach.*

She didn't even have the good sense to question that because he stood there, handsome and sweet, and she'd never been so certain of Jordan. She'd convinced herself she was in love with Jordan, convinced herself to love him because of his act. But she'd never *felt* it wash over her as some irrefutable fact.

She'd had to work at loving Jordan and believing in that love. This thing inside her that waved over her whenever she looked at Zach was different, and it was real—no matter how little she understood that.

Zach wasn't an act. She'd *seen* him act. The real him was the man who'd made love to her last night.

She wished she could rewind time—stay right back there—where she didn't have to deal with loose ends or her brother.

But both had to be dealt with. Standing in this kitchen, looking at Zach, wishing this could be normal life without her safety in question—she realized for the first time in this whole nightmare year that at some point her life would be hers again.

She'd lived in the scary *now* for a year, most especially this past awful week. But it would have to end at some point and once it was over she'd have her life back. Completely. She'd be able to visit Vaughn and his family without worry. She'd be able to settle down somewhere and build whatever kind of life she wanted—including one with a partner, a real partner.

Maybe even in Wyoming. Maybe even with Zach.

Why not? It was her fantasy life right now, so why not indulge in all those impossibilities?

"What about trying to ferret out the anonymous tip?" Vaughn asked, singularly focused on the task at hand. "Surely, the cops have some way of tracking it."

Zach turned back to his conversation with Vaughn, so Lucy focused on the coffee and the nice little fantasy of settling down in a ghost town where no one could find her if she didn't want them to. Zach could protect people and she could write music.

She was brought out of the reverie that eased some of that tension inside her by the vibrating of her phone in her pocket.

Lucy slipped the phone out and looked at the message. From Stacy.

She glanced at Vaughn and Zach, but they were deep in computers and papers and theories, so she opened the message.

911. Call back. No ears.

The *no ears* made her uneasy, but what could Stacy do over the phone? Maybe she was calling to warn her about something. Explain something. Hell, maybe she was calling to confess all.

She looked at the two men in her life again. They certainly didn't need her for whatever it was they were doing, and she wasn't so sure she needed them for this.

Part of her knew she should tell them about Stacy's text *before* she made the call, but they were handling everything else. Why couldn't she handle a simple phone call?

She opened her mouth to make her excuses, then

realized neither one of them would come up for air for hours if she left them alone.

She eased her way into the hall. Then toward the back door. Slowly and as quietly as possible, she undid all three locks. She hadn't been out here, but Zach had mentioned a back porch she could use. She just hadn't had a reason to yet.

She stepped out onto it. It was less of a porch and more of a sunroom. The walls were made out of glass, glass she suspected was reinforced with whatever special security measures someone protecting people might use—if the giant keypad lock on the door to the outside was anything to go by.

Still, the day was sunny, and everything outside the glass was a vibrant, enticing green. God, she was tired of being cooped up, of feeling like she had to be in someone else's presence for every second. She hadn't realized how much she missed just stepping outside and lifting her face to the sun.

Which meant this had to end and she had to talk to Stacy. She dialed Stacy's number, staring at the green outside, trying to breathe in the sunshine to offset the nausea roiling around inside her.

"Oh, thank God, Lucy. I don't know what's going on. Everything is so messed up. Jordan's in jail? What is happening?"

Stacy only ever called her Lucy outside work, those occasions they interacted as friends. Stacy had never had any trouble keeping both names straight. Was it because she was a two-faced backstabber?

"I don't know what's happening," Lucy replied flatly.

"Jordan's team is trying to lay the seeds that you've framed him."

Lucy snorted, lowering herself into a cushioned wicker chair and pulling her legs up under her. "The police didn't seem to think that was a possibility." She closed her eyes, trying to ignore the seed of fear and worry that Stacy had planted. God, would he succeed at that, too?

No one could prove she was trying to frame Jordan. Of course that didn't mean the tide of public opinion couldn't turn even further against her. That was what Jordan's team would try to do. Not just a wild, alcoholic cheater, but a murderer, too.

"I mean, Jordan's stupid enough to be set up," Stacy continued. "I'd certainly commend you for your creativity and for getting his big mouth out of the way."

"Are you accusing me of something, Stacy?" Lucy asked coldly, because an unforgiving chill had swept through her. Any conflict she had over not trusting Stacy was fading away with each statement. If Stacy was really worried about *her*, wouldn't this conversation go differently?

"No, God, of course not." Stacy sighed heavily into the receiver. "Everything is so messed up. So confusing. Can we meet for lunch?"

"Not without two bodyguards," Lucy retorted sharply.

"Two?" Stacy asked—the question one of confusion, or was it calculating the odds? Was it filing away information to use later?

It broke Lucy's heart to think Stacy was fishing. Broke Lucy's heart that she had to lie. "To start. You know how overprotective Vaughn is. I swear he's hired half the country to look out for my well-being and investigate what on earth is really going on." She tried to make herself laugh casually, but couldn't muster the sound.

"You don't think Jordan did it?"

"All evidence points to yes, based on what I've heard, but you know, some people are more concerned for my safety than how much information I've got."

"You know, don't you?" Stacy said, her voice hushed and pained.

Lucy had to swallow at the lump in her throat. She waited for the confession, but Stacy didn't speak.

"What do I know, Stacy? Why don't you go ahead and tell it to me straight for once."

"God." Stacy's voice broke. "Don't hate me, Luce. It was an honest mistake. They all were."

An honest mistake. Tom was dead and Stacy had made an *honest mistake*. Lucy couldn't speak past the lump in her throat.

"Okay, okay. Just hear me out, okay? I know I'm the reason Jordan knew you were in town. I would have told you, but I didn't even realize it until someone told me you'd been at dinner together when he got arrested. Then I pieced it all together and—I'm sorry, okay?"

Lucy frowned. That wasn't exactly the grand confession she was expecting, but it was something. "You gave him the information about me coming here? Or going to Wyoming?"

"Here! Of course. You were totally safe in Wyoming," Stacy returned, and it was too hard to try and decide if she was an excellent liar or simply telling the truth.

"Truth be told, I don't understand why you came home when no one knew you were there."

"Because someone knew I was there, Stacy. I wasn't

safe there. Someone found me. Now, what exactly did you tell Jordan? This time and before."

"Nothing before! How can you think that of me?" Stacy muttered a curse. "Listen, listen, okay? I hadn't talked to Jordan in months, but he called me not long after the smoke bomb. He was fishing, I knew he was, but he knew all the right buttons to push. I didn't mean to tell him. I was... He was being irritating, and I was trying to one-up him. I said I'd seen you at my office and you were *fine*. It wasn't until long after I'd hung up that I realized he was goading me and I was just dumb enough to bite."

It sounded plausible enough. God knew Jordan could manipulate. But how had someone found her in Wyoming? And why had Stacy pulled her in the opposite direction of Zach at the office?

Stacy wasn't copping to any of that, so what on Earth was this 911 emergency all about?

"Were you the anonymous tip?" Stacy asked after some beats of silence.

Lucy's blood chilled. "Pretty sure if I had any tips they wouldn't be anonymous, and I would have handed them over when I found Tom dead in my dressing room."

"Jesus," Stacy said, sounding truly sickened by the thought.

"Someone knew I was in Wyoming. You were the only person I told."

"You really think I'm behind this," Stacy said, sounding so shocked and hurt Lucy's own heart twisted in pain. But she had to be strong. Because manipulations were apparently the name of the game, and she'd fallen for too many.

"You were the only one outside my immediate family who knew where I was going," Lucy said, doubling down.

"I didn't tell anyone. Not a soul. Not even Cory. Cory..." There was a long pause.

"Don't try to pin this on Cory. What possible reason would she have for being involved in this?"

"It wasn't me, Luce. Whatever you think. I haven't done anything. I swear to God. I made a mistake in talking to Jordan, but...nothing else. How is this getting so out of hand?"

"What exactly is getting out of hand, Stacy? Because I'm lost."

Stacy swore again. "I might know... I have a bad feeling I know who's behind all this. Jordan told me something a long time ago that I never told you. I know I should have, but you were head over heels for him. If it didn't connect to some things with Cory lately, I might not have even remembered, but..."

"But what? What is it?"

The line was quiet except for Stacy's breathing. "Someone's here," Stacy whispered. "Oh, God, someone's in my house."

Fear bolted through Lucy sharply, and she forgot all of her suspicions at the sheer terror trembling through Stacy's voice.

"Stacy. Hang up. Call 911. Okay? Stacy?" Still shallow breathing. "Stacy!" Lucy yelled. "Hang up and call 911."

"Help m—"

The line clicked off.

# Chapter Sixteen

"Stacy's in trouble!"

Zach jumped to his feet, heart in his throat as Lucy ran into the living room.

"What?" he and Vaughn echoed in unison.

She waved her phone in both their faces. "I was talking to Stacy on the phone and—"

"Why the hell were you doing that?" Vaughn demanded. Which kept Zach from having to demand it.

"Zach," she said, turning to him, clearly thinking he'd be more reasonable than her brother. That wasn't the case, but he'd try to pretend. A sort of good-cop-bad-cop deal.

"She's at her house," Lucy said, panic in her voice and broad gestures. "She said someone was in her house and then the line went dead."

"Go back to the beginning," Zach said, trying to remain calm. "Explain everything."

She looked up at him helplessly. "There isn't time!"

"Lucy." He took her by the shoulders. "Just do it. Quickly, but from the beginning."

Lucy shook her head, still gripping the phone like it was a lifeline to Stacy. "She wanted me to call her. So I did, and she talked about Jordan being arrested, and said she accidentally told him about our meeting and me heading home."

Vaughn and Zach scoffed together.

"Look, I don't know. She seemed fishy and yet not and she was going to tell me something she thought I should know, then she said someone was in her house and her line went dead. She said *help*. Please." Blue eyes looked up at him, full of tears and fear. "Even if she's...part of this, she's in trouble."

Zach wasn't convinced that was true, but it was possible. It was also possible she was trying to lure Lucy to her house, and he'd use that if he could.

"Why didn't you tell us she was calling?" Zach asked, trying to be gentle.

"She wanted to talk privately," Lucy replied, sounding resigned. "But she was scared, Zach. That wasn't an act. I don't... It couldn't have been. I'm not saying it's on the up and up, but this is complicated and she's in *danger*."

Complicated was right.

"Call the cops," Zach instructed. He shook his head at Vaughn, who'd opened his mouth to speak. "Not you or me, her. She's the one who spoke with Stacy, so she's going to give them her account. You two stay put. But call the cops and tell them everything you remember about the phone call."

"You don't know that she's telling the truth," Vaughn said firmly.

"No, but I don't know that she's not," Zach returned, moving for his gun, his holster, keys, wallet. "If this is some sort of plot to get to Lucy, she'll be here, protected by you and out of harm's way. If it's not, then

I get close enough to see what she might be planning. I'll need her address."

"Wait, you're not…going," Lucy said incredulously.

"If she's in trouble, I'm going to help," Zach said, weapon already strapped to his body. "And if she's trying to lure you, I want to be there to figure out why."

"But the cops—"

"I want them to check it out, but I want to get there first in case something is off. The more information I can gather, the better chance we have of putting this away for good."

"But if it's a lure, it could be dangerous. You could be hurt."

"Not if you call the cops." He didn't like Lucy being out of his sight right now, but they were both going to have to deal with their worry. Vaughn would protect her. He was more than capable. "Make sure you tell the cops I'll be there and give my description and that I'll be happy to verify and ID who I am so they don't mix me up with anyone else."

He leaned forward to kiss her goodbye—just on the off chance this was dangerous and things went south—but the presence of her brother gave him pause.

Screw it. He kissed her. Hard. "Stay put. I mean it. Both of you." He didn't need to worry about Vaughn keeping an eye on her. There was no doubt in Zach's mind Vaughn would lay down his own life to save his sister's, just like Zach would do.

So Zach would go, no matter how much uncertainty plagued him. Because this didn't add up and if it was a lead, he'd darn well take it. "Text me the address."

By the time he was in the rental car, Stacy's address

was plugged into his navigation system and he was on his way.

He wished he had more time to plan, but if Lucy sincerely thought Stacy was in trouble there wasn't time for plans. He had to act. Stacy might be involved, like Jordan, and about to be hurt to protect a killer's true identity. Stacy could be luring Lucy to her, or trying to get her alone.

Endless possibilities. So he had to be ready for anything.

He beat the cops to her house, which wasn't too far from the farmhouse. That certainly gave him some pause, but he quickly got out of the car and began moving toward the house.

It was quiet. Stacy didn't have the same amount of property as the place they'd been staying, but it was still secluded from the neighbors by a pristine lawn and thick trees around the perimeter.

Zach glanced into the garage through the windows. There was a car parked inside the tidy building. If someone was here, there was no evidence of a vehicle besides Stacy's own.

He didn't want Stacy to be guilty for Lucy's sake, but believing things for Lucy's sake was bound to get people hurt. He'd already let his emotions get too involved here even after promising himself not to.

That was… Well, it had happened. He couldn't change it.

So he'd have to do better for Lucy than he'd done for Ethan. Neither Lucy nor her brother were getting hurt on his watch, so he'd follow this path wherever it led.

He moved to the front door, glanced around the quiet lawn. Nothing and no one, as far as he could tell.

Carefully, he tried the knob. Locked. He looked around again, hoping for police backup, but still no sign of cops or sounds of sirens.

He'd have to move around the house, looking in what windows he could. Then if there was still nothing— and no cops—he'd simply have to break in and hope for the best.

He moved stealthily around the house, peeking in windows and seeing nothing—no people, no signs of struggle, just a perfectly neat but lived-in-looking house.

Until he got to the back porch. There were two big French doors that led into a dining room and kitchen area.

The bolt of shock at what he saw stopped him in his tracks. Stacy was sitting in the middle of the kitchen— tied to a chair. She had duct tape around her mouth. He could see her profile, and her eyes were wide and terrified.

There didn't appear to be anyone around her— though he could only see part of the kitchen and dining room from his vantage point. He looked around the expansive backyard. No one.

It could be a trap—the way his heart beat hard against his chest warned him that this could all end very, very badly for him.

But a woman was tied up in a kitchen and he was armed. The least he could do was try to help her.

He could tell the doors weren't fully latched—likely where whoever was in there had gotten in—so he began to slowly move forward, watching every inch of the backyard for a flash of movement.

Every last hunch inside him screamed *trap*, but he

couldn't ignore the trickle of blood that started at Stacy's temple and slid down the side of her face and neck.

It was possible she'd done it to herself, possible she was *this* good of an actor, but he couldn't be sure.

Carefully, making as little noise as possible, Zach inched forward. He kept his gaze alert and his movements careful, gun at the ready. He moved up to the door and waited for some kind of movement.

When he reached forward and gave the door a slight nudge, Stacy's head whipped around. Her eyes went wide. Zach could only hope she recognized him as he stepped forward.

She didn't fidget or try to speak past the tape. She just watched him as she breathed heavily through her nose. Slowly, she moved her hand. Though her arms were tied to her sides and the chair, she lifted one finger and pointed upstairs.

At least, that was what he hoped she was pointing at. He moved closer and closer, studying the way she was tied. It would be best to free her arms and legs first, so she could run if need be, but he needed more information first. So the tape had to go.

"Brace yourself, okay?" he whispered, tapping the edge of the tape. "And try not to make a sound."

She nodded, tears trickling down her cheeks. Feeling awful, Zach pulled the tape from her mouth.

She gasped in pain, but she didn't make any extra noise.

"How many are there?" he asked, immediately crouching to untie the rope bonds.

"Just one. Just one. I don't know who he is. I don't know what's going on." She started crying in earnest, and Zach winced at the noise. "He's upstairs. He's looking for something, but I don't know what."

"That's fine. It's all going to be okay." He got the ropes off her and helped her to her feet. "Run outside. The police will be here soon. I'm going to stay right here and make sure he doesn't leave, so you just make sure to tell the police there are two of us in here—and one of us means them no harm." Hopefully, between Stacy's recount and Lucy's call giving his description, he'd avoid accidentally entangling with police.

"What are you going to do?" Stacy whispered, rubbing her arms where the rope had been.

"I'm going to find out what's going on once and for all. You run. Now."

She nodded tremulously, but then she eased out of the back door and left in a dead run.

Zach took a breath and then began to move. He wished he knew the layout of Stacy's house, but he could at least hear someone upstairs. As long as he did, he knew the perpetrator was up there and not on the same level as him.

Zach just needed to find him, get him to talk and then let the police do whatever they had to do.

Easy, right?

He eased closer to the staircase, weapon drawn and ready. Here he couldn't hear the footsteps as well as he'd been able to in the dining area.

Still, he moved slowly and as silently as possible. As he went up the stairs, some of his old FBI training took over—the way his body would cool, tense and let go of the wild fear. Focused on the job—on the end result, and the rest of the chips would fall where they fell.

Doing what he came to do was the most important thing.

When he crested the top, he leaned forward and looked around. There weren't any hallways, just a circle of an area—with four rooms around him.

All four doors were open, but only slightly ajar. If he started to move forward, he'd be able to get a glimpse into them, but he wouldn't be able to do anything else without drawing attention to himself.

Not ideal, but it could be worse, so he started forward. The first room didn't have anyone in it that he could see. Neither did the second room. As he approached the third, his foot landed on a floorboard that made a creak as loud as a bomb.

Immediately, the third door burst open and a gun went off. Zach felt the searing burn of metal hitting flesh, stumbled to his hands and knees and swore, then rolled forward to knock the shooter off his feet.

His arm throbbed, but not enough to be anything more than a flesh wound. The gunman let out a howl of pain as he crashed into the dresser. Violent cursing and threats spewed from the man, but it was drowned out by the thundering of feet and shouted orders to drop their weapons and stay down.

Zach winced at the searing ache in his arm, but praised the timing of the police. The man he'd knocked into wasn't taller than Zach, but he was built like a Mack truck. Zach could take on a bigger man, but in this tiny room he would have been beat to hell in the process, no doubt.

Once the cops verified who he was and cleared him to get up, he moved toward the man he didn't recognize being handcuffed.

"Who do you work for?" Zach demanded.

"We'll handle the questioning, Mr. Simmons."

Zach leveled the officer pushing him back with a scathing look. Zach kept trying to push forward, but the one cop kept pushing him back while two others arrested the thrashing man on the ground.

Zach cursed. Demanded answers. Got nothing but a brick wall of blank-faced cops as they hauled the assailant down the stairs.

The last cop eyed him, nodded toward his arm. "There's an ambulance outside."

Zach looked down. Blood was trickling down his arm and onto the white carpet. He blinked at the tiny pool of blood. For a second he felt a little light-headed, but then he shook it off.

"I'm fine." He had to find some answers before this escalated any further. "I need answers. I need—"

"Nasty gash on his head. He'll be transported to the hospital, and then we'll take him in for questioning. I'd suggest calling one of our detectives tomorrow to get an update on the situation."

Tomorrow. An *update*? He didn't have time to wait until tomorrow. "Where's the woman?" Zach asked.

"What woman?"

Zach's entire body went cold, his gut sinking with dread. "The one who ran out of here a good ten minutes ago."

The cop's eyebrows drew together, and he pulled his shoulder radio to his mouth and muttered a few things into it. After a few seconds of static and responses, the cop shrugged. "No one saw a woman."

*Hell.* "There was a woman here, tied up and mouth taped." He went through the whole event, gave Stacy's name and description, and then rushed back to the farm-house, trying to determine what on earth Stacy had been trying to pull. She'd been hurt, but now she was missing.

What was going on? He couldn't figure it out for the life of him, but one thing he knew for sure.

He had to get back to Lucy and make sure she was okay.

LUCY PACED IRRITABLY. "It's taking too long. Why hasn't he called? Or come back? What if he's hurt and we're just sitting here—"

"If the police are questioning him, it'll take a while," Vaughn replied calmly. "These things take time, and unfortunately going half-cocked is likely what Stacy wanted. We have to stay put and wait and trust the police to do their jobs."

"Why would they question Zach?"

"Because they have to piece together what happened. If Zach sees anything over there, he'll need to explain. Maybe he's giving them more details on the case. You just don't know, and you can't read into the time that passes. Sit. Relax."

She snorted. "How can I relax when…when…" She plopped down on the couch next to Vaughn. She'd never told her brother anything about her personal life, and vice versa, but she didn't have anywhere else to put all this *stuff* roiling around inside her.

"I'm in love with him."

Vaughn leveled her with a bland gaze. "Gee. You don't say."

She frowned at him. She thought she'd get a lec-ture…one that would give her a reason to be mad and rage instead of be sad or worried.

Vaughn offered no such lecture and, in fact, seemed wholly unsurprised and unconcerned.

"You're okay with that?"

"Not *okay* exactly, but I know a thing or two about… falling in love under uncomfortable circumstances."

"He might not be in love with me," Lucy replied petulantly, because she wanted to be petulant about something if she couldn't be mad.

"Lucy, please. He's so head over heels even I can't be big-brother outraged over it. I might not be particularly comfortable with emotion, but I certainly recognize head-over-heels stupid love when I see it."

"It's just the pressure. He feels guilty. He had this thing go wrong when he was in the FBI, and… You don't fall in love over the course of a few days. It's adrenaline and stuff."

Vaughn didn't even have the decency to look away from the computer screen he was still doing research on. "I'll be sure to let Nat know the only reason I fell in love with her was *adrenaline and stuff.*"

"That's not the same."

This time he did look at her, but only to give her his patented condescending older-brother look. "How exactly?"

She didn't have a good answer, so she was more than happy that her phone trilling interrupted the question. She stood and answered without even looking at the caller ID. "Zach?"

"Lucy. No. No, it's me."

"Stacy?" She grabbed Vaughn's arm as he shot to his feet next to her. She was scared to death Stacy was calling to tell her Zach had been hurt or worse.

"What's happening? What is *happening*? I'm so scared. God."

"Stacy. Where are you? Where's Zach?" Lucy demanded through a tight throat.

Vaughn ripped the phone out of her hands. She thought he was going to talk to Stacy himself, demand answers, but he only put the call on speaker.

"He saved me," Stacy was saying over and over again. "He saved me, but… Lucy." Stacy was breathing hard, and the connection was spotty. "Listen to me."

The line cut in and out. "Stacy. Stacy. Stop…running? Or whatever you're doing. Stay in one place. I'm losing you."

"I'm so scared. Zach told me to run, so I ran and now… I don't know where I am. I ran into the trees and now… God, I'm so lost. I know I should have waited for the police, but I was so scared."

She started crying and Lucy's heart twisted, some awful mix of compassion and suspicion. What if this was another fake thing? "Stacy, tell me what's going on."

"I don't know. I don't understand it, but I think… Lucy, Jordan is Don Levinson's grand-nephew."

"What?" Daisy asked incredulously. The only reason she didn't lose her balance was because Vaughn held her up.

"Yes. God. He told me at some party eons ago. I didn't think much of it. You and I had already had a fight about Jordan and I didn't want to make you madder at me over Jordan. But then I mostly forgot about all that. He never brought it up again, and I never saw the old bastard. But I think Cory is involved, Lucy. I really do. I didn't tell anyone you'd been to Wyoming.

Not a *soul*. But Cory could have been listening. It's the only possibility."

Lucy shared a look with Vaughn. He didn't look convinced, but Jordan was related to *Don*? Why would Don want to hurt her after all this time? How did it all connect?

"Okay. Okay. You just stay put," Lucy instructed. They needed her safe and coherent to figure out if her story made any sense. "I'm going to come find you."

Before Vaughn could mount his argument, Stacy gave one. "No, Lucy. You can't. Whoever was in my house… I didn't recognize him or know him. Whoever wants to hurt you is still out there, pulling strings."

Which was when they heard a car squeal to a stop in front of the farmhouse.

## Chapter Seventeen

Zach screeched to a stop in front of the farmhouse. He all but leaped out of the car and ran for the door. Stacy missing, the cops not having seen her at all, made every terrible scenario run through his head.

Stacy had already beaten him here. The whole thing had been a ruse to find out the location of the farmhouse. It was too late and Lucy was—

He stopped on the porch on a dime. What if he'd fallen for it, and led Stacy—or whoever—here right *now*? Stacy was a plant, but not the kind he'd expected. Not trying to lead Lucy to an ambush at her place, but a way to find Lucy at hers.

He turned, looked around the yard, but there was no sign of anyone that he could see. If someone had followed him, they were still far enough away that he could get to Lucy and keep her safe.

Unless they were already here. He jumped forward and shoved his key into the lock. He'd get to Lucy first. Move them out fast. Then they could figure it out, but first they had to be away from any place that could be dangerous and breeched.

The sound of an explosion shuddered through the air in perfect timing with a blast of pain in his thigh.

He staggered forward, the door opening as he did so. He crashed to the ground of the entryway, just barely recognizing the scream as Lucy's.

Lucy. Who he had to keep safe, no matter how his vision dimmed or the pain screamed through him. This wound was worse than his arm, but it wasn't fatal. Probably.

Even if it was, he'd do whatever it took to make sure nothing fatal touched Lucy.

Zach managed to scoot back and kick the door closed, but it wasn't fast enough. Before Vaughn could jump on the lock, it was being flung back open and Vaughn got knocked into the coffee table, which broke and splintered under his weight.

Two men stepped inside, one holding a gun, and one looking very, very smug. They shut the door behind them.

Zach didn't know why he was surprised. He'd known, hadn't he?

Emotion got people hurt and killed. He'd let his worry over Lucy cloud his thoughts, and now they'd all pay for it.


"Well, look at you, Daisy girl. All grown."

Lucy's stomach pitched. The years had not been kind to Don Levinson, and yet that smarmy smile of his was exactly the same and still reminded her of things she'd tried long and hard to forget.

That smile made her remember all too clearly a young girl who'd thought her father would protect her and been wholly, utterly disillusioned.

But Dad was dead, and Don very much wasn't. Old, yes, but not dead, and certainly no less evil than he'd been all those years ago trying to take advantage of young women.

Vaughn sat in the wreckage of the coffee table. Zach lay on the ground, a concerning amount of blood pooling around his leg. Both were armed, but neither reached for their weapon. She supposed they wouldn't as long as Don's little buddy there had a very big and scary-looking gun pointed in her direction.

"I'm very disappointed in you, sweetheart. Your father always told me how smart you were, and yet you never once suspected your old pal Don. You didn't suspect that moron you married until it was too late."

Lucy didn't say anything. She barely let the words register, because she had to think. She had to survive this and get Zach and Vaughn out of this horrible mess.

"Don't worry. You're not half as disappointing as *him*," Don continued. "The time and effort I poured into that boy, and he's still dumb as a post. A bit of a coward, too. If I'd had my way, he would have killed you slowly and quietly when you were married, but *no*."

Killed her. Don and Jordan had plotted to kill her.

"He thought he'd use your fame instead of my know-how. Thought you being a wreck would sell him better than you being dead. Well, look where he is now. Like I said, dumb as a post."

"Yeah, I suppose we both were," Lucy replied, trying not to let the wave of nauseous regret fell her. Zach was bleeding. Vaughn would die to protect her and leave his family without a husband and father.

She couldn't—wouldn't—let that happen.

"What on earth do you have against me, Don?" Lucy asked, trying to sound bored and unaffected.

Don laughed. "Against *you*. Against *you*? As if you don't know. Your father told me what you did."

"Told him you were a dangerous pervert who couldn't keep his hands off teenage girls?"

"If you hadn't gone crying to him, pretending like you hadn't wanted my hands on you, do you know what I would have? He cut me out of his estate, and out of all I'd invested in *you*. So I had to bow and scrape and pay off my debts. The things I had to endure because I didn't get that money, all because you were a lying whore. Well, my hands'll be on you now."

Zach and Vaughn made almost identical sounds of outrage, and Don smiled down at them. "Don't worry," he said cheerfully. "It won't bother you any. You'll both be dead." His gaze went back to Daisy. "And boy, will the press eat this up. I'll have to figure out how I'm going to play it first. You'd think I'd know, with all the planning that's gone into it, but sometimes I do like to wing it. Murder-suicide? Or do I just frame you? So many options. But at least I finally realized I'd have to do it myself. The younger generation just doesn't have the chutzpa to get things done."

He turned to the other man. "Leave the one on the floor." He nudged Zach with his boot. Zach didn't so much as move or groan. Lucy tried not to panic that he'd lost consciousness. "He'll bleed out if he hasn't already." Don then studied Vaughn.

Lucy had to do something. Save her brother. Save Zach. But how? If someone was willing to kill like this, what kind of reasoning would work?

"You want money?" she demanded.

"I want *revenge*, little girl. I was supposed to have a piece of your pie, but your father held your lying story over me for years. Made me jump through all those hoops and then not even a *cent* of his estate? Which should have been rightfully left to me for all I'd done to make him a star, if you hadn't come along."

"I never lied. You grabbed me."

"You begged for it."

"You're delusional. And insane, I think, to have spent your life so obsessed with me—"

"Shoot her," Don ordered of the man with the gun. Then he held up a hand, before Vaughn could lunge to her rescue, and sighed dramatically. "No. That's rash. I want my fun with her first. And yours, as well," he said, nodding toward the man with the gun, who smiled.

Lucy hoped she didn't go gray, because it felt as though the very blood leaked out of her. But she needed to keep Don talking, not acting. She had to make him feel…superior. Anger would make him act, but condescension would keep his diatribes going.

"You were never supposed to have a piece of my career. My career was always separate from Dad's."

Don tipped his head back and laughed, all too heartily. Lucy noted Zach's lifeless body. Vaughn's hesitant, slow and deliberate move for his hand to get closer and closer to his weapon without drawing attention.

She needed a scene. Not just from Don, but from everyone to get the man with the gun's attention.

"You were always meant to be your daddy's pawn. Problem was you got too many ideas, and that uppity assistant of mine fed them. And if your father had listened to me, you both would have been taken down a peg. But he let you go instead. Costing me millions. *Millions.*"

The rage was starting to seep back in and Lucy racked her brain for a way to fix this. Save them. But

Don just kept going, eyes gleaming with vicious rage, spittle forming at the corners of his mouth.

And all the while the man with the gun had the barrel pointed right at Lucy's heart.

"Then he didn't even have the intelligence to be sorry. Every time, every single time I had a better idea for your father's career, one he didn't agree with, what did he say to me? *I guess Daisy going to the police wouldn't be such a good thing for* your *career, would it, Don?*"

"That sounds like a problem between you and my father," Lucy managed, though her throat was tight with fear and pain.

"A problem I solved." He grinned and Lucy's knees nearly gave out.

"You killed him?" she rasped.

Don shrugged, but his smile was sharp. "Not so much. Supply him enough drugs and he killed himself." But his smile turned into a sneer. "Then I started getting your notes."

"I never sent you any notes, Don. I'd forgotten you even existed. That's why I didn't suspect you were behind this, because you're so far beneath me and behind me I didn't give you a second thought." Notes. Notes. As if this wasn't complicated enough, someone had been sending him notes in her name?

"Sure, little girl. Sure."

"Maybe Jordan isn't as stupid as you thought," Lucy shot out. "He knew, you know. About what you did to me." It was a flat-out lie. The only person she'd ever told aside from Stacy was Zach.

Oh, God, it all circled back to Stacy, didn't it?

But she couldn't get caught up on that. She couldn't

let the tears that threatened, fall. She couldn't give in to panic or fear, because Zach was a lifeless, bleeding form on the floor and she had to save him.

Jordan was safe in jail. If she implicated him, if she got Don to believe it…well, he'd kill them all anyway, but maybe it would make him unbalanced for a few minutes.

Don narrowed his eyes at her. "I don't believe it."

"I didn't send you notes, Don. You would have been one of the top suspects if I had. It had to be Jordan. Unless you told someone else about it."

"Or your father did." He shook his head. "It doesn't matter. Result is still the same. This guy is dead." He pointed at Zach. Then he pointed at Vaughn. "That guy is going to be. And we're going to have our fun before you are, too."

No. That was not how this was going to go down, and the best way to get out of a sticky situation with a man who thought he was in charge was always, *always* act the overwrought female.

"Dead?" she moaned. "He's dead?" She made a choking, sobbing noise and flung herself on Zach's body.

She'd hoped it would be enough of an opening Vaughn would shoot, but Don just grumbled something about women. So Lucy sobbed as loudly as she could, moving her hand, discreetly trying to get to Zach's gun without anyone noticing.

It wasn't hard to keep crying when he didn't move. But he was breathing. Unless it was just the movement of her own body making his chest seem as though it was moving up and down. She was almost to his gun when she felt him twitch under her just a little.

She gave herself one second to just press her cheek

to his chest and breathe in some relief. He was alive but he desperately needed help. She'd give it. Get his gun and—

"Scream," Zach whispered through bloodless lips, but he was breathing and talking, so she didn't wait around for anything else. She did exactly what he said.

Lucy's scream shattered through the air and though it hurt like hell, Zach whipped his gun out of his holster and shot the man with the gun—who'd been so intent on Vaughn's lunge he hadn't seen Zach move, and with Lucy sheltering his arm from Don, the old man hadn't been able to warn him.

Vaughn tackled Don to the floor amidst shouts and threats.

Zach tried to get to his feet, but leveling the gun had taken all his energy and focus. His vision wavered, and he wasn't all that certain he could feel his legs. There was only pain and a fog that he kept trying to fight.

It was starting to win.

"Get some pressure on the wound," he thought he heard Vaughn shout. Was Lucy hurt? No, she hadn't been—had she?

Zach had shot the right guy, and Vaughn had taken care of the rest. Lucy was safe. He relaxed a little into the fog, except there were still so many unanswered questions.

"Loose ends," Zach muttered.

Gentle hands were on his face. "Only a few. You just stay with me so we can figure them out, all right?"

"Lucy."

"That's right. That's right." There was a catch in her throat and even though he could only see black, he knew she was crying. But she was here and safe and that was what mattered.

He hissed out a breath, eyes opening as pain shot through his leg. Pressure, he supposed, but it hurt too much to hold on to consciousness. He tried not to slide away while Lucy whispered things in his ears.

"You're okay, baby. I promise."

Something floated around in his head, a feeling he had to tell her. But the words didn't form. Yet, it was imperative. He had to tell her so she knew, but every time he tried to speak it all floated away.

"Zach, stay with me. We need you here."

"I'm here." But he wasn't. He kept losing hold on himself, on her.

There was noise, and he was being jostled. Lucy faded away, and so did he, but words floated with him.

"I love you, Zach. I love you. So you just hold on to that or I'm going to be really pissed."

Those were the words he'd meant to find—*I love you, I love you*—if only he could manage to say them back.

## Chapter Eighteen

Everyone insisted she go to the police station. Vaughn was with her, but no one was with Zach. No matter what Vaughn said about him being in surgery and her not being able to be with him anyway, she could only think about him being alone.

The detective who sat at the desk across from them looked frazzled, which wasn't exactly comforting. "It doesn't add up. Let's go over it again."

"She's gone over it enough," Vaughn said firmly. "You have to find Stacy Vine. She'll fill in some of these missing pieces."

"Yes, I know. We're searching for her. We've got a team combing the woods as Ms. Delaney described to us from their phone call, and we've got someone watching her office as well as her car." The detective sighed, and then tapped a few things on his computer. "We've got someone searching Don Levinson's place of residence for evidence of these letters allegedly from you. Also, obviously, any evidence pertaining to the murder of Tom Perelli, the break-in at Stacy Vine's house or any connection to the three hired men that have been involved in attacks on Ms. Delaney."

"That's all well and good, but it isn't answers."

"Answers take time, Ranger Cooper," the detective returned, losing some of his control as irritation snaked into his tone.

Lucy couldn't blame him. It seemed no matter how they dug, no one could find all the answers. And her being here wasn't changing that, so she had to go to the hospital.

Before she could thank him for his time, make her excuses to go to the hospital, a knock sounded at the door to the detective's office.

Lucy didn't know how long they'd been sitting here, but it felt interminable.

And then Cory, Stacy's assistant, was being walked in. Handcuffed.

"Cory?"

"I didn't do anything! I didn't do a *thing*." But Lucy's stomach sank as she noticed anger more than fear in the depths of Cory's eyes. The same kind of anger that had been in Don's.

"She was found in Ms. Vine's house. An officer found her placing these in Ms. Vine's belongings." The officer held out a ziplock bag and the detective studied them. Then he turned them to Lucy.

"Is this your handwriting, Ms. Delaney?"

Lucy studied the words. *You spineless lowlife, you owe me for what you did. I'm going to make you pay worse than my father did.*

"No. Not my handwriting and I didn't write those."

Cory started screaming, blaming Don and Lucy and Stacy at equal turns, not making much sense in the process. The officer who'd led her in led her back out.

Lucy closed her eyes against the roil of nausea. She felt…sorry for the girl, almost. It was too easy to be manipulated by powerful men who'd always trusted their own influence, when you always questioned your own.

Vaughn's arm came around her and she leaned into it.

Hours passed as she sat in the awful police station. They finally found Stacy, and Lucy didn't know how to repair the damage of the past few days. But the police seemed to believe Stacy was innocent—that Cory's connection to Don had led her to ferret out information and supply Don with it.

Cory, a woman Don had groomed from the time she'd moved to Nashville with a dream of becoming a country music star. He'd pushed her into getting a job for Stacy, pumped her for information about Daisy over the years. Don had used that information to supply bits and pieces to Jordan. Who had, in the end, not used it quite the way Don had wanted.

But Don also hadn't helped Cory the way she'd expected, so Cory had begun using the information *she* knew about Don against him—writing threatening letters supposedly from Daisy.

Which had finally forced Don to act, instead of just stew. Especially when Daisy had filed for divorce from Jordan.

Jordan, who hadn't been released from jail yet, but it was looking like he would be.

Vaughn was insisting the detectives look into the legality of him getting off scot-free when he'd known Don had wanted her dead, but Lucy didn't care about that.

"I just want to see Zach. And then I want…" She wanted to go home. Only she didn't have one.

"We'll take it one step at a time, and I'll be here for every step. Whether you want me to be or not. That's a promise for the rest of your life."

Lucy smiled, but she also cried. And Vaughn held her through the tears, no matter how uncomfortable he was. He always would have, but now she was promising herself to always let him.

ZACH WOKE UP, groggy and gray. Pain snaked through a void of numbness. He didn't know where he was or why he was here, except he was clearly hurt.

When he managed to open his eyes, blue ones stared right back at him. Something inside him eased. She was all right.

"Your mother will be so upset with me. I just convinced her to go back to her hotel and get some sleep and here you are waking up."

"Aw, hell. My mother?" Zach grumbled, his voice raw.

Lucy took his hand in hers. "She likes me, don't worry. Cam and Hilly wanted to come, too, but I think your mother told them to stay put so they could take shifts."

"Cam's probably pretty pissed I went dark."

"Cam will probably forgive the man who's been shot twice."

He looked at her, really looked, as he came back to himself. He didn't remember much of what had happened, and based on the itchy and uncomfortable scruff on his face, he'd been out for a while.

But he remembered her saying she loved him, like one bright, shining beacon in the middle of foggy dark.

"Supposed to be a Delaney that gets shot," he managed to say, earning one of her patented raised eyebrow looks that made the love sweep through him so hard, so fast, he'd never question anyone's view on meant-to-be again.

"You see, back in Bent, there's a feud," he said over the wave of pain.

"You've been holding another good story from me?"

A story she'd love. A story that didn't scare him anymore. Because when it came to love, there were lots of things to worry about, but none to be scared of. "Carsons and Delaneys. They don't like each other. My mother was a Carson. Your grandmother was a Delaney."

"Are we Romeo and Juliet, Zach?"

"No, because I'm willing to die for you, Lucy, but I'm not willing to kill myself over you. Besides, the past year or so it's been something of a…hate to love deal. Carsons and Delaneys kept pairing off. Until I was the only one left."

"So we're meant to be."

"I've never believed in meant-to-be," Zach replied, holding her hand in his. She was looking worse for the wear herself, worrying over him. So many loose ends, but she was here and okay, and he was here and okay, so the most important loose end was love. "But I believe we got thrown into each other's life for a chance at something I never really thought I'd have."

"A country duo?"

"You're on quite the comedic roll, aren't you?"

"If I don't laugh I might break down and cry, and I've cried myself dry. So, I'd rather laugh, if you don't mind."

"I don't mind. I don't mind anything, if you're here. I love you, Lucy."

She swallowed, eyes shining. "I want it to go down on the record I was brave enough to say it first."

"Or at least smart enough to realize it first. I needed to get shot. Twice."

"You're just more stubborn than me."

"Ha!" The scoffing laugh hurt and he winced.

"I need to call the nurse in."

"No, not just yet. Come here."

She scooted closer and brushed a gentle kiss across his cheekbone.

"Going to come visit me? A lot?"

"Nah."

The pain of getting shot had nothing on the simple slice of horror that cut through him, until he noted she was smiling and leaning forward.

"I'd rather come home with you instead. I've got some ideas for your little ghost town."

Relief coursed through him like a river. "Do you now?"

"I'll still make music, and tour, and you'll work with Cam and keep people safe even if it puts you in danger. Because my songs and your protection is who we are."

"Yes, it is."

"But I want to build a life with you where I can come home and be Lucy Cooper when Daisy Delaney wears me out."

"I want that, too." God. More than he could express.

"So you'll have to heal up quick. Nashville's got too many prying eyes, and one too many men named Jordan Jones."

"All right. I'm ready. Tell me the whole thing."

He fell asleep halfway through her explanation of Don's plans, Cory's role, Jordan's half guilt and Stacy's innocence. It took him another few days to make it through the whole story, and more time after that to get out of the hospital, and then back onto a plane to Wyoming.

With Lucy Cooper at his side. Just where she belonged.

## *Epilogue*

Zach Simmons was not a sentimental man, or so he'd thought. The sight of his mother carefully assisting Hilly with her wedding dress outside the church that had been restored in Hope Town—the name Lucy had come up with for their little ghost town—shifted something inside him.

Hilly made a beautiful bride, and their mother's elegant form standing next to her, openly crying, made his heart swell—a mix of sweet and bitter. He knew Mom was missing Dad, but also happy for Hilly, who'd been through so much and deserved this pretty wedding.

"Mom, you're supposed to go take your seat."

She nodded, dabbing at her eyes. She gave him a quick hug, beaming at him.

"You're looking good," she offered before slipping out of the room.

*Good* was probably a tiny exaggeration. He still had a ways to go on his recovery for his leg, but even Lucy had gotten to a place where she didn't get irritated about his jokes over it. After all, only Delaneys got shot in their pursuit of happily-ever-after. He'd bucked tradition—being the best of the Carsons and all that.

"You look beautiful," he said to Hilly once Mom had gone.

Hilly shook her head. "Don't say nice things to me. I'm trying not to cry until I see Cam. Is he nervous?"

"Cool as a cucumber." Which had been true on the surface, but his obsessive attention to detail at the church had been a sure giveaway Cam wasn't as calm as he pretended.

Lucy had called it cute. Zach had scoffed at her.

Zach offered an arm and then walked out of the small room Hilly had gotten ready in. They moved into the lobby of the church. Hilly and Cam had foregone bridesmaids and groomsmen since they had so many family members they would want to stand up with them. They'd said a church full of people they loved was enough—and that was exactly what they were getting.

So Zach waited for the signal—a text from Jen—and when it came, he opened the door. He led Hilly down the aisle.

There were people missing from the wedding. Their father and brother. The man Hilly had considered a father growing up. But Hilly and Cam were surrounded by family—Carsons and Delaneys, and the offspring of such calamitous pairings—and Zach was going to walk his baby sister down the aisle.

So he did, bringing her to a man he loved like a brother anyway. And he watched two people pledge their love to each other with the woman he loved seated next to him.

When the wedding ended, and the interminable pictures that tested his leg's endurance were done, they all drove back over to Bent to have the reception at

Rightful Claim—filled to the brim with couples. Laurel and Vanessa made rounds with their girls in their arms before handing them off to Grady and Dylan respectively. Noah's adopted son ran around squealing as Addie looked tired with a little baby bump popping more each day. Jen had looked suspiciously nauseated for the past week—at least that was what Lucy had told him that Laurel had told her.

Lucy had jumped into Carson and Delaney life like she'd been born into it, and no one here called her Daisy Delaney, because she was Lucy Cooper here.

Except to Cam, on occasion.

Speaking of which, Grady and Lucy took the small makeshift stage shoved into the corner of the saloon's main room.

"All right, folks, we're going to have the first dance for Cam and Hilly, with our very, *very* special guest to serenade our couple. You all know her as Lucy Cooper, but let's give a warm round of applause for Daisy Delaney."

Everyone clapped, Zach cheered and whistled and Lucy took to the stage with her guitar. She grinned at the crowd and spoke into the microphone.

"When Hilly asked me if I'd sing Cam's favorite song at their wedding, I promised I would. But I also thought something as momentous as a first dance should be about two people, two families, coming together. A song about love and promises. So with Hilly's permission, I wrote a song not just for this moment, but for all of you, too. For love and family and hope. We'll save Cam's favorite song for later, and here's a tip. Get me drunk enough, I'll sing anything. But for now, this one's for all of you."

The crowd laughed, but it didn't take long for them to settle. For Daisy's amazing voice to fill the saloon. What's more, the words of the song Lucy had written, about love and forever and even a few lines about breaking curses, settled over a group made up of people who'd been brave enough to buck tradition and expectation and fall in love with the person they were never even supposed to tolerate.

Silence, tears, happy and hopeful smiles. Even the babies were quiet until Lucy finished her song.

She slid off the stage as Cam and Hilly still swayed to their own music while Grady hooked up the speakers to Hilly's curated playlist for the evening.

Though Lucy stopped and talked to anyone who called out her name, her eyes were on Zach's as she slowly made her way over.

When she finally reached him, she sized him up. "How's the leg, champ?"

"Good enough for a dance."

"So long as it's one and only one," she returned, letting him pull her into his arms. They swayed to the slow song, and Lucy rested her temple on his cheek.

"I wrote the song for Hilly and Cam, for all of them really, but I never would have had the words if I hadn't found you," she murmured into his ear.

He pulled her closer, overwhelmed by his love for her and the love in the air. "I never believed in curses. I still don't, but you convinced me to believe in meant-to-be."

And from that day forward in Bent, Wyoming, people didn't mention curses anymore. But they did talk about a love strong enough to stand the test of murder, loss, greed, terror and evil.

And a little bit about how some things are just meant to be.

\* \* \* \* \*

# HER FORBIDDEN
# COWBOY

**CHARLENE SANDS**

To our own Zane William (Pettis), the bright little light in our family. And to his mommy, Angi, and daddy, Kent, with love to all!

# One

The heels of Jessica's boots beat against the redwood of Zane Williams's sun-drenched deck overlooking the Pacific Ocean. Shielded by the shade of an overhang, he didn't miss a move his new houseguest made as he leaned forward on his chaise longue. His sister-in-law had officially arrived.

Was he still allowed to call her that?

Gusty breezes lifted her caramel hair, loosening the knot at the back of her head. A few wayward tendrils whipped across her eyes and, as she followed behind his assistant Mariah, her hand came up to brush them away. Late afternoon winds were strong on Moonlight Beach, swirling up from the shore as the sun lowered on the horizon. It was the time most sunbathers packed up their gear and went home and the locals came out. Shirt-billowing weather and one of the few things he'd come to like about California beach living.

He removed his sunglasses to get a better look at her. She wore a snowdrift-white blouse tucked into washed-to-the-millionth-degree jeans and a wide brown belt. Tortoiseshell-rimmed eyeglasses delicately in place didn't hide the pain and distress in her eyes.

Sweet Jess. Seeing her brought back so many memories, and the frigidness in his heart thawed a bit.

She looked like…*home*.

It hurt to think about Beckon, Texas. About his ranch

and the life he'd had there once. It hurt to think about how he'd met Jessica's sister, Janie, and the way their small-town lives had entwined. In one respect, the tragedy that occurred more than two years ago might've been a lifetime ago. In another, it seemed as if time was standing still. Either way, his wife, Janie, and their unborn child were gone. They were never coming back. His mouth began to twitch. An ache in the pit of his stomach spread like wildfire and scorched him from the inside out.

He focused on Jessica. She carried a large tapestry suitcase woven in muted tones of gray and mauve and peach. He'd given Janie and Jessica matching luggage three years ago on their birthdays. It had been a fluke that both girls, the only two offspring of Mae and Harold Holcomb, were born on the same day, seven years apart.

Grabbing at the crutches propped beside his lounge chair, Zane slowly lifted himself up, careful not to fall and break his other foot. Mariah would have his head if he got hurt again. His casted wrist ached like the devil, but he refused to have his assistant come running every damn time he wanted to get up. It was bad enough she'd taken on the extra role of nursemaid. He reminded himself to have his business manager give Mariah a big fat bonus.

She halted midway on the deck, her disapproving gaze dropping to his busted wrist and crutches before she shot him a silent warning. "Here he is, Jessica." Mariah's peach-pie voice was sweet as ever for his houseguest. "I'll leave you two alone now."

"Thanks, Mariah," he said.

Her mouth pursed tight, she about-faced and marched off, none too pleased with him.

Jessica came forward. "Still such a gentleman, Zane," she said. "Even on crutches."

He'd forgotten how much she sounded like Janie. Hearing her sultry tone stirred him up inside. But that's about all Janie and Jessica had in common. The two sisters were different in most other ways. Jess wasn't as tall as her sister. Her eyes were a light shade of green instead of the deep emerald that had sparkled from Janie's eyes. Jess was brunette, Janie blonde. And their personalities were miles apart. Janie had been a risk-taker, a strong woman who could hold her own against Zane's country-star fame, which might've intimidated a less confident woman. From what he remembered about Jess, she was quieter, more subtle, a schoolteacher who loved her profession, a real sweetheart.

"Sorry about your accident."

Zane nodded. "Wasn't much of an accident. More like stupidity. I lost focus and fell off the stage. Broke my foot in three places." He'd been at the Los Angeles Amphitheater, singing a silly tune about chasing ducks on the farm, all the while thinking about Janie. A video of his fall went viral on the internet. Everyone in country music and then some had witnessed his loss of concentration. "My tour's postponed for the duration. Can't strum a guitar with a broken wrist."

"Don't suppose you can."

She put down her luggage and gazed over the railing to the shore below. Sunlight glossed over deep steely-blue water as whitecaps foamed over wet sand, the tide rising. "I suppose Mama must've strong-armed you into doing this."

"Your mama couldn't strong-arm a puppy."

She whipped around to face him, her eyes sharp. "You know what I mean."

He did. Fact was, he wouldn't refuse Mae Holcomb anything. And she'd asked him this favor. *It's huge*, she'd said to him. *My Jess is hurtin' and needs to clear her head. I'm asking you to let her stay with you a week, maybe two. Please, Zane, watch out for her.*

He'd given his word. He'd take care of Jess and make sure she had time to heal. Mae was counting on him, and there wasn't anything he wouldn't do for Janie's mother. She deserved that much from him.

"You can stay as long as you like, Jess. You've got to know that."

Her mouth began to tremble. "Th-thanks. You heard what happened?"

"I did."

"I—I couldn't stay in town. I had to get out of Texas. The farther, the better."

"Well, Jess, you're as far west as you could possibly go." Five miles north of Malibu by way of the Pacific Coast Highway.

Her shoulders slumped. "I feel like such a fool."

Reaching out, he cupped her chin, forcing her eyes to his, the darn crutch under his arm falling to rest on the railing. "Don't."

"I won't be very good company," she whispered, dang near breathless.

His body swayed, not allowing him another unassisted moment. He released her and grabbed for his crutch just in time. He tucked it under his arm and righted his position. "That makes two of us."

Her soft laughter carried on the breeze. Probably the first bit of amusement she'd felt in days.

He smiled.

"I just need a week, Zane."

"Like I said, take as long as you need."

"Thanks." She blinked, and her eyes drifted down to his injuries. "Uh, are you in a lot of pain?"

"More like, I'm being a pain. Mariah's getting the brunt of my sour mood."

"Now I can share it with her." Her eyes twinkled for a second.

He'd forgotten what it was like having Jess around. She was ten years younger than him, and he'd always called her his little sis. He hadn't seen much of her since Janie's death. Cursed by guilt and anguish, he'd deliberately removed himself from the Holcombs' lives. He'd done enough damage to them.

"Hand up your luggage to me," he told her. With his good hand, he tucked his crutches under his armpits and propped himself, then wiggled his fingers. If he could get a grip on the bag...

Jessica rolled her eyes and hoisted her valise. "I appreciate it, Zane. But I've got this. Really, it's not heavy. I packed light. You know, summer-at-the-beach kind of clothes."

She let him off the hook. He would've tried, but fooling with her luggage wouldn't have been pretty. The doggone crutches made him clumsy as a drunken sailor, and he wasn't supposed to put any weight on his foot yet. "Fine, then. Why don't you settle in and rest up a bit? I'm bunking on this level. You've got an entire wing of rooms to yourself upstairs. Take your pick and spread out."

He followed behind as she made her way inside the wide set of light oak French doors leading to the living room. "Feel free to look around. I can have Mariah give you a tour."

"No, that's not necessary." She scanned over what she could see of the house, taking in the expanse—vaulted ceilings, textured walls, art deco interior and sleek contemporary furniture. He caught her vibe, sensing her confusion. What was Zane Williams, a country-western artist and a born and bred Texan, doing living on a California beach? When he'd leased this place with the option to buy, he told himself it was because he wanted a change. He was building Zane's on the Beach, his second restaurant in as many years, and he'd been offered roles in several Hollywood movies. He didn't know if he was cut out for acting, so the pending offers were still on the table.

She sent him an over-the-shoulder glance. "It's...a beautiful house, Zane."

His crutches supporting him, he sidled up next to her, seeing the house from her perspective. "But not *me*?"

"I guess I don't know what that is anymore."

"It's just a house. A place to hang my hat."

She gave his hatless head a glance. "It's a palace on the sea."

He chuckled. So much for his attempt at humble. The house was a masterpiece. One of three designed by the architect who lived next door. "Okay, you got me there. Mariah found the house and leased it on the spot. She said it would shake the cobwebs from my head. Had it awhile, but this is my first summer here." He leaned back, darting a glance around. "At least the humidity is bearable and it never seems to rain, so no threat of thunderstorms. The neighbors are nice."

"A good place to rest up."

"I suppose, if that's what I'm doing."

"Isn't it?"

He shrugged, fearing he'd opened up a can of worms. Why was he revealing his innermost thoughts to her? They weren't close anymore. He hardly knew Jessica as an adult, and yet they shared a deeply powerful connection. "Sure it is. Are you hungry? I can have my housekeeper make you—"

"Oh, uh...no. I'm not hungry right now. Just a bit tired from the trip. I'd better go upstairs before I collapse right here on your floor. Thanks for having a limo pick me up. And, well, thanks for everything, Zane."

She rose on her tiptoes, and the soft brush of her lips on his cheek squeezed something tight in his chest. Her hair smelled of summer strawberries, and the fresh scent lingered in his nose as she backed away.

"Welcome." The crutches dug into his armpits as they supported his weight. He hated the damn things. Couldn't wait to be free of them. "Just a suggestion, but the room to the right of the stairs and farthest down the hall has the best view of the ocean. Sunsets here are pretty glorious."

"I'll keep that in mind." Her quick smile was probably

meant to fake him out. She could pretend she wasn't hurting all that badly if she wanted to, but dark circles under her eyes and the pallor of her skin told the real story. He understood. He'd been there. He knew how pain could strangle a person until all the breath was sucked out. Hell, he'd lived it. Was still living it. And he knew something about Holcomb family pride, too.

What kind of jerk would leave any Holcomb woman standing at the altar?

Only a damn fool.

Jessica took Zane's advice and chose the guest room at the end of the hallway. Not for the amazing sunsets as Zane had suggested, but to keep out of his hair. Privacy was a precious commodity. He valued it, and so did she now. A powerful urge summoned her to slump down on the bed and cry her eyes out, but she managed to fight through the sensation. She was done with self-pity. She wasn't the first woman to be dumped at the altar. She'd been duped by a man she'd loved and trusted. She'd been so sure and missed all of the telling signs. Now she saw them through crystal clear eyes.

She busied herself unpacking her one suitcase, layering her clothes into a long, stylish light wood dresser. Carefully she set her jeans, shorts, swimsuits and undies into two of the nine drawers. She plucked out a few sleeveless sundresses and walked over the closet. With a slight tug, the double doors opened in a whoosh. The scents of cedar and freshness filled her nostrils as she gazed into a girl cave almost the size of her first-grade classroom back in Beckon. Cedar drawers, shoe racks and silken hangers were a far cry from the tiny drywalled closet in her one-bedroom apartment.

Deftly she scooped the delicate hangers under the straps of her dresses and hung them up. Next she laid her tennis shoes, flip-flops and two pairs of boots, one flat, one high-heeled, onto the floor just under her clothes. Her meager collection barely made a dent in the closet space. She closed the double doors and leaned against them. Then she took her first real glimpse at the view from her second-story bedroom.

"Wow." Breath tunneled from her chest.

Aqua seas and the sun-glazed sky made for a spectacular vista from the wide windows facing the horizon. She swallowed in a gulp of awe. Then suddenly, a strange bone-rattling feeling of loss hit her. She shivered as if assailed by a winter storm.

Why now? Why wasn't she reveling in the beauty surrounding her?

*Nothing's beautiful. You lost your sister, her unborn baby and your fiancé.*

"Would you like to go out onto the balcony?"

She whirled around, surprised to find Mariah, Zane's fortyish blonde assistant standing in the doorway. She'd worked for him since before he had married Janie. Jessica and Mariah's paths had crossed a few times since then. "Oh, hi." She glanced at the narrow glass door at the far end of the wall that led to the balcony. It was obviously situated there to keep from detracting from the room's sweeping view of the Pacific. "Thanks, but maybe later."

"Sure, you must be tired from the flight. Is there anything I can do for you?"

"I don't think so. I've unpacked. A shower and a nap and I'll be good to go."

Mariah smiled. "I'll be leaving for the day. Mrs. Lopez, Zane's housekeeper, is here. If you need anything, just ask her."

"Thank you… I'll be fine."

"Zane will want to have dinner with you. He eats dinner just before sunset. But he'd make an exception if you're hungry earlier."

"Sunset is fine."

Mariah studied her, her eyes unflinching and kind. "You look a little like Janie."

"I doubt that. Janie was beautiful."

"I see a resemblance. If you don't mind me saying, you have the same soulful eyes and lovely complexion."

She was pale as a ghost, and ten freckles dotted her nose. Yep, she'd counted them. Though, she'd never had acne or even a full-fledged zit to speak of in her teens. She supposed her complexion wasn't half-bad. "Thank you. I, uh, don't want to cause Zane or you any trouble. I'm basically here because it would've been harder to convince my mother otherwise, and I didn't want her to worry about me off in some deserted location to search my soul. Mama's had enough on her plate. She doesn't need to fret over me."

"I get it. Actually, you might be exactly what Zane needs to get his head out of the sand."

That was an odd statement. She narrowed her eyes, trying to make sense of it.

"He's not been himself for a while now," Mariah explained without spelling it out. Jessica gave her credit for the delicate way she put it.

"I figured. He lost his family. We all did," Jess said. She missed Janie something awful. Sometimes life was cruel.

Mariah nodded. "But having family around might be good for both of you."

She doubted that. She'd be a thorn in Zane's side. A kink in his plans. She would bide her time here, soak up some fresh sea air and then return home to face the music. Humiliation and desperate hurt had made her flee Texas. But she'd have to go back eventually. Her face pulled tight. She didn't want to think about that right now.

"Maybe," she said to Mariah.

"Well, have a good evening."

"Thanks. You, too."

After Mariah left, Jessica plucked up her shampoo and entered the bathroom. Oh, boy, and she'd thought the closet was something. The guest bathroom came equipped with a television, a huge oval Jacuzzi tub and an intricately tiled spacious shower that was digitized for each of the three shower heads looming above. She peered closer to read the monitor. She could program the time, temperature and force of the shower and heaven knew what else.

After she punched in a few commands, the shower spurted to life, and water rained down. Jess smiled. A new toy. Peeling off her clothes, she opened the clear glass door and stepped inside. Steamy spray hit her from three sides, with two heads spewing softly and one pulsing like the pumping of her heart. She turned around and around, using the fragrant liquid soap from a dispenser in the wall. She lingered there, lost in the mist and jet stream as pent-up tension seeped out of her bones, her limbs loose and free. Eventually, she got down to business and worked shampoo into her hair. Much too early, the shower turned off automatically. As she stepped out, the steam followed her. She dried herself with a cushy white towel. How nice.

She dressed in a pair of tan midthigh shorts and a cocoa-brown tank top. She hoped dinner with Zane wasn't a formal thing. She hadn't brought anything remotely fashionable.

After blow-drying her hair, she lifted the long strands up in a ponytail, leaving bangs to rest on her forehead. A little nap had sounded wonderful minutes ago, but now she was too keyed up to sleep. The time change would probably hit her like a ton of bricks later, but right now, the sandy wind-blown beach below beckoned her. She slipped her feet into flip-flops and headed downstairs.

Lured by the scent of spices and sauce wafting to her nose, she headed in that direction. Inside a magnificent granite-and-stone kitchen, she came face to face with an older woman, a little hefty in the hips, wearing an apron and humming to herself.

The woman turned around. "*Hola*, Miss Holcomb?"

"Yes, I'm Jessica."

"*Hola*, Jessica." She nodded. "I'm Mrs. Lopez. Do you like enchiladas?"

She was Texan. She loved everything Mexican. "Yes. Smells yummy."

Mrs. Lopez lowered the oven door, and a stainless-steel rack automatically pushed forward.

"They will be ready in half an hour. Can I get you a drink? Or a snack?"

"No, thank you. I'll wait for Zane. Well, it's nice to meet you," she said, retreating from the kitchen. "I'll be back in—"

A boom sounded. "Double damn you!" Zane's loud curse echoed throughout the house.

Jessica froze in place.

Mrs. Lopez grinned and shook her head. "He cannot dress himself too well. He will not let anyone help him. He is not such a good patient."

They shared a smile. "I see." But when she'd first arrived, he was wearing jeans and a casual cotton shirt. Was he dressing up now? "Do I need to change my clothes for dinner?"

"No, no. Mr. Zane spilled iced tea on his shirt. You are dressed nice."

"Thank you." Okay, great. She felt better now. When she'd packed her clothes, she hadn't given much thought to her wardrobe. All she hoped for was to clear her head a little while here. "I thought I'd go for a walk on the beach. I'll be back in plenty of time for dinner. See you later."

Mrs. Lopez nodded and focused on the stove. Jess's stomach grumbled as she left the spicy smells of the kitchen and walked out the double doors to the deck. From there, she climbed a few more stairs down, until warm sand crept onto her flip-flops.

There were no lakes or rivers back home that compared with the balmy breezes whipping at her hair, the briny taste on her lips or the glistening golden hues reflecting off the ocean. Her steps fell lightly, making a slight impression in the packed wet sand until the next wave inched up the shore and carried her footprints out to sea. Even with the sun low over the water's edge, her skin warmed as she walked along the beach. To her right, beachfront mansions overlooking the sea filled her line of vision, each one different in design and structure. She was so intent on gauging the houses, she didn't notice a jogger approaching until he'd stopped right in front of her.

"Hi," he said, his breaths heaving.

"Hello." A swift glance at his face made her gasp silently. He was stunning and tanned and one of the most famous movie stars in the world. Dylan McKay.

He hunched over, hands on knees, catching his breath. "Give me a sec."

For what? She wanted to ask, yet she stood there, feet implanted in the sand, waiting. He was easy on the eyes, and she tried not to stare at his bare chest and the dip of his jogging shorts below a trim waist.

He righted his posture, and blood drained from her body as he aimed a heart-melting smile her way. "Thank you."

Puzzled, she stared at him. "For?"

"Being here. For giving me an excuse to stop running." He chuckled, and white teeth flashed. Was the sun-gleaming twinkle from his smile real? Could've been. Dylan McKay was every red-blooded woman's idea of the perfect man.

Except hers. She knew there was no such thing.

"Okay. But…you could've just stopped on your own, couldn't you?"

He shook his head. "No, I'm supposed to run ten miles a day. It's a work thing. I'm preparing for a role as a Navy SEAL."

No kidding? She wasn't going to pretend she didn't know who he was. Or that his bronzed body wasn't already honed and ripped. "Gotcha. How many did you do?"

His lips twisted with self-loathing. "Eight."

"That's not bad." Judging by the pained look on his face, he was a man who expected perfection of himself. "There aren't too many people who can run eight miles."

His expression lightened and he seemed to appreciate her encouragement. "I'm Dylan, by the way." He put out his hand.

"Jessica." It was a one-pump handshake.

"Are we neighbors?" he asked, his brows gathering. "I live over there." He pointed to a trilevel mansion looming close by.

She shook her head. "Not really. I'm staying with Zane Williams for a short time."

When his brows lifted ever so slightly and his eyes flashed, she read his mind. "He's…he's *family.*"

He nodded. "I know Zane. Good guy."

"He is. My sister…well, he was married to Janie."

A moment passed as he put two and two together. "I'm sorry about what happened."

"Thank you."

"Well, I think I've gotten my second wind. Thanks to you. Only two miles to go. Nice meeting you, Jessica. Say hi to Zane for me."

He about-faced, trotted down the beach in the opposite direction and soon picked up his pace to a full-out jog.

She headed back to the house, a smile on her lips, a song humming in her heart. Maybe coming here wasn't such a bad idea after all.

She spotted Zane braced against the patio railing and waved. Had he been watching her? She was hit with a surge of self-consciousness. She wasn't a beach babe. Her curvy figure didn't allow two-piece bathing suits, and her pale skin tone could be compared only with the bark of a birch tree or the peel of a honeydew melon.

As she climbed the stairs, her gaze hit upon his shirt, a Hawaiian print with repeating palm trees. She'd never seen

Zane look more casual and yet appear so ill at ease in his surroundings.

"Nice walk?" he asked, removing his sunglasses.

"It beats a stroll to Beckon's Cinema Palace."

Zane laughed, a knowing glint in his eyes. "You got that right. I haven't thought about the Palace in a long time." His voice sounded gruff as if he'd go back to those days in a heartbeat.

There wasn't a whole lot to do in Beckon, Texas, so on Saturday night the parking lot at the Palace swarmed with kids from the high school. Hanging out and hooking up. It's where Jessica had had her first awkward kiss. With Miles Bernardy. Gosh, he was such a geek. But then, so was she.

It was also where Janie and Zane had fallen in love.

"I met one of your neighbors."

"Judging by the glow on your face, must've been Dylan. He runs this time of day."

"My face is not glowing." She blinked.

"Nothing to worry over. Happens all the time with women."

"I'm not a wom—I mean, I am not gawking over a movie star, for heaven's sake."

He should talk. Former brother-in-law or not, Zane Williams was a country superstar hunk. Dark-haired, six foot two, a chiseled-jawed Grammy winner, Zane wasn't hard on the eyes, either. The tabloids painted him as an eligible widower who needed love in his life. So far, they'd been kind to him, a rare thing for a superstar.

He picked up his crutches and lifted one to gesture to a table. "This okay with you?"

Two adjacent places were set along a rectangular glass table large enough for ten. Votive candles and a spray of flowers accented the place settings facing the sunset. "It's nice, Zane. I hope you didn't go to too much trouble. I don't expect you to entertain me."

"Not going to any trouble, Jess. Fact is, I eat out here

most days. I hate being cooped up inside the house. Just another week and I'll be out of these dang confinements." He raised his wrapped wrist.

"That's good news. Then what will you do?"

Inclining his head, he considered her question. "Some rehab, I'm told. And continue working out details on the restaurant." He frowned, and the light dimmed in his eyes. "My tour's not due to pick up until September sometime. *Maybe*."

She wouldn't pry about the maybe. He hobbled to the table. Leaning a crutch against the table's edge, he managed to pull out her chair—such chivalry—and she took her seat. Then he scooted his butt into his own chair. Plop. Poor Zane. His injuries put him completely out of his element.

Mrs. Lopez appeared with platters of food. She set them on the table with efficient haste and nodded to him. "I made a pitcher of margaritas to go with the enchiladas and rice. Or maybe some iced tea or soda?"

"Jessica?" he asked.

"A margarita sounds like heaven."

He glanced at the housekeeper. "Bring the pitcher, please."

She nodded. Within a minute, a pitcher appeared along with two bottle-green wide-rimmed margarita glasses. "Thanks," he said. Zane leaned forward and gripped the pitcher with his wrapped hand. His face pinched tight as he struggled to upend the weighty pitcher. He sighed, and she sensed his frustration over not being able to perform the simple task of pouring a drink with his right hand.

"Let me help," she said softly.

She slipped her hand under the pitcher and helped guide the slushy concoction into the glasses. She gave him credit for clamping his mouth shut and not complaining about his limitations.

"Thanks," he said. He reached out, and the slide of his rough fingers over hers sent warm tingles to her heart. They were still connected through Janie, and she valued his friendship now. She'd made the right decision in coming here.

The food was delicious. She inhaled the meal, emptying her plate within minutes. "I guess I didn't know how hungry I was. Or thirsty."

She reached for her second margarita and took a long sip. Tart icy goodness slid down her throat. "Mmm."

The sun had set with a parfait of swirling color, and now half the moon lit the night. The beach was quiet and calm. The roar of the waves had given way to an occasional lulling swish.

Zane sipped his third margarita. She remembered that about him. He could hold his liquor.

"So what are your plans now, Jess?" he asked.

"Hit the beach, work on my tan and stay out of your way. Shouldn't be too hard. The place is huge."

Tiny lines crinkled around his eyes, and he chuckled. "You don't need to stay out of my way. But feel free to do whatever you want. There are two cars parked in the garage, fueled and ready to go. I can't drive them."

"So how do you get around?"

"Mariah, usually. When I'm needed at the restaurant site or somewhere, she's drives me or I hire a car. She's been a trouper, going above and beyond since my accident."

Mrs. Lopez picked up the empty dishes, leaving the margarita pitcher. A smart woman.

"Thank you, Mrs. Lopez. Have a good night," Zane said. "See you tomorrow."

"Good night," she said to both of them.

"Thanks for the delicious enchiladas."

On a humble nod and smile, she exited the patio.

Zane pointed to her half-empty glass. "How many of those can you handle, darlin'?"

"Oh, uh…I don't know. Why?"

"'Cause if you fall flat on your face, I won't be able to pick you up and carry you to your room."

He winked, and a sudden vision of Zane carrying her to the bedroom burst into her mind. It wasn't as weird a notion as she might've thought. She felt safe with Zane. She truly liked him and didn't buy into his guilt over Janie's death. He wasn't to blame. He couldn't have known about faulty wiring in the house or the fire that would claim her life. Janie had loved Zane for the man that he was, had always been. She wouldn't want Zane's guilt to follow him into old age.

"Well, then, we're even. If you got pie-eyed, I wouldn't be able to pick you up, either." She took another long sip of her drink. Darn, but it tasted good. Her spirits lifted. Let the healing begin.

Zane cocked a crooked smile. "I like your style, *Miss Holcomb*."

"Ugh. To think I would've been Mrs. Monahan by now. Thank God I'm not."

"The guy's an ass."

"Thanks for saying that. He sure had me fooled. Up until the minute I was having my bridal veil pinned in my hair, I thought I knew what the future had in store for me. I saw myself married to a man I had a common bond with. He was a high school principal. I was a grade-school teacher. We both loved education. But I was too blind to see that Steven had commitment phobia. He'd had one broken relationship after another before we started dating. I invested three years of my life in the guy, and I thought surely he'd gotten over it. I thought I was the one. But he was fooling himself as well as me." A pent-up breath whooshed out of her. A little bit of tequila loosened her tongue, and out poured her heart. The unburdening was liberating. "My friend Sally said Steven looked up his old girlfriend seeking sympathy after the wedding that never happened. Can you imagine?"

Zane stared at her. "No. He should be on his knees begging you for forgiveness. He did one thing right. He didn't marry you and make your life miserable. I hate to say it, darlin', but you're better off without him. The man doesn't deserve you. But you're hurt right now, and I get that. You probably still love him."

"I don't," she said, hoisting her glass and swallowing a big gulp. "I pretty much hate him."

Zane leaned back in his seat, his gaze soft on her. "Okay. You hate him. He's out of your life."

She braced folded elbows on the table and rested her chin on her hands. The sea was black as pitch now, the sky lit only with a few stars and clouded moonlight. "I just wanted...I wanted what you and Janie had. I wanted that kind of love."

Her fuzzy brain cleared. Oh, no. She hadn't just said that? She whipped her head around. Zane's expression of sympathy didn't change. He didn't flinch. He simply stared out to sea. "We had something pretty special."

"You did. I'm sorry for bringing it up."

"Don't be." His tone held no malice. "You're Janie's sister. You have as much right to talk about her as I do."

Tears misted in her eyes. "I miss her."

"I miss her, too."

She sighed. She didn't mean to put such a somber mood on the evening. Zane was gracious enough to allow her to stay here. She didn't want to bring him down. It was definitely time to call it a night. She put on a cheery face. "Well, this has been nice."

She rose, and her head immediately clouded up. The table, the railing, the ocean blurred before her. She batted her eyes over and over, trying to focus. Two Zanes popped into her line of vision. She reached for the tabletop, struggling to remain upright on her own steam. She swayed back and forth, unable to keep her body still. "Zane?"

"It just hit you, didn't it?"

"Oh, yeah. I think so." She giggled.

"Don't move for a second."

"I'll...try." A tornado swirled in her head. "Why?"

He rose and hobbled over to her. Using one crutch, he

tucked it under his left arm. "I'm going to help you get inside."

"But, you said…you c-couldn't. Uh…" She giggled again.

Zane wrapped his right arm around her shoulder. "Okay, now, darlin', I've got you. Your body will be my other crutch. We'll help each other. Move slowly."

"W-where are we g-going?"

"I've got to get you to bed."

Her head fell to his shoulder. Somewhere in the back of her mind, she thought how nice it felt to have him hold her. He smelled good. He would take care of her.

"Focus on putting one foot in front of the other."

She tried.

"That's good, honey."

Hobble-hopping, they moved together. It seemed to take forever to go a short distance in the dark shadows of the night. Keeping her eyes down, she watched her feet move. Then blinding light appeared in a burst. She squinted. "What's that?"

"We're inside the house now," Zane was saying.

"That's g-good, right? I'll be in b-bed soon." A warm buzz spread through her like soft, sweet jelly.

"Not upstairs. You'll never make it. We're going to my room."

She couldn't wait to lay her head down someplace. She didn't care where. More careful steps later, they entered a room. A ray of moonlight beamed like an arrow, aiming straight at the bed.

"Okay, we made it," Zane said. He sounded weird and out of breath. "You'll sleep here tonight."

He guided her down. The bed hit her bottom quickly and cushioned around her. She swayed sideways and was immediately set to right. Zane held her steady as the mattress dipped again and he sat next to her. Dizzying waves bombarded her head. She'd sat too quickly.

"Think you can take it from here?" he whispered.

No. Aware of Zane's eyes on her, she waited until the twister in her head calmed. "Yeah, I think so."

"Good."

Her giddiness fading, her lighthearted high dropped to a pitiful low. It hadn't taken her long to become a burden to Zane. If only she hadn't sucked down that second margarita. Zane had warned her to go slowly. Expensive tequila and jet lag had done her in. Man, chalk another mistake up to her lousy intuition.

"I'm sorry."

"Nothing to be sorry for," he said.

But she was, and an urge to thank him wiggled through the fog in her head. Pursing her lips, she leaned forward toward his cheek. Her aim off, she missed and caught the corner of his mouth instead. As she brushed a soft kiss there, he tasted of tequila and the sea. So good. Inside, a warm sprinkling of something wonderful spread through her body. "Thank you," she whispered, not sure if her words slurred.

Then his arms wrapped around her and gently lowered her down. Her head was enveloped in a large, fluffy pillow, and a silky sheet came to rest over her body.

She heard a whispered, "Welcome," right before the world finally stopped spinning.

# Two

Jessica gazed at the digital clock on the nightstand. Eight-thirty! She flashed back to last night and drinking those two giant margaritas, then slowly looked around. She was in an unfamiliar bed.

She'd finally let go and given herself permission to have a good time, and where had that gotten her? She'd made a fool of herself. Zane had hobbled her inside the house and slept heaven only knew where. Was there another bedroom on this floor? Maybe a servant's quarters? She'd seen an office, a screening room and a game room. No beds, just couches. "Oh, man," she mumbled.

She scanned the stark but stylish bedroom where she'd slept. A flat-screen TV, a dresser and a low fabric sofa were the only other furniture in the room. If it wasn't for a shelf that housed Zane's five Grammys, as well as a couple of CMA and ACM awards, she wouldn't have guessed it was his master suite. There was nothing personal, warm and cozy about the space.

Hitching her body forward, she waited for signs of pain, but there was nothing. Thank goodness—no hangover. She grabbed her glasses from the nightstand, tossed off the covers and rose. Seeing she was still dressed in her shorts and tank top, she emitted a low groan from her throat as she slipped her feet into her flip-flops. How reckless of her. She'd abused Zane's hospitality already.

She entered the bathroom, another ode to magnificence, and glanced at herself in the mirror. Smudged mascara and rumpled hair reflected back at her. She washed her face and finger-combed her long wayward tresses. She'd take care of the rest once she reached her own room.

Exiting Zane's room, she made her way down a short hallway. Voices coming from the kitchen perked up her ears.

Mrs. Lopez spotted her and waved her inside. "Just in time for breakfast."

Mariah and Zane sat at the kitchen table, coffee mugs piping hot in front of them. Upon the housekeeper's announcement, both heads lifted her way. Blood rushed up her neck, and her face flamed.

"Morning," Zane said, peering into her eyes and not at her wrinkled mess of clothes. "You ready for some breakfast?"

"Good morning, Jessica," Mariah said. They'd obviously been deep in concentration, poring over a stack of papers.

"Yes, yes. Sit down," Mrs. Lopez insisted.

"Oh, uh…good morning. I don't want to intrude. You look busy."

"Just same old, same old," Mariah said. "We're going over plans for Zane's new restaurant. We could use your input."

She'd given Zane her input last night. God. She'd kissed him. Remembering that kiss sent a warm rash of heat through her body. She'd missed his cheek and gotten hold of his lips. Was it the alcohol, or had her heart strummed from that kiss? The alcohol. Had to be. He must have known it was a genuine miscalculation on her part. She hadn't meant to kiss him that way.

"Yes, have a seat, Jess," he said casually. "You need to eat. And we sure need a fresh perspective."

Before her shower? Luckily Zane hadn't mentioned anything about her lack of discretion last night or her state of dress today. She'd overslept, that much was a given. Back home, she rose before six every morning. She loved to go through the morning newspaper, take a walk in the back-woods and then eat a light breakfast before heading to her classroom.

There were a platter of bagels with cream cheese, a scrambled egg jalapeno dish and cereal boxes on the table. The eggs smelled heavenly, and her stomach grumbled. Seeing no other option, she sat down and reached for the eggs as Mrs. Lopez provided her with a bowl and a cup of coffee.

"*Bien.*" She gave a satisfied nod.

Jessica smiled at her.

As Zane and his assistant finished up their breakfast, she ate, too, complimenting Mrs. Lopez on the food she'd prepared.

Zane told Mariah, "Janie and Jessica worked at their folks' café in Beckon. They served the best fried chicken in all of Texas."

"That's what most folks said," she agreed. She couldn't claim modesty. Her parents *did* make the best fried chicken in the state. "My parents opened Holcomb House when I was young. They worked hard to make a go of it. It wasn't anything as grand as what you're probably planning, but in Beckon, the Holcomb House was known for good eats and a friendly atmosphere. When Dad died five years ago, my mom couldn't make a go of it by herself. I think she lost the will, so she sold the restaurant. I'm no expert, but if I can help in any way, I'll give it a try."

"Great," Mariah said.

"Appreciate it," Zane added. "This restaurant will be a little different than the one in Reno, in cuisine and atmosphere. The beach is a big draw for tourists, and we want it to be a great experience."

Zane probably had half a dozen financial advisors, but if he needed her help in any way, she'd oblige. How could she not? She cringed thinking that Zane slept on a sofa last night. A quick glance at his less than crisp clothes, the same clothes he'd worn last night, meant that he probably hadn't got to shower this morning, either. Because of her.

Once the dishes were cleared, Mariah pushed a few papers over to her. "If you don't mind, could you tell us what you think of the menu? Are the prices fair? Do the titles of the dishes make sense? We're working with a few chefs and want to get it just right. These are renderings of what Zane's on the Beach will look like once all done, exterior and interior."

For the next hour, Jessica worked with the two of them, giving her opinion, voicing her concerns when they probed and offering praise honestly if not sparingly. Zane's on the Beach had everything a restaurant could offer. Outside, patio tables facing the beach included a sand bar for summer nights of drinking under the moonlight. Inside, window tables were premium, with the next row of tables raised to gain a view of the ocean, as well. It wasn't posh, but it wasn't family dining, either. "I like that you've made it accessible to a younger crowd. The prices are fair. Have you thought about putting a little stage in the bar? Invite in local entertainment to perform?"

Mariah shot a look at Zane. "We discussed it. I think it's a great idea. Zane isn't so sure."

Zane scrubbed his chin, deep in thought. "I've got to get a handle on what I want from this restaurant. My name and reputation are at stake. Do I want ocean views and great food or a hot spot for a younger crowd?"

"Why can't you have both?" Jessica asked. "Quality is quality. Diners will come for the cuisine and ambiance. After hours, the place can transform into a nightspot for the millennials."

Amused, Zane's dark eyes sparked. "Millennials? Are you one?"

"I guess so."

His head tilted, and his mouth quirked up. "Why do I suddenly feel old?"

"Because you are," Mariah jabbed. "You're cranking toward forty."

"Thirty-five is a far shot from forty, and that's all I'm saying."

"You're wise to stop there," Mariah said playfully, yet with a note of warning. Jessica could tell that Mariah Jacobellis wasn't a woman who put up with age jokes. Although Mariah was physically lovely, she seemed to take no prisoners when it came to business or her personal life. Jessica admired that about her. Maybe she could take a lesson from her rule book.

Zane leaned way back in his seat. "You got that right."

Mariah stacked the papers on the table and rose, hugging them to her chest. "Well, I'm off to make some phone calls. Zane, think about when you want to resume your tour. I've got to let the event coordinators know. They're on my back about it. Oh, and be sure to read through that contract that Bernie sent over the other day."

Zane's lips pursed. "I'll do my best."

"Jessica, have a nice morning. And if you're around Zane today, please give him a hand. He may look like a superhero, but he's really not Superman."

Could've fooled her. Last night, he'd been super *heroic*.

Mariah pivoted on her heels and strode out the door.

Zane chuckled.

"What?"

"The look on your face."

"I'm mortified about last night. Where on earth did you sleep, and does Mariah know what happened?"

"First off, don't be upset. It's our little secret. Mariah doesn't know that you're a margarita lightweight." He smiled. "That woman's been babying me for weeks. Doesn't do a man a bit of good being so dang useless. For the first time in a month of Sundays, I was able to help out and do something useful with this banged-up body."

"I took your bed."

"Glad to give it up."

"Where did you sleep?"

"The office sofa is the most comfortable place in the whole house."

"Oh, boy. I'm sorry. The first night I'm here, I give you trouble."

He smiled again, a stunning heart-melter. "If livening up my life some is trouble, then bring it on. Fact is, I'm glad you're here. You bring a bit of home with you. I miss that."

She needed to believe him. She'd been afraid coming here would remind him of Janie and all that he'd lost. To have him say he was glad she'd come made a big difference. "Okay."

He put his palms on her cheeks and leaned forward. Her heart stopped. Was he going to kiss her? His touch sent tingles parading up and down her chest. Oh, wow. It wasn't alcohol this time. Probably wasn't the alcohol last night, either. She'd been dumped by a scoundrel, and now a man she had no right responding to made her feel giddy inside. How screwed up was that?

She gazed into his eyes. He was looking somewhere above her eyeglasses. Then he lowered his mouth—she stilled—and he brushed a brotherly kiss across her forehead. Breath eased from her chest, and her foolish heart tumbled. Of course, Zane wasn't going to kiss her *that* way.

"And thanks for the input about the restaurant," he said. "I respect your honesty and what you have to offer."

She swallowed hard. Tamping down her silly emotions, she offered a quick smile. "Anytime."

Beaming sunshine simmered over Jessica's body, the invading heat soaking into her bones. Salty air, a cushion of sand beneath her and the soothing sounds of waves crashing upon the shore gave her good reason to forget her disastrous relationship with Steven Monahan. He didn't deserve any more of her time. But the sting of his rejection stayed with her, leaving her hollowed out inside, afraid to trust, questioning her intuition. She feared she'd never fully recover the innocence of her first love. Good thing she didn't have to make any decisions here on Moonlight Beach. She could just be.

Drenched in sunscreen, she lay on a beach blanket in a modest one-piece bathing suit, a folded towel under her head. Slight breezes just outside Zane's beachfront home deposited flecks of sand onto her arms and legs. Children's giggles and adult conversations drifted to her ears. For the first time in days, her nerves were completely calm.

She promised herself to keep out of Zane's hair, and she had for the most part these past three days. He spent hours inside his office working with Mariah, and occasionally they would ask for her input on the restaurant. She figured it was just a way for him to keep her entertained and make her feel welcome. Each morning, under an overcast sky that would burn off before noon, she walked a three-mile stretch of beach, loosening up her limbs and clearing her head. At night, she'd dine with Zane on the patio facing the ocean, and except for having an occasional glass of white wine or a cold beer, she kept her alcohol consumption to a bare minimum. The Pacific Ocean and fresh air were her balm. She didn't need to rely on anything else.

She wiggled her tush into the sand, carving out a more comfy spot on her blanket, and closed her eyes. The flapping of wings and piercing squawk of a seagull overhead made her smile.

"Glad to see you've taken to Moonlight Beach."

Blocking rays of sunlight with a hand salute, she opened her eyes. The handsome face of Dylan McKay came into view.

"Hi, Jessica." He stared at her with his million-dollar smile. "Don't let me disturb you."

Gosh, he remembered her name.

Wearing plaid board shorts and a muscle-hugging white

T-shirt, and fitting into beach society with the casualness of a megastar, he sort of did disturb her. Yet he did so in such a friendly way, she didn't mind the intrusion. As she sat up on her elbows, his gaze dipped to her chest. To his credit, his eyes didn't linger on her breasts, and that was more than she could say about most men.

"Hello, and I am enjoying the beach. When in Rome, as they say." She chuckled at the cliché. It was Mama's favorite saying, and she'd used it a zillion times over the years. The most recent was last night when they'd talked on the phone. Did others in her generation get that phrase?

Her eyes fell on a black portfolio tucked under his arm. It looked odd there, as if he should be wearing a three-piece suit while carrying that austere leather case. Instead of moving on, he squatted down beside her, his tanned knees nearly in her face. Obviously, he wanted to chat.

"I see you sometimes in the morning, walking along the beach."

"You've inspired me," she said. "Of course, I only do three miles. How are your runs going?"

"Killing me, but I'm getting in the ten miles."

His legs were taut, like those of a natural runner, and the rest of his body, well…it would be hard not to notice his muscles and the way his T-shirt nearly split at the seams around his shoulders and upper arms. "Good for you."

"So, how's it going?" he asked. "Other than sunbathing and taking long walks, are you having a good time?"

"Yes. It's nice here. I'm working on some new lesson plans for my class. I teach first grade back home."

"Ah…a teacher. Such an honorable profession."

She waggled her brows. Was he poking fun at her? Or was he being genuine?

"My mother taught school for thirty-five years," he added, his smile wistful, pride filling his voice. "She was loved by her students, but she wasn't a pushover. It wasn't easy pulling my antics on her. She was too savvy. She knew when kids were up to no good."

"I bet you gave her a run for her money."

He laughed, the gleam of his lake-blue eyes touching her. "I did."

"What grade did she teach?"

"All grades, but she preferred fourth and fifth. Then, later on, she became dean of a middle school, and eventually, the principal of the high school."

She nodded. She didn't have much else to add to the conversation. Not that Dylan McKay wasn't easy to talk to. He was. And she loved talking about education to anyone who would listen. It was just that he was fabulous, famous Dylan McKay. And he kept smiling at her.

"Hey, I'm having a party on Saturday night. If you're still here, I'd love for you to come. Maybe you can get Zane to get out and have a little fun."

"Oh, thanks." He'd caught her off guard. Wasn't that what she needed right now, to be a wallflower at an A-list party? "I'm…uh, I'm not the partying type. Especially now."

"Now?"

She shrugged. "I'm going through something and need a little R and R."

"Ah…a breakup?"

She nodded. Her pride aside, she opened up a little to make her point. "Broken engagement as the wedding guests were taking their seats in church."

"Ah…gotcha. I've been there once, a long time ago, when I was too young to know better. It turned out for the best, so believe me, I understand. Listen, I promise you, the party is low-key. Just a few friends and neighbors for a barbecue on the beach. I'd love to see you there."

"Thanks."

He smiled, and she smiled back. Then he pointed to her upper thigh, on the right side, closest to him. "Uh-oh. Looks like you missed a spot. You're starting to burn."

Grabbing the sunscreen tube from the blanket, his long fingers brushed the soft underside of her hand as he set the sunscreen into her palm. "Better lather up and—"

"Stop corrupting my little sis, McKay."

Jessica whipped her head around. Zane stood on the sundeck railing, staring at Dylan. His voice was a far cry from menacing, but the cool look he shot Dylan made her wonder what was up.

Dylan winked at her. "Maybe she wants to be corrupted."

"And maybe you want to turn tail and go home. I don't have to read that script, you know."

"Whoops," he said, flashing a charming smile. "He's got me there. Maybe you can help me convince him to take this role. Wanna try? Since you're about to turn into a fried tomato out here."

Under normal circumstances, she was probably the least starstruck person in Beckon, Texas, but how could she not take Dylan up on his offer to go over a movie script? The notion got her juices flowing, and excitement buzzed around her like a busy little bee.

She glanced down at her legs. Oh, wow. Dylan was right. There were more than a few splotchy patches on her body. Time to get out of the sun. "Sure, why not?"

"Great." He swiveled his head in Zane's direction. "We're coming up right now."

Gallantly, he offered her his hand. She couldn't very well refuse the gesture. She slipped one hand into his and simultaneously clutched her cover-up with the other as they rose together. He was too close for comfort, his eyes smiling on her, their hands entwined. Gently she pulled away, making herself busy zipping herself into a white cotton cover up and ignoring his rapt attention. He was a charmer, but thankfully his touch hadn't elicited a jolt of any kind. She glanced at Zane, leaning by the railing, his sharp gaze fixed on her.

Something hot and unruly sizzled in the pit of her belly.

She ignored it and pushed on, climbing the steps with Dylan McKay following behind.

"Did he ask you out?" Zane probed the minute Dylan McKay exited the house. Looming over her, Zane was a bit foreboding, as if he was her white knight protecting her from the wicked prince of darkness. Geesh.

"Wh-what?"

"The guy couldn't take his eyes off you down on the beach."

She shrugged and picked up three empty glasses, reminiscent of her waitress days at Holcomb House.

After coming back into the house she'd left the two men to take a quick shower and slip on a sundress. She'd listened to Dylan's script proposal to Zane with keen interest in a spacious light oak–paneled office on the main level of the house. The meeting took almost an hour. Then they'd had drinks in the cool shade of the patio. Iced tea for her. The men were content to knock back whiskey and soda.

Dylan was a charming lady's man to the millionth degree, and she knew enough to steer clear. The idea that he'd be interested in a little ol' school teacher from Beckon, Texas, was ridiculous. She had no illusions of anything else going on between them, and Zane should know that.

Her mama's image flashed before her eyes. That was it. She bet her mother put Zane up to watching out for her, making sure her tender heart didn't get broken again. Well, heck. She'd let him off the hook, but not without giving him some grief. Her chin up, she said, "He invited me to his beach party Saturday night. It was just a friendly invitation."

Zane's mouth tightened into a snarl and he snorted. "Doubtful."

"I told him I probably wouldn't go."

"Good." Zane nodded, satisfied. "You don't need to get involved with him. He's—"

"Out of my league?"

His eyes widened. "Hell, no."

"Well, he is. And I know it all too well. Heck, my life is messy enough right now. There's no room for romance, though it's absurd to think of Dylan McKay actually being into me."

Zane immediately reached out to grab her arm. Surprised, she jerked from his touch, and the glasses she held nearly slipped from her hand. "Don't put yourself down, Jess."

A jolt sprang to life, spiraling out of control where the strong fingers of his bandaged hand pressed into her skin. Sharpness left Zane's dark eyes, and he gave her a bone-melting look. "I was going to say, he would never appreciate you. You're special, Jess. You always have been."

Because she was Janie's sister.

Zane held dear her sister's memory, closing his heart around it and not allowing anyone else into his life. He was a sought-after hunky bachelor, but he'd been true to Janie's love even now, years later. Jessica understood she was only here because Zane was too nice a guy to refuse her mama a favor. "Thank you."

He nodded and released her to go lean against the railing.

Free of his touch, she marched the glasses into the kitchen, handing them to Mrs. Lopez one at a time. She had to do something to quell her pounding heart. What the heck was wrong with her?

"*Dios*, you do not do the work around here. That's my job, no?"

"Yes. But I like to help."

It was the same conversation she'd had with Mrs. Lopez since she'd arrived here. Jessica saw nothing wrong with putting clothes in the washer and turning the thing on, or clearing the dishes, or helping slice potatoes for a meal. Today, especially, she needed to do something with her hands.

"*Sí*, okay." A relenting sigh echoed in the kitchen.

She picked up dirty dishes on the counter, loaded them in the dishwasher and put things back in the refrigerator. A few chores later, after scanning the clean kitchen they'd both worked on, she gave Mrs. Lopez a bright smile. The woman was shaking her head, but with a twinkle in her eyes. Progress.

Jessica strode out the kitchen door and was immediately knocked against the doorjamb. Pain shot to her shoulder. The jarring bump brought Mariah's face into view. "Oh, sorry."

Mariah was equally shocked from the collision. "I didn't see you."

"My fault. I should learn how to slow down."

She chuckled. "I'm the same way. I've got to get where I'm going fast, no matter if it's just to sip coffee and read the newspaper." Mariah, always impeccably dressed, rubbed her shoulder through her cognac-colored silk blouse. "Guess we're alike in that regard. Where were you going in such a hurry?"

"Nowhere. Just outside. I left Zane hanging and I wanted to go back to talk to him."

"Good luck with that. I just left him, and he's a bear right now."

"Oh, really? Why?" It couldn't be the Dylan McKay thing, could it?

"I don't know exactly what set him off other than he hates being confined. He feels like a caged animal. Though he doesn't make an effort to go anywhere, other than for business."

"I can see how that would make him restless."

Mariah smiled. "That's the perfect way to describe it. He's restless. But I'm afraid that came on well before his fall. I think a change of pace is good for him. I've helped him make the decision to open this second restaurant, and now he's thinking about movie roles. It might be just what he needs."

Or maybe he was running away from his past, the same way she was. Zane loved music. He loved writing lyrics and composing songs. He was meant to entertain. His sexy, deep baritone voice made his fans swoon. That's the only Zane she'd known.

"Dylan invited you in to hear his pitch, I understand. What did you think of the movie?"

"Me? Well, I, uh…to be honest, I think the idea of Zane and Dylan being estranged brothers coming home after the death of their father might work. If Zane can act, he'd be great in the role. The only issue I see is the love triangle about the girl back home. I saw Zane's reaction to Dylan's description of the romantic scenes he'd have to do. Zane instantly shut down. I'm not sure if Zane's up to that."

"That's exactly what I think, too. Zane's not going to do something he's not comfortable with. Believe me, I know. I've had plenty of discussions with him about his recent decisions. He bounces things off me. He asks me a question, and I tell him the truth."

"Which is?"

"I will say this. Zane can act. He's been doing so for over two years now. His public persona is far different than the real Zane." Mariah was ready to say more and then clamped shut. Her eyes downcast, she shook her head. "Forgive me. I keep forgetting who you are."

Jessica drew her brows together. "It's because of Janie. He's still hurting."

Mariah nodded. "I'm afraid so."

Mariah's eyes fell on her softly, her genuine warmth shining through. "Please forget I said anything. It's none of my business."

The idea that after two years, Zane was still making decisions based on the love he had for Janie, nestled deep into her heart. It was beautiful in a way, but also incredibly sad. "You're Zane's personal assistant. You spend a lot of time together. I can see that you care about him as a friend, too, so maybe it's more your business than mine."

"Zane thinks of you as family. He's said so a dozen times since you've come here."

"I'm the little sis he never had." Wasn't that the term he'd used this afternoon with Dylan McKay?

*Stop corrupting my little sis.*

Zane's loyalty to her family was very sweet. She didn't take it lightly, but she also didn't want him to think of her as a pity case. From the moment her shocked guests walked out of the church on her wedding day, weeks ago now, something harsh and cold seeped into her soul. Trust would be a long time coming, if ever again. So Zane didn't have to worry over her. She wasn't a woman looking for love. She wasn't on the rebound. He could sleep well at night.

"So, what are you up to today?" she asked Mariah. She was learning the ins and outs of Zane's superstardom. Mariah sifted through a dozen offers a day for special appearances, television interviews and charity events on Zane's behalf. She'd learned that Zane was a generous contributor to children and military charities, but lately, he'd declined any personal appearances. Mariah worked with his fan club president on occasion and took care of any personal business, such as setting up medical appointments or shopping trips. It was a different world, one that her sister, Janie, had resigned herself to because she'd been with Zane from the launch of his career. They'd grown into this life together.

"More restaurant business to do today. We've got a decorator working on the interior design, but Zane's not sure about the motif." Mariah's cell phone rang, and she excused herself.

Jessica walked over to the French door leading out to the deck. Zane was sprawled out on a lounge chair, shaded from the sun, his booted foot elevated, reading the script Dylan had brought over. Keen on the subject matter, he seemed deep in thought. As her gaze lingered, she watched him close the binder and stare out to sea, his expression incredibly wistful.

She followed the direction of his gaze and honed in on the vast view of the ocean. The sounds of the sea lulled her into a soothing state of mind. It was a place to find infinite peace, if there ever was such a thing. Her nerves no longer throbbed against her skin. These past few days, she'd been much calmer. Were time and distance all she'd needed to get over Steven Monahan? Geesh, Jessica felt at one with nature and started to believe. A chuckle rose from her throat at the notion. She was beginning to sound like a true Californian.

"Crap! Damn things."

Out of the corner of her eye, she witnessed Zane's crutches fall to the ground. The slap echoed against the wood deck. Zane was off the chair, bending to pick them up and trying to keep weight off his bad foot. It looked like a yoga move gone bad. She moved quickly, her legs eating up the length of the deck to get to him.

"Zane, hang on."

He stumbled and fell over, landing on his bad hand. "Ow!"

By the time she reached him, he was on his butt, cursing like the devil, shaking out his wrist. She kneeled beside him. "Are you okay?" she asked softly.

He tilted his head toward her. "You mean other than my pride?"

She smiled. "Yes, we'll deal with that later. How's the hand?"

"I managed to catch the fall on the tips of my fingers, so the wrist should be fine."

He moved his fingers one by one as if he was playing keys on a piano. So much for keeping his hand immobilized. "Maybe your doctor would be a better judge of that."

"Now you sound like Mariah."

"I knew an old goat like you once," she said, putting his right arm over her shoulder. "Let me help you up."

"I knew the same goat," he bounced back. "Smart critter."

"Pleeeze. Okay, are you ready? On three." She swung her arm around his waist. "One. Two. Three."

His weight drew her toward him, the side of her face against his chest, her hair brushing his shirt. He smelled like soap and lime shaving lotion. His heart pounded in her ear as she strained to help lift him.

Zane did most of the work, his brawny strength a blessing. Together, they managed to stand steady, Zane keeping weight off his foot by using her as his right crutch. Once again, just like the other night, she was wrapped tight in his arms. Ridiculous warmth flowed through her body. She couldn't explain it except she felt safe with him, which was silly because this time she'd done the rescuing. "There," she said, satisfied she'd gotten him upright. "Now, we're even."

His arm over her shoulder, he turned to her with eyes flickering. "Is that so?"

Well, maybe not. She was getting drunk on him, minus the alcohol. "Yes, that's so."

"I could've gotten up on my own, you know."

"It wouldn't have been pretty."

He laughed. "True."

"So, I'm glad I was here to help. Show a little gratitude."

He wasn't a man who liked taking help. That was part of the problem. His gaze roamed over the deck where he'd spent most of his day, and she sensed his frustration.

"Wanna get out of here?" he asked.

"Sure. Where would you like to go?" Mariah said he didn't like to go out, so she couldn't let this opportunity pass by. If he needed some breathing room, away from his gorgeous house and his familiar surroundings, who was she to deny him?

"Anywhere. I don't care. Are you up to driving my car?"

"I can manage that. I'm going to get your crutches now, okay?" She didn't wait for an answer.

She released him and he stood there, balancing himself for the two seconds it took her to pick up both of his crutches and hand them over. Tucking one under each arm, he pointed a crutch toward the door. "After you."

# Three

To her surprise, Zane picked his silver convertible sports car for her to drive over the black SUV sitting in his three-car garage. The other car, a little blue sedan, had to be Mariah's car. Jessica helped him get into his seat, taking his crutches and setting them into the narrow backseat before closing his door.

As soon as she climbed behind the steering wheel, she understood why Zane didn't venture out much. Sitting in the passenger seat, he was encumbered by his foot, broken in three places, which required him to be extremely careful. He also put on a disguise. Well, a Dodgers baseball cap instead of his signature Stetson and sunglasses wasn't much of a disguise, but she knew where he was coming from. He couldn't afford to be recognized and surrounded by fans or paparazzi. In his condition, he couldn't make a fast getaway.

"Why am I driving this car?"

"More fun for you."

"You mean more scary, don't you? How much is this car worth, just in case I wreck it, or—heaven forbid—put a scratch on it?"

He smiled. "Don't worry. It's insured."

Stalling for time, she fidgeted with her glasses and took several deep breaths before she turned to Zane. He was still smiling at her. At the moment, she didn't enjoy being his source of amusement.

"Here goes." With the press of a button, the engine purred to life. Zane showed her how to adjust her seat and mirrors using the control buttons. Once set, she supposed she was as ready as she would ever be. She pumped the gas pedal and gripped the steering wheel. She'd never driven anything but a sedan, a boring four-door family car with no bells and whistles. This car had it all. A thrill shimmied up her legs…all that power under her control.

She backed the car out of the garage and made the turn into a long driveway that reached the front gate. Upon Zane's voice command, the gate slid open, and she pulled forward and onto the highway. She drove along the shoreline, keeping her eyes trained on the road and her speed under thirty miles per hour.

His back was angled against the passenger door and his seat. She sensed him watching her. He'd opted to keep the top up on the convertible, for anonymity, she supposed. Even though he'd not had a hint of scandal to his name, every time Zane went out, he risked being photographed. Putting the top down on his car in the light of day would be like asking for trouble.

She didn't dare shoot him a glance, keeping her focus on the road.

"What?" she asked finally. "Your grandmother drives faster than me?"

"I didn't say a word." His Texas drawl seeped into her bones. "But now that you mention it, I think my great-grandmother drove her horse and buggy a mite faster than you."

"Ha. Ha. Very funny. Maybe I'd drive faster if I knew where I was going."

He sighed. "I've learned that sometimes, it's better not to know where you're going. Sometimes, planning isn't all it's cracked up to be. Some roads are better not mapped out."

After that cryptic statement, she did look his way and found him resting his head against the window. His sunglasses hid his eyes and his true expression. The mood in the car grew heavy, and she didn't know how to answer him, so she buttoned her lips and continued to drive.

After five minutes of silence, Zane shifted in his seat. "Wanna see the site of the restaurant? The framework is up."

"I'd love to."

He directed her down a side road that wound around a cove. Then the beach opened up again to a street that faced the ocean. Unique shops and a few other small restaurants sparsely dotted the shoreline before she came upon the skeletal frame of a building.

"There it is. You can park along the side of the road here." He gestured to a space, and she swung the car into the spot.

"This is a great location."

"I think so, too. On a clear day, there's visibility for miles going in either direction."

The beach was wide where the restaurant would sit, far enough from the water to avoid high tides. A rock embankment jutted out to the left, where pelicans rested, scoping out their next meal. Above them and across the road, far up on the cliffs sat zillion-dollar homes overlooking the coastline.

"Do you want to get out?" she asked.

"Yep."

"Hold on," she said, killing the engine and climbing out. She reached into the backseat and grabbed his crutches, then strolled to his side of the car. He was lifting himself out of his seat by the time she got there. "Here you go."

"Thanks."

She waited for him to get his bearings, and they moved through the sand until they reached the beach side of the restaurant. "So this is Zane's on the Beach."

"Yep. Gonna be."

"I suppose it's good that you're branching out. You've become a regular entrepreneur."

"Can't sing forever."

Why not? Willie Nelson, George Strait and Dolly Parton weren't having career problems. And neither was Zane. "Why do I get the feeling you're not eager to go back to doing what you love to do?"

It was a personal question. Maybe too personal, given that Zane didn't react to it at all. He simply stared at the ocean, thinking.

"I'm sorry. It's none of my business."

"Don't apologize, Jess," he rasped with a note of irritation. "You can ask me anything you want."

Okay, she'd take him up on that. "So, then, why are you searching for something else when you've established yourself as a superstar and you have fans all over the world waiting for your return?"

He closed his eyes briefly. "I don't know. Maybe I'm tired of being in my own skin."

It was the most honest answer he could've given her. Zane was hurting. Still. And he didn't know how to deal with it. "I get that. After my disastrous breakup with Steven, I felt totally out of options. I didn't know who to trust, what to believe. I couldn't make a decision to save my life. That's why when I had to get out of Dodge, I let my mother take over and make arrangements. After she did, I didn't have the gumption to argue with her. No offense, but visiting you wasn't even on my radar."

He chuckled. "Should I be insulted?"

She softened her voice. "You made a point of keeping away from the entire family after Janie…"

He winced at her honesty. Maybe she shouldn't have been so blunt. "It's not for the reasons you think."

"I know why you did it, Zane."

He put his head down. "I was having a hard time."

"I know." He'd been swallowed up with guilt. Janie was five months pregnant when she lost her life. Zane was touring in London, and Janie wanted desperately to travel with him. Zane had given her a flat-out no. He didn't want her away from her doctors, on a whirlwind schedule that would sap her energy. They'd argued until Zane had gotten his way. He'd loved Janie so much, trying to protect her and keep her safe. It was a tragic irony that she'd died in her own home on the night Zane had performed for Prince Charles and the royal family. Momentary grief swept over his features. He'd probably feel the guilt of his decision until his dying day. But there was no one to blame. No one could've known that Janie would've been safer in London than resting in her own sprawling, comfortable ranch house while Zane was gone. Her mother had recognized that. Jessica recognized that, but Zane wouldn't let himself off the hook.

Braced by the crutches under his arms, Zane let go of one handle and took her right hand. Lacing their fingers, he applied slight pressure there, squeezing her hand as they stared at the ocean. "I'm glad you're here, Jess."

Peace and pain mingled together, a bittersweet and odd combination of emotions that she was certain Zane was experiencing, too. They'd both lost so much and shared a profound connection.

Afternoon winds blew her hair onto her cheek and Zane touched her face, removing the wayward strands, tucking them behind her ear. "It's good to have someone who understands," he whispered.

She nodded.

"You can trust me," he said.

"I do." Strangely, she did trust Zane. He wasn't a threat to her, not the way every other man in the universe might be. She had learned some harsh lessons about men and about herself. She'd never overlook the obvious the way she had with Steven. She'd never allow herself to be fooled into believing a relationship would work when there were three strikes against it from the get-go.

"This is nice," she murmured.

"Mmm," he replied.

Zane released her hand, and they fell into comfortable silence, watching wave upon wave hit the shore. After a minute, he turned her way. "Do you want to see the inside of the restaurant?"

Her gaze was drawn to the framed, unroofed, sandy-floored structure behind her. "I sure do!"

He laughed. "Follow me, if you can keep up." He hobbled ahead of her. "I'll give you the grand tour."

Zane folded his arms and leaned back in the booth of Amigos del Sol—friends of the sun—watching Jess pore over the menu items of his favorite off-the-beaten-path Mexican restaurant. It was a small hacienda-style place known for making the most delicious, fresh guacamole right at the table. "Everything is great here, but the tamales are out of this world."

And the guacamole was on its way.

Jessica's head was down, and her glasses dropped to the tip of her nose. With her index finger, she pushed them up to the bridge of her nose. He grinned. It was a habit of hers that he found adorable.

"Tamales it is. I will bow to your vast culinary taste. But I'm even more impressed at how you managed to sneak us in the back way and get this corner booth."

"I shouldn't give away my secrets, but while you were navigating turns and learning how to gun the engine on my car, I texted Mariah to call the owner and let him know we needed a quiet spot and we'd appreciate coming in through the back door."

"Ah…Mariah. Your secret weapon."

"She makes things happen."

"I've noticed. She anticipates your every move and watches out for you."

"Yeah, like a mother hen," he said. "Not that I'm ungrateful. She's like my second right arm." He lifted his broken wrist. "And in my condition, that's important."

A uniformed waiter pushed a food cart to their table. Zane practically salivated. He'd been craving the home-made guacamole since earlier in the day. The waiter set out a *molcajete* and *tejolote*, a mortar and pestle carved from volcanic rock, to begin preparations. Squeezing lime juice into the bowl first, he added cilantro, bits of tomato, garlic and other spices. Next he used the pestle to grind all the flavors together and scooped out three perfectly ripe avocados. The aroma of the blended spices and avocados flavored the air. Once done, the guacamole and warm tortilla chips were placed on the table.

After the waiter took their dinner order, he walked off with his cart. Zane grabbed a tortilla chip and dipped it into the fresh green mixture, offering it to Jess first. "Taste this and tell me it's not heaven."

She leaned in close enough for him to place the chip into her mouth. As she chewed, a beautiful smile emerged, and her eyes closed. She sighed. "Oh, this is so good."

Drawn to the sublime expression on her face, he forgot about his craving for a few seconds. Eyeing her reaction distracted him in ways that might've been worrisome, if it hadn't been Jess. As soon as she finished chewing, she snapped her eyes open. "You didn't have one yet?"

"No…it was too much fun watching you."

"I seem to be a source of your amusement lately."

That much was true. Jess being here brightened up his solemn mood. That wasn't a bad thing, was it? He dipped a chip in and came up with a large chunk of guacamole. He shoved it into his mouth and chewed. On a swallow, he said. "Oh, man. That's good."

Jess's eyes darted past him, focusing on something happening behind his back.

"Uh…oh. Don't turn around, Zane," she whispered.

As soon as her words were out, two twentysomething girls approached the table, giddy and bumping shoulders with each other. "Hello. Excuse me," one of them said. "But we're big fans of yours."

"Thank you," he said.

"Would you mind signing a napkin for us?"

He glanced at Jessica and she nodded.

"Sure will."

They produced two white napkins and a pen, which made things a little less awkward. Zane hated waiting around while fans scrambled for something for him to autograph. They gave him their names, and he signed the napkins and handed them back.

"Thank you. Thank you. You're our favorite country singer. I just can't believe we've met you. Your last ballad was amazing. You have the best voice. I saw you in concert five years ago, when I was living in Abilene with my folks."

Zane kept a smile on his face. The girls were clueless that they were interrupting his meal with Jessica. "Well, that's nice to hear."

They stared at him, hovering close.

Jessica stood up then. Bracing her hands on the table, she smiled at the girls. "Hello. I'm Jessica, Zane's sister-in-law." The girls seemed baffled when she shook both of their hands. "We were having a little family talk, and we're limited on time. Otherwise I'm sure Zane would love to speak to you. If you give me your names and addresses, I'll see that you get a signed CD of his latest album. And please be discreet when you leave here," she whispered. "Zane loves meeting his fans, but we really need a few private moments during our meal tonight."

"Oh, okay. Sure," one of them said congenially.

The other girl wrote their addresses on the napkin Jessica provided before she wished them well. Giggling quietly, the two women walked away.

Zane stared at Jessica. "I'm impressed."

"I've been listening to how Mariah deals with your fan club members. I hope it's okay that I offered them a CD."

"It's fine. Happens all the time. I wish I'd have thought of it myself."

"They were persistent."

Zane shook his head. "I could tell you stories." But he wouldn't. Some of the things that had happened to him while touring on the road weren't worth repeating. "Actually, these two were a little subtle compared with some of the people who approach me."

"You mean, compared with the *women* who approach you."

He scrubbed his chin, his fingers brushing over prickly stubble. "I suppose."

Jessica snorted. "You don't have to be modest on my account. I know you're in demand."

He tossed his head back and laughed. "In demand? What are you getting at?"

"You're single, available, successful and handsome. Those two women who left here would probably describe you as a hottie, a hunk, a heartthrob and a hero. You're in the 4-H club of men."

His smile broadened. "The 4-H club of men? You just made that up."

"Maybe," she said, taking a big scoop of guacamole and downing the chip in one big swallow. "Maybe not."

"You constantly surprise me," he said, sipping water. He could use something stronger. "I like that about you."

"And I like that you're decent to folks who admire you."

Their eyes met, and something warm zipped through his gut. Jessica's compliments meant more to him than ten thousand wide-eyed, giddy fans. He admired her, too. "Ah, shucks, ma'am. Now you're gonna make me blush."

Another unladylike snort escaped through her mouth. Zane grinned and leaned way back in his seat just as his cell phone rang. Dang, he didn't want to speak to anyone now, but only a few close friends and family knew his number. He fished the phone out of his pocket. "It's Mariah," he said to Jessica. He turned his wrist to glance at his watch. It was after eight. "That's odd. She usually texts me if she needs me for something after hours. Excuse me a second."

"Hi," he said. "What's up?"

"Zane, s-something terrible's h-happened." Sobs came through the phone, Mariah's voice frantic and unsteady. Zane froze, those words instilling fear and flashing a bad memory. "My mother had a stroke. It's pretty b-bad."

"Oh, man. Sorry to hear that, Mariah."

"I have to fly home right away. Th-they don't know… oh, Zane…she's so young. Only sixty-four. She never had health problems before. Oh, God."

"Mariah, you just do what you have to do. Don't worry about a thing." Her voice broke down, her sobs growing louder. "Where are you?"

"At Patty's h-house in Santa Monica." She shared a place temporarily with an old college roommate. The situation was perfect while he was staying on Moonlight Beach. She was close by without living under his roof.

"Pack up a few things and try to stay calm. Do you have a flight?"

"Patty got me on a midnight flight to Miami."

"Okay…I'll send a car for you in an hour. Hang in there, Mariah."

"It's okay, Zane. I a-appreciate it, but Patty offered to d-drive me. I'll be fine." A deep, sorrowful sigh whispered through the phone. "Are you going to be all right? I don't know how long I'll be gone."

"Don't worry about me." He stared at Jessica. Her eyes were softly sympathetic and kind. "Take all the time you need. And call if there's any way I can help, okay?"

"Okay. Thanks. Goodbye, Zane."

Zane hung up the phone. "Man, that's rough. Mariah's mother had a stroke. She's on her way to Florida now."

"Gosh, I'm sorry to hear that. Is it serious?"

"Seems that way." He ran a hand down his face, pulling the skin taut. "I've never heard her so unraveled before. She may be gone a long time."

"I would think so. Will you find a replacement for her?"

Zane wasn't thinking along those lines. Not yet. He kept hearing the disbelief and pain in Mariah's voice and understood it all too well.

*Your wife didn't make it, Zane.*

*Didn't make what?* he'd asked the doctor over and over, screaming into the phone. Then, all the way home from London, he kept thinking, hoping, praying it had been a mistake. A horrible, sick mistake. It wasn't until he saw the desolate ruins of his once proud home in Beckon that it finally sank in Janie was gone. Forever.

The meal was served, and as his gaze landed on the plate of saucy cheese-topped tamales, blood drained from his face, and his gut rebelled. For Jessica's sake, he pushed his haunting memories aside. He didn't want to ruin her meal.

Jessica reached for him across the table, her fingertips feathering over his good hand gently, comforting him with the slightest touch. When he lifted his lids, he gazed into her knowing, sensitive eyes, and she smiled. "Let's have them pack up this food. We'll eat it later on."

"Do you mind?" he asked.

"Not at all. I'm ready to go anytime you are."

He felt at peace suddenly, a glowing warmth usurping the dread inside his gut.

And then it hit him. Sweet Jess. She was good for him. She understood him, perhaps better than anyone else on this earth. She was a true friend, an authentic reminder of home, and he needed her here.

"You asked me before if I'd find a replacement for Mariah."

"Yes, I did. Hard shoes to fill, I would imagine."

"Yeah, I agree." He looked her squarely in the eyes. "Except I've already found someone, and I'm looking straight at her."

# Four

Jessica woke to a glorious sunrise, the stream of light cutting through early morning haze and clouds in a host of color. Every morning brought something new from the view outside her bedroom window, and she was beginning to enjoy the variance from fog to haze to brilliance that took place before her eyes.

She stretched her arms above her head, working out the kinks, not so much in her shoulders and neck, but the ones baffling her brain. Last night, Zane told her to keep an open mind and sleep on his suggestion of replacing Mariah as his personal assistant. Her mouth had dropped open, and she thought him insane for a few seconds, but then he pointed out that he wasn't working, he had no gigs lined up, and he wasn't doing interviews right now. Most of what she had to do was hold off the press and postpone anything pending to future dates.

She wouldn't go into it cold. Mariah would be in touch to give her the guidance she needed to get her through anything remotely difficult.

"You're an intelligent woman, Jess. I'm convinced you'd have no problem, and I'm right here to help you," he'd said.

Zane's assurances last night gave her the push over the edge she'd needed this morning. Her head was clear now, and she valued the challenge and even looked forward to it. She wasn't ready to return to Texas anyway. Zane wanted freedom from his agent and manager's constant urging to get back on the horse. Zane wasn't ready yet and she could understand that. He needed more time, just as she did.

The new, bronzer Jessica no longer had freckles on her nose, thanks to a wonderful suntan that had connected those freckly dots and browned up her light skin. How many more hours could she feasibly sunbathe her day away? Staying on for a few weeks and helping Zane out would give her a new sense of purpose.

Jessica showered and dressed quickly. Putting on a pair of khaki shorts and a loose mocha-brown blouse, she slipped her feet into flip-flops and strode toward the kitchen. There were no wickedly delicious aromas drifting from the kitchen this morning. Mrs. Lopez had yet to arrive.

"Sonofabitch!"

A string of Zane's profanities carried to her ears. She grinned. Poor guy. He hated being confined.

She ventured into his bedroom. "Zane?"

"In here!"

She followed the sound of his cursing. He was standing over the bathroom sink, and their eyes met in the mirror. A scowl marred his handsome face, and three blood dots covered with bits of tissue spotted his cheeks and chin. Remnants of lime-scented shaving cream covered the rest of his face. "Damn hand. It's impossible to get a good shave."

"Whoops." With her index finger, she caught a drop of blood dripping from his chin before it landed on his white ribbed tank. "Got it."

He peered at her in the mirror and handed her a tissue. "Thanks."

"Thank me later, after I shave you. We'll see if I can't do a better job."

"You?"

"I used to lather up my dad and shave him when I was a kid." She hoisted herself up onto the marble counter to face him and picked up his razor. "It used to be a game, but darn it, I did an excellent job. Dad was surprised. Seems I'm pretty good with one of these."

Doubtful eyes peered at the razor in her hand.

"What? You don't trust me? It's a guarantee I'd do a better job than what I see on your face now. Or, I can drive you to the local barbershop. Since I'm going to be your new personal assistant and all."

The scowl left his face immediately, and her heart warmed at seeing approval in his eyes. "You've decided, then?"

"Yes, I'm on the clock now. So what will it be? A shave by your PA or a drive to the barber?"

"Try not to cut me," he said.

"You've already done a good job of that." She handed him a towel. "Wipe your face clean. We'll start from scratch."

Zane's eyes widened.

She chuckled at her bad choice of words. "You know what I mean." Pressing down on the canister, she released a mound of shave cream in her hand and leaned forward to rub it over his cheeks, chin and throat.

Zane leaned a little closer, his body braced by the counter. Her heart did a little dance in her chest. His nearness, the refreshing heady lime scent, her position sitting on the counter, *touching him*—suddenly she was all too aware of the intimate act she was performing on her brother-in-law.

What on earth was she doing?

Zane needed help and she'd rushed to his aid. But she hadn't thought this through.

He still towered over her, but only by a few inches now. She lifted her eyes and found him, waiting and watching her through the mirror.

Her hand wasn't so steady anymore.

She couldn't fall down on her first official act as Zane's personal assistant, intimate as it was.

"Okay, are you ready?"

He kept perfectly still. "Hmm."

Her legs were near his hip, and she angled her body to get closer to his face. Bracing her left hand on his shoulder to steady herself, she was taken by the strong rock-hard feel of him under her fingertips. She stroked his face, and the razor met with stubble and gently scraped it away. Carefully she proceeded, gliding the razor over his skin in the smoothest strokes she could manage.

His breath drifted her way as heat from his body radiated out, surrounding her. Cocooned in Zane's warmth, she fought an unwelcome attraction to him by thinking of Steven, the man who'd shattered her faith. And that reminder worked. Thoughts of Steven could destroy any thrilling moment in her life. She dipped the razor into the sink and shook it off. Zane's gaze left the mirror, and as she lifted her eyes to his, there in that moment, a sudden surprising sizzle passed between them.

One, two, three seconds went by.

And then he focused his attention back on the mirror, keeping a silent vigil on her reflection.

"How are you holding up?" she asked, breaking the quiet tension.

"Am I bleeding?"

Her lips hitched at his intense tone. "No."

"Then, I'm good."

Yes. Yes, he was.

"Okay, now for your throat. Chin up, please."

He obeyed without quarrel. Gosh, he really did trust her. Something warm slid into her belly, and the feeling clung to her as she finished up his shave.

"All done," she said after another minute. "Not a nick on you, I might add." At least one of them had come out of this unscathed.

"I think I hear Mrs. Lopez tinkering in the kitchen now." She handed him his razor and jumped down from the counter. "Do you want breakfast? Coffee?"

She was partway out the door when Zane caught her arm

just above the elbow. He looked gorgeous in his white ribbed tank, his face and throat shaved clean but for the last traces of shave cream. "Just a sec. I haven't thanked you. And you don't have to worry about breakfast for me."

"I don't?"

"No. That's not part of your job description."

Well, duh. She knew that. Mariah hadn't served him his meals, but Jessica couldn't very well tell him she'd run her mouth in order to get away from him as quickly as possible.

"We'll go over what I expect of you as my assistant this morning. Thanks for the shave." He slid his hands down his smooth face, and his eyes filled with admiration. "Feels great. You're pretty good."

She swallowed. Did this mean she'd have to shave him every day?

Gosh, she really didn't think this through thoroughly enough.

"Thanks. Well, I'll see you at breakfast."

"Oh, and Jess?"

"Yeah?"

He released her arm. "I'm glad you'll be staying on. I do need your help. And I think you'll enjoy it, but whenever you're ready to head home, I'll…understand."

"Thanks, Zane. I'll do my best."

Four hours later, Jessica sat behind the desk in Zane's office, satisfied she had things under control. It had been a little scary at first. What did she really know about Zane's celebrity life? But Mariah had been acutely efficient, keeping good records and documenting things, which made it easier for Jess to slide into the role of personal assistant. She seemed to live by a detailed calendar, and Zane's appointments, events and meetings were clearly labeled. *Thank you, Mariah, for not being a slouch.* In the day planner she came to regard as The Book, Mariah had jotted down phone numbers next to names and brief reminders of what needed to be said or done.

No to the *People* magazine interview.

Yes to donating twenty thousand dollars to the Children's Hospital charity. Zane would make an appearance in the future.

No to an appearance on *The Ellen DeGeneres Show*.

And so on.

With a little help from Zane earlier this morning, she was able to field a few phone calls and make the necessary arrangements for him. It was clear Zane was in a state of celebrity hibernation. Other than opening a new restaurant, Zane was pretty much in a deep freeze. Maybe he needed the break away from the limelight, or maybe he wasn't through running away from his demons.

In a sense, she was doing the same thing by being here, afraid to go home, afraid to face the pitfalls in her own life. She, too, was hiding out, so she had no right to judge him or try to fix the situation. It wasn't any of her business. That was for sure.

"How're you doing?" he asked.

She glanced up from The Book to find him standing at the office threshold, leaning on his crutches. She flashed back to shaving him this morning and the baffling emotions that followed her into breakfast. Her heart tumbled a little.

"Good, I think."

He smiled. "Anything I can help you with?"

"No, not at the moment."

He didn't leave. He didn't enter the room.

"Is there anything I can do for you?" she asked.

"Sort of." His lips twisted back and forth. "You see, Dylan's bugging me about this script. Fact is, I don't know if acting is right for me. I never had an acting lesson in my life. So I want to say no to him. But…"

She braced her elbows on the desk and leaned forward. "But, just maybe it's something you want to do?"

He stared at her. "Hell, I don't know, Jess. I guess I need a reason to say no."

"And how can I help you with that?"

"Dylan's got this idea that if I had someone run lines with me, I'd feel better about accepting the role. Or not. I didn't ask Mariah, well…because she works for me and I'm not sure she would be—"

"Honest?"

"Objective. She tends to encourage me to try new things, so she might not be the person to ask."

"So you're saying I'd have no problem telling you 'you suck'?"

He chuckled. "Would you?"

"No, no problem at all."

His brows gathered. "I'm not sure how to take that."

"I'd have only your best interests at heart. But honestly, Zane, what do I know about acting? What if my instincts aren't dead-on? What if I get it wrong?"

"Bad acting is bad acting. You can tell if someone sings off-key, can't you?"

"Sometimes, but my ear for music isn't as good as yours."

"But you're *real*, Jess. You would know when something is authentic. That's all I'm asking you to do."

His faith in her was a heady thing. She couldn't deny she was flattered. And as his personal assistant, she couldn't really tell him she didn't want to do it.

"Okay. What did you have in mind?"

"We read through some scenes. See if I can grasp the character."

"Where?"

He pointed to the long beige leather sofa—the most comfortable place to sleep in Zane's world. "Right here." He hobbled into the room on his crutches and sank down, resting the crutches on the floor. "The script is behind you on the bookcase. If you could get it and bring it over…"

"Sure." She turned and found it quickly. *"Wildflower?"*

"That's the one. You know most of the story."

She did. She was there when Dylan explained the premise of the romantic mystery to both of them the other day. It was about a man who comes home to his family's ranch after a long estrangement and finds his brother romantically involved with the woman he'd left behind. There's a mystery surrounding their father's death and a whole cast of characters who are implicated, including both brothers. "I think it's a good story, Zane."

"Well, let's see if I can do it justice."

"Sure."

She walked over to the couch and took a seat one cushion away from him.

"I don't think that's going to work," Zane said. "You have to sit next to me." He waved the script in the air. "There's only one of these."

"Right." As she scooted closer to him, Zane's eyes flicked over her legs and lingered for half a second. Oh, boy. The back of her neck prickled with heat. In a subtle move, she adjusted her position and lowered the shorts riding up her legs to midthigh. Zane didn't seem to notice. He'd focused back on the script and was busy flipping through story pages.

"Okay, here's a scene we can do together. It's where Josh and Bridget meet for the first time since his return."

She peered at the pages and read the lines silently. It was easy enough to follow. There were one or two sentences of description to set up the scene and action taking place. The rest was dialogue, and each character's part was designated by a name printed in bold letters.

"You start first," he said, pointing to the top of the page. "Where Josh speaks to Bridget in front of her house."

"Okay, here goes." She glanced at him and smiled.

He didn't smile back. He was taking this very seriously. She cleared her throat and concentrated on the lines before her. "Josh? You're home? When did you get back? I…I didn't know you'd come."

"My father is dead. You thought I wouldn't return for his burial?"

"No. I mean…it's just that you've been gone so long."

"So you wrote me off?"

A note of anger came through in Zane's voice. It was perfect.

"That's not how it happened. You left me, remember? You said you couldn't take living here anymore."

"I gave you a choice, Bridget. You didn't choose me."

"That wasn't a choice. You asked me to leave everything behind. My family, my friends, my job and a town I love. I don't hate the way you do."

"You think I hate this place?"

"Don't you?"

"Once, I loved everything about this place. Including you."

Jessica stared at him. The way he dropped his voice to a gravelly tone and spoke his lines was so real, so genuine, it impressed the hell out of her.

"But you've moved on." Now Zane's voice turned cold. He had a definite knack for dialogue. "With my brother."

They read the next three pages, bantering back and forth, learning the characters and living them. The scene was intense, and Zane held his own. He had a lot of angst inside him and found his release using the screenwriter's words on the page.

The scene was almost finished. Just a few more lines to go.

"Don't come back here, Josh," she said, meeting Zane's eyes. "I don't want to see you again."

Zane was really into the character now. "That's too bad, Bridget." The depth of his emotion had her believing. "I'm back to stay."

"I'm going to marry your brother."

"Like hell you are," Zane said fiercely, leaning toward Jessica, his face inches from hers.

"Don't…Josh…don't mess with my life again."

"This is where he grabs her and kisses her," Zane whispered. His breath swept over her mouth, and she found herself wanting to be kissed. By Zane. Heat crept up her throat and burned her cheeks.

Zane glanced at her mouth. Was he thinking the same thing? Did he want to kiss her?

He was a man she trusted. He was a man she truly liked. "Do you want to, uh, bypass the kiss?"

He shook his head, his gaze dropping to her mouth. "No," he rasped. "I don't."

Her pulse pounded as he took her head in his hands and caressed the sides of her overheated cheeks with his long, slender fingers. Her head was tilted slightly to the left, and then his mouth lowered to hers. He touched her lips gently, and she felt the beautiful connection from the depths of her soul. Was she supposed to stay in character? How would she accomplish that? Everything inside her was spinning like crazy.

The script called for a brutal, crushing kiss, but this kiss was nothing like that. His lips were firm and giving and generous…pure heaven.

"I'm not through messing with your life, Bridget." The gravel in his voice convinced her. He did *harsh* perfectly. "I might never be through."

As Zane backed away, his gaze remained on her. He blinked a few times, as if coming to his senses, and then cleared his throat.

The air sizzled around her. Was Zane feeling it, too? She didn't know where to look, what to say.

"It's your line," Zane whispered.

Oh! She glanced at the page and read her last line. "I—I can't do this again, Josh."

Zane paused for a second, glaring at her for a beat. "I'm not gonna give you a choice this time."

There. They'd made it through the entire scene. Zane flipped the script closed, and as he braced his elbows on his knees, he leaned forward.

Her heart was zipping along. She needed space, a few inches of separation from Zane. She flopped back against the sofa and silently sighed.

"Thank you," Zane said quietly.

"Hmm."

"Now for the hard part. I respect your opinion. No hard feelings either way, so lay it on me."

He'd convinced her he could act. Aside from the kiss that still had her reeling, she was completely enthralled with his character. He'd stepped into Josh's shoes without a bit of awkwardness. "I'm no expert, but I know when something's good. I'd say you were a natural, Zane."

He leaned back and looked into her eyes. Oh, God. She didn't want him to notice how nervous she was. "You really think so?"

"I do. You dove into that character and had me believing."

He stroked his jaw and sighed.

"I'm sorry if you wanted to hear you stink at acting. But I don't think so."

A crooked smile lifted the corner of his mouth. "I admit, I was hoping that was the case. Makes my decision harder now."

"Sorry?" she squeaked.

He released a noisy breath. "Don't be. I asked for your opinion. I appreciate you, Jess," he said. "I trust your judgment. I, uh…sort of got caught up in the scene. Hope you didn't mind about the little kiss I gave you."

Little kiss? If that was his little kiss, what would a real, genuine, from-the-heart kiss feel like from her one time brother-in-law? He didn't know the kiss had sent her senses soaring, and it would have to stay that way.

She'd never admit she'd wanted to kiss him. He was her brother-in-law, for heaven's sake. He was her employer now. And he was a good, decent man who'd never take advantage of her situation. She knew all that about Zane.

Of course he'd wanted to stay true to the script. He'd delved so deeply into character that he didn't want to lose the momentum of the scene. But, oh…for that brief moment when he'd looked into her eyes and her heartbeat soared, she believed he, Zane Williams, really wanted to kiss her.

And it had been a wow moment. "No, I didn't mind at all."

Her cell phone on the desk rang and she jumped up to answer it. "Oh, uh, excuse me, Zane. It's Mama."

"Sure."

He began to rise, and she put up her hand. She wasn't going to have him leave his own office. "No, don't get up. I'll take it in my room." Her mother's timing couldn't have been better. She needed to get away from Zane and the silly notions entering her head.

She walked out of the office and climbed the stairs. "Hi, Mama."

"Hi, honey. How're you doing this afternoon? Oh, I guess it's still morning there."

"Yes, it's just before noon. I'm doing fine." Her heartbeat had finally slinked down to normal since Zane's kiss a few minutes ago.

"Really?"

"Yes, I'm fine." It was weird how distance and the new surroundings made her see things differently. She wasn't thrilled with the way her life was turning out—she'd invested a lot of time on Steven Monahan—but she didn't need to worry her mother over it. Right now, she was taking it one day at a time. "Actually, I'm glad you called this morning. I have news. Zane's personal assistant, Mariah, had to take a leave of absence. Her mother's very ill and, well, since I'm here and Zane needs help, he's asked me to take over the position. It's temporary, but I won't be coming home this week or the next, probably. I might be here longer than that."

"Oh, that's good, honey."

"It is?" There was something in her mother's too-cheerful tone that raised her suspicions. She entered her bedroom wondering what was up? "What I mean to say is, I'm sorry Mariah's mother is ill. Bless her heart. I'll be sure to say a prayer for her. But you staying there for a little longer might be best for you, after all."

Really? Her overprotective mother—the woman who had set her alarm at 3 a.m. every night to get up and check on her two sleeping little girls when they were young, the woman who'd worried and fretted during their teen years, and the woman who, after Jessica's disastrous nonwedding, arranged for her to move into Zane's house just so he could keep an eye on her—*that mother* was actually glad that she wasn't coming home anytime soon?

Now she knew something was going on.

She lowered herself onto the bed. "Why, Mom? What's happened?"

"I hate to tell you this, honey. But better it come from me than you hear about it another way."

Her heart nearly stopped. Was her mother ill? Was it something severe? She flashed back to Janie's death. How the news had seemed unreal. She'd gotten physically sick, acid drenching her stomach and her breaths coming in short, uneven bursts. Now she held her breath. "Please, just tell me."

"Okay, honey. I'm sorry…but I just found out that your Steven eloped with Judy McGinnis. They just up and left town two nights ago. Went to Vegas, I hear. The whole town's crackling about it."

"W-with Judy?"

"I'm afraid so. I never expected that from Judy. Honey, are you okay?"

She might never be okay again. She'd just learned that the man she'd banked on for three full years, the man who had sworn up and down in her dressing room on their wedding day that he wasn't ready for marriage and that it wasn't anything she'd done, had just gotten married. The fault was all his for not recognizing his problem sooner, he'd told her. She'd believed he had commitment issues. But now she knew the truth. He wasn't ready for marriage to *her*. Instead, he chose one of her bridesmaids to speak vows with.

Judy had been her friend since grade school. Oh, God. She'd accepted losing Steven and any future they might've had together, but losing Judy's friendship, too? That was a double blow to her self-esteem. They'd both betrayed her. Made a fool out of her. She hadn't seen the signs. How long had Judy and Steven been hooking up behind her back?

Her eyes burned with unshed tears.

Being here and having a new sense of purpose in helping Zane, she was beginning to feel better and gain control of her emotions. But now, fresh new pain seared her from the inside out. What an idiot she'd been. That was the worst part of all, this hopeless sense of loss of *herself*. Her heart ached in a way it never had before. She felt herself slipping away.

She couldn't give in to it. If she did, she'd be totally lost. She couldn't dwell. She wouldn't let their betrayal dictate her life. She wouldn't curl into a pitiful ball and let the world spin without her.

"Jessica?"

"I'm going to be fine, Mama. I just need some time to digest this."

"I'm here if you need me, honey. I'm so, so sorry."

"I know. I love you. I'll call you tonight. Bye for now."

Jessica pushed End on her cell phone and faced the mirror. Her mousy-brown-haired reflection stared back at her through tortoiseshell-rimmed glasses. "What's happened to you, Jess?" she muttered.

She was tired of feeling like crap. Being a victim didn't suit her. She wasn't going to put up with it another second. The old Jessica had to go.

It was time for her to take hold of her life.

Afternoon breezes whispered through Zane's hair as he sat on his deck, gazing out to sea. Dylan McKay sat beside him, sipping a glass of iced tea. He didn't mind Dylan's company as long as he wasn't pressuring him about taking on an acting role.

"How soon before you're all healed up and ready to start living again?" Dylan asked.

Not soon enough for him. The confinement was getting to him. The only good thing about being temporarily disabled was that he didn't have to make any decisions right away. And he was milking that for all it was worth.

"The blasted boot comes off on Monday."

"And how's the wrist doing?"

His wrist? He flashed to trying to shave himself this morning. He'd been hopeless. Mariah usually took him to the barber twice a week. He hated being so damn helpless, and Jess had rescued him. She'd given him a clean, smooth shave and for a second there, as she leaned in close to him, her honeyed breath mingled with his and his body zinged to life. Electricity stifled his breathing for those few moments.

Jess?

He'd written it off as nothing and gone about his business.

Then he'd asked Jess to read lines with him. He'd gotten so caught up in the scene that when it came time to kiss her…he didn't want to deny himself the opportunity. Had it been only because the scene demanded a kiss? Or had it been something more?

A tick worked his jaw. It damn well couldn't be something more.

Though kissing her soft giving mouth packed a wallop. He'd forgotten what it felt like to have a sweet woman respond to him. He'd backed off immediately and didn't dare take it any further. The complication was the last thing either of them needed.

"My wrist should be healed soon, too…with any luck." He wiggled the tips of his fingers unencumbered by the cast. "I can't do a damn thing left-handed. You have no idea how uncoordinated you really are until you lose the use of your right hand."

"I hear you. How long will Mariah be gone?"

"Not sure. I spoke with her this morning. Her mom might have some permanent paralysis. Mariah's pretty torn up about it."

"So it's just you and Jessica now, living in this itty-bitty ole house?"

Zane rolled his eyes. The house was enormous, much more than he needed. He was hardly bumping into her in the hallway in the middle of the night.

Now, there was a thought. He struck that from his mind.

"She's taken on Mariah's duties here."

"You hired her?"

Zane nodded. Dylan didn't need to know that having Jessica around made him feel closer to Janie. She, above everyone else, understood the loss he felt. They shared that horrific pain together. Jess was *home* to him, without him having to return to Beckon. He liked that about her. So maybe it was selfish of him to ask her to stay on, but he hadn't pressured her. Much. He'd like to think she wanted to stay.

"I did. I didn't have a backup for Mariah. You know as well as I do it's hard to find a replacement for a trusted employee. I trust Jess. She'll do her best."

Dylan eyed him carefully. "You sure sing her praises."

"She's bright and learns quickly." He shrugged. "She's family."

"You keep saying that."

"It's true. Why wouldn't I say it?"

Dylan flashed a wry smile and then shook his head. "No real reason, I guess. Any chance I can convince you to be my costar before you head back on tour?"

"I haven't made up my mind yet, McKay. I told you I'm not making you any promises."

"Yeah, yeah. So I've heard. Remember what they say about people who drag their feet."

"No, what the hell do they say?"

"They risk getting them cut off at the ankles."

He laughed. "I should be flattered you're so persistent. Honestly, if I lose the role to someone else, so be it. I'm not sure." About anything, he wanted to add.

"Buddy, you're not going to lose the role to someone else. I'm the executive producer, and I see you doing this character."

"You want my fan base."

"That, too. I'd be a fool not to want to reel in your fans. I know they'd turn out for you. But I have no doubt in my mind you'd be—"

"Zane?" A sultry voice carried to the deck. His heart stopped for a second. Sometimes, when he was least expecting it, Jess would call out his name and he'd swear it was Janie asking for him.

"Out here," he called to her.

Jessica popped her head out the doorway. "Oh, sorry. I didn't realize you had a guest."

"Hi," Dylan said. "How're you doing, Jess?" Dylan sent her a brilliant smile. The guy could charm a billy goat out of a field of alfalfa.

"Hi, Dylan."

"Come on out here, Jess." Zane hadn't seen much of her since they'd run lines and *kissed* earlier in the day. He'd heard her working in the office, but she hadn't asked for his help, and he'd let her be. "Have a cool drink with us?"

"Uh, no thanks," she said, taking a few steps toward them. She wore a loose-fitting flowery sundress. Her hair was up in a ponytail, and a straw satchel hung from her shoulder. "Actually, I finished up what I could this afternoon. I was hoping to go shopping now. I wanted to see if you needed anything while I was out."

"Oh, yeah? What are you shopping for?" Was he so dang bored that he had to nose into Jessica's private business?

"I, uh, didn't bring enough clothes with me. I thought I'd pick up a few things."

"Hey, I know a great little boutique in the canyon," Dylan said. "I'd be happy to drive you there."

Zane swiveled his head toward Dylan. Was he kidding?

Jessica chuckled. "Thanks, that's a kind offer, but I'm good. I'm anxious to explore and see what I can find."

"Gotcha," Dylan said. "A little me time. I hope Zane hasn't been working you too hard."

"Not at all. I'm enjoying the work." With her finger, she pushed her sunglasses up her nose. She did that when she was nervous, and obviously, Dylan McKay made her nervous. Zane wasn't sure that was a good thing. He inhaled deep into his chest. Jessica was vulnerable right now, and she didn't need Dylan hitting on her.

"But you're both coming to the party tomorrow night, right?" Another charming smile creased his neighbor's face.

"Nope, sorry," Zane said. "We're not available."

Jessica faced him a second and blinked, then shifted her focus to Dylan. "Actually, I've changed my mind. I'd love to come. What time?"

Dylan's grin seemed to spread wider than the ocean view. "Six o'clock."

"I'll be there."

"You will?" Zane asked. They'd both decided on not going.

She nodded. "Sure, why not? Sounds like fun."

Zane couldn't argue the point. If she wanted to go to Dylan's little party, he had no right to stop her. "Well, then... I guess we're coming."

"We?" Jessica asked. A genuine spark of delight lit her expression. "You're going now? That's great, Zane."

He shrugged it off but couldn't stop his chest from puffing out. Why did it make him so doggone happy that Jessica wanted him around?

"Well, I'd better be off. Zane, is it still okay that I take one of your cars?"

"Yep. You know where the keys are in the office."

"Okay, thanks. I'll take the SUV. Bye for now," she said. She pivoted and walked back into the house.

"She's nice," Dylan said.

"Very nice. "

"Too nice for me? Are you warning me off?"

"Damn straight I am." Zane eyed him. "You know darn well Jessica isn't your type. So stay away. I'm serious. She's had it rough lately."

The patio chair creaked as Dylan leaned over the arm and focused on him. "You like her?"

"Of course I like her. She's like my..." But this time Zane couldn't finish his thought. He couldn't say she was like a sister to him. An image of taking her mouth in a daring kiss burst through his mind again. In that moment, he'd forgotten she was Janie's sister. All that filled his mind was how sweet and soft her lips were. How much he wanted to go on kissing her. He'd felt at peace with Jess, yet electrified at the same time.

He'd had women in the past to satisfy his physical needs. He hadn't been a total saint after Janie died, but he hadn't had a real relationship, either, and he sure as hell wasn't going in headfirst with Jessica. So why in hell was the memory of kissing her earlier torturing him?

"I meant you want her for yourself."

Zane snorted. "Are you not hearing what I'm saying? She's off-limits. To everyone. She has a lot of healing to do. Until then, no one gets near her." He'd promised her mother he'd protect her and make sure she didn't get hurt again.

"Okay, okay. I get it, Papa Bear. Now, let's get back to the script. I think Josh's character is perfect for you, like it was written with you in mind."

For once, Zane was grateful the subject changed to his possible acting career.

# Five

Thank goodness for credit cards. They gave Jessica the freedom to spend, spend, spend at the boutique Mariah had once raved about. She scoured the golden wardrobe racks at Misty Blue, and every time something struck her as daring and unlike her small-town schoolmarm image, she handed it to Misty Blue's *attire concierge* to put aside for her to try on. Sybil, the thirtysomething saleswoman, was dogging her, making suggestions and flattering her at every turn.

"Oh, you must have that," and "you'll never find a better fit," and "you'll be the envy of every woman on Moonlight Beach," were her mantras.

Jessica ate up her compliments. Why not? She needed them as much as she needed to buy a whole new wardrobe. The old Jessica was put to rest the minute she'd heard about her so-called good friend eloping with her fiancé. So be it. Jessica would return to Beckon a new woman.

Her clothes would be stylish. Her attitude would brook no pity. And she'd have a few thousand dollars less in her very tidy bankroll.

Saving money wasn't everything.

"I'll just put these items in your dressing room," Sybil announced. "Take your time looking around. When you're ready, you'll be in the Waves room."

Jessica blinked. Even the dressing rooms had names. "Okay, thank you."

She moved around the boutique slowly, taking her time perusing the shelves and racks. She picked out a two-piece bathing suit, a few hip-hugging dresses, two pairs of designer slim-cut jeans, and four blouses in varying colors and styles.

Sybil came racing forward. "Let me take those off your hands, too. I'll put them in the dressing room."

She transferred the clothes into Sybil's outstretched arms. "Thanks."

"Would you like to keep shopping?"

Jessica eyed several pairs of shoes on top of a lovely glass display case. "Yes, I'll need some shoes, too."

"I'll have Carmine, our shoe attendant, help you with that."

Thirty minutes later, Jessica glanced around the Waves dressing room. Clothes hung on every pretty golden hook, and shoes dotted the floor around her feet. She'd gone a bit hog-wild in her choices and needed guidance from someone who knew her well. She punched the speed dial on her cell phone and was relieved when her best friend, Sally, answered.

"Help me, Sally. I need your honest opinion," she whispered. "I texted you pictures of five of the dresses I've tried on. Did you get them?"

"Sure did. I'm looking at them now."

"Good." The inventor of cell phone technology was a genius. It made shopping a whole lot easier. "Which ones do you like?"

"Gosh, none of them look bad on you. You have a great figure," Sally said, almost in disbelief. "You've been hiding it."

"I guess I have." She'd never been comfortable with her busty appearance and had always chosen clothes to hide rather than highlight her figure. Now, all bets were off.

"Did you like the red one?"

"Definitely the red. That's a given," Sally said. "Whose eyeballs are you trying to ruin?"

"What do you mean?"

"That dress is an eye-popper."

She pictured Zane. Why had he come to mind so easily? It was ridiculous and yet, something had hummed in her heart when he'd kissed her today. He'd been caught up in the scene. She shouldn't make a darn thing out of it. But she was having a hard time forgetting the feel of his lips claiming hers. As short as the kiss was, it had been potent enough to shoot endorphins through her body. That wasn't necessarily a good thing.

"Do you think maybe I shouldn't be doing this?" she asked Sally, her bravado fading.

"Doing what? Pampering yourself? Spending some of your hard-earned money on yourself? Indulging a little? I'm only sorry I'm not there to help you with your TLC gone wild. Believe me, if I could swing it, I'd hop on a plane today."

She chuckled. "TLC gone wild? That's a new one, Sal."

"I'm clever. What can I say? Buy the clothes, Jess. I'll let you decide on the shoes, but those red stiletto heels will kick some major butt. Oh, and while you're at it, lose the eyeglasses. You brought your contacts, didn't you?"

"Yes, I have them."

"Well, use them. If you're going to do it, do it right."

Of course, Sally was dead-on. If she was going to invest in these clothes, she had to go all the way. She'd already decided to ditch her tortoiseshell glasses. Her hair could use some highlights, and her California tan was coming along nicely. Already she felt better about herself.

"And Sal, I wish you could come out here. It's really… nice."

"I bet. Zane's place sounds like heaven. Right on the beach. I bet you don't even have any swamp heat and humidity."

"Nope, not like home."

"Tell me you haven't met any big movie stars and I swear I won't be jealous."

"I, uh, well," her voice squeaked.

"Who? Tell me or I'll haunt you into forever."

"Would you believe Dylan McKay lives two doors down?" Jessica squeezed her eyes shut, anticipating the bombardment. No one was a bigger fan of the Hollywood heartthrob than her bestie Sally.

"You've met him?"

"Yes, I sort of ran into him on the beach." Or rather, the other way around—he'd run into her. "He's a friend of Zane's."

"No way! I can't believe it. Tell me everything."

A knock on the dressing-room door startled her, and she jumped. She'd forgotten where she was.

"Miss Holcomb, can I help you with anything?" Sybil asked.

"Whoops, gotta go," she said in a low voice. "I've got to get dressed. I'll call you later."

"You better!"

Jessica smiled as she ended the call and answered the saleswoman. "No thanks. I'm doing great."

"I'll be out in one minute."

"You sound happy. Find anything to your liking?"

"Just about everything," she answered.

She imagined the attire concierge who worked on commission smiling on the other side of the door.

Her purchases today would make both of them happy.

Zane had received a text message from Jessica half an hour ago telling him not to wait for her to have his meal. She was going to be late. But he didn't feel much like eating without her. It had taken Jessica living here for him to realize he'd eaten too many meals alone.

She must've gotten carried away on her little shopping spree.

When Jessica finally pulled through the gates, driving toward the garage, Zane made his way to the living room and, with the grace of an ox, plunked down onto the sofa.

A minute later the door opened into the back foyer, and he heard the crunch of bags and footsteps approaching. He picked up a magazine and flipped through the pages.

"Hi, Zane," Jessica said. Her voice sounded breezy and carefree. "Sorry I'm so late."

When he lifted his head, he found her loaded down with shopping bags. "Did you buy out the store?"

She chuckled from a warm and deep place in her throat. "Let's just say the store manager couldn't do enough for me. They offered me a vanilla latte and a chocolate mini croissant, and the shoe salesman almost gave me a foot massage."

His brows gathered. "A foot massage?"

"I told him no. I didn't have time. Is that done here?"

"I don't know if it's done *anywhere*," Zane said. For heaven's sake, she was buying shoes, not asking for a damn foot rub. His nerves started to sizzle. He studied the assortment of shiny teal-blue bags she held. "Where did you go?"

"Misty Blue. Mariah recommended the shop to me. It's just up the coast."

"Leave it to Mariah," Zane muttered. She had impeccable taste, but she could be indulgent at times.

"Speaking of Mariah, have you heard from her today?"

"Yes, we spoke earlier this morning. Do you need to talk to her about anything in particular?"

She shook her head and lowered her packages to the floor, releasing the handles. "I'm managing for right now." She walked over to lean her elbows on the back of his angular sofa. From his spot on the couch, he had a clear view of her face. "How is her mother doing?"

Zane shook his head. "Not great." He was lucky his mother and father were in their seventies and still quite active living in a retirement community in Arizona. He saw them several times a year. And when something like this happened, he thought about spending more time with them. "Mariah said her mom might have some permanent damage from the stroke, but it's too soon to tell. She spends most of her day at the hospital or meeting with doctors."

"I'm sorry to hear that."

"Yeah, me, too. And with all that, she asked about you. She made me promise to have you call her with any questions."

Jessica sent him a rigid look. "Unless it's an emergency, I'm not going to call her, Zane. You and I both know what it's like having to deal with a family crisis."

A lump formed in his throat. "Yeah. I agree, and I told her as much. There's nothing so important that it can't wait. Between the two of us, we'll figure out what needs figuring from this end."

"Right. Hey, I almost forgot. I bought you a present."

His heavy heart lightened. "You did?"

She bent to forage in one of the bags and came up holding a long, shiny black box. It wasn't a gift from Misty Blue, that was for sure. She stretched as far as her arms could reach, eyeing the box carefully one last time, before handing it over. "I, uh, hope this doesn't upset you, but I know how much you loved the one Janie got you, and, well...this one is from me."

Her fingers gently brushed over his hand, and her caring touch seized his heart for a moment. With his good hand, he managed to lift the lid and gaze at his gift. He found himself momentarily speechless. It was an almost identical replica of a bolo tie with a turquoise stone set on a stamped silver backing that Janie had given him on the anniversary of their first date. It had been lost in the fire, and he'd never replaced it. It wouldn't have had the same sentimental meaning. But the fact that Jessica gave it to him meant something. He lifted the rope tie out of the box and shifted his gaze to her. "It's a thoughtful gift, Jess."

"I know you treasured the first one. I helped Janie pick it out, so I remember exactly what it looked like."

"You didn't have to do this." But he was glad she had.

"You're putting a roof over my head and feeding me, but more importantly, being here is helping me heal. It's the least I could do for you. And I wanted it to be…something special."

"It is. Very special."

He rose from the sofa, found his footing and, using his crutches, shuffled over to her. He gazed through the lenses of her glasses to dewy, softly speckled green eyes. They were warm and friendly and genuine. He bent to kiss her forehead the way a brother would a sister, but then awareness flickered in her eyes, and he felt it, too. He lowered his mouth, heady in his need to taste the giving warmth of her lips again. When he touched his mouth to hers, he savored her sweetness and assigned this moment to memory for safekeeping. He backed away just in time to keep the kiss to one of thanks. "Thank you."

"You're welcome." Her deep, sultry voice thrilled him and churned his stomach at the same time. She sounded so much like Janie.

"I haven't had dinner yet. I waited for you. Mrs. Lopez put our meal in the oven to keep warm. Are you hungry?"

"Starving," she said. "Shopping is tough. I worked up an appetite."

He laughed. The women he knew loved to shop and spend endlessly. He'd never heard one remark about hard work.

"I'll put the bags away in my room. Meet you in the kitchen?"

He nodded. He hated that he couldn't offer to help her. He watched her climb the stairway holding three maxed-out shopping bags in one hand and two in the other. The next time she wanted to shop, he'd be damn ready to take the packages off her hands and carry them upstairs for her.

Zane made his way into the kitchen. Mrs. Lopez had left chicken and dumplings warming in the oven. Zane lifted a periwinkle-striped kitchen towel tucked over a basket and eyed cheesy biscuits, still warm. He dipped into the basket and sank his teeth into a biscuit. Warmth spread throughout his mouth and reminded him he was ready for a hearty meal.

"Wow, smells good in here." Jessica entered the kitchen.

"Mrs. Lopez made one of my favorites tonight."

"In that case, I'm surprised you waited for me."

"I figured a Southern girl like you would appreciate sharing chicken and dumplings. It's my mother's recipe."

"You figured right. Well, then. Have a seat." She gestured to the table. "I'll dish it up. Unless you want to eat outside?"

He shook his head. The sun had already set, and winds howled over the shoreline, spraying sand everywhere. "Here is just fine."

Before he knew it, the table was set, plates were dished up and he had the company of one of his favorite people sitting across from him.

The chicken was tender, the dumplings melted in his mouth and Zane spent the next few minutes quietly diving into his meal. He liked that he could sit in silence with Jess without feeling as though he had to entertain her. She was as comfortable with the quiet as he was.

"Mmm, this was so good." Jess took a last bite of food, and as she wiped her mouth, his gaze drifted down to where the napkin touched her lips. "I'll have to steal the recipe from Mrs. Lopez and make it for my mother when I get home."

"No problem." He shouldn't be noticing the things he was noticing about Jess. Like the cute way she pushed her glasses up her nose, or the way she smelled right after a shower, or how her light skin had burnished to a golden tone from days of sunbathing. The sound of her voice dug deep into his gut. Janie and Jess were the only two women he knew that had a low, raspy yet very feminine voice. Janie had been sultry, sexy, alluring, but…Jess?

"Zane?"

He lifted his gaze to her meadow-green eyes.

"You went someplace just now."

"I'm sorry."

"No need to be sorry. Are you okay?"

He nodded and cleared his throat. "So, did you have fun shopping today?"

"Fun?" Her head tilted as a slow, easy smile spread across her face. "I had an attire concierge help me. That was weirdly entertaining. She dogged my every step but was nice as can be. Actually my best friend, Sally, helped me make the right choices. Sally was my maid of honor in the wedding that never was."

"Is your friend in town?"

She laughed and shook her head. "No, not at all. I texted her pictures of the clothes I tried on, and she helped me decide. I'm *so* not a shopper."

"Ah, the power of technology."

"Yeah, ain't it great?"

It beat having Dylan McKay help her shop. Zane wasn't about to allow that to happen.

A heartbreaking ladies' man was the last thing sweet Jess needed in her life right now.

"Actually, it is pretty great. I'm glad you had a good day."

"I plan to have a lot of good days from now on." A glint of something resolute beamed in her eyes, her face an open expression of hope.

Jess was healing, and that was a good thing. He liked seeing her feeling better. That was the whole point of her coming here. But it seemed too soon. And she seemed a little too happy for a woman who'd been betrayed and heartbroken. Right now, Jessica Holcomb looked ready to conquer the world, or at least Moonlight Beach. Instincts that rarely failed him told him something else was going on with Jess.

And he didn't know if he was going to like it.

"Hi, Zane." Jessica stepped into the living room, dressed and ready for Dylan's party.

Zane turned from the window… His hair was combed back, shiny and straight, the stubble on his face a reflection of not having a shave in two days. He looked gorgeous in a white billowy shirt and light khaki trousers. When his gaze fell on the *new* her, his lips parted and his eyes popped as he took in her appearance from the top of her head to her sandaled toes. Pain entered his eyes, and he blinked several times as if trying to make it go away. Relying on the two crutches under his arms, he straightened to his full height and sighed heavily.

"Zane?" Her lips began to quiver. What was wrong with him? "Are you all right?"

He stared at her, his expression unreadable. "I'm fine."

"Are you? Have I done something? Don't you like the dress?" Her mind rushed back to the clothes she'd laid out on the bed. She'd chosen the cornflower-blue sundress that accented her slender waist in a scoop-neck design that, granted, revealed more cleavage that she was comfortable with, but wasn't indecent by any means.

His mouth opened partly, but no words tumbled forth, and then he gulped as if swallowing his words.

"What is it?" she pressed.

"You look like Janie," he rushed out, as though once pressured, he couldn't stop himself from saying it.

"I…do?"

How could she possibly look like Janie? Janie was stunning. She had natural beauty, a perfectly symmetrical face. She wore stylish clothes, had the prettiest long, silken hair, and oh…now she understood. Of course she and Janie resembled each other—they were sisters—but Jessica had always stood in Janie's shadow where beauty was concerned. Her blonde-from-a-bottle hair color had turned out a little less dark honey and much more sweet wheat, similar to Janie's hair color. Jessica didn't usually wear her contacts, but she imagined her eyes looked more vibrant green than ever before. Like Janie's brilliant gemstone eyes. Did Zane think he was seeing a ghost of his former wife? She didn't believe she looked enough like Janie for that and never thought about how it might appear. "I, um, wasn't trying to, but I take that as a compliment." She shrugged, compelled to explain. "I guess I needed a change."

An awkward moment passed between them, which was weird. They didn't do awkward. Usually they were completely at peace with each other.

"You didn't need to change a thing," he said firmly.

Was he trying to make her feel better? Even she had to admit, after looking at herself in the mirror today, that her new look made her appear revitalized and well, better than she had in years. Zane had no idea what she was really going through right now, the pain, rejection, anger. He didn't know, because she hadn't told him. He wasn't her shrink, her sounding board. And call it pride, but she wasn't ready to talk about Steven's quick marriage to her once-friend/bridesmaid to anyone, much less him. "I'm sorry if I upset you. Obviously you don't approve. I don't have to go tonight."

The last thing she wanted to do was cause Zane any upheaval in his life. He was still in love with Janie. She got that. No one knew what a special person her sister was better than she did.

She was staying here thanks to Zane's generosity. He was her employer now, too, and she had to remember that, yet underlying hurt simmered inside her. He had no idea how hard this was for her. She'd come into this room hoping for some sort of approval. She'd made a change in her appearance, but it was more than that. She looked upon this makeover as a fresh start, a way to say "screw you" to all the Stevens in the world. She'd come into this room with newfound confidence, and Zane's dismal attitude had caused her heart to plummet. Why did it matter so much to her what Zane thought?

She pivoted on her heels, taking a step toward the staircase, and Zane's voice boomed across the room. "Damn it, Jess. Don't leave."

She whirled around and stared at him. A dark storm raged in his eyes.

Was he angry with her? Maybe she should be angry with him. Maybe she'd had enough of men dictating what they wanted from her. "Is that an order from the boss?"

"Hell, no." His head thumped against the window behind him once, twice, and then he lowered his voice. "It wasn't an order."

"Then what was it?"

Zane's gaze scoured over her body again, and as he took in her appearance, approval, desire and *heat* entered his eyes. Her bones could have just about melted from that look. Then, with a quick shake of his head, he said, "Nothing, I guess. Jess, you don't need my approval for anything. Fact is, you look beautiful tonight. You surprised me and, well…I don't like surprises."

She didn't move. She was torn with indecision.

From the depth of his eyes, his sincerity came through. "I'm a jerk."

Her lips almost lifted. She fought it tooth and nail, but Zane could be charming when he had to be.

"Blond hair looks great on you."

She drew breath into her lungs.

"The dress is killer. You're a real knockout in it."

His compliments went straight to her head. He'd finally gotten to her. "Okay, Zane. Enough said." She'd been touchy with him, maybe because she'd hoped to impress him a little. Maybe because, in the back of her mind, she'd wanted to please Zane or at least win his approval. "Let's forget about this." She didn't like confrontation, not one bit.

"You'll go to the party?"

She nodded. "Yes. I'm ready."

They'd had their first real argument. Granted, it wasn't much of one. A few minutes of tension was all. But she'd stood her ground, and she could feel good about that. One thing that loving Steven had taught her was never to turn a blind eye. From now on, she wanted to deal in absolute truth.

"You mind driving?" he asked.

"I should make you trudge through the sand all the way to Dylan's place."

"I'd do it if it would put a smile back on your face."

"It's tempting. But I'm not that cruel."

Amused, Zane's mouth lifted, and they seemed back on even footing again.

Whatever that was.

# Six

Zane stood outside in the shadows, his shoulder braced against the wall of Dylan's home. The setting sun cast pastel colors across the cobalt sky, and waves pounded the shoreline. The Pacific breezes had died down and no longer lifted Jessica's blond locks into a flowing silky sheet in the wind. She stood in front of a circular fire pit on the deck. Her flowery summer dress had been a victim of the wind, too, and hell if he hadn't noticed her hem billow up, *every single time*. And every single time, something powerful zinged inside him.

He couldn't figure why Jessica had made such a drastic turnabout in her appearance. He wouldn't have called her an ugly duckling before—she'd been perfect in her own natural way—but tonight, she'd bloomed into a beautiful swan and he feared he was in deep trouble.

He liked her. A lot. And he knew damn well she was as off-limits to him as any woman would ever be. The old Jess he could deal with. She was like his kid sister. But now, as he watched the predusk light filter through her hair and heard the sound of her sultry laughter carry to him as she spoke with Dylan and his friends, she seemed like a different woman.

Sweet Jess was a knockout, and every man here had noticed.

Dylan popped his head up from the group and gestured to him. "Come on over and join the party."

Well, damn. He couldn't very well stay in the shadows the entire night. He'd have to shelve his confused thoughts about Jessica and join them. He pushed off from the wall using his crutches for balance and made his way over to the fire pit.

"I thought Adam was the only recluse on the beach," Dylan said.

"There's a difference between savoring one's privacy as opposed to hiding out from the world," Adam said.

Adam Chase was his next-door neighbor, the architect of many of the homes on the beachfront and a man who didn't give much away about himself. He'd been featured in *Architectural Digest* and agreed to a rare magazine interview, but mostly the man's astonishing work spoke for itself. The one thing he'd learned about Adam in the time he'd known him was that he shied away from attention.

"He's got you there, Dylan. Being someone who craves attention, you wouldn't understand." Zane zinged him because he knew Dylan was a good sport and could handle the teasing.

Dylan took Jess's hand, entwining their fingers. "They're ganging up on me, Jess. I need someone in my corner."

Jess's giggles swept over Zane, and he eyed the half-empty blended mojito she held in her other hand. She freed her hand and inched away from Dylan. It was hardly a noticeable move, except maybe to Zane, who was eyeballing her every step. "You boys are on your own. I'm staying out of this."

Dylan slammed his hand to his chest. "Oh, you're breaking my heart, Jess."

Adam's eyes flickered over Jess and touched on the valley between her breasts in the revealing sundress she wore. She was dazzling tonight, and Zane had a hard time keeping his eyes off her, too. He shouldn't fault the guys for flirting, yet every inappropriate glance at her boiled his blood.

"You're a smart woman, Jessica," Adam said.

"The smartest," Zane added. "She's going home with me tonight."

All eyes turned his way. Ah, hell. He'd shocked them, but no more than he'd shocked himself. He spared Dylan a glance, and the guy's smug grin was bright enough to light the night sky. Adam's face was unreadable, and the four others around the fire pit became awkwardly silent. "She's my houseguest and she's…"

"I think what Zane meant," Jess chimed in, "was that I've had a tough time lately. I'm getting over a broken engagement and, well, he's sweet enough to want to protect me." Her eyes scanned the seven people sitting around the fire pit. "Not that I'd need protecting from anyone here. You've all been so nice and welcoming."

They had. And now Zane felt like an ass for staking his claim when he had no right and for putting her in an awkward position.

"But I do make my own decisions. And I'd love to get to know each of you better."

"You *are* a smart woman." Dylan turned to Zane with genuine understanding. He and Dylan had had this conversation before. "And we all knew what Zane was getting at."

Zane clamped his mouth shut for the moment. He'd said enough, and he had a feeling that Jessica wasn't too thrilled with him right now. His big brother act had probably started to wear thin on her. He didn't say boo when she walked down to the water deep in conversation with Adam Chase for a few minutes. He didn't register an inkling of irritation when Dylan offered to give her a tour of his house. But darn if he wasn't keenly relieved when Jessica made friends with three of the women at the party. She'd spent a good deal of time with them. He recognized one woman as an actress recently cast in a film about a Southern girl. She'd gobbled up a good deal of time asking Jess questions about Texas.

"You look like you could use a beer." Adam handed him one of the two longnecks he clasped between his fingers.

"You read my mind. That sounds good." Adam's mouth twitched. The man didn't often smile, but obviously Zane had amused him. "Right. How's the restaurant coming?"

Zane had asked Adam for a recommendation of someone whose specialty was designing shoreline commercial establishments since Adam didn't work with small restaurants. "We've broken ground. The framework is up, and we should open our doors in a few months. I'm hoping for Labor Day."

"Glad things are going smoothly."

He nodded. Last year, he'd opened a restaurant in Reno, and his friend and CEO of Sentinel Construction had overseen the building. But Casey's business didn't reach the west coast, and Adam had connections all over the world. He wound up hiring a builder Adam said was top-notch. "They seem to be."

Adam sipped his beer. "Jessica seems like a nice girl. She said she's indirectly related to you."

Indirectly? Though those were true words, it still stung hearing them coming from her mouth secondhand that way. There was something painful in the truth, and if he was being gut-honest with himself, it was liberating, as well. "Uh, yeah. She was my wife's little sis. She's staying in Moonlight Beach for a while."

"With you. Yes, you made that clear earlier." Adam's mouth hitched again. It was more animation than Zane had seen in the guy practically since he'd met him. "I'm going out on a limb here, but either you're hooked on her, or you've got a bad case of Big Brother syndrome."

Zane peered over Adam's shoulder and caught a glimpse of Jessica speaking with a man who looked enough like Dylan to be his twin. "Who the hell is that?"

Adam swiveled his head and gave the guy a once-over.

"Dylan introduced him to me before you arrived. That's Roy. He's Dylan's stunt double."

Roy and Jessica stood in the sand under the light of a tiki torch and away from the crowd of people beginning to swarm the barbecue pit, where a chef prepared food on the grill. Zane didn't like it, but he couldn't very well pull her away from every guy who approached her.

"So, which is it?" Adam asked.

"Which is what?" He watched Jessica laugh at something Roy said.

"Are you playing big brother? Cause if you're not, I think you have to amp up your game, neighbor. Or you're going to lose something special, before you know what hit you."

Zane stared at Adam. The guy had no clue what he was talking about. Adam had no idea how hard he'd loved Janie. He had no idea how he couldn't get past what happened. He'd tried over and over to put his emotions to lyrics, to gain some sort of closure in a song meant to honor his love for Janie, but the words wouldn't come. "I've already lost—"

Adam began shaking his head. "I'm not talking about the past, Zane. I'm talking about the future."

"Spoken by a man who rarely steps foot out of his house."

Now Adam did laugh. "I'm here now, aren't I?"

"Yeah, that surprises me. Why are you?"

He shrugged. "I've got a temperamental artist painting a wall in my gallery. It's going to be fantastic when he's through, and he insists on complete privacy. I'm staying at Dylan's for a few days."

"Well, damn. You're sorta here by default, then."

"It's not so bad. At least I got to meet Jessica and all her Southern charm."

"Why, that's very nice of you to say, Adam."

A sweet strawberry scent wafted to his nostrils, announcing Jessica's presence even before she'd uttered a word.

He'd come to recognize her scent, and every time she approached, a little bitty buzz would rush through his belly. She took a place by his side, and he refrained from puffing out his chest.

"Just speaking the truth," Adam said.

"Hey, Jess," Zane said.

"Hey, yourself," she said to him. He wasn't sure if she'd been deliberately avoiding him since his dopey remark earlier, or if she was flitting around like a butterfly to make new friends. Either way, he was glad she'd come over to him.

"Having fun?"

"Sure am. I'm meeting some great people here. It was sweet of Dylan to invite me. Sorry if I abandoned you."

He raised his beer bottle to his lips. "No problem. I spent my time keeping Adam amused."

Jessica shot a questioning glance at Adam.

"He's quite a party animal these days," Adam explained, tucking his free hand into his trouser pockets.

Zane gulped the rest of his beer. He wouldn't be here if Jessica hadn't changed her mind about coming. "C'mon Jess. Looks like the meal's being served. I've got me a hankering for some barbecue chicken."

"Adam, will you join us?" she asked.

Adam shook his head. "I'll see you over at the table later. I'm going to have another drink first."

Zane began moving, and Jessica kept by his side as he headed for a table occupying the far corner of the massive patio. "Chances are we won't see much of Adam tonight. He keeps to himself pretty much."

"Does he?" she asked. "Why?"

"I don't really know. We got friendly when I leased the house from him. And we had some business dealings, but I sensed he's a loner. It's probably why he was standing with me, over against the wall."

"Well, he was cordial to me."

"Yeah, I know." Zane dipped his gaze to the swell of her breasts teasing the top of her frilly sundress. Her skin looked creamy soft and—Lord help him—inviting. With that blond hair flowing down her back and her eyes as green as a grassy meadow, she made his heart ache. "I saw the two of you walking out to the water."

"All I did was ask him about his designs. Architecture has always fascinated me."

"Yeah, that's probably why he spent time with you. He loves talking shop." Lucky for him, Jess didn't notice the sarcasm in his voice. He managed to pull a chair out for her, crutches and all.

Man, he'd be glad to rid himself of them.

It couldn't happen soon enough.

They'd stayed at the party a little too long. Zane was smashed, going over his liquor limit an hour ago, and now she struggled to get him out of the car. He obviously didn't take his own advice. Hadn't he warned her of not drinking too much, because in his handicapped state, he wouldn't be able to help her? Well…now the shoe was on the other foot. "Hang on to me," she said, reaching inside the car.

"Glad to, darlin'."

He slung his arm around her shoulder, nearly pulling her onto his lap.

"Zane!"

An earthy laugh rumbled from his throat.

"Not cute."

"Neither are y-you," he said.

After a few seconds of maneuvering, she managed to get him upright.

"You're b-beautiful."

Oh, boy. She rolled her eyes and ignored his comment.

He swayed to the left. Sure-footed he was not. She leaned him up against the car. "Here." She shoved a crutch under his arm, tucking it carefully but none too gently. "Please, please, try to concentrate."

Maybe she should've taken Dylan up on his offer to drive Zane home. But Zane wouldn't have any of it, insisting he could manage.

Men and their egos.

Now she had two hundred pounds of sheer brawn and muscle to contend with. "Lean against me, Zane. Try not to topple. Ready?"

He nodded forcefully, and his whole body coasted away from her. "Whoa!" She gripped him around the waist and tugged with all of her might to bring him close. Letting him go right now would be a disaster. "Don't make sudden moves like that."

"Mmm."

He sounded happy about something. She was glad someone was enjoying this. When he seemed secure in his stance, she took a step and then another. With his body pressed to hers and one shoulder supporting his arm, she managed to get him through the garage and inside the house. By the time she made it to his bed, her strength was almost sapped. "Here we go. I'm going to let go of you now."

"Don't," he said.

"Why? Are you feeling dizzy?"

He shook his head, and his arm tightened around her shoulder. She was trapped in his warmth, his heat. And as she gazed up into his eyes, they cleared. Just like that. The haze that seemed to keep him in a woozy state was gone. "No. I'm feeling pretty damn good. Because you're here with me. Because I can't get you out of my head."

As if his own weight was too much to bear, he sat down, taking her with him. She plopped on the bed, and the mattress sighed. Streaming moonlight filtered into the room, and their reflection in the window bounced back at her. Two souls, searching for something that they'd lost. Was that what the attraction was?

"Are you drunk?" she asked.

"Not too much anymore." He pushed aside her hair at her nape, his touch as gentle as a Texas breeze. He nipped her there, his teeth scraping around to the top of her throat and the sensation claimed all the breath in her lungs.

"You sobered up fast," she whispered, barely able to form a coherent thought. Having his delicious mouth taking liberties on her neck was pure heaven.

"I know when I want something."

His nips were heady, and she tilted her head to the side, offering him more of her throat. "Wh-what do you want?"

With his good hand under her chin, he turned her head, and then his lips were on hers, pressing firm against her softness, igniting fireworks that started with her brain and rushed all the way down to her belly. She turned to him, roping her arm around his neck, kissing him back. He smelled like pure male animal, his scent mingling with whiskey and heat. Her breasts perked up, and her nipples pebbled against the silky material of her dress.

"I want to kiss you again and again," he rasped over her lips. "I want to touch your body and have you touch mine. I need you, too. So badly, sweetheart."

Oh, wow. Oh, wow. Oh, wow. A fierce physical attraction pulled at her like a giant magnet. She couldn't fight the force or the combustible chemistry between them. And Zane didn't give her time to refuse. With his left hand, he began unbuttoning his shirt and did a lousy job of slipping the buttons free until she came to his rescue.

"Let me." She shoved his hand away and quickly finished for him. With his shirt open now, his chest was a work of art, muscled and bronzed. She itched to touch him, to put her hands exactly where he wanted her to. She inhaled, and as she released a breath, she spread her palms over his hot, moist skin. From the contours of his waist up his torso to where crisp chest hairs tickled the underside of her fingers, she savored each inch of him.

A guttural groan exploded in the room, and she wasn't sure if she'd made that sound, but one look into Zane's eyes darkened by desire and she knew it wasn't her.

He was on fire. His skin sizzled hot and steamy, his breathing hitched and all of that combined was enough to blanket her body with burning heat. "We can't," she said softly.

She had to say it. Because of Janie. Because of Steven. She and Zane were both trying to heal, but none of that resonated right now. None of it seemed powerful enough to derail the sensations whipping them into a frenzied state.

Maybe this was what both of them needed.

One night.

His mouth claimed her again as he lay down on the bed, tugging her along with him. She fell beside him. Promptly he snaked his arm under her waist and flipped her on top of him.

She had his answer. Yes, they could.

His good hand cupped her cheek, and his eyes bored into her. "Don't question this, Jess. Not if it's what you want right now."

That was Zane. The man who didn't plan for the future anymore, the man who'd said it was better sometimes not to know where you were going. And Jessica certainly didn't have a clue what her future held or where the heck she was going from here.

But she knew what she wanted tonight.

How could she not? Her breasts were crushed against Zane's chest, her body trembling and so ready for whatever would come next. Zane was a good, decent man who also happened to be sexy as sin but he had also been her sis— She stopped thinking. Enough. She might talk herself out of this. "It's what I want."

He gave her a serious smile and kissed her again, his lips soft and tender, taking his time with her, making her come apart in small doses.

In the moment, Jessica gave herself permission to let go completely. He pushed the straps down on her dress and her breasts popped free of restraint. Zane caressed her, running his hand over her sensitive skin, lightly touching one wanton crest that seemed made for his touch.

A deep moan rose from her throat. She closed her eyes and enjoyed every second of his tender ministrations. "You have a beautiful body, sweetheart," he said, then rose up to place his mouth over one breast, his tongue flicking the nub, wetting it in a flurry of sweeps. He moved to the other side and did the same, a little more frenzied, faster, rougher. She squealed, the exquisite pain sending shock waves down past her belly.

Zane reacted with a jerk of his hips. "Get naked for me, Jess."

She pulled her dress over her shoulders, and he helped as much as he could to lift it the rest of the way off. She gave it a gentle toss to the floor and straddled him, bare but for her panties, and looking into eyes that seemed distant for a moment. "Are you sure about this?" he rasped, his brows gathering.

He was giving her a way out, but she was in too deep now. Her body hummed from his touch and the promise of the pulsing manhood beneath her. She wanted more…she wanted it all.

She was the *new* Jess.

"I'm sure, Zane."

He nodded and blew out a breath in apparent relief, but there was something else. A part of him seemed undecided. It was only a feeling she had, a vibe that worried her in some small part of her consciousness. Don't think. Don't think. Don't think.

The new Jess wasn't a thinker. She was a doer.

She bent to his mouth, her sensitized nipples reaching his chest first. He bucked under her. "Oh, man, babe." She smiled at him and opened her mouth, coaxing his tongue to play with hers. His strokes made her dizzy, and her desire for him soared. She was almost ready. She reached for his zipper.

"No," he said. He gently rolled her to her side and leaned over her. "There might be something I'm good at with my left hand."

A smile broke out on her face, but Zane wiped the smile away the second his fingers probed inside her panties. He cupped her there, and a melodic sigh escaped her throat. He kissed her, swallowing the rest of her sounds as he stroked her with deft fingers. Her body moved, arched, reached as he became more and more merciless. "Zane," she cried.

She climbed over the top immediately, her limbs shaking, her breathing quickened and labored. A drawn-out, piercing scream rang from her throat. She was cocooned in heat. Zane held her patiently while her tingles ebbed and she came down to earth.

"Reach over to the bed stand, sweetheart," he said as she caught her breath. "Dig deep in the drawer." He nuzzled her ear and said softly, "It's been a while."

Seconds later, with a little of her help, he was sheathed. She reeled from the passion she witnessed in his eyes. It wasn't lust, but something more. Something she could feel good about when she remembered this night. They were connected, always had been, and right now all things powerful in the universe were pulling her toward this man.

"Ready?" he asked.

As she nodded, boldly she lifted her leg over his waist to straddle him. Both of his hands came around her back, encouraging her to lean down. She did, and he pressed a dozen molten kisses to her mouth before he set her onto him.

Instinctively she rose up, and he helped guide her down. The tip of his shaft teased her entrance, and she closed her eyes.

"So beautiful," she heard him say softly as he filled her body.

They moved together as one, his thrusts setting the pace. Her heart beat rapid-fire; she was in the Zane zone now and offered to him everything he wanted to take.

He was all she could ever hope for in a lover. His kiss drove her crazy, and he was more adept with one good hand than the men she'd known in the past who'd had the use of both. He explored her body with tender kisses and bold touches, with harmonious rhythm and unexpected caresses. He was wild and tender, sweet and wicked. And when he pressed her for finality that he seemingly couldn't hold back another second, her release astonished and satisfied her. "Wow," she whimpered, her body still buzzing. She lay sated and spent on the bed.

"Yeah, babe. Wow." Zane sighed heavily, an uncomplicated sound telling her how much pleasure she'd brought him. She wasn't sorry. She had no regrets. But then, she hadn't let her mind wander since she'd entered Zane's bedroom. She didn't want to think. Not now.

Zane wrapped his arm around her, tucking her into him, and soon the sound of his quiet breaths steadied. With all that he'd consumed tonight, there was no reason to hope that he would wake soon.

She closed her eyes, savoring the safety and serenity the night brought to her.

Zane's eyes snapped open to the ceiling above. It was funny how the crater-like texture seemed odd to him this morning. He'd never noticed it before. Back home, solid wood beams supported the house. The rich smell of pines and oaks and cedar lent warmth and gave him a true sense of belonging. He missed home, longed for it actually, but how in hell could he complain? He lived in a rich man's paradise, on a sandy windswept beach with dazzling pastel sunsets and beautiful people surrounding him.

He didn't have to look over to know Jess wasn't beside him on the bed. He'd heard her exit the room in the wee hours of the morning. He should've stopped her. He should've reached out and tugged her back to bed. If he had, she'd be here with him now, and he would nestle into her warmth again.

Sweet Jess. *Sexy Jess.*

Oxygen pushed out of his lungs. He was still feeling the effects of last night. The alcohol, the soft woman—the entire night played back in his mind. He was in deep now.

He hinged his body up and swiveled his feet over the bed to meet with the floor. He made a grab for his crutches that lay against the wall and luckily hung on to them. Rising, still wearing the pants he'd worn last night, he ambled from the bedroom to the living room. From there, he spotted Jess pressed against the deck railing in a pair of sexy shorts and a ruffled blouse, gazing out to sea. It was just after dawn, and the beach was empty but for a few seagulls milling about. Low curling waves splashed against the shore almost silently. It was a beautiful time of day.

Made even more beautiful by his golden-haired houseguest.

As quietly as a man on crutches could, he made his way out the double French doors and headed toward her. Her concentration was intense, and she didn't hear him approach until he was behind her. He put his crutches near the wall and braced his arms on the railing, trapping her in his embrace.

She stood with her back to his chest. Her hair whipped in the breeze and tickled his cheeks as he nibbled on her nape. She tasted like a woman who'd had a delicious night of sex. She smelled like a woman who'd been sated and well loved. He breathed her in. "Mornin', Jess."

"Hmm."

"Wish you hadn't left my bed. Wish you were still in there with me."

As she nodded, she leaned her head against his shoulder. "I don't know what we're doing," she said softly.

"Helping each other heal, maybe." He nipped the soft skin under her ear. "All I know is, I haven't felt this alive in a long time. And that's because of you."

"It's only because I remind you of—"

"Home." He wouldn't allow her to think for a second she was a replacement for his dead wife. He wasn't certain in his own mind that wasn't the case—her transformation last night had knocked the vinegar out of him, she'd looked so much like Janie—but he didn't want Jess believing it. What kind of a scoundrel would that make him? "But it's more than that. You remind me of the good things in my life."

"You're romanticizing about Beckon. It's really not all that."

In a way, they were both in the same situation. She'd had her heart broken. Of course she wouldn't look upon home with fond memories now. He couldn't go home because it wouldn't be the same. He blamed himself for Janie's death, and the guilt wracked him ten ways to Sunday, each and every day. "Maybe you're right, sweetheart."

Memories being what they were, he couldn't deny he held Beckon close to his heart. But he didn't need to win this round with Jessica today.

"I don't have a single regret about last night. Well, except that I had the damn boot and cast still on."

She turned away from the ocean and captured his attention with her pretty fresh-meadow eyes. "Not one, Zane? Not one regret?"

He blinked at the intensity of her question. This was important to her. "No."

What he had were doubts. He wasn't ready for anything heavy, with her or anyone else. The thought of entering into a relationship gave him hives. He might never be ready. He'd removed himself from any thoughts of the future and lived in the present. He'd shut himself off for two years. It was safe. His haven of sanity.

"Are you regretting what happened last night?" He wasn't sure he wanted to hear her answer.

Her chin lifted as she thought about it for an eternity of seconds. "*Regret* isn't the right word. I think you're right. We both needed each other."

"We don't have to attach any labels to last night," Zane said. "It just happened." He wanted it to happen again. But it wasn't his decision. He was smart enough to know that.

"But where do we go from here?"

Breezes blew her hair off her shoulders, the golden strands dancing in the morning light. Her face was clean of makeup, glowing with a fresh-washed look. All of Zane's impulses heightened.

"First," he said, dipping his head to her mouth, "I give you a good morning kiss." He pressed his lips to hers and kissed her soundly. She made a tiny noise in the back of her throat that made him smile inside. He could kiss her until the sun set and wouldn't tire of it. He inched away from her face as her eyes opened, glowing with warmth. God, she was sweet. "If you're inclined to do some cooking this morning, we have breakfast. Mrs. Lopez doesn't work on Sunday. And then we do whatever comes natural. No pressure, Jess."

He'd had sex with Janie's younger sister. He should be beating himself up about that now, but oddly he wasn't. He couldn't figure the why of it. Why was being with Jess making him feel better about himself instead of worse? He had nothing to offer her but strong arms to hold her and a warm body to comfort her, if she needed them. He couldn't pursue her. It wouldn't be fair to her, but that didn't stop him from wanting her.

A soft, relieved breath blew from her lips. "That sounds good to me, Zane." She gave him a sweet smile and handed him his crutches. "Meet me in the kitchen in half an hour."

His gaze landed on the curvy form of her backside as she strode inside the house. He hung his head. Oh, man. He was in deep.

Life at 211 Moonlight Drive wasn't going to get any easier.

# Seven

Two and a half months after his accidental fall off a Los Angeles stage, Zane had gotten a good report from his doctor. His foot had healed nicely and was now out of the cast. His wrist had taken longer than expected to heal, but that, too, was in great shape and cast-free. Jessica was almost as relieved as he was, hearing the news today after driving him to his appointment. Zane had never gotten used to the crutches and now, with a little physical therapy, he'd be back to normal, good as new. And her duties wouldn't be so up close and personal with him any longer. She could concentrate on work and try to forget about making love with him two nights ago.

The new Jess would've let it go by now.

But traces of the old Jess were resurfacing, and she wanted to kick her to the curb. Falling in love with Zane would be a bonehead stupid move. He was still in love with Janie, and nothing much could persuade her otherwise. How could she be sure that the night they'd had sex wasn't more about her resemblance to her sister than any intense affection Zane had for her?

"I feel like celebrating," Zane said as she drove toward the gates of his home.

"I bet you do. But you can't go dancing just yet. You have to get through physical therapy."

From out of the corner of her eye, she spied Zane flexing his hand. "I'm fine. Just dandy. Even wearing my own boots for a change."

She took her eyes off the road for a split second to gaze at his expensive boots. Snakeskin. Gorgeous. Studded black leather. They made her mouth water. "You do know you live on the beach. Sandals are expected. Even admired."

A belly laugh rolled out of his mouth. "I could say the same about you. Lately, you've been wearing those high-falutin heels."

"Me?" Yes, it was true. The new Jess wore pricey heels when she wasn't in her morning walk tennis shoes.

"Yeah, you. Admit it. You're happier in a pair of soft leather boots with flat heels than those skyscrapers you've taken to wearing. Not that I mind. You look hot in those heels."

The compliment lit her up inside, but she couldn't let him see how it affected her. She lowered her sunglasses and gave him a deadpan look.

He grinned.

The man was in a great mood today, happier than she'd seen him in days. It was certainly better than putting up with his sourpuss, like on Sunday afternoon when he'd balked at her going to Dylan's house for the screening of *Time of Her Life*. She'd thought he'd be okay with it. After all, he'd said to do what came natural, and she had promised Dylan she'd be there. When she'd walked in past nine, missing dinner with him, he'd been sullen and distant, none too pleased with her.

Yes, they'd had sex the night before, and it had been amazing. Surely Zane had to know that Dylan McKay, handsome as he was, didn't strike her fancy. She'd gone because she'd promised and because she needed time away from Zane to clear her head, yet that entire afternoon and evening, she'd wondered if she'd made a mistake by going to Dylan's.

"You know what I feel like doing?" Zane asked, breaking into her thoughts.

"I'm afraid to ask."

"I feel like taking a dip."

"In your Jacuzzi? That's a good idea. I bet the warm water—"

"In the ocean, Jess. Tonight, after dinner."

She pulled through the gates and drove along the winding road to his house. "I don't know if that's wise, Zane. You shouldn't push it. You only just—"

"I'm going, Jess." He set his face stubbornly, and she couldn't think of anything to say to change his mind. "I've been confined long enough."

Pulling into the garage, she cut the engine. "I get that, but I won't be—"

Oh, shoot. He wasn't going to like this.

"Won't be what?"

"Home after dinner."

"Another shopping trip?"

A lie could fall from her lips very easily. But she wasn't going to lie to Zane. "No. I'm invited over to your neighbor's house."

Zane's lips thinned. "Dylan again?"

"Adam Chase."

Zane's eyes sharpened on her. "You're going over to Adam's tonight?"

"I kind of didn't give him a choice the other night. He was telling me about his new artwork, and I hinted at wanting to see it. I guess he was just being nice by inviting me over." She'd been a little stunned and humbled when he'd asked her since, according to Zane, invitations from Adam were rare.

Zane closed his eyes briefly. "That's Adam. Mr. Nice Guy."

"You don't think he is?"

Zane snorted. "I think he's a genius. But I don't know much about his personal life."

"I don't want to know about his personal life, either. This isn't anything, Zane." If only she could melt the disapproval off his face with an explanation. "It's just me, being curious. The teacher in me loves learning."

They'd been carefully dancing around what had happened between them. It seemed neither wanted to bring the subject up. So how could she admit that she'd rather be home with him? That after making love with him, it was better that they spend time apart. Too much alone time with him could prove disastrous. One disaster per decade was her limit. One disaster in her entire life would be preferable.

She cared deeply for Zane, thought he was gorgeous and more appealing than any man she'd ever met, but she couldn't be dumb again. And that meant not reading too much into having sex with him, wonderful as it was. She rationalized it was all about healing. Isn't that how Zane passed it off?

"I'm sure Adam wouldn't mind if you joined me."

He reached for the door handle. "I've seen his house, Jess. You go on. Have a nice time," he said through tight lips.

She didn't buy his comment for a second, but she clamped her mouth shut, and as he opened the car door, she rushed around the front end to meet him. Putting his good foot down, he braced his hands on the sides of the car and brought himself up and out.

"Lean on me," she said. "I'm here if you need me."

"I'll make it just fine."

She moved out of his way, and he walked slowly but on his own power, his boots scraping the garage floor as he made his way into the house.

Her shoulders fell, and black emptiness seemed to swallow her up. She wanted Zane to need her.

Or maybe, she just plain wanted Zane. Either way

wasn't an option. She couldn't very well count the days until Mariah returned. Nobody knew when that would be.

But for the first time, she hoped it would be soon.

Zane leaned his elbows over his deck banister, grateful to be on his own two feet now. His gaze focused on Jess as she made her way down the deck steps to the beach. "Bye, Zane. I won't be long."

Her sultry voice hammered inside his brain. It was unique, and he was beginning to hear the slight nuances that differed from her sister's. There was more sugary rasp and a lightness in her tone that made him think of only good things.

She held the straps of her heeled sandals up by two fingers and waved at him once her bare feet hit the sand. In her other hand, she held a flashlight to guide her way over to Adam's house. It wasn't too far, just about one hundred yards from back door to back door, but the half moon's light wasn't enough illumination on the darkened beach, so the flashlight was a good idea.

Her blond hair touched the top of a nipped-at-the-waist snowy white dress that flared out to just above her knees. She looked ethereal in a delicate way that would turn any man's head.

"Bye" he heard himself growl, and lifted his hand up, a semiwave back, watching her trudge through the sand and out of his line of vision.

She was determined to go, yet he'd noted a flicker in her eyes earlier, a moment of doubt as if she waited for him to tell her to stay. He wanted her, and his newly healed body was in a state of arousal around her most of the time now, but he held back. He let her go off to another man's house tonight instead of giving in to his lust.

Was he an idiot or being smart, for her sake?

His cell phone rang, and he plucked it from his pocket. It was probably Mariah. She'd been a saint, checking in and worrying about him when she was the one who needed the support. He'd had Jess send her flowers this morning to cheer her up.

He answered the ring. "Hello?"

"Hello, Zane. This is Mae."

His brows rose. It wasn't Mariah after all, but Jessica's mother. "Hi, Mae. This is a nice surprise."

"I hope so. Zane, how are you feeling these days?"

"Better. I'm out of my cast and healing up real good. And how are you, Mae?"

"I could be better. You know I'm an eternal worrier. And I'm worried about my Jess. I haven't heard from her in three days."

"Is that unusual?"

"Yes, very. She usually checks in with me every day or every other day. We've been playing phone tag over the weekend, and I can't seem to reach her. She didn't answer my call today. I wondered if something was wrong with her phone. Thought it'd be best to check in with you."

"Well…I can assure you, she's doing fine."

"Really?"

"Yes, ma'am."

"That's a relief. I thought after I gave her the news, she'd be crushed. My dear girl has been through a lot this past month. She can't be happy about Steven."

Steven? Just hearing the guy's name made his hand ball into a fist. "What news is that, Mae?"

"I couldn't hide it from my sweet girl. She didn't need to hear it from anyone else but her mama."

"Yes, I think you were right." Zane hadn't a clue what she was getting at, but he knew Mae. She'd eventually get around to telling him what was going on.

"Can you imagine her bridesmaid, Judy, running off with Steven to get married? Why, she'd been like a member of our family when the girls were younger. And Steven? I thought I knew that boy. I'd like to wallop both of them for the hurt they put my daughter through."

His face tightened and he squeezed his eyes shut, wishing like hell he could give that jerk a piece of his mind. And to add to the insult, he'd run away with one of Jess's good friends. A woman who'd vowed to stand up for her at her wedding.

Something clicked in his head. "Wait a minute, Mae. When did you tell Jess about this?"

"Oh, let me see. It must have been on Thursday. Yes, that's right. I remember, because I was getting my hair done at the salon and, well, it was the talk of the entire beauty shop. I felt so bad when I heard, I walked out after my cut with a wet head, didn't bother having my hair styled. All I kept thinking about was my Jess and how she would take the news. But you know, when I told her, I was surprised at her reaction. She seemed calm. I think she was in shock. Have you noticed anything different about her, lately?"

Had he? Hell, yeah. Now he understood her transformation. She'd dyed her hair blond, gotten rid of her eyeglasses, starting wearing provocative clothes. Was it rebellion? Or worse yet, had Jess decided to throw caution to the wind and... No, he wouldn't let his mind go there. She wasn't promiscuous. She was a woman who'd been betrayed by people she trusted. He could only imagine what hearing that news did to her.

And what had he done? She'd come into the room the night of party and he'd shot her down, doing the unthinkable by telling her she looked like Janie in a voice that held nothing but disapproval. He'd been selfish, thinking only about how much it hurt to look at her that way. If he was damn honest with himself, seeing that daring side of Jess had excited him. He hadn't known how to handle his initial reaction to her. She almost didn't go to the party because he'd given her a hard time about the way she looked, gorgeous as she was.

And he'd been jealous because he couldn't have her, and yet he didn't want any other man going after her, either. Wow. What a revelation.

"Zane, I asked if Jessica has been acting differently lately?"

Uh, yeah. But in this case, he saw no reason not to bend the truth a little. "She's been keeping busy, Mae. She tells me she likes the work. And she's made a few friends here, too. She seems to fit in real nice. In fact, she's visiting my neighbor now. When she comes in, I'll be sure to tell her you called."

"I'm happy about that, Zane. I knew coming to stay with you would be good for her."

Zane scrunched his face up. He'd taken Mae's daughter to bed, and if he had his way, he would do so again. His mind muddied up, and he didn't understand any of it other than that Jess was under his roof and getting under his skin. He felt for her and the hurt she'd gone through. Nothing about liking her seemed wrong, even though he could count the bullet points in his mind why he shouldn't.

"I can't thank you enough. You know how much I love my girls."

Her comment dug deep into his heart. Mae would never stop loving Janie. She always spoke of her as if she were still with them. Zane loved that about her. "Yep, I know, Mae."

"So tell me what you've been doing. That's if you have the time."

"I have the time. Let's see, the restaurant is coming along as scheduled and…"

Thirty minutes later, after he'd hung up with Mae, he sat down with his guitar and strummed lightly to reacquaint himself to the feel of the instrument in his hands and the resiliency of the strings. He had words in his head struggling to get out, lyrics that were just beginning to flow, and he jotted them down as he struck chord after chord. The pick in his hand felt awkward at first, but he pressed on.

Thoughts of Jess distracted him. He couldn't stop thinking about her and what Mae had revealed. He wanted to
protect her. Yet he desired her. Her heartache scored his
heart. He felt sorry for her, but not enough to keep his distance. He was *conflicted*, as Dylan would say. He needed
some release.

Only a dunk in the ocean would help clear his mind and
cool his body.

And minutes later, dressed in his swim trunks, he made
his way to the shoreline and dived straight in, propelling
his arms and legs past the shallow waters, pushing his body
to the limit.

After enjoying a pleasant visit with Adam and declining
his offer to walk her home, she trudged across the beach
alone. Cool sand squished between her toes as she made her
way to the shoreline, where the moist grains under her feet
became smoother, making it much easier to move. She knew
this beach; she'd walked it in the mornings many times.

As she entered Zane's home, silence surrounded her. It
was too quiet for this time of the evening. Zane never turned
in before ten. "Zane? Are you here?"

Nothing.

"Zane?" She stepped into the office, then the kitchen,
and peeked into his bedroom.

There was no sign of him.

She sighed wearily and shook her head. He must have
gone for a swim in the ocean. Half a dozen worries entered
her head about his night swim. Geesh, he'd just gotten his
cast off. What was the doggone rush?

Hurrying to her room, she flung off her clothes and put
on her bathing suit. In her haste to rid herself of the old Jess,
she'd tossed out her one-piece swimsuits she'd brought from
Texas, which left her with the daring bikini she'd bought
the other day. She slipped into it and then wiggled a T-shirt
over her head. Without wasting a second, she strode down

the stairs, grabbed her flashlight and ventured out the sliding door.

If she were lucky, she'd find Zane walking toward the house, whistling a happy tune.

Who was she kidding? Luck wasn't with her lately. Zane's towel was on the beach, which meant he was out there somewhere. The crashing waves that usually lulled her to sleep made her wary now. Her flashlight pointed out to sea illuminated only a narrow strip of water at a time. She squinted, trying to make out shapes, searching corridors of ocean, back and forth. "Zane! Zane!"

She couldn't find him. Nibbling her lip, she paced the beach, aiming her flashlight onto the water over and over. She'd never swum in the ocean before coming to California, but she'd quickly learned how the currents could take you away, making you drift in one direction or another. She'd start out in front of Zane's house and wind up hundreds of feet away when it was time to come in. Those currents had to be stronger at night, more powerful and...

She spotted something. A head bobbing in the water? She pointed the flashlight and struggled to focus. Yep, someone was out there. But then the form dropped down as if being swallowed up by the sea. She ran into the surf, targeting that bit of water with the flashlight. "Zane!" she shouted, but her voice was muted by the crash of the waves.

He couldn't hear her. He was out past the shallows. She waited several long seconds for him to reappear. She prayed that he would. She couldn't see much, only what the moonlight and stars and her flashlight allowed, but she'd always had a good sense of direction. She knew the exact spot where she'd seen him go down.

"Oh, God. Zane!"

With no time to waste, she dived in, her arms pumping, her feet kicking, fighting against the tide. She swam as fast as she ever had in her life, her eyes trying to focus on the spot she'd seen him. She was almost there, a little farther, just another few strokes.

A thunderous sound boomed in her ears. She looked up. Oh, no. A monstrous wave was coming toward her like a coiling snake. It was too late to get out of its path. The pounding surf reached her in midstroke. The force slammed her back. She flew in the air and belly-flopped facedown against a sheet of ocean as hard as a slab of granite.

Waves buried her, and she sputtered for breath.

Seconds later, she felt herself being lifted, her head popping above the water. She gasped.

"Jess."

Zane. He'd come for her. How did he get here? As she struggled to catch her breath, he half dragged, half swam her to the shallows by floating on his back and keeping her head above water. Once he got his footing, he stopped and stood upright in the water, then scooped her into his arms, carrying her to the beach.

He laid her down carefully away from high tide. The sand granules scratched at her back, but she was never happier to be on dry land. And Zane was safe. That mattered just as much.

He fell to his knees beside her. Huffing breaths, he shook his head. "You gave me a scare."

He bent to her, pushing aside the locks of hair hiding her face, and his magnificent eyes were soft and concerned. "Are you okay?"

She nodded. "I'm okay. Got the wind knocked out of me."

"You almost drowned, sweetheart. What on earth were you doing?"

She filled her lungs with oxygen, this time without gulping water along with it. "Saving you," she said quietly. "I thought I saw you out there, going under."

Zane's eyes were warm on her face, the heat enough to keep the cool drops on her body from freezing. His hands were working wonders, too, caressing her cheeks and stroking her chin, heating her up in ways no other man ever had. He rasped softly, "You mean you thought I was drowning, and you risked your life to save me?"

She nodded.

"That wasn't me, sweetheart."

"It wasn't? I saw someone go under. I thought for sure you were out there."

"I was. I lasted only ten minutes before I came in. What you saw was probably a school of sea lions. They frequent the shallower waters here at night. I've seen one of them pop a head up and then go under and, yeah...I guess in the dark, it might look like a swimmer out there."

"Then how...how did you find me?"

"After my swim, I took a long walk. Thankfully, I returned just in time to hear you calling my name. Took me only a second to figure out where you were."

He began to rub her arms and legs. She was cold, but that didn't stop her from reacting to his touch. As warmth spread through her body, her gentle cooing seemed to draw Zane's attention to her lips. "That feels good," she said.

"Tell me about it." The corner of his mouth crooked up.

His palms heated her through and through, her skin highly sensitized to his touch. She was overwhelmed with relief that he hadn't drowned and grateful that he'd saved her, but there was more...so much more that she was feeling right now. "Thank you, Zane."

She touched his shoulder and felt his cool skin under her fingertips. His eyes gleamed with a fiery invitation to do more. Bravely, she wound her arms around his neck. It didn't take an ounce of effort to pull him close. His mouth hovered near hers.

It was crazy. They were on the beach under the moonlight and dripping wet after the rescue, and nothing seemed amiss in her world. She wouldn't trade places with another living soul right now.

"I'd give you what-for," he said, "but that will have to wait."

"It will?"

"Yep. Cause I think you're about to kiss me."

"Smart man."

She ran her fingers through his thick wet hair and lowered his head down to her lips. Oh…he tasted warm and inviting and salty. His kiss made her tremble in a good way, and she opened her mouth for him.

He plunged inside and swept her up in one burning kiss after another. What was left of her body when he finished kissing her was a pulsing bundle of need. "Zane," she whispered over his lips.

"I need to get you inside the house…"

He didn't have to finish. She knew. They'd get arrested if they acted on their impulses right here on the beach.

"Can you walk?" he asked.

"Yes, with your help."

"Okay, sweetheart. Seems one of us is always leaning on the other."

She smiled. How true.

He bounded up and then entwined their hands. Gently he helped her to her feet. The world didn't go dizzy on her—well, except for the hot looks Zane was giving her. "I actually feel pretty good."

"Glad to hear it." He kissed her earlobe. "Ready?"

"Ready."

Side by side, bracing each other, they walked through the sand and up the steps that led into the house.

As soon as they entered the house, Zane did an about-face and walked her backward until she was pressed against the living room wall. He trapped her there, his body pulsing near hers, his gaze generating enough heat to burn the building down.

"Are you about to give me what-for?"

A low rumble of laughter rose from his throat. Her senses heightened. He was one sexy man. "You know it, Jess." He glanced down at her dripping wet T-shirt plastered to her body and sighed as if he was in pain. "Do you know how incredibly perfect you are?"

His hands wrapped around her waist, and thrilling warmth penetrated through her shirt to heat her skin. "I'm not."

His mouth grazed her throat. "You are. You can't let what those two did to you change who you are. That guy was about the stupidest man on earth."

She stilled. "What do you mean, 'those two'?"

Zane's lips were doing amazing things to her throat. And his body pressing against hers made it hard to think. Her breasts were ready for his touch. Her nipples pebbled hard and beckoned him through the flimsy T-shirt and bikini.

She had to ignore her body. She needed to know what he meant. "Zane?"

He stopped kissing her and inched away enough to gaze into her eyes. "Oh, uh. Your mama called while you were out. She was worried about you, and well…she told me about Steven running off with a friend of yours."

She'd told him about Judy?

All the wind left her lungs, and a different kind of burn seared through her stomach. She wished Mama hadn't revealed to Zane her latest humiliation. She felt so exposed, so vulnerable. Did she have an ounce of pride left?

"You have every right to feel hurt, Jess. But don't let what he did change the person that you are."

"You think that's what I'm doing?"

"Isn't it? You changed your hair, wear your contacts all the time. You dress differently now. Don't get me wrong. You look beautiful, sweetheart. But you were beautiful before."

She shrugged. She found it hard to believe. It was a platitude, a cliché, a way to make her feel better about herself.

"I need the change." Tears misted in her eyes. She really did. She needed to look at herself in the mirror and see a strong, independent woman who had style and confidence. She needed to see that transformation, more than anything else.

"I get that." Zane took her into his arms and hugged her, as a friend now. She felt safe again, protected. And just being with him made her problems seem trivial. "But promise me one thing?"

"What?"

"Don't try to find what you need with another man. Makes me crazy."

*Makes me crazy.* Oh, wow. There was no mistaking what he meant. Not from the genuine pain she found in his eyes, or the intensity in his voice. "You mean like Dylan or Adam? I told you, they're not—"

He shushed her with a kiss, right smack on the lips. Her body instantly reacted, and goose bumps rose on her arms.

"*You* make me crazy, too," he rasped and began rolling the hem of her T-shirt up. With his coaxing, she raised her arms as he brought the wet garment over her head and her breasts jiggled back into place. Zane's hot gaze touched her there and lingered, then traveled over the rest her body clad in a skimpy New Jess bikini. He made a loud noise from sucking oxygen into his lungs. "From now on, sweet Jess, I want to be the man you go to when you need something."

"You mean, like my rebound guy?"

"Call it whatever you want, honey."

Jess didn't have to think twice. Zane just abolished all deprecating thoughts she'd had about herself and totally wiped out any pain she'd felt about Steven. Even her pride was restored somewhat. The Steven ship had sailed, and she wasn't going to waste another second thinking of him. Not when she had Zane offering her the moon.

He was a real man.

If she had any doubts before about her feelings for him,

they were banished the second she'd thought he was drowning. She'd rushed in to save him, praying that God wouldn't take him from her. And she wasn't going to feel bad about it or apologize to anyone. Forbidden or not, she wanted him.

"I promise."

He hooked his fingers with hers. "Your room or mine?"

"Neither," she said. Her confidence soaring and her heart melting, she let go of every inhibition she'd ever had. "I think we need a hot, steamy shower to warm up, don't you?"

"As long as I get to peel this bikini off you, you've got yourself a deal."

# Eight

The peeling was blissful torture. Jessica lay her head against cool slate, her arms behind her. Steam rose up as the customized shower streams poured down, warming her bones. It was like being tucked inside a large waterfall, cascading water all around her. Zane came to her naked, his sculpted, bronzed beach body equal to that of an ancient god. There was enough room for twelve people in the master shower, but she knew Zane would make good use of the space for the two of them.

"You're beautiful, Jess."

His mouth covered hers as both of his hands came under her bikini top. Weighing her full breasts, he groaned deep in his throat, and his appreciation of her body flowed to her ears. She roped her arms around his neck and continued to kiss him even as he unhooked the back of the bathing suit, releasing her breasts. Warm spray moistened them and he worked magic on her, gliding his hands over her bare, wet skin and arousing her in tortuous increments. His thumb caressed her already pebbled nipples until she muted a cry.

He was amazingly gentle, but brutal in his determination to make it good for her. As he removed the bottom half of her bikini, his hands shaking with need, she'd never felt more desirable and powerful.

Drizzling kisses along her throat, his hands came to the small of her back, and she bowed her body for him. He took one jutted breast in his mouth and suckled her, his tongue swirling and flicking. She screamed then, but the pleasured sounds were drowned out by the thunderous showerheads. He gave the other breast equal treatment, and it was almost too much.

"Are you warm yet?" he asked, nuzzling her throat.

"Just getting there."

"Let me help you with that."

He picked up a bar of soap and lathered her from head to toe, bathing her in a soft and subtle flowery scent that reminded her of a spring afternoon. He didn't miss one inch of her, paying special attention to the crux of her womanhood, stroking, washing, cupping her, making her moan.

"Oh, oh, oh."

Jess thought every woman should experience a shower this way, just once.

She smiled, gritted her teeth and savored the pleasure he brought her.

His hands moved to her backside and slid over the rounded halves of her derriere, molding her form, spreading his fingers wide as if savoring the feel of her. His manhood pressed her belly, rock-hard and pulsing. She shuddered, unable to hold back another second. Her body released gently, in beautifully timid waves that nudged her forever toward him. His mouth covered hers, and she enjoyed the sweetly erotic taste of his passion.

Wow.

She'd never had an orgasm like that before.

She clung to him and let the full force of her feelings consume her.

"Did you like that, sweetheart?"

"So much."

She sensed his smile, and it made her heart nearly burst.

She moved down on him, letting her mouth and breasts caress the middle of his chest, his belly, and then she touched his full-fledged erection.

"Oh, man," he uttered. "Jess."

He fisted a handful of her hair and helped move her along the length of him. Water pounded her back, the showerhead pulsing now. It was deliciously sexy, and when she was through, she rose to meet him. The hungry look on his face, teeth gritted, eyes gleaming like a wolf about to devour his prey, would have been almost frightening if it wasn't Zane.

He lifted her, and on instinct she wrapped her legs around his waist. He held her tight and murmured, "Hang on."

She clung to him, and his manhood nudged into her, filling her with gentle force. He was patient and oh, so ready. She moved on him, letting him know she was okay with whatever he wanted to do. The beat, beat, beat of the raining drops set the pace of his thrusts. He arched and drove deeper.

"Oh." She sighed. "So good."

He kissed her throat, her breasts, and continued to thrust into her, hard, harder.

It was pure heaven. She'd never made love like this before. Her heart pounded in her chest, and her body soared. Spasms of tight, sweet pain released, and she cried out softly "Oh, Zane."

His eyes were on her, burning hot. He waited for her to come down off the clouds, and then he began to thrust into her again. He set a fast rhythm, and she gave back equally. She wanted to make it good for him, too.

Guttural groans rose up his throat, and she knew he was close. He impaled her one last, amazing time, his reach touching the very core of her womanhood. And waves of his orgasm struck her, one after the other, until he was spent, sated.

He took her with him as he sat down on the stone shower bench, raining kisses all over her face, cheeks, chin, throat. He pushed her hair away from her face. "Are you okay, sweetheart?"

How could she not be? She was overjoyed. "It was beautiful, Zane."

"It was," he said, leaning way back.

She stroked his face, running her hand over his stubbly cheek. He grabbed her wrist and planted a kiss on her palm.

The shower turned off. Perfect timing. It was a perfect night. Well, except for those few minutes she thought Zane was drowning. He'd taxed his body tonight. "You must be tired," she said.

His eyes darkened, and he hiked a brow. "I'm ready to be in bed with you."

"Sounds good."

She didn't want the night to end. She no longer worried about what tomorrow would bring. She was living in the moment, and these moments had been pretty darn spectacular.

Zane lifted her off him and grabbed two giant towels. He took his time drying her off, sneaking kisses on parts of her body, arousing her. She did the same to him, teasing him with her mouth.

They entered his bedroom clean, dry and exhausted.

She took a few steps toward his door, and his arm snaked around her. "Where do you think you're going?"

"To my room. I need to get my nightie."

"No, you don't. Come to bed. I promise to keep you warm."

"Part of your duties as my rebound guy?"

"You know it, honey. Now get in."

Spooning with Zane in his big, comfortable bed, Jessica's eyes eased open. It was slightly after dawn, and the usual early morning cloud cover allowed a smidgen of struggling sunshine into the room. Zane stroked her hip, lightly, possessively, his touch becoming familiar to her, and she purred like a kitten given a big bowl of cream.

"I'm giving you the day off," he murmured, his breath whispering over her hair.

"Mmm." A lovely thought. "I have work to do today."

"It'll keep, Jess. I want to spend the day with you."

"You already do."

He nipped her earlobe, then planted tiny kisses along her nape. His hand traveled deliciously to her waist, just under her belly. "Not the way I want to."

They'd made love twice last night. It was incredible and frightening at the same time. Every so often, thoughts of her future would break through her steely resolve to live in the moment. She'd shudder, and sudden panic would set in. What was she doing? Where was all this leading? They hadn't used protection in the shower last night, but Jess was on birth control, sort of. She'd skipped a few days during the height of her wedding fiasco, but she'd resumed when she'd arrived here to keep her hormones from getting out of whack.

She turned to Zane, roping her arms around his neck. "What did you have in mind?"

He kissed her quickly and then tugged her closer. "A day of play. We can get out of here. Have fun."

A lock of his thick hair fell to his forehead. In many ways, he looked like a little boy, eager to play hooky. He lived in this dream house on the beach and spoke of getting away, as if he'd been in living in the slums all this time. The irony made her smile, and she toyed with that wayward lock of hair, curling it around her finger, mesmerized by the man she shared a bed with.

"You're the boss," she whispered.

"I'm not your boss," he said softly. "Not when it comes to this."

He began kissing her shoulder, her throat, her chin. And then he stopped suddenly and inched away. He shot her a solid, earnest look. "Would you like to spend the day with me?"

Oh, wow. Like a date? "Yes." She yanked the lock of hair. "Of course, silly."

He gave her backside a gentle squeeze. "Then we'd better get up and get showered. You first. If we share another shower, we'll never make it out of here this morning." He waggled his brows. "On second thought, maybe…"

She laughed and jumped out of bed. "I'm going in first."

Less than an hour later, Zane was sitting behind the wheel of his SUV and pulling out of the gates of his home. "Feels good to be driving again. I hated feeling helpless, having to rely on someone to take me places."

A few days of stubble on his face had led to a short, sexy beard. The new look turned her on. Everything about him seemed to do that. All she had to do was think about making love with him last night and tingles fluttered inside her belly.

He wore a baseball cap instead of his Stetson. The beard and sunglasses also helped disguise him. He'd healed so well, she would've never guessed he'd broken his foot, except for his slight limp as he tried not to put too much pressure on it. She already knew she'd be arguing with him about going to his rehab appointments.

He'd told her to wear her boots, dress in jeans and not question where they were going. He wanted to surprise her. She sat in her comfortable clothes, watching the stunning landscape go by as they left the blue waters behind and drove up a mountain road. The scenery lent itself to light conversation and soft music. Zane sang along with the tune on the radio, his voice deep and rich, her own personal concert. She couldn't help but grin.

Thirty minutes later, they were atop the mountain at a sprawling ranch-style home overlooking the city to the south and the valley to the north. The air was clean up here, the smog of the day blown away by ocean breezes. "Where are we?" she asked.

"My friend Chuck Bowen owns this place with his mother. It's called Ruby Ranch."

She glanced around and spotted white-fenced corrals, vineyards off in the distance and acres and acres of hilly, tree-dotted land. The sound of horses whinnying and snorting reached her ears.

"C'mon."

Zane exited the car and walked around to help her out. He took her hand. That little boy excitement once again lit his expression. "We're going riding."

"Riding?" She hadn't been on a horse since she was a teenager. She'd go riding every weekend with her good friend Jolie Burns when she wasn't working at Holcomb House. Jolie lived on a cattle ranch ten miles outside of Beckon. Jessica had the use of a pretty palomino named Sparkle, and she'd learned how to wash down and groom a horse back then, too. It was expected. If you exercised a horse, got him lathered up, then it was your responsibility to see to his needs after the ride. Jessica had fallen in love with Sparkle. She never minded the hard work that came with him.

She rubbed her hands together. This could be fun. "Oh, boy!"

Zane chuckled and kissed the tip of nose. "That's what I thought."

A fiftysomething woman with hair the color of deep, rich red wine walked out of the house. She was flawless in her appearance, neat and tidy, and her pretty face must have stopped men in their tracks when she was younger. Even now, she was stunning and dressed in Western clothes that looked as if they'd just come off a fashion runway.

"Hi, Ruby," Zane said.

"Zane. It's good to see you again."

Zane took Jessica's hand as he moved toward the house. Ruby tried not to react, but her eyes dipped to their interlocked hands for a second before she gave them both a smile. "Ruby, I'd like you to meet Jessica Holcomb. Jess, this is Ruby Bowen. She and Chuck own this amazing land."

They came to a stop on her veranda. "Hello," Jessica said. "The place is lovely. You have vineyards?"

"Thank you. Yes, we grow grapes and raise horses. It's a rare mix, but it works for Chuck and me. We don't bottle the wine here—we're too small for that—but we do have our own label. It's fun, hectic and keeps us plenty busy."

"I bet," Jessica said.

"I met Ruby and Chuck at a charity auction six months ago," Zane said. "Being original Texans, they've been gracious enough to offer their stables for whenever I wanted to ride."

"Absolutely. We've got over a thousand acres and plenty of horses that need exercising. We figured Zane was like a fish out of water, living at the beach these days. We're happy he took us up on the offer. Chuck's out of town and due back later. He'll be sorry he missed you. But please, make use of the grounds. The stables are just down the hill a ways. Our wrangler, Stewie, is waiting for you. He'll find a good fit for both of you."

"Thanks, Ruby. Would've been by sooner, but it's hard to ride with a broken foot and wrist. Just recently got the dang cast off."

"Well, you're here now, and that's all that matters. Have a good time. Be sure to stop by afterward. Chuck may be home by then."

"Will do, and thanks again," Zane said.

Just minutes later, Jessica rode atop a sweet bay mare named Adobe, and Zane sat a few hands taller on a black gelding named Triumph. In her hometown of Beckon, the terrain was flat as the tires in Jeb's Junkyard. But here at Ruby Ranch, set in the Santa Monica Mountains, the powder-blue sky seemed nearly touchable. They ambled along a path that led away from the house into land that rose high and dipped gently alongside a creek.

"No rain lately," Zane offered. "I bet this creek was a rushing stream at one time."

"It's still pretty awesome up here."

"It is. You miss riding?"

She nodded, holding on to the silver-gray felt hat Ruby's wrangler had offered her. Zane kept his ball cap on his head, but there was no doubt he was a cowboy, through and through. He may have great wealth and live in a contemporary beach house, but you couldn't take Texas out of a Texan. And that was fact. "I do. I love horses."

Zane gave a nod of agreement. "Yeah, me, too."

It was a sore subject and one Jess didn't want to press at the moment. Zane had abandoned his home after the fire that took Janie and their unborn baby's life. The place still stood as it was. Acres and acres of land gated off, going to waste. He hadn't had the heart to demolish what was left of his house or improve upon the land. He'd had an agent sell off the livestock, and that was that.

Heartbroken, Zane had picked up roots, leaving memories he couldn't deal with behind. Losing him had taken a big chunk out the hearts of the fine people of Beckon. Zane was their golden boy, a singer whose talent brought him great fame. The townsfolk were darn proud of their hometown hero. He'd had no more loyal fans in the world.

"I'm glad you brought me up here, Zane."

He eyed her, studying her face as if trying to puzzle something out. "I'd have never come without you. Fact is, Chuck's been after me to ride for months, and I never took him up on it." His voice seemed sort of strange, and then he took a giant swallow. "I didn't want to, until now."

She shouldn't read too much into it, but her heart jumped in her chest anyway. Hope could be just as drastic as despair to her right now. She shoved it away and took a different approach. "You were confined a long time. I bet getting up on a horse and riding is just what you needed. It's freeing."

"Maybe," he said. His index finger pushed at the corner of his mouth, contemplating. He gave his head a shake. "Maybe it's something else. Having to do with you."

Oh, God. Out in the open air, in these beautiful surroundings, anything seemed possible. *Don't hope. Don't hope.* "Me?"

He slowed his horse to a stop.

She did the same.

His dark eyes grazed her face. "Yeah, you," he said, his voice husky.

Her cheeks burned, and she hoped her new suntan along with the brim of her hat hid her emotions. Zane didn't need another groupie. They'd already established he was her rebound guy, whatever that really meant. She was his bed partner, for sure. But after that…she had no clue where she stood with him.

Maybe her crazy heart didn't want to know. Maybe she couldn't survive another disappointment. It was better not knowing, not thinking at all.

She clicked the heels of her boots and took off. "Race you to that plateau up ahead. First one to the oak tree wins!" She was already three lengths ahead of him when she heard his laughter.

"You're on!"

Westerly winds blew cool air at her face, her hair a riotous mess, as she leaned low on her mare and pressed the animal faster. The path was wide enough here for two horses, but branches hung low, and she expertly navigated through a thick patch of trees to reach the innermost edge of the clearing. Another fifty yards to go.

From behind, resounding hooves beat the ground, and she sensed Zane catching up.

"C'mon girl!" The mare was shorter, her legs not quite as long as Triumph's, and of course, Jessica was rusty as a rider.

It was a valiant effort, even if she'd cheated at the starting line, but Zane caught her. His gelding made the pass just five yards out, and yet Adobe wrestled to move faster. Her mare didn't like to lose, it seemed. They reached the oak tree, Triumph just nosing Adobe out.

Jess reined her mare in and circled around to the base of the oak tree. Zane sat atop his horse, grinning wide. His joy seared her heart. He was so dang happy. How could she not join in?

He dismounted and sauntered over to her, his confident strides stealing her breath. His recovery looked damn good on him, the smile on his face, the gleam in his eyes, the breadth of his shoulders…

"I win, Jess."

"Just barely." She gave a good fight.

"Still, a win is a win."

He reached up and helped her off, his large hands handling her with ease as she slid down the length of him. Tucked close, she didn't mind being in his trap. The exhilaration of the race and the handsomest darn face she'd ever seen brought on palpitations. Her heart pounded like crazy.

"So what do I win?" he asked.

"Is this a trick question?"

"Not even close."

"What do you want?"

A soap-opera villain couldn't have produced a more wicked grin. "A kiss, for starters."

"For starters?" Her gaze darted to his beautiful mouth, and a delicious craving began to develop. She didn't think she could play coy. She wanted him to kiss her, more than anything.

He nodded and bent his head. The second his yummy lips met hers, her mind rewound to last night and how his mouth had trailed pleasure all over her body. He'd tasted every inch of her. "Oh," she squeaked.

She sensed his smile from her noisy outburst as he continued to kiss her. Then he plucked the hat from her head and angled his mouth over hers again and again.

Backing up an inch, she gulped air to catch her breath and gazed into his mischievous eyes.

"You cheated in the race, sweetheart. You're gonna have to pay for that."

A dozen illicit notions popped into her head regarding how he'd make her pay, and a hot thrill spread like wildfire in her belly.

He tugged on her hand, and she followed as he led her behind the solid base of the sprawling oak tree. Hidden by drooping branches and fully shaded by overlapping leaves, he sat down, his back to the tree, and spread his legs. "Sit." He gestured to the place between his legs. "Relax."

Hardly a position that would have her relaxing, but she sat down, facing out, and rested her head on his chest. His arms wrapped around her, and he whispered in her ear, "Comfortable?"

She snuggled in deeper, her butt grazing his groin. A groan rose from his throat, and she chuckled. "Very."

His hands splayed across her ribcage. "Close your eyes." She did.

"Now for your punishment."

He began to kiss the back of her neck, but it was what his hands were doing that made her dizzy. Deftly the tips of his fingers glided just under her breasts. Through the rough plaid material of her shirt, her nipples puckered in anticipation of his next move.

The snaps of her blouse popped open, his doing, and a startled gasp exploded from her lungs. "Zane!"

He brought his head around and kissed the corner of her mouth. "Shh. I'm pretty sure we're alone out here, but just in case, keep your shrieks to a minimum."

"You mean there's going to be more?"

He laughed quietly. Dipping into her bra, he flicked the pads of his thumbs over her responsive nipples. Her mouth opened, and he immediately stymied her next shriek with another kiss. "You are a loud one."

"You didn't mind last night," she breathed. He was doing amazing things to her with his hands.

"I don't mind now, but we're not on my turf anymore."

Damn it. She was his turf. It was becoming clearer and clearer to her. "So, maybe we should stop before someone sees us?"

"No one's out here, Jess. But I'll stop if you want me to. And that would be *my punishment*. I didn't think I could go all day without touching you again."

With a confession like that, how in the world could she tell him to stop? "You won, fair and square, Zane. I'm a big girl. I can take whatever you dish out."

# Nine

"I like playing hooky with you," Zane said to Jessica over dinner at an exclusive, out-of-the-way nightspot overlooking the beach. He'd heard about this place from his neighbors, who commended the food, the privacy and the music. He sat beside her in a booth, listening to smooth jazz from a sax player with a powerful set of lungs.

Every time his gaze landed on Jessica tonight, he was reminded of the way she fell apart in his arms under that oak tree this morning. He hadn't planned on taking it as far as he did, but there was something about Jess that made him do wild things.

Maybe it was the sweet, squeaky sounds she sighed when he kissed her.

Or maybe it was the forbidden lust that came over him when she entered a room.

Or maybe it was her vulnerability and her honesty that drew him to her the most.

Those sexy shaves she'd given him didn't hurt, either.

"I like playing hooky with you, too." Her deep, sultry tone fit the atmosphere in the nightclub, reminding him every second he needed to finish what he'd started up on that plateau today.

She wore red tonight, a daring dress with a scoop neckline, the hem hiking up inches above her knees. The dress fit each sumptuous curve of her form to perfection. There were times when he forgot who she was, that he'd been married to Jessica's sister and that she wasn't ready for another relationship. He was her go-to guy, and he'd wanted it that way, but where it led from here, he didn't know. He didn't think past the present these days. He couldn't hope, didn't want to hope for more. He'd been sliced up pretty badly when Janie and his child died. The guilt ate at him every day.

He raised his wineglass and sipped, turning his gaze to the scant number of people dancing. He hadn't disguised himself tonight. He'd relied on the dimly lit surroundings and the back booth to keep his privacy. Sometimes his fame came at too high a price, and tonight he wanted to show Jess a good time. He wanted to hold her again. He roped his arm around her shoulder and spoke into her ear. "Dance with me?"

Her gaze moved to the dance floor and the amber hues focusing on couples sharing the spotlight. Yearning entered her eyes, and he'd be damned not to deliver her this little bit of pleasure.

"Are you sure?"

"Positive."

He rose and grabbed her hand, leading her to the center of the room. As soon as he stepped foot on the wood floor, he turned and tugged her to his chest. She fit him, her curves finding his angles, and they moved as if they were born to dance together.

"How's your foot?" she asked.

"It's floating on air right now. Fact is, both feet aren't touching the ground."

She chuckled. "Sweet, but I'm serious. You rode today, and now you're dancing."

"Thank you for your concern." He kissed her temple. "But I'm fine. Feels darn good doing some normal things again. And with the most beautiful woman in the room."

"How do you know? Have you checked all the other women out?"

"I, uh…not going to answer that one."

"Smart man."

He laughed, wrapping his arms tighter around her slim waist. Her breasts touched his chest, and he imagined her nipples pebbling for him, hardening through the delicate lace of her dress. Her hand wove through his hair, her fingertips playing with the strands as her arm lay on his shoulder, and it was the most intimate thing she'd done to him this entire day. His groin tightened instantly, and he backed away from her, fearing they'd get thrown out for an X-rated dance. Her gaze lifted, and pools of soft pasture green questioned him.

He shrugged, helpless.

She smiled then, and nodded.

He and Jess were on the same wavelength lately. They *got* each other, and everything felt right when he held her in his arms. He wasn't ready to let that feeling go. Luckily, he didn't have to think about that now.

Two dances later, they noticed their meals were being delivered to their table.

"Ready for dinner?"

Jessica nodded. "I think I've worked up an appetite."

"For food?"

"Among other things."

Jessica scooted into the booth, and he took his seat beside her as the waiter set down plates of pasta and petite loaves of garlic bread. Jess had chosen penne with sweet pesto sauce, and he'd ordered linguine with meat sauce. Steam rose up, the air around them flavored with spicy goodness.

"Looks heavenly," Jess said, picking up her fork.

"Yep," he said, staring at her. "Sure does."

He didn't think Jess would blush over such an easy compliment, but color rose to her cheeks, and she blinked and wiggled in her seat. He liked flustering her.

"Hey, you two." A familiar voice sounded from the shadows, and Dylan McKay's smug face came into view. "I hope you don't mind me coming over to say hello. Saw the two of you dancing a minute ago. Didn't have the balls to cut in, Zane. Excuse my language, Jessica, but the two of you looked hot and heavy out there. And Zane, it's good to see you without those crutches."

"Hi, Dylan," she said with enough damn cheerfulness for both of them.

"Hey, you," he said, giving Jess a wink.

Zane kept a smile plastered on his face. He liked Dylan, but damn his keen perception and his untimely interruption. "Dylan."

"So, how do you like this place?" the actor asked.

"Very much," Jess said.

"We were just about to dive into our meal." Zane picked up his fork.

"Yeah, the food's pretty good here. And you can't beat…"

Lights flashed, and cameras snapped, one, two, three clicks a second. Zane caught sight of a trio of paparazzi, kneeling down, angling cameras and snapping pictures of Dylan. Damn it.

Dylan turned, giving them a charming smile as Zane wrangled Jess into his arms, turning away from the cameras. Shielding Jess, his first instinct was to protect her from the intrusive photographers. He hated paparazzi ambushes. But Dylan didn't seem fazed. He posed for a few shots, and then the manager rushed over, shooing the photographers away from his customers.

"So sorry, Mr. McKay. This usually doesn't happen."

"I know, Jeffrey. It's okay. It must be a slow news day. I'm here with some buddies. No hot chicks on my arm tonight."

The manager didn't smile at Dylan's attempt at humor. He took his job seriously. "I apologize to you as well, Mr. Williams," he said.

"No harm done." He had to be gracious. The manager couldn't have prevented this from happening. It happened all the time in every place imaginable, especially to Dylan.

The guy was a walking magnet for the tabloids. He seemed to love the attention.

After the manager walked off, Dylan shrugged. "What can I say? I'm sorry. This place used to be off their radar."

"It's not your fault," Jess was quick to say. "Like Zane said, no harm done."

Dylan stared at Jess for a moment, his eyes smiling, and then focused on Zane. "It's good to see you two together like this."

*Like what?* Zane was tempted to ask. Instead, he sent him his best mind-your-business look.

"O…kay," Dylan said. "Well, I'll be getting back to my friends now. Have a nice evening. Oh, and Jess, I'll see you on the beach."

Jess smiled.

"Bye, Dylan," Zane said, and the guy walked off. If only Dylan's flirty relationship with Jessica didn't grate so much on his nerves.

She touched his arm. "Are you angry?"

Dylan pissed him off, but that's not what she meant. "No. But I don't like having our time together interrupted like that. You don't need to be exposed to my real world. It's bad enough I have to deal with it."

"It's okay." Her face went gooey soft. "It wasn't so bad."

They'd never set boundaries or labeled what was happening between them, except to say she was on the rebound and he was the guy enjoying the privilege. But he wanted to spend every minute with her while she was here. She would go home soon. And he'd have to deal with it. She was forbidden fruit, and at times, his conscience warred with his desire for her. She was vulnerable right now and had come to live with him to heal her wounds. The last thing he wanted was to add to her pain. He'd never knowingly take advantage of her, but was he leading her on or helping her heal? He had to think it was healing for them to be together.

Right now, things were simple, but when the time came for her to return home, he'd have to let her go.

Her palm caressed his cheek. The touch was gentle, caring, and her eyes simmered with enough warmth to light a fire. When she leaned in and kissed him, something snapped in his heart. He wouldn't name it, didn't want to think about it. The sensations roiling in his gut scared the stuffing out of him. The mistake he'd made had cost his wife her life, and he wasn't going back there again. Falling in love was already checked off his bucket list.

Leaning back in his seat, he gave her a smile. "Our food's getting cold, sweetheart."

She blinked, and the heat in her eyes evaporated.

He hated disappointing her, but he had nothing else to say on the subject.

Jessica loved working for Zane. It gave her a sense of purpose, and she enjoyed gaining a new perspective on life. As a grade-school teacher, her world revolved around children, shaping and molding them into good students and eager learners. But this work had its own rewards. This morning she'd already spoken to Zane's fan club president, made a list of devotees she needed to send autographed photos to, and spoken with Mrs. Elise Woolery, a senior citizen who wrote to Zane every month. Yes, at the age of eighty-four, the woman was a Zane Zealot. She was his Super Fan. Mariah had made a special point to make sure Zane read and answered this woman's letters. Jessica would do no less.

Sitting at the office desk, she was reading her heartwarming letter when her cell phone rang. She glanced at the screen and smiled before answering. "Hi, Mama."

"Hi, honey."

"Is something wrong? Your voice…"

"Honey, I'm fine. It's not that, but how are you?"

She was flying high, happy as a clam, strolling on Moonlight Beach shores and spending time with Zane. Last night had been incredible. Except for the crazy camera goons coming out of the woodwork and some odd moments afterward, it had been a picture-perfect day and night. Riding at Ruby Ranch, dinner, dancing and making love with Zane afterward was up there on her Top Ten List of Best Days. What more could a girl ask for?

*A lot,* a voice in her head screamed.

She ignored it.

"I'm fine, Mom. What is it? Did Steven make another stupid move? Is Judy pregnant or something? I'm telling you right now I'm over it, whatever it is."

"No, honey. I haven't heard anything more about Steven. It's just that…well, have you read the *Daily Inquiry* this morning?"

"Mama, you know I don't read that stuff. And neither do you. What's this all about?"

"I mean, I was sort of used to it with Janie. Zane protected her mostly, and the press loved them. But you, honey. Well, there's a picture of you and Zane, and it's quite shocking."

"There's a picture of me and Zane?"

"On the front page. My neighbor Esther showed it to me this morning. And after that, my phone hasn't stopped ringing."

"It hasn't?" It was noon in Texas. Damn those photographers. She'd thought they were only after Dylan. She should've known better, not that she had any way of stopping the invasion of privacy. "Mama, it's nothing, really. You know the life Zane leads. We were dining out and were ambushed by the Hollywood nut jobs. That's all."

"You changed your hair. You're blonde now. And the dress you were wearing…well, it was quite revealing. Zane had you in his arms, baby girl, and it looked to me as if—"

"He was protecting me from the cameras, that's all."

"Is that *all*, honey?"

She nibbled her lip. What could she say to her mother?

That she'd been sleeping with Zane and they'd been helping each other come to terms with their own personal demons? Could she honestly tell her mother that? No. Her mother would worry like crazy. She didn't know that the new and improved Jessica could handle anything that came her way. God, she only hoped she wasn't wrong about that.

"Jessica, that picture of you…well, do you know how much you look like Janie now?"

Something powerful stung her heart. The subtle implication wasn't anything she hadn't already thought of a hundred times in her head. Was that the attraction Zane had to her? She looked enough like Janie for him to gravitate her way.

"I don't want you to get hurt again."

"I know, Mama. I don't plan to."

Swinging her chair toward the computer, she keyed into the *Daily Inquiry* site on the internet. The front-page picture came up, and there she was, her neckline plunging and Zane's arms around her shoulders possessively, his body half covering hers in a proprietary way. But the headline was what grabbed her the most. "Zane Williams Dating Wife Look-alike." The subtitle wasn't much better. "Who Is His Mystery Love?"

"Holy moly, Mama. I just looked it up." Good thing the paparazzi didn't do much investigating. She could only imagine the headline if they knew she was Janie's younger sister.

"See what I mean?"

"I do. But this will pass. Tomorrow someone else will be their fodder."

"I know that. I'm not worried about the picture or the headline. I'm only worried about you and what you're feeling right now."

"Mama, just know I'm happy. Zane has been incredible, and I'm making friends, enjoying the work I'm doing here."

"Is Zane there now?"

"No, he's having physical therapy." She gasped as a

thought struck her. "Mama, you're not going to call him about this, are you?"

Her mother paused long enough to worry her. "Mother?"

"No, not if you don't want me to."

"I definitely don't want you to. Promise me you won't."

Gosh, the last thing she needed was her mother intervening in her love life. She was the one who had insisted Jessica come here. The damage was already done. Her mama could only make things worse. She hung up on a cheery note, convincing her mother she was fine, and resumed her work.

An hour later, she heard Zane's car pull up. Giddiness stirred inside her, and her heart warmed. She was becoming a lovesick puppy dog where he was concerned. She heard him enter the house, and his footsteps grew louder on the slate flooring as he approached. Seconds later, he was standing in front of her, a newspaper in his hand. He tossed it onto the desk, and she gave it a glance. "Sorry, sweetheart. I've got my manager doing some repair on this. Ideally, he can keep your name out of it." He studied her a second. "You don't look surprised."

"Oh, I was very surprised when my mama called to tell me about it," she said softly.

"Your mama saw this?" he nearly shrieked.

She nodded. "Just about all of Beckon has seen it by now."

He ran a hand down his face, pulling his skin tight. "Oh, man."

"Zane? What are you worried about?" Looking into his pained eyes frightened her.

He came around the desk and, taking her arms, pulled her up against him. "You. I'm worried about you," his said softly into her ear. He tucked her into an embrace while his breath warmed her skin and her spine got all tingly.

"Don't. I'm okay."

"Your mama must think I'm a jerk, subjecting you to this.

You have to go back to Beckon one day. I don't want it to be harder on you than it has to be. I'm so sorry, sweetheart."

*You have to go back to Beckon one day.*

He was right, she would have to return to her hometown one day. Her mind rebelled at the thought. He kissed her again and eased the battle going on inside her head. Oh, boy.

She gazed at him and was floored by the genuine look of concern on his face.

"How was your appointment?"

He pulled away from her and shrugged. "Fine. I don't think I needed it, but—"

"You need it. So you did okay. It wasn't too hard?"

"I've been swimming, riding and dancing on this foot. Seems I'm doing my own rehab."

"You're lucky you haven't reinjured yourself, babe."

He grinned.

"It's not funny."

"I'm not laughing at that. I like it when you call me 'babe.'"

"Well, if you like that, I have an idea I think you might enjoy."

"Does it involve a bed and soft sheets?"

"No, it involves being poolside with some beautiful hot chicks."

One week later, at the Ventura Women's Senior Center, an hour's ride from Moonlight Beach, Jessica sat poolside in the audience of geriatric hot chicks. The scent of chorine was heavy in the air of the enclosed pool area that opened into the center's recreation center. Zane had his butt in a chair, facing his eager fans with guitar in hand—he'd been brushing up at home—and it sounded to her as if he hadn't lost his touch. Playing guitar was probably like riding a bicycle. Once you mastered it, you never forgot.

Zane's Super Fan Elise Woolery, was all smiles today. She sat in the front row next to her friends, all of whom she'd coaxed into becoming great fans of Zane's, as well. As smokin' hot as Zane appeared to his younger audience, he had the wholesome good looks and Southern charm that any of these women would admire in a son.

Zane had balked at the idea of coming here, not because he wasn't charitable. Nothing was further from the truth. But he didn't know if he had the chops or the will to get back onstage and entertain the masses anymore. It had taken only one little ole note from Elise, saying she'd had a bad week physically, her arthritis so painful she couldn't get out of bed in the mornings, and listening to Zane's songs had helped her get by. That letter and Jessica's urgings had convinced him to play this private concert. He insisted on no press, and Jessica agreed. This wasn't a photo op. It wasn't done for his public image, either. He'd agreed because basically he'd been humbled by her letter and wanted to help.

Zane faced his audience. "Well, now. It's nice to be in such fine company. I guess you all are stuck with me for the next hour or two, so let's start things off." He nodded for Jessica to bring Elise up front and center. There was an empty chair beside him.

"Elise?" She helped the woman sit down next to him. The older woman waved her hand over her chest as the silvery-blue in her eyes gleamed.

"How are you this afternoon?" he asked.

Giddy as a school girl, she nodded and spoke softly. "I'm just fine."

"Yes, you are," Zane said. "Ready for a song?"

She gazed out at the envious women in the audience, her friends in the front fidgeting in their seats, too excited to sit still.

"I am, Mr. Williams."

"Zane," he corrected her, taking her hand. "May I call you Elise?"

"Oh, my, yes."

Zane performed for over an hour, and he'd never sounded

better. Just Zane and his guitar, without all the usual fan-fare, lights or band to back him up. His voice was clear and honest and mesmerizing.

After the performance, one by one the seniors said their goodbyes and thanked him, often offering kisses on the cheek before leaving the facility. Elise stayed until the end and chatted with Zane. Jessica didn't contribute much to the conversation. It seemed as though through her letters, Elise and Zane knew each other pretty well, but Jessica did take a number of photos, promising Elise she'd send them to her home address as soon as she could.

"You can thank Jessica here for arranging this," Zane was saying.

"Thank you, Jessica. This made my whole year. I swear today, my arthritis just vanished. I think I'll go home, put on one of Zane's records and dance a jig."

And later, sitting in the backseat of a limo, Zane reached for Jessica's hand as they headed down the highway. He didn't say much as he stared out the window, and every once in a while, he'd give her hand a squeeze.

If she could put a name on this sense of peace and total belonging, she'd call it bliss.

The sea glistened in the moonlight, calm tonight, the placid waves grazing the shore. It was a night like many she'd shared with Zane these past weeks, walking the shore in the dark, holding hands, enjoying the beach after the lo-cals went home.

"You're quiet tonight," Zane said as they strolled along.

She wasn't a complainer. She didn't want to mar the per-fection they'd seemed to achieve lately.

"I think I ate something that didn't agree with me."

Zane squeezed her hand lightly. "We can head back. We're only half a mile from the house."

"No, it's okay. The fresh air is doing me good."

"You sure?"

"I'm sure."

"'Cause you know, now that my rehab is done, I could pick you up and carry you all the way."

She chuckled, and the movement caused her stomach to curl. "Oh."

She wanted desperately to put her hand to her belly, but she didn't want to draw his attention there. They were having such a wonderful evening. She managed a small smile instead. "That won't be necessary."

"Could be fun."

"I don't doubt it. You'd probably dunk me into the ocean first or deliver me into your shower, like you did the other night."

"And you enjoyed every second. But I wouldn't do that to you tonight, sweetheart. I can see on your face that you're exhausted." He pivoted, taking her with him. "C'mon. You should get to bed."

"Okay, maybe you're right."

She didn't have the strength to argue with him. Zane had a charity event at the children's hospital in the city tomorrow, and she didn't want to miss it. It wasn't an extravaganza by any means, just an artist making the rounds and singing songs with the kids She hadn't had any difficulty convincing Zane to do it. When it came to making children feel better, Zane was all in.

"Excuse me? You said I was right about something?"

"Very funny." Gosh, her voice sounded suddenly weak. Whatever strength she had left seemed to seep right out of her. Her limbs lost all their juice. "Zane, I'm, uh, really tired." A wave of fatigue stopped her steps in the sand.

Zane halted and gave her a quick once-over, his eyes dark with concern. He lifted her effortlessly, and she wound her arms around his neck. "I've got you. Hang on, honey."

"I don't know what hit me all of a sudden."

"Just rest against me and close your eyes. I'll have you home in no time."

And minutes later, they entered the house. She insisted Zane deposit her in her own bedroom. He balked at first. He said he wanted to keep an eye on her tonight. "Are you sure?"

She needed a place to crash. And if she had a bug or the flu, she could be contagious. Zane didn't need to get sick on her account. "I'm sure. Thanks for the lift." Literally. She smiled, and his eyes grew sympathetic in response.

"Anytime."

"I just need to sleep this off."

"Can I help you get ready for bed?" he asked.

"I'll manage, Zane. Thanks for the thought."

"Okay if I come in to check on you later? I won't wake you."

She could see it meant a lot to him by the protective look in his eyes. "Yes, I'd like that."

"If you need anything during the night, just call for me."

When she'd had the flu during spring break last year, Steven hadn't so much as offered to bring her a bowl of soup. He'd told her he'd keep his distance so she could rest up and get better. He couldn't afford to get sick. She'd received a total of one phone call from him during her recuperation. What a fool she'd been. The signs were all there, but she'd refused to see them.

"Thank you, Zane."

He smiled, but the worry in his eyes touched her deeply. "Good night, sweet Jess." He placed a kiss on her forehead, tossed the sheets back on the bed and gave her a lingering smile before he walked out of the room and closed the door.

Her hands trembled as she put on her nightie and tucked herself into bed. She hadn't lasted but a minute when her belly rattled and the turmoil reached up into her throat, gagging her. Her stomach recoiled, and she covered her mouth, clamping it shut as she raced to the toilet.

It wasn't a pretty sight, but she emptied her stomach in just about thirty seconds.

Sitting back on the floor, she closed her eyes and took big breaths of air in order to calm her stomach. Whatever it was, she hoped it was gone.

Bye. Bye.

*Arrivederci.*

Good riddance.

She rose slowly and leaned against the marble counter. One look at her chalky face in the mirror told her to wash up and get her butt back into bed. She splashed water on her cheeks, chin, throat and arms, cooling and cleansing herself, and then headed back to bed on wobbly jelly legs. Her eyes closed to the distant serenade of Zane's beautiful voice coming from downstairs as he rehearsed his music for tomorrow's event.

In the morning, her weakened body felt bulldozed. Her head was propped by the pillow and her limbs lay flaccid on the bed as she absorbed the comfort of the luxurious mattress. She missed having Zane's arms around her, but she needed these hours of privacy to rest up.

A soft knock at her door snapped her eyes open. "Jess, are you awake?"

She sat taller in the bed, ran her fingers through her hair and pinched her cheeks, hoping she still didn't look like death warmed over. "Yes, come in."

Zane entered the room, assessing her from top to bottom, and took a seat on the side of the bed. "Morning. Are you feeling any better today?"

"Yes. Just a little tired still. But I'm sure once I get up and eat something, I'll perk right up."

He looked like a zillion bucks. Dressed in crisp new jeans, his signature sterling silver Z belt buckle and a Western shirt the color of sea coral decorated tastefully with rhinestones that outlined a horse and rider, Zane resembled the superstar that he was. His concert shirts were custommade by a trusty tailor, and this one was perfect for a day with children. "Glad to hear it. Mrs. Lopez has breakfast ready whenever you are."

The mention of food riled her stomach. And blood drained from her face. Her eyes drifted toward the digital clock inside a wall unit near her bed. It was almost ten! "Zane! I had no idea how late I slept. Give me a few minutes to get dressed and I'll—"

As she hinged her body forward, Zane's arms were on her shoulders, pressing her back down. "Whoa, Jess. Slow down."

Dizziness followed her as her head hit the pillow. The world spun for a second, and when it stopped, a soft sigh escaped her. "But I'm supposed to go with you today." It was her job, her duty as Zane's personal assistant. Zane wasn't used to making appearances on his own. He always had an assistant to usher him through the process.

"I didn't have the heart to wake you. I'm leaving in just a few minutes. What I want you to do is take the day off and relax. I'll be back in a few hours."

"I don't want to miss it."

He took hold of her hand. "I wish you could come, too."

"I'm sorry."

"Don't be. I'm sorry you're not feeling well."

"I'll be sure to call Mrs. Russo this morning. She's in charge at Children's Hospital, and I made all the arrangements through her. I'll tell her the situation."

"Don't go to any trouble. I'm sure I'll be fine."

"No trouble." She picked up her cell phone. "I've got the number right here."

Zane's gaze swept over her rumpled sheets and the spot where she'd conjured up her phone. "You sleep with your cell phone?" His incredulous voice tickled the funny bone inside her head.

"When I'm not sleeping with you."

He grinned and kissed the top of her head. "Feel better."

"Thanks."

As soon as Zane left, she made the call and was relieved that Mrs. Russo was amenable to sticking by Zane's side today, keeping him on schedule. She was a fan and was looking forward to the day, as well. Jessica hung up, convinced Zane would enjoy himself, doing what he loved to do. He'd be fine on his own. He liked being around children. Singing to them and with them would be second nature to a guy who'd lived and breathed country music as a boy.

A short time later, ringing blasted in her ear, and she lifted her eyelids. When had she drifted off? How long had she been in sleep land? She squinted to ward off the sunshine blazing into her window. The last thing she remembered was speaking with the director at the hospital regarding Zane's appearance. She took a few seconds to awaken fully, blinking and stretching. Gosh, she felt better, her stomach didn't ache and her head cleared of all the fuzz.

All systems go.

She grabbed her phone and greeted her caller on the third ring. "Hello, Mariah. It's good to hear from you."

Mariah had been calling in at least once a week to make sure things were going smoothly for her and checking in on Zane. Jessica appreciated her diligence and thoughtfulness, but she'd already spoken with Mariah earlier in the week. "Is everything alright?"

"Everything is actually better than I hoped." Enthusiasm that had been vacant in Mariah's voice since her mother's ordeal was making a sparkling comeback. "The last time I spoke with Zane, I told him my mother was being re-evaluated by the doctors. Well, the good news is that even though Mom has something of a long road ahead of her, she's recovered enough to come home from the transitional facility. My sister plans on taking over from now on. She'll have the help of a caregiver during the week. And I'll come home on the weekends whenever I can to help out. I tried to reach Zane to tell him I'll be coming back to work starting Monday morning, but I think he shut his phone off."

Mariah was coming back in five days? The news pounded Jessica's skull. Five days. She'd known this day would come, but she'd been too busy living in the moment to worry about it. "Oh, uh...yes. He's not here. He's doing a show at the children's hospital."

"That's where he really shines," Mariah was saying. "Anyway, you don't have to pinch-hit for me anymore. You, my savior, are off the hook."

She was off the hook? But she liked being on the hook. She *was* hooked on Zane.

Wow. Just like that, her life was about to change again. Mariah would return to work, and things would go back to the status quo. No more sunset dinners with Zane or moonlit strolls or making love on his big bed during the night. The happy place in her heart deflated. Like when the air inside a balloon was released, she fizzled.

"I'm happy to hear your mother's doing well, Mariah." She really was. It was good news, and she focused on that and what Mariah had gone through to get to this point. "And I'll be sure to tell Zane."

"Thanks, hon. I know you've done a great job in my absence. Zane sings your praises and tells me not to worry about a thing."

"Well, there wasn't all that much to do." Except to fall for the boss. "And you left impeccable notes."

"It's a flaw of mine. I'm a detail person. Makes most people crazy, but it comes in handy for the kind of work that I do. I'm happy Zane had you these past weeks. And I'm eager to come back to work. What about you, Jessica? How's your summer going?"

The summer was more than half-over. If she stayed, nothing would be the same. She wouldn't be working alongside Zane, and she couldn't very well carry on with him right under Mariah's nose. She had no name for her relationship with Zane. She wasn't his girlfriend. He hadn't made a commitment to her in any way. Did he look at her as a forbidden fling? He wanted to be her rebound guy, and he'd accomplished that and more. He got an A for effort.

"My coming back doesn't mean you have to leave, you know. Please don't on my account," Mariah was saying. But in fact, her coming back meant that very thing. Zane hadn't spoken about the future with Jessica. He wasn't one to plan anymore. He took things as they came now. Hadn't he encouraged her to do the same? "I would love to get to know you better."

"I feel the same way, Mariah. But unfortunately, I can't promise you that. I…should be getting home soon. There are things I have to do."

Prepare her lesson plans for the new school year.

Avoid Steven at all costs.

Fall back in step with single life in Beckon.

Try not to think about Zane.

"I understand. When home is calling, you must go."

"When Beckon beckons."

Mariah chuckled.

"Sorry. It's a dumb joke the locals think is clever. Small-town humor."

"Sounds kinda sweet. Will you tell Zane I'm sorry I missed him? It was nice talking to you, Jess."

"Sure, I'll tell Zane as soon as he gets back, and same here. Good talking to you."

Bittersweet emotions snagged her heart. She was thankful Mariah's mother was on the mend, but the thought of leaving Zane to return to Beckon was killing her. He'd be home soon.

And she'd have to tell him the news.

# Ten

"**Y**ou're staying," Zane said resolutely. His handsome face was inches from hers as she lay on a beach blanket on the sand right outside his back door, her head propped by a towel. She'd needed some sun to put color on her sickly cheeks while she tried to figure out where in heck her life was headed.

"How can you say that so easily?"

He'd plopped down beside her just minutes ago, wearing shorts and an aqua Hawaiian shirt. He'd been in a good mood since coming back from the children's hospital, and she'd had to spoil it by giving him the news that she'd be returning home.

"It is easy. You're my summer guest. What's so hard about that?"

He made it seem so simple, and he'd brought along his arsenal of secret weapons to convince her. His ripped chest grazed her breasts, teasing and tormenting her. Powerful arms braced on either side of her head surrounded her with strength, and that amazing mouth of his hovered so close she could almost taste it. His presence surrounded her, sucking oxygen from her rational brain.

"It'll be awkward. These past weeks it's been just us, and now that Mariah will be here most of the time, it won't be the same. She'll guess what's going on."

As he cupped her head with both hands, she had nowhere

to look but deep into his eyes. "She probably already knows, Jess. Mariah keeps up on everything, and I'm sure she's seen that tabloid photo of us. But if it makes you feel any better, I'll be up-front with her and explain the situation." Zane lowered his head and brushed his lips over hers. "It won't matter if she knows, as long as you stay."

Yes, yes. His kiss was a potent persuader. Oh, how she wanted to agree with him. She shouldn't care what people thought. But darn it, she did, and her heart was at stake, too. "I'm not… I don't do… Never mind."

"Jess," he said softly, his finger outlining the lips he'd just kissed. His touch seeped into her skin as he curved his fingertips around and around the rim of her mouth as if he'd never touched anything so fascinating. She'd hoped he'd ask her to stay, but she wanted more. She wanted the happily-ever-after that wasn't bound to happen.

He claimed her lips and took her into another world. When he was through kissing her, his deep, dark eyes were hot, heavy and filled with desire. "You can't go yet. This is new and real, and right now I can't offer you more than that." His words were raw with emotion. "But I'm asking you to stay."

*New and real?* Those were promising words. Hope began to build in her, but she warned herself not to be a fool. She couldn't get blindsided again. She had to face the truth head-on. She didn't know if Zane had the capacity to love again. He was and always would be devoted to her sister. Could she live with that? Could she spend the next five weeks with him and enjoy herself? The new Jess said yes. *Go for it, you idiot!* But the old Jess buried deep down wasn't quite so fearless, and she rose up occasionally to plant dire warnings in her ear. "I want to…but—"

"Sweetheart, you don't have to make up your mind right this minute. Take time to think it over."

Her shoulders relaxed as she blew breath from her lungs. "Okay, I can do that," she said softly.

"Good." He rose and offered her his hand.

"Where are we going?"

"One guess." He waggled his brows. He was six feet two inches of gorgeous, rugged, tan and aroused.

"You don't play fair, Zane Williams."

"*You* don't play fair. That bikini does things to my head and…" He looked down past his waistband. "If I don't get inside soon, I'll be arrested for indecent exposure."

She took his hand, and he yanked her up. She fell against him, her hands landing on his broad, bronzed chest. He smelled of sunshine and sand and sunscreen, and at this moment, she couldn't imagine not being with him.

"What would the residents of the Ventura Women's Senior Center say to that?"

A smile spread wide across his face. "They'd probably invite me back with an engraved invitation."

She laughed along with him, and her day brightened.

Jessica gave her body and soul to Zane, and the past three days had been magical. They rode horses, had moonlight swims, dined and danced together. Zane took her to the new restaurant, and they'd surveyed the progress, sharing ideas. He helped her answer fan mail, giving attention to questions and signing the letters personally. At night their lovemaking was intense, the heat level rising above anything she'd ever experienced before, but it was more than that. Emotions were involved now, their time together precious. Each night before they drifted off to sleep, Zane would hold her close and whisper in her ear, "Stay." In the morning, they'd rise at the crack of dawn to walk along the beach before the world woke up.

Except for a growing suspicion she might be pregnant, everything was perfect.

The idea of carrying Zane's baby made her glow inside, the beaming light of hope strong. It wasn't an ideal situation, but how could she not embrace the new life she might be carrying? She'd been queasy in the mornings ever since her bout of illness, but she managed to hide it from Zane for the most part. She ate little in the mornings, to his raised eyebrows, claiming she put on weight fast and needed to be disciplined. "You haven't got an ounce of fat on you," he'd said.

"And I want to keep it that way." Not entirely true. She wasn't a big believer in stick-thin female bodies, especially since she might be described as voluptuous. But most men bought that explanation, and for now, feminine vanity was a white lie that was necessary.

She'd been overly tired, too, but when Zane noticed, she attributed her fatigue to the energetic pace they'd been keeping in and out of bed. And she was overdue on her monthly cycle.

Locked inside her bathroom, she held the pregnancy test in her hand, waiting those precious few minutes that might change the course of her life. Zane was out shopping—which was bizarre since the man would rather break his other foot than step into a store—and she would use this time alone to deal with whatever came her way. Admittedly, it had taken her half an hour to muster the courage to break open the package and pee on the stick. And now that she had, her pulse pounded in anticipation.

Seconds ticked by, and then she glanced down and got the news.

She leaned against the sink and pressed her eyelids closed.

"Okay." She took a breath.

The new Jess was strong. She could do this.

Tears stung behind her eyes.

"Jess?"

Oh, no. Zane was home. What was he doing back so soon?

"I'll just be a minute." Her voice wobbled from behind the bathroom door.

"Okay, mind if I wait for you in here?"

"Uh, no. It's okay." Shaking, she scrambled to toss all signs of the pregnancy test away. She wrapped everything in toilet paper and shoved it into the bottom of her trash container. She took another few seconds to wash her face and straighten herself out mentally. Then she opened the door.

Zane was lying across her bed, staring out the window. He sat up the minute he saw her and smiled, a winning, charming, loving smile that seared straight into her heart.

"Everything okay, sweetheart?"

She nodded and bit her lip to keep herself from saying more.

Zane studied her face. Did he see the truth in her expression? She lowered her eyes, and that's when she saw a small, square, sapphire-blue velvet box on the spot next to him.

"Sit with me?" He picked up the box and patted that same spot for her to take a seat.

She did and turned his way. He had something to say, and she was all ears.

"Recently, you gave me a gift that was especially meaningful. And now, it's my turn to give you something. Not in reciprocation but because, well, you deserve this. I had this made for you."

His eyes contained a genuine spark of excitement as he placed the box in her hand. Whatever it was, Zane was eager for her to see it. She didn't make him wait. Gently she opened the lid and lifted out a unique charm bracelet. She'd never seen one made with diamonds before. "Oh, Zane." She was truly swept away. "This is…" A lump in her throat blocked her next words. She was speechless.

The silver-and-diamond bracelet held three charms and glittered brightly enough to light all of Moonlight Beach. The charms were well thought-out and special to the person that she was. The first charm was a teacher's apple that reminded her of her students, the second was a schoolbook with opened pages and the third was a pair of eyeglasses, which, up until a few weeks ago, were her mainstay. Every charm was exquisitely outlined by small diamonds. A tiny heart hung from the clasp, engraved with one word in italic script: *Stay*.

"Let me try it on you," Zane said, and she put out her hand.

"Thank you," she said finally. She couldn't have been more surprised. Zane fastened the clasp around her wrist. The fit was perfect, and there was something about a personalized gift, no matter what it was, that made her feel cared for. There were no words to express how meaningful this gift was to her. Zane had outdone himself. "It's very special."

"Just like you. I'm glad you like it," he said.

"I do. You don't play fair, Zane." It was getting to be his signature move. Make her want him even more than she already did.

"I swear to you, I had this bracelet ordered weeks ago, and then, well, the heart was just added on this week. You can't fault a guy for trying."

She put her hand to his cheek and gazed into his eyes. "That's sweet." And then she kissed him, quickly and passionately, before she pulled away, her heart in her throat.

She loved this man with all of her heart.

And she *wasn't* carrying his child.

Sadness blanketed her body, a shallow sliver of sorrow of what wasn't to be.

"Are you sure you're okay, Jess?" Zane studied her movements as she approached his bed. He lifted his sheets and welcomed her. He wanted her with him tonight, sex or no sex. She was special to him, and he didn't want to press her if she needed more rest.

After he returned to the house today, he couldn't wait to see her. His gift was burning a hole in his pocket, so he'd waited for her on her bed. When she'd stepped out of the bathroom and he'd looked at her, he'd seen a haunted expression on her face, and she'd been overly quiet. He worried over her health, but he sensed it was something more than her having an upset stomach. She'd looked sad, and a transparent sheen of despair seemed to cover her eyes.

She'd liked the gift—he could tell that much—and that brightened her mood, but her eyes never really returned to the Jess sparkle he was used to. She'd kept the bracelet on during the day, and there were moments when he'd catch her touching the links, tracing her fingertips over the charms tenderly. After what she'd been through this year, if the gift told her she was appreciated, she was worthy of beautiful things and she was desirable as a woman, then mission accomplished. Zane wanted her to feel all of those things. He'd wanted her to know what she had come to mean to him.

"I'm feeling better tonight," she said. She climbed in and scooted close to him. His arms tightened around her automatically, and he rolled so that her back was up against his chest.

Like it or not, Mae Holcomb put him in charge of her daughter. His first responsibility was to see to her health. Precious little else mattered. He'd failed where Janie was concerned, and he certainly wasn't going to let something happen to Jess while she was here with him. Not on his watch.

"Glad to hear it."

She still looked weary, as if a burden weighed her down. Was she deliberating about staying with him for the rest of the summer? Right now, breathing in the sweet scent of her hair and having her body cuddled up against him, he couldn't imagine her leaving in two days, but he wouldn't pressure her. She needed to come to the conclusion that they were good together, on her own. He'd done everything he could do, short of begging, to convince her to stay, but ultimately it was her decision.

Pushing silken strands away from her face, he kissed her earlobe. "If you need to sleep, I can just hold you tonight, babe. Or…"

She turned around in his arms, her features softening and her eyes tender and liquid. "Or," she said. "Definitely or."

Zane made slow, easy love to her, and she fell in sync with his body movements. He savored every inch of her with gentle strokes and touches. And she did the same to him. He loved the feel of her hands on him, exploring, probing and possessing him in small doses. Little by little, hour by hour, minute by minute, Jess was filling his life.

He cared about her. Worried when she was sick. Praised her accomplishments. Was impressed by her feisty spirit. Wanted to see her happy.

She mattered to him.

And after the explosion that burst before his eyes in warm colors, Jessica's sighs of contentment, completion and satisfaction settled peacefully in his heart. He never remembered being so in tune with another person before. *Except with Janie.*

A wave of guilt blindsided him. Up until now, he'd been able to separate the two, but was he disparaging his deceased wife's memory by finding comfort and some joy with her sister? Was he hurting Jessica and dishonoring his wife?

Zane carefully removed himself from a sleeping Jess and padded away from the bed. Words he hadn't found before came rushing forth, pounding inside his head. He had a song to finish, and the lyrics blasted in his ears now. The song that had haunted him for months would finally see the light of day.

Jessica just put on the finishing touches on her makeup, a hint of pale-green eye shadow and toner under her eyes to conceal the dark shadows from the ungodly remnants of whatever bug she'd had. Her appetite was coming back, thankfully, and she put on a lemon-yellow sundress decorated with tiny white daisies to make her feel human again. She looked at her reflection in the mirror. The dress did the trick. She had a dash of color in her face now, and wearing something fun perked up her spirits.

As she walked into the kitchen, Mrs. Lopez was just setting out her morning meal.

"Thank you," she said, taking a seat. She could definitely handle hard-boiled eggs, toast and a cup of tea. "You always know exactly what I want to eat. How do you do that?"

"I am like a little mouse, observing, watching. I can see you are feeling better, but the stomach needs time to rest. Today, you eat a little. Tomorrow, a little bit more. If you want something more, you just need to tell me."

"No, no. This is perfect. Exactly what I feel like having. It's…late."

"*Sí*. You've been waking late."

"The bug I had wore me out."

Minutes later, just as she was finishing up her last bite of toast and sip of tea, a knock on the deck door brought her head up.

Mrs. Lopez was there before Jessica pushed her chair out to rise. "Hello, Mr. McKay," she said politely, her olive face blossoming. Even Zane's housekeeper was starstruck. Dylan McKay had the same effect on all women, young and old, happily married or not.

"Hello, Mrs. Lopez. I took a walk down the beach to see if Zane could spare a few minutes for me this morning."

"He is not here."

"But I am." Jessica walked over to the door. "Dylan, hi! Is there something I can help you with?"

Dylan had a briefcase tucked under his arm, yet dressed in plaid board shorts and a teal-blue muscle shirt, he looked like a walking advertisement for sunscreen or surfboards. Hardly businessman attire, but that was Dylan.

"Hey, Jess."

"Thanks, Mrs. Lopez," she said, and the woman backed away.

"What's up?"

He brushed past her and stepped into the kitchen. "Looking beautiful as always," Dylan said. It wasn't a line with Dylan. He had a genuine appreciation for women, and he seemed to love to compliment them.

"You're looking fit yourself," she said. "Still running?"

He scrunched up his face. "Yeah. It's getting old."

"Why don't you break it up? Do five miles in the morning, five miles at night?"

His brows rose. "Wow, smart and beautiful. Does Zane know what a treasure you are?"

"I don't know. Why don't you ask him?" She grinned.

"Well, I like your idea, Little Miss Smarty Pants. I might just try breaking up the run and see how it goes."

Mrs. Lopez stood by the oven with a coffee pot in hand, reminding Jess of her manners.

"Would you like a cup of coffee? Water? Juice? Anything?" How comfortable she felt in the role of hostess to Zane's friends. It was something she didn't want to end.

"No, thanks. I'm good right now. Actually, I brought a revised script for Zane to look over. The screenwriter made some adjustments that I think really enhance the story. I've highlighted the parts that would affect Zane. Would you like to see them?"

"Of course!" It sounded better than watching her nails dry, and she was still on the clock as far as work went, even if it was Saturday. "I'd love to. Why don't you come into the office?"

He followed her, and as she entered the office, she went to the wood shutters first, opening them and allowing eastern light to enter the room. "Have a seat."

"Wow, looks like Zane's doing some writing."

Dylan was eyeing Zane's desk littered with sheet music

crumpled into tight balls. Ready to clear away the mess, she noticed the waste basket was full to the brim with the same. Mrs. Lopez worked her way through the rooms every morning. It was evident she hadn't made it to this room yet. "Yeah, I guess he is."

"That's good, right? As far as I know, he hasn't written a song for years."

Since Janie's death.

"I suppose so."

Dylan sat down on the sofa and opened his portfolio. "Do you know where he keeps the original script I gave him? We can compare the two. I'm eager to see if you think the changes work as well as I do."

"Sure. I think Zane locked it up in his desk for safekeeping. Just give me a second to get the key."

"No problem. I'm a patient man."

She doubted that. She moved quickly to retrieve the key from a set Zane kept in his bedroom dresser drawer. She came back to find Dylan with head down, making notes on the script. "Okay, here we go."

She unlocked the bottom drawer, and sure enough, there was the script. She made a grab for it and did a rapid double take at the folder that lay beneath it. In black lettering and handwritten by Zane, the title was spelled out. "Janie's Song. Final."

Zane never mentioned he was writing a song about Janie.

All that sheet music? She had to guess that Zane had been working on this recently. As recently as last night, maybe? She'd woken in the middle of the night and opened her eyes to an empty pillow beside her. She'd heard distant strumming and figured Zane was practicing his guitar again. She thought nothing of it and had fallen right back to sleep. But now, as she glanced at all the rejected papers strewn across his desk and bubbling up from his trash, she knew it had to be true.

It was and always had been all about Janie.

How could she be jealous of her dead sister?

Tears welled in her eyes. She felt sick to her stomach again.

She handed Dylan the first version of the script and went back to the drawer to lock it up. Instead, her profound sense of curiosity had her giving Dylan her back. She opened the manila folder and slipped out the first page of new, unwrinkled sheet music.

She shouldn't be prying. It wasn't her business. Yet she had to know. It was killing her not to know. Her hands trembling, she scanned the lyrics. "I will always love you, Janie girl." She'd forgotten he used to call her that. His Janie Girl. "Without you here, my road is bleak, my path unclear. My heart is yours without a doubt…"

Dylan cleared his throat. The innocent sound reminded her she wasn't alone. She slapped the folder shut. She'd seen enough. She didn't need to see more. What good would it do to torture herself? She was already torn up inside.

She locked the drawer before Dylan grew suspicious and turned to give him a smile. His head was still buried in the script. Then she heard the familiar sound of boots clicking down the hallway.

"Jess?"

She didn't answer. Dylan gave her a look and then called out. "We're in here, Zane. Your office."

Zane popped his head inside the doorway before entering. He shot Jess a questioning stare. She averted her eyes. She couldn't look at him right now, and he was probably wondering why she hadn't answered him. Was Zane jealous of Dylan? Did he think something was going on behind his back? It would serve him right, but that was a small consolation for her.

"Hey, Dylan. What's up?" Zane asked.

She had to get her mental bearings. She needed out of this room, pronto.

Dylan rose to shake his hand. "Hi, buddy. I came by looking for you with a new and improved version of the script. Jess invited me inside, and I was just about to go over it with her to get her opinion."

"Looks like you two don't need me now," she said. "Dylan, you can go over it with Zane. I just remembered I've got some urgent phone calls to make. See you, later."

"Sure. Later," Dylan said, distracted. He turned to his friend. "Zane, is this a good time?"

She dashed away before Zane could get any words out to the contrary. But his completely baffled expression rattled her already tightly strung nerves.

Jessica refused to shed a tear. She refused to cave to her riotous emotions. What good would it do? She'd wasted a lifetime of tears on Steven. Her well was dry. But her heart physically hurt, the kind of pain that no tears or aspirin or alcohol could cure. She marched into her room, closed the door and walked over to her bed. Plopping down, she stared out the window to majestic blue skies glazed with marshmallow tufted clouds.

She liked California. Everything was beautiful here. The people were easy, friendly and carefree. The near-tropical summer consisted of windswept days and warm, balmy nights.

But suddenly, and for the first time since coming here, she missed home. She missed her small apartment and tiny balcony where she grew cactus in a vertical garden and the jasmine flourished over the rail grating. She missed her little kitchen, her bedroom of lavender blooms and country white lace.

She missed her mama.

And her friends.

She didn't see a future with Zane. As much as it broke her heart to think it, Zane wasn't available to her emotionally. He was hung up on her sister and losing her and their baby had scarred him for life.

"You can't get blood from a stone," she muttered. It was

one of her mama's ageless comments on life. It was right up there with another Holcomb favorite: You can take a horse to water, but you can't make him drink.

*Ain't that the truth?*

Jessica rose and eased out of her sundress. She opened the vast walk-in closet that doubled for a black hole and selected a pair of running shoes, shorts and a top. She redressed quickly and lifted her long locks into a ponytail. Giving herself a glimpse in the mirror, she saw someone she didn't recognize. She'd become a California girl like the ones the Beach Boys sang about: the blonde, tanned, skimpy shorts-wearing chicks who adorned the shores of the Pacific coastline.

Jess wasn't sure how she felt about that. She wasn't sure about anything right now.

She headed down the staircase and heard male voices. There was no way to avoid Dylan and Zane since she had to walk past the office to get out the back door. She stuck her head inside the room. "Hey, guys. I'm going for a run."

Zane glanced up, but she couldn't look him in the eye, and it dawned on her in that very second, that the sick feeling invading her belly was betrayal…the lyrics of a song hurting her more than perhaps being left at the altar by the wrong man. "We're almost through here. If you wait a sec…"

"I'll join you, too," Dylan was saying.

"Uh, no thanks. I think I'll go this one alone. You guys finish up your work. I'll see you later."

She turned, but not before she saw Zane's eyes narrow to a squint, trying to figure her out.

She cringed as she walked away. She'd been borderline rude, but she couldn't help it. She needed some time alone, away from the house and the influences that could very well blindside her again. She hurried out the door and raced down the steps. She headed to where the tide teased the sand under the glorious Moonlight Beach sunshine and began to jog.

She ran at a pace that would keep her feet moving for the longest amount of time. She dodged and weaved around Frisbee-tossing teenagers, small swimsuit-clad kids digging tunnels in the wet sand and boogie boarders crashing against the shore. Sea breezes kept her cool as she dug in, jogging farther and farther away. She headed to a cove, a thin parcel of land surrounded by odd-shaped rock clusters called Moon Point that extended into the sea, forming a crescent.

The rocks looked climbable, and she was in the mood for a challenge.

Up she went, gripping the sharp edge of one rock and then finding her footing on another. Winds blew stronger here, but she held on and worked her way up. She'd heard the view from Moon Point was the best. On a clear day you could see the Santa Monica Pier. Once she got the hang of it, she was pretty good at climbing, and best of all, she was alone. She had no competition for viewing rights. She reached the top in fewer than five minutes and planted her butt on a flat part of a rock.

A hand salute kept the sun from her eyes, and she looked out at the vast ocean view. It was amazing and peaceful up here. Quiet, as if she had the entire ocean to herself.

She could stay up here all day.

Waves rocked the Point, and the sea spray sprinkled her body. The drops felt cool and refreshing, but also woke her to the time. She'd been up on the Point for three hours. She'd hardly noticed the others who'd decided to join her. They'd come and gone, but she'd stayed.

She climbed down from the rock, a deceivingly much harder proposition than going up, and she walked along the shore that was slowly and surely becoming deserted by summer school buses and mothers eager to get on the road before traffic hit. She reached the strip of beach in front of Zane's house half an hour later, and her heart somersaulted when she spotted him on the deck.

He stood with feet spread wide as if he'd been there a long time. His beige linen shirt flapped in the breeze, and his eyes, those beautiful, deep, dark eyes, locked directly on her. There was no need to wave. They'd made their connection. She stifled a whimper and headed toward him.

He started to move toward her, climbing down the steps to the sand, a loving smile absent on his lips. This was not going to be an easy conversation. For either of them.

"Where in hell did you go?" he asked.

She blinked. He'd never spoken to her in that tone. "I took a run."

"You were gone for almost four freaking hours, Jess."

"Well, I'm back now."

His bronzed face reddened to deep brick. "I can see that. Why you'd go off in such a damn hurry?"

"I needed to be alone."

"On the beach? Must've been a thousand people out today."

That was an exaggeration. "Okay, fine. I needed to get away from you for a little while."

He jerked back. "Me? What did I do? And don't change the subject. I was worried."

"Why were you worried, Zane?"

"Because, damn it. I had no idea where you were. You could've gotten swept up by a wave, or some lunatic could've grabbed you, or you might have fallen and gotten hurt. You didn't have your cell phone with you. How was I supposed to know if you were all right? Who goes jogging for four hours?"

"I needed to think."

"So, did you?"

"Yes, up on Moon Point."

Zane rolled his eyes. "You climbed the Point?"

"It wasn't hard."

The sound of teeth grinding reached her ears, but he didn't say another word.

A sigh wobbled in her throat before she released it. She laced her fingers with his and he gazed down at their hands entwined.

"Zane," she said, softening her voice. "You were worried because you care some about me, but also because you feel responsible for me. You promised my mom that you'd watch out for me. Don't deny it. I know it's true. You didn't want to fail her. I get that. I actually appreciate that. But you don't have to worry about me. I'm not the same weak, heartbroken Jess that showed up on your door more than a month ago. I've changed."

A genuine spark of sincerity flickered in his eyes. "You're amazing, Jess. Strong and smart and funny and beautiful."

She hesitated a beat. His compliments nearly destroyed her. "Don't say nice things to me."

"They're true."

"There you go again, Zane."

"Can't help it."

"I'm leaving tomorrow." She had to be strong now. She couldn't show him how her heart was cracking at this very second.

"No, you're not."

She nodded. She wouldn't be persuaded.

"What can I say to make you stay?"

She could think of a dozen things, but she remained silent.

"Why, Jess? What's happened? You owe me an explanation."

In a way, she did. "You asked what you could say to make me stay? Well, I've got something to tell you to make you rethink that."

He squeezed her hand. "Never going to happen, Jess."

"I took a pregnancy test yesterday." The words were hard to get out, and tears burned behind her eyes unexpectedly. She was through with crying. Yet one lonely drop made its way down her cheek.

Breath rushed out of his mouth. The gasp was loud enough to wake the dead. He blinked several times, staring at her as if trying to make sense of what she'd just said. His hands dropped to his sides. He probably didn't even know they had. Just like that, she had her answer.

All remnants of anger left his eyes. They filled with... fear. And he began shaking his head as if he'd heard wrong. "You took a pregnancy test?"

"Yes. I've been feeling tired and nauseated and, well, I had some other symptoms."

The fear spread to his face, which seemed to turn a putrid shade of avocado green. At any minute, he might be the one upchucking. His body, on the other hand, became one rigid piece of granite.

"I'm not pregnant."

A sigh from the depths of his chest rushed out uncontrollably fast, his breath tumbling nosily. The relief on his face drifted down to the rest of his body, and his form sagged heavily. He looked like a man who'd been given a reprieve from the worst fate in the world.

Sadly, his reaction didn't really surprise her. She'd known all along. He didn't want her child. He couldn't handle the commitment of loving another human being more than anything else in the world. He'd been there, done that once in his life. He was still plenty scarred up on the inside, but his scars also showed in his lack of commitment to his career, his floundering around, trying to reinvent himself as an actor, maybe? Or a restaurant entrepreneur. He had clipped wings, and breaking his foot had served as a means for Zane to put a temporary halt to his life.

"Maybe I shouldn't have told you," she whispered. "Kept my trap shut."

"No, no. I'm glad you did." He straightened, the gentleman and dutiful decent man that he was taking hold. But nothing could've hurt her more than seeing, *living* his response. Witnessing the somber truth in his frightened eyes for those brief moments had dissected her heart.

Yet a ridiculously hopeful part of her wished he might have been glad or even receptive to the idea of her having his child. Even if it wasn't planned. Even if it hadn't been conceived in wedlock.

When Janie had told Zane about her pregnancy, he'd been over-the-moon happy. He sent her flowers every day for a week. He hired a decorator and told her to fix up a nursery any way she wanted. He'd written a song for the baby, a soothing lullaby meant only for their new family. He'd told his friends, his fans and the press. The town of Beckon had rejoiced. Their golden boy was going to be a father.

Now Zane reclaimed her hands. His were cold and clammy, and another pang singed her heart. "I wouldn't want you to go through something like that without telling me. I, uh, want you to know that if things had turned out differently, we would've worked it out, Jess."

She didn't want to know what he meant by *working it out*. How did one work out having a baby? It didn't sound like flowers and sweet lullabies. "I know. And now you understand why I have to leave tomorrow."

She couldn't find fault with him. She knew if he could've made her feel better, he would have. But the man didn't have it in him. He didn't love her. He was through with commitment. He'd already had the one great love in his life. The stony expression on his face said it all.

A cold blast coated her insides. The frost would linger even through the Texas heat of home. She loved Zane and wanted to have his child. But he would never know her feelings. He would come to think of her as his wife's sister again.

Sweet Jess.

She wasn't destined for love.

"I'll pack my bags tonight, Zane. Don't bother to see me off. I'm leaving before dawn."

# Eleven

Jessica was all about change now, moving the desks around her classroom in a new way. She wanted to see each of her students' faces when she taught in front of the blackboard. Making a connection to them was of the utmost importance. She didn't want to see their profiles but look directly into their eyes to gauge their level of attention and encourage their participation. She had her lesson plans all laid out, her mind spinning about the mark she would make on her students' lives. Who didn't remember their first-grade teacher? And she hoped they would one day think upon her fondly and know she cared.

School started in Beckon just after Labor Day, one week from today. She was eager for the semester to begin, eager to put the past behind her. Scraping sounds echoed in the classroom as she moved chairs across the linoleum floor. She was actually working up a sweat. The summer heat hadn't relented yet. September was just as hot as June in Texas.

Just minutes ago, Steven had knocked on her door. She'd been surprised to see him, but one look at his sheepish face and she knew she'd never really loved him in that forever kind of way. He'd offered her excuse after excuse and finally apologized to her. She'd listened patiently and let him have his say, all the while thinking he'd actually done her a favor by not marrying her, brutal as it had been. When he was through, it was her turn to speak. She didn't swear, didn't get angry, but calmly and very systematically gave him a piece of her mind and then dismissed him.

The new Jess had finally been heard, and it had been liberating.

She kept her hands busy maneuvering desks, not wasting another minute on Steven. But in the silence of her classroom, her mind drifted back to Zane, as it always seemed to do, and her last day in California.

Zane wouldn't let her leave on her own that morning. He'd gotten up before dawn, insisting on driving her to the airport. He had no clue how terribly hard it was for her to say goodbye. He had no way of knowing that her rebound guy had become her Mr. Right and that he'd taught her what love was truly about.

Thanks to airport regulations, Zane couldn't walk her to her boarding gate, but he'd handled her luggage and helped her get as far as he could without garnering a reprimand from security. Luckily, it was the butt crack of dawn, as her friend Sally would put it, and the Zane Williams fan club members obviously weren't early risers. Zane had told her in the car that he didn't care if he was recognized or if the paparazzi were following them—which they weren't. He wanted to see her off.

"Well," he said, dropping her luggage at his feet and taking both of her hands. His dark lashes lowered to her, framing beautiful brown eyes that seemed to give her a view into his soul. "I'll miss the hell out of you, sweetheart."

He had a way with words. The corner of her mouth lifted. How could she not love this man who'd braved Homeland Security, a possible rash of Super Fans and the ungodly early hour to wish her farewell?

"Thank you, Zane." She looked away, into the street that was starting to swarm with taxicabs and buses. She couldn't tell him she'd miss him. That would be the understatement of the century. "I appreciate you letting me stay with you. I'll miss…California."

She'd become a California girl, by Beach Boy standards.

He moved his hands up her arms, caressing her skin, and she began to prickle everywhere he touched.

"Won't you miss me a little?"

"I can't answer that, Zane." *Don't make me.*

He nodded, and his magic hands continued up her arms. "I won't ever forget the time we've spent together. It's meant a lot to me."

Her eyes squeezed shut to hold back tears. She filled her lungs, steadied herself and stared right back at him. "I won't forget, either. I'd better go. They'll be boarding soon."

"Just a sec," he said and then planted a kiss on her lips that would've brought her to her knees if he hadn't been holding her arms. He kissed her for all he was worth. And then he moved his hands to her face and cradled her cheeks, lifting her chin to position his mouth once again and stake a claim in a whopper of a kiss that brought her up onto her toes.

When the kiss ended, he pressed his forehead to hers, and they stood that way for a long time with eyes closed, their breaths mingling.

Over the loudspeaker, her flight was announced. It was time to board.

"Damn," Zane muttered and stepped back.

She lifted her luggage and began the trek that took her away from the man she loved.

He didn't ask her to stay this time.

They both knew it was over.

She had walked away from him and never did look back.

Jess shook off that memory and after accomplishing what she set out to do in the classroom, she climbed into her car and turned on the radio. Zane's melodic voice came across the airwaves. "Great, just great." She didn't need any reminders of how much she missed him. She punched off the radio and cruised along the streets of Beckon, aiming her car for home.

She needed a good soak in the tub.

Or better yet, she'd go soak her head and be done with it.

"Happy birthday, Jessica. How's my girl today?"

"Hi, Mama." Jessica left the curb in front of her apartment and bounded around the front end of her mother's car. Climbing into the passenger seat, she leaned in for a kiss. Mama planted one right smack on her cheek. The none-too-subtle scent of Elizabeth Taylor's White Diamonds perfume matched the heavy humidity in the air, but it was comforting in a way, since the classic scent defined her mama to a T. And today of all days, Jess and her mother needed the comfort.

Mama wasn't the best driver, but she insisted on picking her up and driving today. Thankfully the roads in Beckon weren't complicated or crowded, because the way her mother drove scared the daylights out of her. She clutched the steering wheel like a lifeline and rocked the darn thing from side to side with nervous jerks. Amazingly the car continued down the road in a straight line.

She looked over her shoulder at an arrangement of bubblegum-pink daylilies and snow-white roses. "Pretty flowers, Mama."

"Janie's favorites. I've got a bunch for you back at the house, sweet darlin'." It had become a ritual to visit Janie's grave on their mutual birthday. Neither of them would have it any other way.

The cemetery was on the edge of town, and it didn't take long to get there. They both stepped out of the car and walked fifty feet to the beautiful monumental headstone that Zane had had constructed. "Looks like someone's already been here today," Mama said.

More than a dozen velvety red and white roses shot up from the in-ground vase. "Zane probably had them sent." He wouldn't forget Janie's birthday. He'd always made a big deal of it when she was alive, hunting for the perfect gift for her, making her day special in any way he could.

"I don't think he had them sent," Mama said, pointing to one rose in particular. "Look at that."

"His guitar pick," Jessica said softly. Black with white lettering, the pick placed between opened petals read, "Love, Zane."

"He's in town, Jess."

"Don't be silly, Mama. Zane doesn't come here. If he was in Beckon, it'd be all over the news by now. You know how the town loves him."

"And so do you, Jessica."

"Mama," she breathed quietly. "No."

"Yes, you do. You love that man. There's no need denying it. He's a fine man, decent, and oh, boy, he loved your sister like there was no tomorrow, but Janie's gone. And Lord knows I wish she wasn't, but if you two have something—"

"Mama, I wish Janie wasn't gone. I really do, with all my heart. But you've got it wrong." She wished her sister had lived. Her baby would've been almost two by now, and she'd be the favorite aunt. Aunt Jess. Janie and Zane were meant for each other.

She was a poor substitute for the real thing.

"We'll see."

Jess ignored her mama's ominous reply and hoped that Zane wasn't within one hundred miles of Beckon. Make that one thousand.

Mama laid the flowers down, and both said a silent prayer. They stayed like usual, half an hour, talking to Janie, catching her up on news. Then, with tears welling in their eyes, said goodbye. It was always the hardest day of the year, sharing a birthday with her sister and being able to live out her birthdays while Janie's were cut short.

Mama pulled through the cemetery gates and onto the road. "How about some barbecue for your birthday dinner? I invited Sally and Louisa and Marty to join us."

Her mother, bless her soul, didn't get to grieve for Janie fully on a day that would maybe bring about some healing. Because it was Jessica's birthday as well, she had to put on a cheery front, plaster a smile on her face and pretend her heart wasn't breaking.

"Sure, Mama, that sounds good."

Sally, her best friend, and Louisa, her mama's dear friend, would be there. Marty was Louisa's daughter and also a schoolteacher. Jessica sort of got Marty's friendship by default, which was okay by her. Marty was a wonderful person.

The parking lot at BBQ Heaven was full by the time they got there. Odd for a weeknight, and though the place had new owners who'd changed the name of the restaurant from Beckon Your Bliss BBQ, it still served the best barbecue beef sliders and tri-tip in three counties. There were times back in California when she'd craved those smoky, hickory-laced meals. Now her mouth watered.

They met their friends outside and entered the place together. Seating for five wasn't a problem, it seemed. Her mama must've made reservations. They were seated at the best crescent-shaped Red Hots candy-colored booth in the restaurant. Mama and Louisa sat in the middle so they could gab, and Jessica and her friends shared the end seats.

"Thank you all for coming," Jessica said. She was getting her life back in order. Seeing Marty and Sally helped. Of course, Sally knew all. She'd picked her up from the airport when she'd returned from Moonlight Beach, and Jessica had spilled the beans. She'd sworn Sally to secrecy that day, as if they were in high school, Jess finding a way to trust a friend again. It was all good.

"Sure thing, friend. Happy birthday. Wish I was twenty-six again," Marty said with a lingering sigh.

Louisa rolled her eyes. "You're only twenty-eight, sugar."

"I know, Mom, but twenty-six was a good year for me."

Sally gave Marty a look, and all three of them laughed.

"Happy birthday, Jessica," Louisa said, her voice somber. "I hope you can find some joy today."

"I'm sure she will," Mama said with enough certainty to make Jess turn her way. Her mother's light emerald eyes were dewy soft and smiling. It was great to see her so relaxed.

The waitress came by their table. Everyone ordered a different dish for sharing, with five different sides as well, garlic mashed potatoes, white cheddar mac and cheese, bacon baked beans, almond string beans and corn soufflé. No one would go home hungry.

Bluegrass music played in the background, but no one could hear a word. The place was hopping, conversations from crowded tables going a mile a minute.

She was halfway through her salad when someone tapped on a microphone, the screeching sound check enough to bust an eardrum. Finally, the sound leveled out, the background bluegrass was history, and George, the restaurant manager, spoke into the mike. "We have a little surprise in store for you tonight," he said from the front of the room. She had to crane her neck to see him above the heads bobbing to catch a look. "Our own Zane Williams is back in town, and he's got a new song he wants to sing for all of you. Sort of a trial run, so to speak. I know not a single one of you will mind being serenaded tonight. So let's give Zane a big Beckon welcome."

Applause broke out, and just like that, Zane stepped up with a guitar strap slung over his shoulder. His six-foot-two frame, black hat and studded white shirt made him stand out from the crowd like no one else could, especially since a spotlight miraculously shone on him like a sainted cowboy who traveled with his own glow.

Lord, help her. He was amazing. She'd almost forgotten how much. And her heart did a little flip. She faced her mother who refused to look at her. And suddenly it clicked.

The innuendo at the cemetery, her mother's suspicious behavior today, the *we'll see*s and the *I'm sure she will*s.

*Oh, Mama, what did you do?*

Sally was beaming and mouthing, *Did you know?*

She shook her head.

And then Zane commanded his audience with simple words. "Thank y'all for letting me interrupt your meal and try out my new song on you. George, I owe you one, buddy," he said, smiling at the man standing to his side. "This one here, it's intended to wish someone I love a happy birthday. So here goes. Oh, it's called 'Janie's Song.'"

*Oh*s and *ah*s swept through the crowd. Everyone knew about Zane's undying love for Janie. A cold rash of dread kicked Jessica in the gut. Her belly ached. Bile rushed up to her mouth. How could she sit here and listen to the lyrics of the song she'd secretly read, a tribute to the love Zane still had for Janie? His voice was a beautifully rich torture instrument that would crumble her heart to powdery dust.

Her gaze darted to the door. Could she make an escape without being noticed?

Zane began to sing. Too late for an escape. He had the floor and a captivated audience. The words she'd remembered, words she'd repeated inside her head a hundred times, poured out of his mouth in a ballad pure and honest, just Zane and his guitar.

"I will always love you, Janie girl. Without you here, my road was bleak, my path unclear. My heart was yours without a doubt..."

Her mama took her hand from underneath the table and squeezed. Jessica glanced at her and found warmth brimming in her eyes. Her mother nodded toward Zane with her chin, her gaze fondly returning to him. Jessica looked down. She couldn't bear to see him sing a love song to another woman, not even to Janie. Not now, not after what they'd shared together. Was that terrible of her?

He crooned, mesmerizing everyone in the place with his

deeply wrought emotions. The pain in his voice was unmistakable, but the lyrics that filled the now quiet room were new, different, changed.

"I loved you once, and it was fine. The finest love I'd ever known. But I'm movin' on, my Janie Girl, with a love so true, I know you'd approve. You see, my girl, you love her, too. You love her, too. You love her, too. You love her, too."

Jessica snapped her head up. Zane's eyes were closed, his head tilted, his hand strumming the chords on the guitar gently as the song eased out of him. He seemed free, liberated, somehow unburdened, even as he put his heart and soul into that song.

She stared at him, unable to shift her eyes away, her mind in an uproar. When he lifted his lids, he focused on her. Only her. He removed his hat in a gallant gesture, and the dark soulful depths of his eyes reeled her in further. All heads in the restaurant turned around. Some people were gaping, others smiling. She recognized quite a few who'd attended her almost-wedding. Her face flamed. What was he doing to her?

He removed the guitar strap from his shoulder and held his instrument with one hand now. He didn't seem to care that he was making a spectacle of himself. And her.

She rose from her seat. The spotlight swiveled to her and flashed in her eyes, making her squint.

Zane took a step toward her.

Her heart was beating so fast, she thought she'd faint.

There was only one thing she could manage right now.

She bolted.

Out of the restaurant.

Into the street.

And kept on running.

"Ah, hell," Zane muttered, ignoring the applause from the crowd and granting Mae Holcomb an apologetic shrug before he took off after Jess. It hadn't gone as he'd planned, that was for doggone sure. His chin held high, he walked out of the restaurant matter-of-factly as if women ran from him every day of the week. As soon as he made it to the street, he darted his head back and forth. Once he spotted Jess nearly a half a football field away, he took off at a sprint. If Doobie Purdy, his track coach, had seen her, he would've signed her up.

But he wasn't anything if not determined, his long legs no match for her. He caught up to her in no time but slowed to a few paces behind, rethinking what he wanted to say to her. He couldn't blow it. Not again. Jess meant the world to him.

"Go away," she tossed over her shoulder.

"That's not nice." What was nice was seeing her tanned, coltish legs making strides. Lifting his gaze higher to her beautiful backside reminded him of how soft and supple she was, how amazingly gifted she was in the female department.

She didn't slow her pace, not for a second.

"Ouch, damn it. I hurt my foot," Zane yelped.

She stopped then and turned, her eyes focused on his fake injury. He saw the depth of her compassion, the love she had for him glowing in her eyes—Dylan hadn't been wrong—and loved her so damn much right now, he could hardly breathe.

"You're not hurt, are you?"

"My heart is bleeding."

She gasped. A good sign.

"But your foot is fine, right?" She stared at his feet.

"Well, my foot could be hurt, Jess. Running like a bat outta hell to catch you in these boots isn't the kind of therapy I need."

She shook her head, and the gorgeous mass of blonde hair curled around her face. The run had put a rosy blush on her face, and the material of her coral dress lifted her ample chest with every breath she took, nearly killing him.

He inhaled now and was grateful she wasn't moving again. "You *really* don't play fair, Zane."

"I needed to see you today. On your birthday."

"Zane, what were you thinking? You made a spectacle of me in that restaurant. You of all people know I don't need another scandal in my life. I've had enough of being the laughingstock in this town. I... Why are you really here?"

"I came for you."

Hope popped into her eyes. Another good sign.

"You changed the words of the song."

"Dylan said he thought you'd seen those lyrics. He was right, wasn't he? Is that why you wouldn't stay with me?"

"Dylan? Are you taking advice from the Casanova now?"

"Don't knock Dylan. He's the one who made me see how much I missed you. How stupid I've been. And yes, after you left, I reworked the song, the lyrics coming easy and straight outta my heart. I sang it tonight just for you."

She folded her arms, and a warm glint entered her eyes. "But why there, in front of half the town?"

"I let you go. I was running scared. When you told me you might've been carrying my child, I couldn't deal with it, Jess. I've been blaming myself for Janie's death all this time, feeling guilty about losing her and our child. Deep down, I hated myself. I didn't think I'd ever want again, or love again. It was easier to live in the moment and not look to the future. But then you left, and I was hollowed out, gutted to my sorry bones. I missed you something fierce. I didn't think me saying it would be enough. I didn't know if you'd believe me unless I shouted it from the rooftops.

"I'm not doing the movie, and the restaurant is the last one I'm building. I'm going to finish up my tour, Jess. I'm through hiding my head in the sand. I'm through not being me."

The corners of her mouth lifted. He wanted to see her pretty smile again, but it wasn't there, not yet. "That's good, Zane. I'm happy for you."

Cars swerved around them. Someone honked a horn. Zane took her hand and guided her out of the middle of the street, to the sidewalk in front of the Cinema Palace. Ironically, it was nearly the same spot where he'd fallen in love with Janie. And now, here he was coming full circle, praying that her sister would agree to spend her life with him.

"Do you love me, Jess?"

She stared at him as if he were a three-headed monster.

"Do you?"

She pulled her hands free of him. "Yes, you idiot."

His face split wide open, and he didn't care if he looked like a grinning fool. Joy rushed out so fast he couldn't stop himself from telling her his plans. "I'm selling off my place, Jess. Finally. The land where I lived with your sister will belong to someone else one day soon. I'll never forget Janie, but it's time to move on. There's this beautiful parcel of land I've got my eye on. But I want you to see it, too. I want you to love it as much as I do. I'm digging in and putting down roots again, here in Beckon."

"But you said you're going back on tour."

"I have to finish it up. I'm bound by the contract, but after that, Jess, I'll stay here in Beckon and tour only during the summer months, when you're not teaching."

The smile he was praying for was almost there. "Zane, what are you saying?"

"Oh, yeah, got ahead of myself, didn't I?" He inhaled deeply and took hold of her hands. "I've already spoken to your mama, Jess. She and I worked things out, and she's given me her blessing. Sweet Jess, my Jess, you've helped me heal my body and my heart. And I can't imagine my life without you. Jessica Holcomb, I'm getting down on one knee," he said, his knee hitting the pavement. He tilted his head up and gazed into her eyes. "You taught me to look toward the future again. Knowing you, loving you the way I do, has given me the courage I needed to find my true self. I'm not afraid anymore. And I'm asking you for a second chance. I'm asking you to share your life with me. I'm asking you to be my wife, Jess. And Lord knows, have my baby one day. I want that. I really do. I love you with all my heart. Will you marry me, sweet Jess?"

Her beautiful, soft, grass-green eyes teared up, but her smile was real and genuine and the most beautiful thing about her. She hesitated so long he thought he'd blown it, but then she pulled him up and he stood facing her, his heart in her hands. "No girl marries her rebound guy," she said, her smile widening. "But me. I love you, Zane. I want to be your wife and spend the rest of my life with you."

"I'm so happy you said yes. 'Cause I wasn't gonna take no for an answer. It's all sorta weird and wonderful and unexpected, sweetheart, but my love is true. You have to know that."

"I do. And I think just like you said in your song, Janie would approve. She's looking down on us now and giving her blessing, too."

Holcomb women sure had a hold on him. "I'd love to believe so."

"I believe it, Zane. Let's go back to the restaurant and share our good news. Mama looked worried when I walked out."

"She wasn't the only one." Zane took her into his arms and pressed a kiss onto her soft, sweet lips. Planting his stake, claiming his woman. He was gonna hold on tight and never let her go.

Ever again.

\* \* \* \* \*

# COMING SOON!

We really hope you enjoyed reading this book.
If you're looking for more romance
be sure to head to the shops when
new books are available on

## Thursday 23rd April

To see which titles are coming soon, please visit
**millsandboon.co.uk/nextmonth**

MILLS & BOON

# FOUR BRAND NEW BOOKS FROM
# MILLS & BOON MODERN

Indulge in desire, drama, and breathtaking romance – where passion knows no bounds!

# OUT NOW